I0788141

keys
and
KISSES

Foreword & Dedication

Here we are at book three. Sometimes, I'm flat out amazed that this story has unfolded the way it has. I've said before that when I first began *Rules and Roses*, I had no idea how much I would fall in love with Frankie, Coop, Jake, Ian, and Archie. Nor did I have any idea how much their day to day lives or how they were facing such tremendous upheaval in their personal relationships would come to mean to me. *Changes and Chocolates* captivated and pushed me as Frankie struggles alternately made me laugh aloud, sniffle, and sometimes just get plain pissed off. Frankie is the kind of girl I'd have been friends with in high school and she's the kind I want to protect now.

Which brings us to our current tale. *Keys and Kisses* takes us on another leg of her journey including the personal struggle she faces with her varying relationships from Archie to Jake to Coop and finally, Ian. I laughed aloud in some of these chapters while others made me cry. I *love* writing this story and I cannot wait to dive into the next one.

This series wouldn't be complete without the enormous support of Blake Blessing, Rebecca Royce and Sara Vermillion. They've been tremendous as cheerleaders (and in Sara's case, cracking the whip), as sounding boards, and even pushing back in places where I needed to dig deeper and let me tell you, this book is so much the better for it.

Thank you to every single reader who has given this series a shot and to those who left reviews. Thank you to the readers who recommend the series to their friends and to every single person who has reached out to me about it. I see and hear all of you.

Thank you. Thank you. Thank you. This book is for all of you, too.

Finally, just a couple of housekeeping notes!

For those of you who have never read a reverse harem before, first let me thank you for picking this up and giving it a shot. Second, a reverse harem means the heroine will not make a choice in this book or any other between the guys in her life. It may take her a while to reach that conclusion, but it's the journey that drives it. There are many ways to frame this kind of relationship, currently reverse harem fits it very well.

Also, this is the third book in a series. If you haven't read *Rules and Roses* and *Changes and Chocolates*, I encourage you to pause here and go grab them. While there may be no specific happy endings at the end of each of these books, there will be one to the whole series, that I promise you. Some of these books will have cliffhangers, largely due to the size of the story, but the happy ending has to be earned as part of the journey.

Thank you again for reading Frankie's story and I truly hope you enjoy it!

Chapter One
EVERY NIGHT IS ANOTHER STORY

"**Y**ou have to try the blue one," Cheryl said, holding up the dress toward me. It was a skinny strapless number that would probably hit me mid-thigh.

"Not really my style," I said.

"No, it's perfect. You have a great body and the ruching hides anything you might think you need to hide." A half-snort and laugh later, she added, "Not that you need to hide anything. Does she, Coop?"

Going through a different rack of dresses behind us, Coop glanced over and grinned. "Nope. She's perfect."

Exasperated, I took the dress from Cheryl and held it up to me as I faced Coop. "Really?"

He cocked his head to the side. "Do they have it in green? It would match your eyes better."

I did not roll my eyes.

"But this matches Bubba's eyes, and he may not notice," Cheryl argued, catching my arm to pull my gaze back to her. "Trust me, guys don't notice it consciously when you do it, but their subconscious? It's the perfect prey, it recognizes the colors, and then they're drawn in by the symmetry."

What the hell did that mean? It wasn't in any psychology book I'd ever read. However… "Right color or not, I don't wear skimpy dresses."

"It's not skimpy," Cheryl said, her exasperation punching up each syllable. "Just add it to our rack there."

Our rack.

Turning, I stared at the single rack the lady had brought out for us to hang our "selections" on, and when we were ready, she would wheel it to the changing room.

Over a dozen dresses already hung on it—for Cheryl. I'd hung precisely one before this one. A simple, straightforward, black cocktail dress Cheryl had given me a singular look of disgust followed by one of sympathy before she'd waved me on to hang it up.

Leaving her flicking through the racks, I carried the strapless dress over to hang it up.

"What do you think of this one?" Coop asked, holding up some tulle-infested nightmare of lace and satin. Despite his vain attempts to contain a smirk, his eyes practically danced with laughter.

"I think you'd look great in that," I deadpanned.

He snorted, and Cheryl let out a giggle. "Oh, do we get to dress Coop up, too? Why didn't you say so!"

"I'm good," Coop said. "Let's focus on Frankie." Thankfully, he put the monstrosity away, and when Cheryl held her hand up for a high five, I gave it to her gratefully. "But seriously, what about this one?"

Ready to lampoon him for that dress again, I shut up as I turned to see him holding what looked like a two-piece outfit—a lacy high neck crop top and satin miniskirt. It was also in the deepest green. Although really pretty, that was a short skirt and the lacy top was kind of provocative.

He eyed the dress and then me.

"Oh, I like that," Cheryl said. "Find it in blue, too." She immediately dove into the racks with him. "We may have found your calling, Coop." Biting my tongue, I drifted to another rack, even as Cheryl let out a whoop. "Royal blue. This will match Bubba's eyes, right?"

"How the hell would I know?" Coop scoffed.

"Hang on, I have a picture, let me check…" Cheryl had a picture?

I stole a glance over as she whipped out her phone. Coop made a face, and I gave him a little smile. Dress shopping hadn't been high on my list, especially after Ian disappeared that morning. Jake had gone after him, but I hadn't heard from or seen either of them—until just after work when Jake sent me a text that everything was gonna be okay and happy hunting for a dress tonight.

Right up until then, I'd almost managed to make the mental block about the dress shopping. Coop waited for me by my apartment door when I got home, and he'd followed me inside. Thankfully, Mom wasn't home and Coop kept it upbeat. He even fed the cats while I grabbed a shower. But even a half-hour of extremely invested making out couldn't quite chase away the half-sick sensation left in the wake of Ian's absence.

I'd texted him before I went to work. Then at lunch. I debated sending him one before we went out to get the dress and then decided against it. If he wanted to answer me, he would.

For the last forty-five minutes, it had been look at dresses and find some to try on. The price tags on them were not cheap. I found a rack with dresses that had longer skirts. The gold one was kind of pretty.

"No, Frankie. You need to work on your tan if you want to go for that. Too cold and pale. It will wash you out."

Yeah, I didn't ask, Cheryl. But I kept that comment to myself as I looked past the pink and the yellow. There was a pale, almost silvery blue that made me think of Jake.

I tugged it out and held it up to me. It would hit right at my ankles. There was a slit at the side, and the bodice had an illusion gap. It would look open almost to my navel but the sheer mesh would disguise it some.

"That's not bad," Cheryl commented as she breezed past me with three other dresses. "I'll add it." She snagged it out of my hands and then was on the move.

"It's like watching a hurricane in action," Coop said as he drifted over to where I searched.

"Kind of feels like one." A force of nature. That description fit Cheryl to a T. "She had a picture of Ian?" I hadn't meant to ask, I wasn't going to ask. I was going to keep the inquiry to myself and yet…

"Yeah," Coop said as he ran his hand over his hair then rubbed the back of his neck. "It's just from one of the parties over the summer."

One of the parties. Cheryl had been at one of the parties.

Of course, she had. They'd all been at the parties. The guys invited everyone. I'd been invited. I just hadn't gone. "Cool."

"Frankie…"

Shifting away from the sympathy in his voice and his expression, I started wading through the rack again. A midnight purple mermaid dress caught my eye, and it was stunning.

Coop sighed. "That's beautiful," he said. "You'd look great in it. 'Course, you'd pretty much look great in anything here." He pretended to look around before he leaned close and whispered, "Even the cold and pale colors."

The corner of my mouth tugged up. "Thanks, Coop." I bumped his shoulder, and he hip checked me gently.

"Anytime. Want me to go add that to the rack?"

I blanched at the price tag. No way I could afford it. I mean, I could, but no way in hell was I spending that much.

"Come on," Coop said, bumping my shoulder again. "Try it on. I bet it looks amazing."

He'd been doing his best to be upbeat and cheerful, and all I'd done since I got home was sulk. Sucking it up, I held up the dress to myself again and glanced down. It really was gorgeous. "You know what…why not?" I didn't have to buy it.

"That's the spirit." He snagged the dress and went to add it to our collection. Surely we had enough. But Cheryl made a shooing motion toward the rest of the area.

"We have to make sure we look at everything available. Go on."

Turning away from her, I rolled my eyes. I didn't want to look at everything available. There were dresses out the wazzoo in here. Animal print. Chiffon. Lace. Tulle. So. Much. Tulle.

Ballerinas didn't use this much tulle.

I bypassed the animal print because I did not have the wherewithal to pull it off, for one. And for two—every single one seemed designed to be slinky and sexy. So not me.

Then again, I didn't really know what *was* me. I owned very few dresses and spent less time than most of them worrying about it. At this point, I'd also worn both of my nice dresses—on dates with Archie—so that meant I *had* to get something different for Homecoming.

Okay.

I needed a dress. We had dresses everywhere. Surely something would work. I wandered away from where Cheryl currently plundered and made my way to a different set of racks—oh, clearance! Perfect. Even twenty-five percent off some of these prices would be better than nothing.

The colors varied from a plum wine spaghetti strapped dress that included two long slits to a deep fuchsia wrap dress. I skipped right past those and then hesitated on a midnight blue sequin midi dress. It had a slit, but most of the skirt hit about mid-calf and it had a halter top with a triangle in the center. It would show some boob but not a lot of it.

And it had no back whatsoever.

Huh.

A hand snagged it out of my grip, and Cheryl grinned. "Normally, I'd fuss at you for sneaking over here, but this is a steal and it's gorgeous. I might have to fight you for it." She tossed it over her arm with three others and headed for the rack.

Relentless.

And stealthy.

"Someone needs to put a bell on her," Coop commented, and I grinned.

"Don't be mean."

"As if you weren't thinking the same thing," he charged, and then crossed his eyes. Laughing, I shook my head.

Because—well, yeah I had been thinking the same thing.

Still…

"Keep looking, Frankie," Cheryl said as she breezed past. The effervescent cheer in her voice grated less as the first hour dragged into the second.

Uh oh.

She was wearing me down.

In the end, I had twenty-seven dresses to try on.

Twenty-seven.

Coop and I were *never* getting out of here.

I would apologize to him, but he'd been the one to insist we go when I wanted to bail in the first place.

"Divide and conquer," Cheryl said. "We walk out in every dress. Coop, you are going to be the tie breaker if we can't agree."

"Oh. Joy. I was about to offer to get you ladies something to drink."

"Nope." Cheryl pointed him toward the puffy flat square seats. "Park it. You have to give us feedback."

He shot me a look, and I shook my head. "You said this would be fun, remember?" If I had to suffer, then so did he.

There might have been a little bit of hate in his eyes when I said that. A very little bit. Cheryl turned away, and Coop and I both stuck our tongues out each other and shot the middle finger.

Chuckling, I felt better and pushed my way into the cubicle with its metric ton of dresses. We'd divided them by length and hung some behind the door and on each of the walls. I also had a large three-panel full-length mirror to see how I looked in them.

Stripping out of my comfortable clothes, I debated which set of dresses to start with. Twenty-seven dresses.

Ugh.

There was a movie with that title and a couple of these reminded me of all of hers.

Blowing out a breath, I turned to my left and started with the short dresses. The first one—the strapless dress with the short skirt and the rusching—wouldn't work with my bra, so I had to lose it too. I squeezed into the dress and did a little hop shimmy before zipping up the last bit.

It hugged every part of me.

I had towels that covered more real estate.

"C'mon," Cheryl called. "Let's see it. I absolutely hate mine."

That boded well. After checking to make sure it actually covered my ass in the mirror, I sucked in my tummy and then opened the door. I made it two steps before I caught the snap of a camera phone.

When I glared at Coop, he just grinned. "And now my fun begins."

Ass.

Still, I laughed as he cocked his head to the side and gave me a critical look. Trying to ignore the nervous flutters, I glanced at Cheryl and then did a double take.

"Um…"

"It's fine," the blonde admitted as she swept a hand down as though indicating the whole poofy—thing. Yeah, I didn't have words for the dress. It was awful. "I hate it. It's not even a contender, and our boy over there flinched. You, though…" She twirled her finger, and I sighed before doing a little pirouette. "Three-inch heels, pull your hair up, and get a nice choker, and girl, you would slay in that dress. The blue is really working for you."

"Not really a fan," I admitted. I was not comfortable. At all. "It's too tight."

"No such thing," Cheryl said. "What do you think, Coop?"

"Nope," he said flatly, and we both glanced at him. Despite a scorching and intense stare, he gave me a lazy smile. "Homecoming *dance*. You dance in that outfit, and everyone is going to see your ass. So no, I think not."

"See, this is a no," I said, probably way too brightly. Admittedly, I liked the way he was looking at me, but the dress was just *too little*. Seriously, too little.

"I think it's a maybe," Cheryl countered. "It's too form fitting to show your ass. You can move in it, right?"

I really didn't intend to find out.

"C'mon, Coop. I know for a fact you can dance. Front and center." Cheryl clapped her hands. "Come dance with our girl, and let's see how it moves."

A startled look crossed Coop's face before he shoved off the seat and headed toward me. "Just pretend the music in here is louder," he offered, before crooking his finger.

They were killing me.

Laughter eddied upward. This was ridiculous.

But I caught Coop's offered hand and let him pull me to him. Wrapping my arms around his neck, I just hoped like hell the top didn't slide down.

Thankfully, it stayed firmly in place. Hands on my hips, Coop started to sway. This close, it was hard to miss the firm muscle where I brushed against him. He was also a lot warmer than I was. They had the air conditioning turned way down.

Oh, there was a benefit of ruching, my perking nipples were not on display. I might like this dress—a little. Especially since Coop looked at me like that. It was easy to move with him as he drifted in a simple box step.

We'd learned this one together in sixth grade gym when our school had its very first dance. Coach had taken pity on all of us and taught everyone a simple way to dance. Coop had been a great partner. Except, he had belched every time we got too close and then would crack up as I glared.

Thankfully, he made no such gesture now. With my hands that close to his hair, I curled my fingers to trace from his scalp to his nape. Faintly, somewhere, the music played overhead seemed a bit faster but we just kept moving slowly. Coop trailed his gaze down to my lips…

Cheryl's sudden burst of laughter sucked me right out of the moment. "Real dancing guys, though you look adorable at the moment."

"I'm good," I said, slipping my hands free and trying not to respond to the quirk of his lips. "We still have twenty-six dresses to go."

"Fine," Cheryl said, throwing up her arms. "Next ones then." She marched back into her changing room, and Coop snaked his arms around my middle and pulled me back before I could head into mine.

Lips next to my ear, he said, "I'm sorry."

Twisting to look at him, I raised my brows. "For what?"

"I thought you were exaggerating," he said in a tight whisper. "This really is going to take all night."

He pressed a kiss to my cheek, and I covered his hand on my abdomen. "Yep." My stomach gurgled. "We will need some major sustenance if I manage to survive this."

"You will," he promised. "I'll be here, every step of the way."

That made me feel better. "Thanks for coming," I said, and he grinned before hugging me against him.

"Glad I could be here, now go find your dress, Cinderella."

I laughed. "That would be shoes."

"Don't worry," Cheryl called. "We'll go out for shoes after we figure out the dresses."

I must have looked as stricken as I felt, because Coop put a hand over his mouth but couldn't quite muffle the snicker. Someday, I was totally getting even for this. It wasn't Coop's fault, but he was here, and he was having too much fun at my expense.

In honor of that, I kissed my finger before I flipped him off. Once I was shut back in the changing room, he cracked up for real. Leaning against the door, I stared at the dresses.

This was going to take forever.

Forever, it seemed, lasted about ninety-nine minutes. Not one hundred. Ninety-nine. Yes, I set a timer on my phone. I wanted something to write about in that journal I had to fill out, and as awkward as this was, it was so much better to try and focus on than the fact there'd been no word from Ian.

Not a peep.

I tried on the skater dress, the mermaid one, the dresses with one slit, dresses with two slits. I fit into the lace crop top and satin mini-skirt—Coop was a serious fan of that. The fact he took multiple pictures said as much.

When I walked out in the pale, silvery blue illusion gap dress, however, Coop and Cheryl both went absolutely silent.

"Wow," he'd exhaled, and leaned forward.

"I'll say," Cheryl commented slowly. "Twirl."

I did, and the skirt had the slightest bit of flare.

"That might be the one." She'd decided on hers, but we were still trying them all on. It was the principle of the thing. And I had to admit—I loved the dress she'd found for her. It was pink, lacy, and had a sheer lace overlay on a satin skirt. It was stunning. While not my favorite color, it looked amazing on her.

I'd left the red dress for last. I had no idea who picked it out—I hadn't seen it before we carried all the dresses in. It was simple, spaghetti straps, a curve bodice and the rest just fell straight down. No fitted waist or body-hugging cut. While I couldn't wear my bra with it, it was the first dress I put on that I actually felt comfortable in.

It clung without being clingy. The skirt moved easily and fell to my calves.

The pair of slits played peek-a-boo with my knees but didn't really gap open unless I moved.

If Coop's reaction to the illusion gap dress had been anything to go on, the red dress blew it out of the water.

"That one," he said without preamble as I stepped out. I grinned and glanced down, then rose up on my toes like I had on pretend heels.

"Yeah?"

I'd actually beaten Cheryl for once, but her door opened as I made a little twirl. She was back in her crop top and shorts. She paused to stare at me and nodded.

"Definitely that one."

Just like that, I had a dress. I ran my hands over the hips on it and then faced Coop again. He nodded as he snapped a picture. "Yes, Frankie. That one. You look great, you look like you feel great, and it's perfect."

Relieved and a little elated, I slipped back into the changing room and took the dress off. As I hung it up, I tugged out the tag and stared at it.

That was two weeks of tips…for a dress.

"Now that you have the colors," Cheryl said. "We can go get shoes."

"No," I answered. "Not tonight."

"But there's a great place…"

"I believe you, but I'm toast. I'm starving. And I've kept Coop up way past his bedtime." I crossed my fingers. *Please play along.*

"Well, she's not wrong. You know, I'm eighteen on Thursday, it's all down hill from here."

I grinned before mouthing *Thank you, Coop* to myself.

"Well, it is almost ten, and we still need to buy these before they close."

Almost ten?

Seriously?

I snagged my phone from on top of my shorts and stared at it. There were some messages from Archie and from Jake. Both giving me ratings on the various dresses.

Jerks.

But I was grinning.

The red dress won their votes, too.

I glanced at the dress and then the phone. Then I tabbed to Ian's message thread.

Ghost silent.

Me

I found a dress. It's red.

I hit send, then waited.

Not even a read receipt.

Sighing, I clicked the screen off and got dressed. The whole time, I argued with myself over the dress. Why would I spend that much on a dress for a dance?

There were others that I'd kind of liked, and they were less expensive. But I kept looking at the dress. It was my first school dance with a date. It was the first thing Ian told me he was going to ask me out to, and he said he would still take me, even if…even if we were only going to be friends.

I lifted the dress off the hook as I popped open the door. Cheryl stood there, grinning. Then she gave me a hug. It startled me, but I hugged her back.

"Thank you," she said with a wider smile.

"For?"

"For coming out tonight and doing this. I had fun, and I know you thought I was crazy, but girl, that dress was waiting for you. You're going to look like a million bucks." Her blazingly bright smile encouraged me to believe her. "That said, you want to go to Mini's or the Shoe Factory, they have the most comfortable heels, and they can color match if you can't find the right ones. So if scheduling is a thing, I want you to know where to go. The Drop Shop also has really great accessories you can pick up, and I'll text you my hair stylist. She does magical things. We should plan a day of pampering before the dance."

Um. No. But I smiled. Cheryl was exhausting me just talking about it, and that was all *before* the dance. "Thanks, I appreciate it. Sorry I'm not more enthusiastic."

"It's okay," she told me. "I know shopping seems like a boring thing, but it is exhausting. So, get your dress and go eat. We'll talk on Monday, okay?"

Coop took the dress from me as we followed Cheryl up to the counter. All the way there, I argued with myself, and Coop didn't say a word. Cheryl paid for hers and then waited for me to take my turn.

Fuck it.

I took the dress and went up there. It was expensive, but gorgeous, and I felt good in it. Coop's face had been worth it. I wanted to go to the dance, and I wanted to feel pretty.

I sucked it up and paid for the dress. Then it was time for another hug. As we left the store, the late hour seemed to hit all at once. I hadn't really slowed down today. I had chores and work the next day. And homework.

Weariness swept through me again. But before we parted… "Cheryl?"

She glanced over as she set her dress inside her little mini cooper. "Yeah?"

"Thank you," I told her. "Seriously. I had—fun."

"You bet. Night, Coop, thanks for being an honorary girl!"

"My pleasure," he said dryly, hooking an arm around my shoulder, and I leaned into him. "Next time, we should do our nails."

Cheryl laughed as she went to slide into the driver's seat. "Oh, my mom usually does the mum the weekend before, so if you want to, I'll give you her number to give your mom so she can show her how to make it—you know, if she needs help."

Oh.

The Homecoming mum. I hadn't even thought about that.

"I'll text it to you," Cheryl said, then waved. "Mitch is waiting for me, so I need to get over there. He's been grumbling for the last two hours since he found out Coop tagged along." She rolled her eyes. "Boys. Bye!"

Then she was out of there.

"Shopping," Coop said. "Sucks."

I laughed.

"Yes, but I wasn't kidding. I did kind of have fun." I glanced up at him. "Thanks for coming along. I know this wasn't what you had in mind for a date."

"I got to spend it with you," he told me serenely. "That's all that matters."

My stomach gurgled rudely.

"Now, let's feed you before you decide to eat me." He made a face, and I laughed.

"I'm not *that* hungry."

"Yet," he teased. He took charge of the dress and got it hung neatly in the back. I'd just spent a fortune on a dress, and I was strangely okay with it.

Whew.

"Food," Coop nudged me.

Yep. Definitely food.

You Went There

Archie

Any word from him?

Jake

No.

Coop

Zip. Just got back.

Archie

Ran late.

Coop

Lots and lots of dresses.

Jake

She looked good. How is she feeling?

Archie

She looked awesome. She got the red, right?

Coop

Yes to the red. Exhausted. Grabbed food, then home.

Jake

Nothing fun?

Coop

She was dead on her feet. Work tomorrow. Her mom wasn't there.

Archie

Good.

Jake

I'll swing by Bubba's tomorrow.

Coop

You went after him earlier. No luck at all?

Jake

He didn't want to talk.

Coop

I get that.

Jake

...

Archie

Explain.

Coop

Bubba's not the guy who wants to start the fight.

Jake

How is it a fight?

Archie

Look, he wants out. Fine. Why is he the one still taking her to Homecoming?

Coop

Not our call. It's hers. He asked. She wants to go.

Jake

Back up to the fight comment.

Archie

Sooner or later, Frankie chooses.

Jake

...

Coop

Yep. He's taking himself out of the fight. I get it.

Next day...

Coop

Homework hell today and I need a job.

Jake

Morning to you, too

Coop

Just need to get this done. Then see about finding a job. Thoughts?

Jake

Fast food?

Coop

Ugh. Thinking something flexible

Jake

I run food.

Coop

What?

Jake

I signed up for the food app delivery. Gets me extra cash.

Coop

...

Jake

Yes, you need a car.

Archie

Yeah, you need a car.

Coop

sigh

Archie

Talk to Frankie...

Coop

She hates people driving her car.

Archie

She really does.

Jake

Talk to your mom. Birthday is this week.

Coop

sigh

Jake

Sorry man, I'd let you use mine, but already busy.

Archie

I can loan you one.

Coop

What?

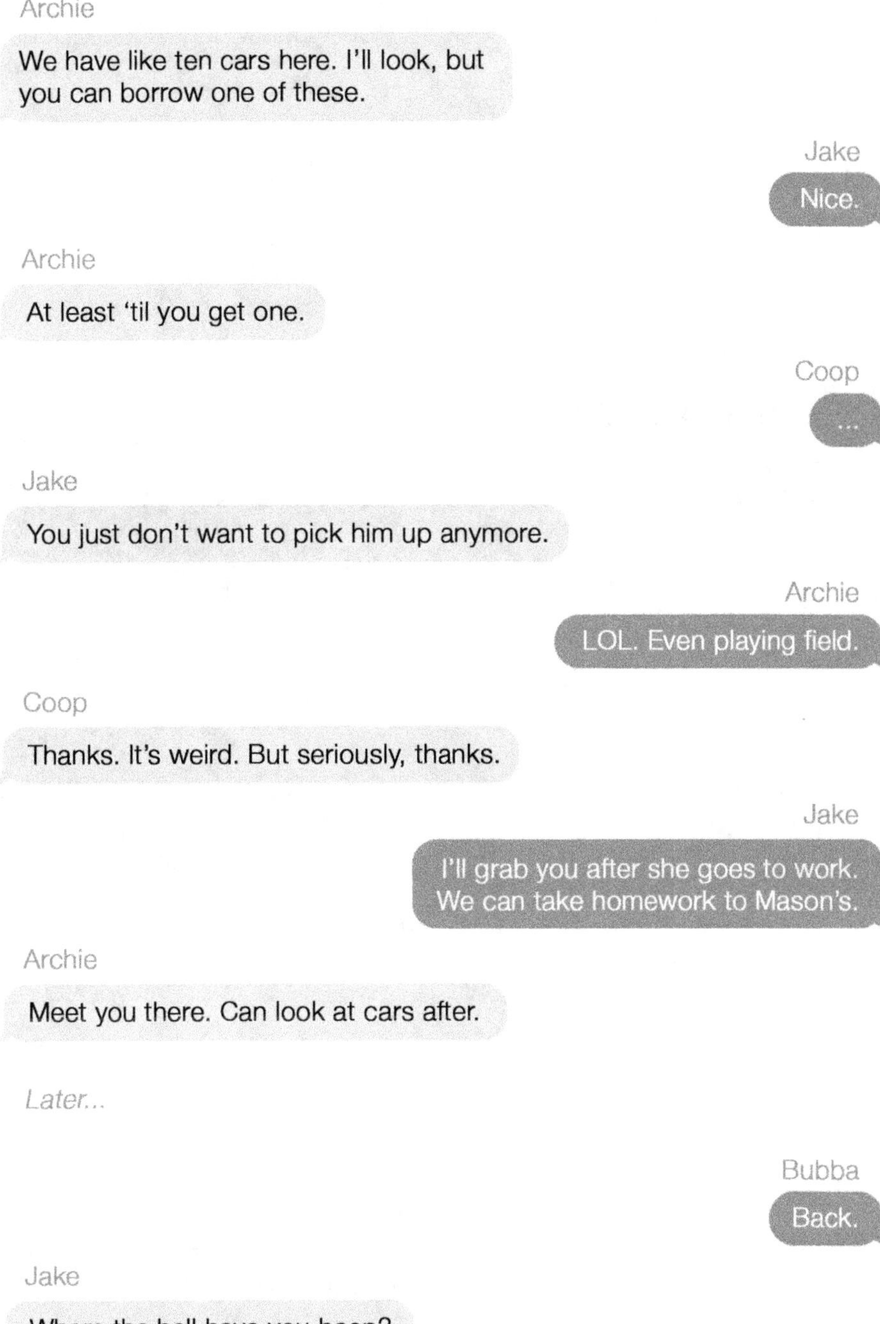
Archie
We have like ten cars here. I'll look, but you can borrow one of these.
Jake
Nice.
Archie
At least 'til you get one.
Coop
...
Jake
You just don't want to pick him up anymore.
Archie
LOL. Even playing field.
Coop
Thanks. It's weird. But seriously, thanks.
Jake
I'll grab you after she goes to work. We can take homework to Mason's.
Archie
Meet you there. Can look at cars after.
Later...
Bubba
Back.
Jake
Where the hell have you been?

Bubba

Went to Dallas with Dad.

Jake

Did your phone break?

Bubba

No. Just needed some time.

Jake

You talk to Frankie yet?

Bubba

I'll talk to her tomorrow.

Jake

You need to call her.

Bubba

She got a dress.

Jake

You need to call her.

Bubba

No.

Jake

Bubba

Bubba

I said no. You guys all went too far, too fast. She's hurting. She needs room to breathe.

Jake

Yes, she is. She thinks you broke up with her.

Jake

Now you're ghosting me again.

Look, I don't know what all is going on,
but talk to us.

Chapter Two
NOBODY TAUGHT US TO QUIT

"Wrap up your last order," Marsha said, nodding to the shake I had mixing. "Then you can close out." It was literally fifteen minutes early. Not that I was complaining, but I shot my manager a quizzical look. Marsha was awesome. Had been awesome last weekend when I was coming apart at the seams. Had covered for me to get out away from the guys and promised me time off when I needed it, because she didn't want me to miss anything in my senior year.

She definitely rated as one of my favorite people ever. Hard not to when she took the time to check on me—all this *after* giving me this job almost two years earlier when I really had zero experience.

"After you wrap up, come in the back, okay?" She patted my shoulder and then hustled on. Most Sundays, we were busy as all get out with the post-church crowd, and today had been no exception. But the hustle diminished in the last hour, and the dinner rush hadn't begun. It was a good time to call it done. I'd managed to get most of my sidework done, so I didn't even have to finish that.

The guys had been in earlier—well, three of them. Ian was still a no show, and I forced myself to focus on something else. Radio silence on his part was unusual. The fact Jake, Archie, and Coop avoided mentioning him was also telling. Shake finished, I dropped it off and let the customers know someone else would be looking after them and wished them a great rest of their day.

A couple of minutes later, I weaved past the cooks on the line and headed past the freezer to Marsha's office. Her door was open, and music spilled out. The familiar country twang was not my first choice, but my boss tended to listen to it while doing paperwork. It kept her relaxed.

Or so she claimed. The tears in my beer and the truck took off with the horse tunes tended to wax and wane between desperately sad and almost painfully upbeat about how awful life was—different strokes for different folks. Better that than focus on the fact the pitiful woman described in the current song could be me.

"Come on in," Marsha said, pushing her rolling chair back as I slid into the office. She reached around me and hooked the door closed. "Did you grab yourself a drink?"

"I'm good," I assured her. Seriously, I was more tired than hungry or thirsty. Jake was supposed to meet me later for a date, but he hadn't mentioned what we were doing, and I was kind of hoping for enough time to make a side trip beforehand—even if I smelled like burgers.

"Well, sit down then," Marsha said, waving me toward the hardback chair propped next to her desk. The cushion was old vinyl, and there was a split in it from years of use. Weirdly, this was more comforting than the bad music, which she thankfully turned down.

"Okay," she said after I perched. I still had on my work apron with the order pad and tips in my pockets. It needed to be washed, but I'd deal with that later.

Despite the awkward beginning, Marsha didn't continue. I raised my brows. "Okay?"

With a smile that creased her cheeks and a half-laugh, she said, "You got a dress last night?"

"Oh, yeah. I did." I'd mentioned going out the day before.

"Well c'mon, let's see it." Enthusiasm churned in every word. I gaped for a second, but she made grabby hand motions, and I laughed.

"Yeah, Coop went with me, and he took a lot of pictures…" Dragging out my phone, I stole a look at Ian's text thread, it was still dark, no red numbers. Swallowing that lump, I tabbed down to Coop's thread. There were a couple of quick messages. One was a question about lit and the other was just a random *what are you wearing* googly-eyed emoji text.

Dork.

I scrolled up to find the photos he'd sent and clicked the red dress before I turned it to show Marsha.

"Oh. I love it." Taking possession of my phone, she blew up a couple of areas to get a look at it. "Did you get shoes? Jewelry? What are your plans for your hair?"

The rapid-fire questions had me gaping all over again. "I hadn't really thought about it. I need to get shoes. Cheryl told me a couple of places to go, and one that will dye the shoes to match the shade of the dress, and I guess—I've got a couple of necklaces that might work."

Jewelry really wasn't my thing.

Eyeing me, Marsha tutted before she handed me the phone back, then reached for a sticky note and scrawled some information. "Go to these shops, they're over off third near the old downtown. They look like junk shops, trust me when I say they aren't. They're vintage stores, and they have some of the best items you've ever seen. If you go into Coat Rack…" Apparently, the name of one of the not-junk stores. "Ask for Carol. She has the best eye and knows every piece in her shop. Show her the dress, and she'll find the most adorable items to accessorize it with."

Tapping her pen against her lower lip, Marsha considered me.

"If I'm being too nosy, tell me, but let's talk hair and make-up, do you have a plan for the day?"

The Homecoming game was on the Friday night. The dance was on Saturday. There was a parade that afternoon. It was a huge thing. "Um… I'm working, so I'll probably go home, shower and throw everything on. It'll be fine."

That got me a narrow-eyed look. She added another name and a phone number. "This is Ms. Liz, she's a dream to work with. You call her and tell her I gave you her number. She'll get you set right up, my treat."

"Wait…no, Marsha."

"Ah." She held up a hand as she snapped out the syllable. "Let me do this. Homecoming may not seem like a big deal, right now."

No, it seemed like a huge deal.

"You have a world of experiences in front of you, after high school ends. But when you look back, I don't want you to have a single regret. Ms. Liz will do all the heavy lifting. She'll style your hair and do your cosmetics, and you won't have to worry. You're also *not* working that day. In fact, let's throw a massage in there, too."

"I'm good," I assured her. "Really. Massages from people I don't know just…" A shudder raced through me. There was something kind of squicky about the idea of some stranger putting their hands all over me. No thank you.

"Fine," Marsha said. "But hair and make-up are still on me." She tapped her lip again. "I feel like I'm forgetting something, but we have time. Just call her soon, all right? I'll send a message to expect to hear from you, so she already has you on the schedule."

Oh, nicely trapped. Now, even if I didn't want to spend Marsha's money, I'd have to call or risk making her look bad and wasting her friend's time.

"I'll call," I promised.

"Good." After peeling the sticky note off, she handed it to me. "That wasn't the only reason I asked you to come back."

"I'm fired?" It was a joke but she didn't laugh.

"Not exactly," she said, and the sudden sober expression had my stomach plummeting. Was the help her way of softening the blow of my dismissal? "I did something for you, and you're going to accept it because while I filled out the paperwork, you won it on your own merit."

What was she talking about?

From under her blotter, she drew out a letter and held it up. "You know Mason's is a franchise, right? I bought into it years ago? I own this store, but we're still part of a larger corporation."

"Um…sure. I think that was in the materials you gave me to read during training." Though it had been a while, and it wasn't like I dealt with corporate. Marsha was the manager and the owner. This was her store, and she ran it her way.

"Well, that part isn't important. What *is* important, is that every year, stores from all over the country are invited to nominate employees for scholarships. You have to be solid students with a good GPA, and you have to have declared intentions to attend or already be enrolled in college, and you need three recommendations."

Excitement threaded at the possibility. I needed all the help I could sew up in advance. "When's the deadline for submitting it?"

"Last May. There will be another one this coming May, but you won't be eligible to apply for that one." The corner of Marsha's mouth tilted up.

"Oh." The syllable came out riding a wave of disappointment. "I guess I should have done my due diligence." In my defense, I'd been hella distracted last April and May, but that wasn't an excuse. "Wait…why wouldn't I be eligible this coming May? You said people could apply if they were in college too, and I'd just be wrapping high school."

"Because you were awarded the scholarship for this year."

The music faded, the room seemed to get bigger, and I was really happy I had already sat down. "But I didn't apply…"

"No sweetie, I applied for you," Marsha told me with a grin. "I nominated you for it, and I talked to some of your teachers at school and they gave me great recommendations. I thought when I asked, I'd get one or two, but every single teacher wrote one for you." She shook the envelope at me. "Go ahead, open it."

Disbelief held me hostage. "You—you applied for me?"

"Yes, I did. You work hard, Frankie. I told you that, and I've got my own kids in college. I know a good opportunity when I see it. They didn't get this scholarship the years they applied, but they didn't have your GPA or your dedication. You make me proud, and I'm so thrilled for you. Now open it." The last came out on a laugh, and I took the envelope. It was thick, though a standard legal-sized envelope. I slit the back of it as Marsha clapped her hands and I glanced at her.

"Do you know what it is?"

"Maybe, but there's nothing like seeing the real thing. C'mon…the suspense is killing me. We're not all young."

I snorted, but pulled out the fat sheaf of papers and unfolded them.

Dear Ms. Curtis,

It is our honor to present you with the James T. Mason Foundation Scholars Award for academic excellence and perseverance. Each award is given individually based on the merit of the applicant and relies heavily on the presentation of recommendations, which our board weighs along with your academic record, stated goals, and history with the company.

You have been deemed an outstanding candidate and in support of that, you are receiving a two hundred and fifty thousand dollar scholarship to be divided amongst four years of your education…

The rest of the words blurred out. A quarter of a million dollar scholarship.

I jerked my gaze up to Marsha, and her grin was a thousand watts all on its own. Dizzy, I held up the papers, and then she just pushed up from her chair and dragged me out of mine.

The hug was even better than the one she gave me last week, and laughter bubbled out me. "A quarter of a million dollars."

"I *know*!" Marsha enthused, and I squeezed her.

"Thank you."

"Oh honey, it was all you, I just made sure they had all the details on just how exceptional you are. I know it's not enough to cover four years of Harvard but…"

Pulling back, I stared at her askance. "Marsha, this is awesome. I know I'm going to have student loans but this—this is so much money, and it means that with this, with my savings, and maybe the other scholarships I applied for—I might be able to take out far less in loans. Thank you."

"I'm delighted for you. I've been sitting on this all day. It came in yesterday's mail, but I didn't see it until this morning, and I couldn't be happier."

Dazed, I could appreciate why she'd waited.

She let out another happy laugh and hugged me. "Now get out of here and go see those boys of yours and celebrate. I'm so proud of you."

I was still trying to digest what this all meant as I clocked out and headed for the doors. I had to count my tips, and I needed a shower in the worst way. But the papers in my hands were like holding onto real gold. The heat outside was a slap as I made my way to the car.

Archie's and Jake's had bracketed it earlier when they came in to do their homework along with Coop. I'd been too busy to hang out, but they'd been great, and it had been nice to have them there. They were still being protective, even if Ian hadn't been with them…

Even if…

Some of the joy of the scholarship waned. There was no even if. I didn't like the fact Ian had taken off. I liked even less that he wasn't answering my texts. Hypocritical, considering I ghosted them over the summer? Maybe.

But he just left the morning before. It had all seemed fine, and then he left. I guess it wasn't fair to expect all of them to be okay with me dating each of them, but they were the ones who'd said it was all right.

Then again, Ian was also the first one to ask me out, and I had sex with Archie and with Jake. So maybe his leaving was my fault.

Sitting down in the driver's seat, I got the car started and opened the windows to let the hot air out. I was already sweating. October was literally right around the corner, but it was still hot.

Sweat already dampened my back, but I just unfolded the scholarship letter and reread it. It seemed surreal. A quarter of a million dollars. Some of the scholarships I applied for were like twenty grand, and that even seemed like spitting into the wind at the idea I'd get it.

Marsha was the best.

I wanted to take a picture of it send it to the chat I had with all the guys, but like the chat with Ian, that one had been quiet all weekend. I'd talked to Archie, Jake, and Coop in our individual threads, but not in the group.

Coop and I hadn't really talked about Ian the night before, and Archie and Jake had been all about the dresses. When I did laundry earlier, Jake and I had debated the latest History Buff video while Coop made a top ten list of all the reasons he was never going shopping again, except he'd enjoyed seeing me in the dresses.

That had been funny.

Archie had just asked how I was doing, and I knew what he really wanted to know was whether I had bad meatloaf at home. Thankfully, that answer had been no. I mean, maybe they were there, except the cats hadn't been locked in my room, so I thought it was a safe bet they weren't.

Speaking of the cats, I needed to go feed them. I also still needed to get Coop something for his birthday. But instead of pulling out and heading home or sending a text to the guys, I re-read the letter for the third time.

My phone buzzed.

Jake

Probably going to be late. 7 okay?

I smiled.

Me

7 is fine. Want me to order takeout?

Jake

Nope. Unless you're still tired from last night. Then I can bring food.

Me

You want to go out, out?

Jake

Duh. Let me know if you don't. That's okay. Gotta run, baby girl. See you soon.

I'd text the guys when I got home. I could celebrate with Jake tonight, but I wanted all of them to know. It wasn't until I got home and fed the cats that the nerves resurged. If I sent the news to the group chat and everyone but Ian responded, that would suck.

But if I changed the group message or created a new one without him in it? That would be worse.

Damned if I did. Damned if I didn't.

By the time I finished my shower, I wasn't so much sad as pissed off. Fine, if Ian wanted to be friends—friends still answered their text messages. When I'd stopped answering their messages over the summer, I'd been angry with them. Angry and hurt.

So if he wasn't answering mine…

Wrapped in a towel with another around my hair, I picked up the phone and opened his text message.

Me

> I know you've been quiet since you left, and maybe you need the time. That's okay. But not answering me is not okay. I am worried about you. I miss you. When I didn't talk to you over the summer, it was because I was mad. I was hurt. I felt betrayed. If you feel that way, I'm sorry. Please tell me what I did wrong.

That last line was pathetic. I backed it up and changed it.

Me

> Please talk to me.

Better.

Hitting send on it before I could change my mind, I tried not to focus on the lack of read receipts on the earlier messages I'd sent him.

In the bedroom, I laid out the scholarship letter, took a picture of it, and then sent it to the group chat with *GUESS WHAT!!!!!* in all caps and lots of exclamation points. Excitement eddied in and out of the worry and the irritation. Could you be excited and pissed off at the same time?

Apparently.

I toweled off and hung those up before I changed into Jake's boxers—a surprise for him if we ended up getting naked—denim shorts, a thin bra, and a tank top. I felt so much better, and I didn't smell like grease and hamburgers.

I blew out some of the dampness from my hair, but didn't dry it all the way and left it down. Then and only then did I go back to check my phone.

Coop

> Holy shit! Go Frankie!

Jake

> Damn! Congrats!

Archie

You're a rock star. Glad the rest
of the world knows it, too.

Coop

We need to celebrate.

Jake

We will.

Archie

You're funny. All of us, tomorrow.
This deserves more than just a text.

There were heart emojis and great answers. But no response from Ian.
None.

My smile faded, and my earlier irritation resurged. There was a read receipt. It said all read. That meant they'd all seen it *including* Ian.

I tabbed over to his text message, and there was a read receipt and three blinking dots.

Sinking onto the bed, I stared at those three dots and waited.

And waited.

Finally…

Ian

Congrats on the scholarship. You
deserve it. I'm not mad. I promise.

That was it. I gave it another minute, but he said nothing else.

Me

But you're hurt?

C'mon, Ian, talk to me.

Ian

I spent the weekend with my dad, Frankie. It's—a lot of this is complicated, and you're on the spot with everyone. We're still friends, I mean that.

Me

That didn't answer my question.

Ian

Getting ready to have dinner with Mom and Dad.

I stared at the message and frowned. If I got up early tomorrow, I could see Ian at school before practice. It would have to be really early. But he couldn't just walk away if I was in front of him.

Ian

Not hurt. I promise. I'm sorry this has been confusing. I meant what I said yesterday morning. Talk tomorrow, okay? You have a date with Jake tonight, and I don't want to spoil it.

I could cancel. Tell Jake I needed to go see Ian. Hell, I could probably ask Jake to go with me to see Ian. He'd been the one who went after him yesterday, but he hadn't said a word about it since. So maybe I should talk to Jake first.

Me

You're not spoiling anything. I just miss you. I don't like this distance.

Ian

Me neither. But I promise, we'll talk tomorrow.

Tomorrow.

Biting my lip, I waited. I mean, I could ask Rachel. I wasn't sure we were at the ride or die stage of friendship here. To be honest, it had been love/hate for years. The fact Rachel had turned out to be Mr. Thorns and said she thought I needed a friend had been a rather shocking, if delightful surprise.

She had a crush on me, but not an unrealistic one. I didn't swing that way, and if I did, she'd have totally won me over with the way she'd sent the roses and the gifts. The last of the roses had already wilted. I'd pressed some of the petals into a book to keep them. I had all the notes, too.

But I thought if I called Rachel and said I needed her help, she'd do it. She liked giving the guys shit. To be honest, I thought she'd liked doing it because she'd had a crush on one of them and they'd blown her off or something.

Nope.

My mistake.

Well, he was talking to me again. That was a good start.

Flopping back on the bed, I stared at the ceiling. I should be doing homework or something, but I kind of just wanted to lie there and savor my two huge successes of the day.

I got a scholarship.

Ian answered me.

Good things.

Ian might be waiting to break up with me for real. Maybe he wanted to tell me he didn't want to ask me to not date the other guys. Or maybe he wanted me to just choose him. That was the stitch, wasn't it? At some point, I'd have to choose between them?

How did I choose between my best friends? I adored all of them. It would be like asking me to pick only one of my cats.

Okay, the guys weren't cats, but the idea was essentially the same. Tiddles leapt onto the bed as if summoned by the thought, and he rubbed along my arm. I'd found him when he was a kitten, hiding under a bush in a downpour. He'd been a miserable little thing.

He'd also bitten the hell out of me when I scooped him up and carried him inside. The vet had said he was young, maybe ten weeks—if that. I couldn't figure out if he'd just gotten lost or if someone had let him go. It didn't matter. From that day forward, he'd been mine. He was the first cat I found. Tabby and Tory came along later.

But I loved all three of them.

The cat rolled over and purred as I stroked him. My phone buzzed, and I picked it up to see Jake's message.

Jake

What are we doing?

Me

Takeout. Mom isn't here. It would be just us.

Jake

Sold. Preference?

Me

Surprise me.

Jake

See you in fifteen.

I smiled, even if he couldn't see me, and glanced at Tiddles. "We're having company tonight."

To say my cat wasn't impressed was an understatement, and I laughed. Then my phone buzzed again.

Mom

Dinner tomorrow evening. You. Me.
No boys. No excuses.

I made a face.

Ugh.

I flopped back against the bed and stared at the ceiling. How many weeks until I turned eighteen and this wasn't my problem anymore?

Chapter Three
I WOULD FOR YOU…

"You didn't have to get up," Jake chided me as I yawned at my cereal for the third time in as many minutes. Somehow, I'd failed to make the connection between Jake sleeping over and crack of dawn football practice. Another reason to avoid sports.

Sports bad.

Sleep good.

"I know," I said. He was already dressed. Normally, he wore his practice gear, but since he had at least another week of sitting it out, he didn't bother. "But you have your first session with Diane today."

I was half-dressed, sitting there in a bra, shorts—his boxers too, because Jake had lost his mind a little bit when he'd peeled off my shorts last night and found me in them.

A little shiver went through me. Sex was a hell of a lot of fun. Even better was the fact Jake could make me laugh, even when he was blowing my mind.

He made a face. "I know. Hopefully, it'll be quick."

The mandatory sessions were going to cut into some of our time. His first session was after lunch when we had study hall.

"She said twice a week. I didn't start last week because she had other crap going on, and I kind of hoped she'd forget about it." He shrugged. "Coop said to just agree with her, listen to her questions, act contrite, and I could probably bounce after a couple of sessions."

"Yes, because Coop's had anger management before." I didn't roll my eyes, but I thought about it. "Not that his advice is bad, but just be careful."

Jake grinned. "Don't worry about me, baby girl, I got this."

Every time he called me that, I got a little flutter. It was ridiculous how much I enjoyed it. "I'm going to worry," I reminded him before I drained the milk from my cereal bowl and he did the same. It was great that we could both sit there and slurp up the milk without missing a beat.

"Because you're you," he said, and kissed me before grabbing the bowls. "Archie's going to swing by to get you and Coop, and I'll see you after practice."

I sighed a little. He'd kiboshed the idea of me going to see Ian before practice. They needed to focus on the game, and while Ian might be acting like a jackass—Jake's word, not mine—distracting him could cause injuries.

"I'll make sure Bubba shows up, too," he promised, and I made a face.

"Don't."

"Excuse me?" He paused in pulling on his backpack as I stood. I still needed to go grab a shirt and finish getting my shit together to go to school. The cats had been fed, and I'd take out the trash on my way to Archie's car. I kind of hated not being able to take my own. The guys were awesome, but even if they were willing to pick me up and drop me off for the rest of the year, I wasn't.

I liked having independence.

Exhaling, I said, "Don't make Ian come to coffee if he doesn't want to."

Jake squinted at me.

"I told him how I felt. I told him I wanted to talk to him. He promised he would talk to me today. If he wants to avoid coffee, that's on him."

"Hey," he said, wrapping an arm around me. "Bubba just needs to get his head out of his ass. That requires assistance sometimes. But this isn't your fault, Frankie. You know that, right?"

"It feels like my fault. Everything seemed—crazy but all right, and then he left and he didn't talk to me. I guess I owe all of you a bigger apology for when I ghosted you."

"No you don't," Jake told me. "We're good. We talked, we worked it out, and you know what? We're in a *much* better place. Maybe we had to get our heads out of our asses too before we could appreciate the good thing we almost screwed up."

"Keyword there," I reminded him as I nuzzled a kiss at his smooth jaw. It had been fun to watch him shave this morning. "We. If I had talked sooner, maybe we would have figured it out sooner." Now I was whining, because instead of four boyfriends, I might only have three. Only. Ian said we were still friends. So maybe I shouldn't complain. "I guess it all worked out."

"Yep, and this will, too. You wait and see." Then with a groan, he gave me another kiss. "I really gotta go. Even if I don't do shit, I'll catch hell if I'm late."

"I know, see you later."

Then he was gone.

I hadn't told Jake about my mother's text. The only thing she hadn't included was a time for dinner. To be honest, I hadn't decided whether I was going to listen to her or not. Archie wanted to celebrate my scholarship, and so did Jake and Coop.

It would be a double celebration, 'cause Jake had gotten a scholarship we both applied for, and I was thrilled for him. He'd been worried about telling me, because he really hoped I'd gotten one from them, too. He was sweet, but I wanted to celebrate his news. This was great.

I glanced at the clock and smothered another yawn. I could actually go lie down for another hour if I wanted. But then I'd have to do my hair again. Bedhead and I were old enemies.

Coffee cup in hand, I retreated to my room and my laptop. I had the time, so I went to work drafting my essay. I had an idea, and I decided to strike while the iron was hot. If it fizzled out, well then, at least I could work on homework.

Ninety minutes later, I had two full essays written. I'd been half-tempted to send them to Ian, since we'd been reading each other's, but I sent them to Ms. Fajardo instead. Until I knew what was going on with Ian, it was probably better to not assume. Ms. Fajardo would give me feedback.

Backpack on and trash bag in hand, I let myself out and locked the door just as Coop was jogging up the steps. He pouted at me. "Aww…what happened to my good morning kiss?"

I busted out laughing at the forlorn expression he wore. Switching the trash bag to my other hand, I rose up on my tiptoes to kiss him. He gripped the bag to take it, even as he slid his free hand around my nape. The gentle stroke of his tongue against my lips had me sighing against his mouth.

Part of why I'd slipped out rather than let him in was because he'd developed this habit for kissing the ever-loving hell out of me against the fridge and then we had to leave. I was wound up enough.

But damn, Coop could kiss. Everything tingled from my head to my toes. You wouldn't know I'd just spent the night with Jake, because heat swept through my system and I half-gasped as he deepened the kiss. The stroke of his thumb against my throat just sent my pulse into overdrive.

When he lifted his head, the faint sounds of traffic in the distance, kids calling to each other as they headed to the bus stops, the beeping of a truck backing up somewhere flooded in, and I blew out a breath.

Heat flushed my face, and my thoughts had scattered like the split on a pool table when the white ball struck the others. Coop grinned slowly, but his chest rose and fell rapidly, and there was definitely a flush high on his cheekbones.

"Good morning," he murmured.

"Wow," was the best I could do. It worked to puncture some of the tension, and his grin grew wider.

"I can do wow."

"Yes, yes you can." I laughed along with him. Then fanned myself. Maybe that was why he saved those kisses for inside. I felt like I'd overheated from running a marathon. Pleasure flashed in his eyes as he clasped my hand and led the way down the steps. Probably a good plan, because I was having trouble getting everything back in order.

All that carefully nurtured focus that let me write up those essays had been utterly decimated. Instead, I was watching Coop's ass. He was in khaki colored shorts today, and his hairy calves were tanned, well flexed with every step. He wasn't big like Ian or Jake, but more lean and rangy. But it was a mistake to think he wasn't strong, he was damn wiry.

How, I had no idea. In all the years we've known each other, Coop always seemed allergic to the gym. I used to be able to do more push-ups than him. So, maybe some of it was a blessing of genetics. Hand in hand, we walked together to the dumpster, where he swung the bag up, over, and in without ever letting go of me.

"Hey," he said, angling us toward the curb where we could wait for Archie. I tried not to look at my car. Apparently, I wasn't that successful. Even still humming from his greeting, there was a pang at the fact I wasn't taking *my* car to school because a few kids had been dicks. "It's not forever," he said, then tugged me closer and wrapped an arm around my shoulders. It was nice—hot, but nice.

"I know, but I *like* having my own car and the freedom to do what I want when I want."

"Yep," he said, pressing a kiss to my temple. "I know. But we like to not have people abuse your car, either. We still don't know what jerk did it."

"So, now we ride with Archie or Jake, and they're trapped to our schedules?" That could get tiresome for anyone real quick. Particularly with Ian being so cagey.

"We'll adjust," Coop said. "It's not forever. Besides—you've been giving me rides forever, have you really minded going out of your way for me?"

"No," I said. "I like to give you crap about it."

"Well, Archie and Jake don't mind doing this for you. I wouldn't mind being able to give you rides, either."

I made a face. "Fine, I'd call you guys overprotective, but last week had some really sucky parts to it."

"Exactly, we're going to apply a concentrated effort to make sure this week and every other week improves. Deal?"

Some of my sour mood fled, and I smiled up at him. "Deal."

"Great, now I congratulated you about the scholarship, and we're celebrating tonight."

"Well, after school." Tonight still had the issue of my mom, but I did *not* want to talk about her.

"Exactly, but I think I need to really congratulate you because that scholarship is awesome."

"Coop…" I didn't get to finish the sentence because he ducked his head and kissed me again. My pulse rabbited, and I was gripping his shirt as he thrust his tongue against mine. The playfulness had turned demanding. Plastered against his side, all I could think was we had on too many clothes, followed swiftly by we were standing out in the open where anyone could see us.

Then he'd suck on my tongue or press more firmly against my lips, and those thoughts fell away. The sharp blare of a horn jerked through me, but Coop shifted slightly and continued the kiss until I relaxed. Then he lifted his head, and I found him aiming his middle finger at Archie, who stared at us with a bemused expression.

"That was congratulations, by the way," Coop said, grinning. "Can't wait to celebrate."

Wow.

"Okay." That I managed those two syllables was a credit to me. Laughing, Coop caught my backpack and eased it off of me before climbing in the backseat with his backpack and mine before I climbed in the passenger seat. The air conditioning was a relief as it washed over me.

Archie held out a velvet jewelry box toward me, and I blinked.

"Hey," Coop protested. "That's cheating."

"Giving her a congratulations present? I think not. Besides, Frankie and I have a deal."

We did?

Then he nodded to my wrist, and I glanced at my bracelet and grinned. "We do have a deal."

"Yep, and I already owed you one new charm, and I picked up a couple more. We can get those added on after school today. I've got the tools to do it, or we can take it to the store."

A little thrill zipped through me as I popped the box open. Archie kept the car idling as he watched me flip it open, and Coop leaned between the seats. Four charms nestled together in the velvet box—a stylized J that matched the A and the F. For Jake. That was both embarrassing and desperately sweet.

A boxed present with a ribbon charm sat next to it, because the bracelet had been one of my very first real jewelry gifts. A movie reel—cause Jake took me to the drive-in. I laughed. The last one was a pair of boxing gloves.

"Why boxing gloves?"

"'Cause you've gone a few rounds the last few days, and you're still standing." The steady gleam in his eyes made me smile. "I gotta get you one for the scholarship. You're achieving things fast, babe. I love it."

"Thank you, Archie," I said, then leaned over and kissed him. It wasn't quite the tense, pulse pounding and almost a make out session kiss I'd been sharing with Coop, but there was a thrill and an effortless sweetness.

Through the insane rollercoaster of the last three weeks, Archie had been right there, throwing his hands up in the air and howling alongside me. I leaned back, biting my lip as Coop grinned at me then Archie and back.

"You need a C for that bracelet."

Archie snorted, but I laughed as I closed the case. I was pretty sure I knew why he'd given me a J. "You do have a birthday coming up," I teased Coop.

"Hey, you're right. How could I forget?" He stretched his arms wide. "Eighteen. Woot. Still have to go school."

Then we were all laughing as I passed the box back to Coop, he secured it in my backpack for me while I pulled on my seatbelt.

"Unfortunately, only Ian got to be born outside of the school year."

"Eh," Archie said. "Jake got Christmas break, there are worse times."

"Yes, but that means everyone gave him combo Christmas and birthday presents."

In unison, Coop and Archie groaned. "That's a crime," Archie declared. "That's why we make a point to *not* give him dual presents."

True.

"And your birthday is in four weeks," I reminded him.

"Seriously?" Archie pressed a hand to his chest. "You mean it really is on the same day every year?"

Snickering, I slapped his arm, and he grinned. "Ass."

"Sometimes," he admitted. "Sometimes."

We swung through and picked up coffee on our way in. I spotted Ian's bike after Archie parked. It wasn't far from Jake's SUV. Still, it made me sad that he'd parked it a couple of slots *away* from the yellow vehicle.

Or maybe Jake had. Jake had been irked with him, too. I made a face.

"Don't worry about Bubba," Archie suggested. "He'll come around. Just let him get it out of his system—whatever it is."

"I told you," Coop started, but Archie glared at him, and Coop raised his hands.

"Told him what?" I glanced between them as we began to walk. When neither was forthcoming, I repeated it. "Told him what, Coop?"

"Arch is right, let Bubba figure it out, Frankie."

"That is not what you were saying earlier." I stared at him, and Coop lifted his shoulders.

"But it is what we should do. It's Bubba, the guy stops and goes out of his way to buy Girl Scout cookies, even if he never eats them."

Yes, that was one bizarre eccentricity. Ian had never liked their cookies. I, on the other hand, had never met a Thin Mint or a Samoa I did not love.

Fuck. Now I wanted Girl Scout cookies, and it was forever until February.

"Jake said to give him time, so I'm giving him time. But I'm worried about him." We were almost to the doors, so I pivoted to face them as we all came to an abrupt halt. "So, if you guys are keeping some other secret…or something you don't want to tell me about him, I'd really like to hear it now and not in some note stuffed in my locker or a post online."

I hadn't been on Instagram in days, and I'd shut off the notifications on my other social media outlets. There were probably messages waiting. Fine. Let them wait.

I'd had enough of having their past rubbed in my face. I knew it happened.

"Let's just say I don't want another bite of the bad decision bagel."

"Bad decision bagel?" Archie lifted his eyebrows.

"Our last summer," Coop surmised, and I nodded.

"For what it's worth, Frankie, I don't know any secrets about Bubba that have anything to do with this. I think it's all him. Now, that said, I haven't seen or spoken to him since Saturday morning."

Coop pursed his lips then scuffed a shoe.

"But apparently Coop has?" Archie's tone held more of a question than a recrimination as he eyed him.

"Just give him some time, Frankie," Coop said. "Okay? We should head in, they should be out of practice and getting changed."

That was it.

When I didn't move right away, he sighed. "I would do anything for you. But they're my friends, too. If Archie or Jake tell me something and trust me with it, I'm going to keep my mouth shut the same way I do with stuff you tell me."

"Except for the parts you decide everyone else needs to know."

"When it comes to you being safe or any of them? Yes."

Uh huh.

"Okay."

Turning, I grabbed the door before one of them could and held it open. Archie had his own bag and the rest of the coffees, and Coop gave me a look as I just stared at him.

"Thank you," he said with a wink, but I didn't feel like smiling much. I lagged a little as we walked, turning over the whole situation in my head. The not knowing was making me nuts. I half wanted to start a fight with Coop over the fact he was keeping a secret.

But that would be the bitchy thing to do. Then again…not talking about how I felt and swallowing my aggravation got us into this mess. The harsh reality of dating all of them hit me as we walked into the cafeteria. I couldn't talk to them about them.

Coop was going to defend him or at least counsel me to be patient—which he did. Archie would be skeptical and wary. Jake wanted to distract me and I think buy Ian some time to come around. But he'd also been pissed on my behalf, too.

Or maybe it was on his.

Truthfully, it wasn't always about me.

"There you are," Rachel said, as if she'd damn near apparated into being next to me. There was no way to disguise my jump, and she grinned. "Someone was lost in thought."

"Yes," I told her. Not like there was any point in lying. "Hi."

She grinned. "Hi. Nice save, you didn't even slosh your coffee." Hooking her arm through mine, she walked with me toward our table. "I'll let you put that down before I demand to see pictures."

"Of my coffee?"

Snorting, Rachel shook her head. "Of the dress…"

We'd made it to our usual table where Archie placed the coffee tray then gave Rachel a dour look. "Why are you here?"

"Not to talk to you, asshat, so shut up." The words just rolled right off of her as she grabbed a chair and pulled it out for me, then dropped into the chair next to it as I sat. "C'mon, Cheryl told me you tried on a bunch of gorgeous ones, but she said I had to wait and see what you picked. So spill…let's see it."

Archie glared at Rachel for a second, then shot a look at Coop, who raised his hands. Nope, he wasn't wading in.

Setting the coffee aside, I slid off my backpack and then pulled my phone out of my pocket. "I'll show you, but try to be nicer to the guys okay?"

Rachel rolled her eyes, then tilted her head. "I'm here to talk to Frankie, asshat, so *please* shut up." The last she added with the barest hint of a smile.

"Meter's running," Archie warned her.

I shouldn't laugh. I really shouldn't, but she had this butter wouldn't melt in her mouth tone, and she'd actually batted her eyes. Across the table, Coop started snickering, too.

"Bitch bitch bitch," Rachel retorted.

"Just what I was thinking," Archie clapped back, then smiled when I raised my eyebrows. He even touched his finger to the corner of his mouth. "See, I'm being nice. I'm even agreeing with the bitch."

I giggled, and Rachel smirked. "Bring it on, asshat, I can take you."

"Yeah, no thanks," Archie informed her. "I'm good right where I am."

"Fantastic, then give us a little less of this." She held up her hand and tapped her thumb to her fingers as if miming talking. "K? Thanx. Bai."

I swore I could almost see the emojis in the too sugary tone. "*Anyway…*" I said before they could launch into each other again. I opened up the photos on my phone. At least I'd saved the image after I showed Marsha the day before. But the first image to pop was my scholarship notice and Rachel leaned a little closer before I swiped to the next one, which was the dress. "This is the dress I picked out."

She studied it critically as she let out a low whistle. "I like it. Simple but sexy. Good color. What are you doing for jewelry? Cheryl said she told you where to get shoes, but you need other accessories.”

Kill me. “I actually know a place.”

“Okay, if you need help, happy to give you backup. What about hair and makeup, have you figured it out?”

From the corner of my eye, I caught Coop leaning toward Archie and throwing an arm around him as he mocked wiped a tear. “Look, she’s turning into a real girl.”

“Yes, actually,” I told Rachel as I flipped Coop off, which set the pair of them laughing their asses off.

“Just ignore them,” Rachel said, tapping the screen with my dress. “How are you doing the hair? Yourself? Your mom? Someone?”

I didn’t flinch at the mention of my mom. While Rachel had really come through for me the previous week to cover up the red mark on my face—which had faded, thank you very much—we weren’t at confiding about my mother stage. I could barely talk about her with Coop and the guys. “Marsha at work made me an appointment with a friend of hers.” Sure, I had to make the appointment, but that was just a technicality. “She even gave me the day off so I could go and get done up right—her words, not mine.”

“Good,” Rachel said. “Perfect. Okay. So, shoes and accessories. I know a couple of other places that Cheryl would never recommend because they aren’t trendy but they do have great shoes and not at kill me now prices.”

That was good to know.

“If you want to get something dyed to match the dress, you’re going to need to order them soon.”

“Cool, well I’ll check the places she gave me…” I could do that later today or tomorrow, I guessed. Did Ian and I still have our standing homework date for tomorrow? I really had no idea.

“Call me,” Rachel said as she glanced to her right, and I followed her look to see Jake striding toward us. “I love the dress,” she said passing the phone back. "Seriously, you're going to look fantastic."

"Thanks, Rach."

"Anytime." She gave my shoulder a squeeze and then headed away. Coop and Archie weren't chuckling anymore. If anything, Archie's frown grew as he stared to where Jake was.

"Bitch," Jake said almost conversationally as he passed Rachel.

"Dickhead," she replied with a smile, then glanced back at me as she kept walking with a finger pointed to her smile like *see, I was polite.*

I groaned and shook my head, even as I laughed.

What was I going to do with them?

"Hey," Jake said, claiming the chair Rachel abandoned and reaching for his coffee.

"No Bubba?" Good thing Archie asked, because I wasn't going to. Not after he promised he would talk to me today.

We had a lot of hours left in today.

"He got waylaid by Coach," Jake said, but it was the worried frown he shot me that had me suddenly wary.

"Is he in trouble?"

"No, not exactly. He'll be here as soon as he can," Jake said, but he needn't have bothered. There was Ian walking through the doors with Patty and Sharon framing him as they chattered away.

Waylaid by Coach?

"I need to go get some stuff done for class," I said as I picked up my coffee. "I want to get ahead this week. I'll see you guys later."

I really didn't want to have this conversation or supposition or anything. Ian hadn't glanced toward us once.

His whole focus was on them.

Wow. That hurt way more than I expected.

I was halfway down the hall before Archie caught up to me. "It may be nothing," he cautioned.

"Yep," I said. "It may absolutely be nothing. But I really do have homework."

Thankfully, he didn't keep pressing the point.

I wouldn't borrow trouble. Ian said he'd speak to me *today*.

Lots of hours left in today.

Lots.

Archie

I don't know what's going on with you. But get your shit together. You're better than this.

Bubba

Long story.

Archie

?

Bubba

Class. Talk after.

Archie

Right.

At the same time...

Jake

She okay?

Archie

Fake it 'til she makes it.

Jake

Fuck.

Archie

Bingo.

Coop

Should I grab her after calc?

Jake

I'm closer.

Coop

K.

Archie

He say anything?

Coop

Just Coach assigned him.

Jake

Homecoming crap.

Archie

Explain.

Coop

No clue, just committee stuff.

Jake

He didn't volunteer.

Archie

Sharon and Patty are on that committee?

Coop

Apparently.

Archie

Fuck.

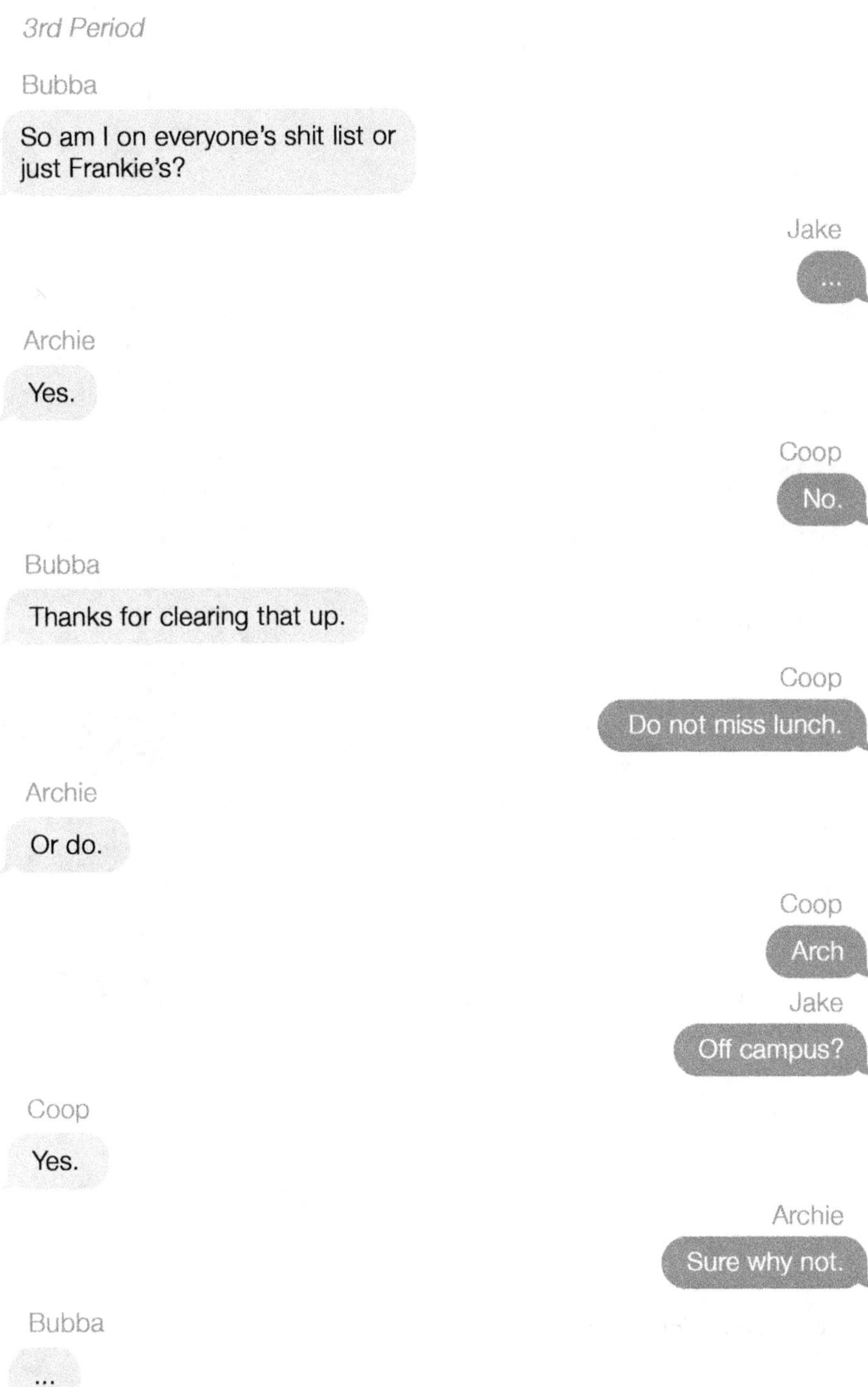
3rd Period
Bubba
So am I on everyone's shit list or just Frankie's?
Jake
...
Archie
Yes.
Coop
No.
Bubba
Thanks for clearing that up.
Coop
Do not miss lunch.
Archie
Or do.
Coop
Arch
Jake
Off campus?
Coop
Yes.
Archie
Sure why not.
Bubba
...

Jake

You can't?

Coop

...

Archie

....

Bubba

Meeting at lunch.

Coop

sigh

Jake

Talk to Frankie...

Coop

Before lunch.

Bubba

Where? In the hall?

Jake

Any fucking where just talk to her before she gets that from someone else.

Archie

You talk to her or we do.

Coop

Arch, that isn't helping.

Archie

Not sure I want to help him.

Coop

What?

Jake

Fuck, just talk to her B.

4th Period

Bubba

I texted.

Coop

You didn't talk to her

Bubba

When?

Coop

Dude, you had 2nd period, why didn't you talk to her then?

Bubba

Pop quiz. Then Jake showed.

Coop

Look, the longer you wait, the worse this is.

Bubba

Don't you think I know that?

Coop

Not sure you do.

Bubba

I thought you understood

Coop

I do. I don't agree. But I understand.
She doesn't.

Bubba

I promised to talk to her today.

Coop

Arch is getting pissy.

Bubba

I noticed.

Coop

Jake doesn't get it either

Bubba

No shit.

Coop

Ever think you're overreacting?

Bubba

No.

Bubba

Look, they've always been the type to
just take what they want. But what they
want is going to end up hurting her. In
no world does this end well for her.

Coop

You don't know that.

Bubba

I know she's more important than a casual
thing. Look what's already happened…

Coop

I have. She needs us.

Bubba

I'm not walking away.

Coop

It looks like you are.

Bubba

I'm not walking away.

Coop

Like I said, I get it. But it also looks like you are. Throw in the thing this morning? What is she supposed to think? Maybe think about that.

Bubba

I'll fix it.

Chapter Four
FIRST CUT'S THE WORST

Maybe I was just being stubborn, but I refused to be distracted today. Seeing Ian with Patty and Sharon had pissed me off. But I buried that down deep, not wanting to admit it aloud. Bad enough Ian had dated the second bitch.

Yes, I said it. The second bitch.

Ugh. I did not want to be one of those girls who blamed other women for her problems. My mother blamed the rest of the world enough for both of us. Things always happened *to* my mother. She was never responsible for her own issues.

Getting pissed at Sharon—and now by extension, Patty—felt a lot like the same thing. Except Sharon took some delight in my misery. That earned her label for me. Patty had just been rude, but the brush seemed to be all encompassing. It didn't help that from the moment Archie left me at calc to when Jake showed up like seconds after class let out—had he just ditched the end of his second period?—Ian and I didn't get to talk. Like at all.

The pop quiz was more of a long test to gauge where we were, and it took nearly the whole hour to work every problem. I worried about Ian when I came across some of the variable formulas. Those were his least favorite, and it took effort to slap my thoughts back on point.

I needed the grades in these classes. My GPA was great, but we only had a short few weeks before class ranks would be announced, and I needed all the lift I could get. That scholarship Marsha secured for me was a gift, but I still had to get into Harvard.

After the bell rang, Ian barely had his mouth open when Jake appeared. With a sigh, he'd said, "I'll find you later, okay?"

If I thought about it too much, it bugged the hell out of me. Worse, was the text Ian sent when later got there almost at the end of third period.

Ian

Don't be upset.

Not an auspicious beginning.

Ian

Can't do lunch today. Coach has me on Homecoming committee helping out as team rep. They are meeting over lunch.

Wow.

Yeah, I tried to not be upset. Wasn't really working.

Me

I understand. See you later.

No, I so didn't understand. But he talked to me, so points for that. Coop hovered during lit. Not literally, but he was sticking close, and when Ms. Fajardo called me up for conference—I wasn't that special she was calling us all up individually for a quiet five minute conference to go over where we were—his stare drilled into me.

Worry radiated off him enough to make me twitchy. Fortunately, Ms.

Fajardo had also had a chance to look at my essays. She loved them both and had some terrific feedback. Her quick skim of my journal earned me a single concerned look, but I told her I was okay.

Like I said once, if I said those words enough, maybe I would begin to believe them.

Lunch wasn't so bad, but it was weird not to be squished in the backseat. Like there was too much room. Archie got shotgun on the way to lunch, and I sat with Coop in the back. The guys tried to make up for the absence, but it was like they were feeling it, too. I kept catching Archie checking his phone.

We made plans for after school, though Archie suggested we bypass our normal diner hangout and head back to his place after for the pool and dinner. We could all celebrate there and just relax. No huge party, just us.

Sounded ideal—except I confessed about the message from my mom. To be honest, I didn't want to run into his dad either.

"I can handle Edward," Archie promised me.

"We'll be there," Coop volunteered. "We can always go lock ourselves in the media room. Archie's got that place fortified for the next twenty years on snacks."

Not really an exaggeration.

"C'mon, baby girl," Jake said with a nudge. "We haven't gotten to celebrate something with you, and this is too good to pass up. Blow your mom off, hang out with us, and we'll have fun."

No lie. That sounded great.

"Okay, but I need to swing home to grab my suit." Yes, Archie had suits I could 'borrow,' but I'd rather wear my own.

"Deal," Jake said. "I'll run you there while Arch gets things ready."

Some of the tension bled off as the guys promised to let Ian know the game plan. Back at school, I spent my study hall time in the library actually getting the next round of homework done. Like missing Ian at lunch, I missed Jake in the library. My TA period just had me in the resource room making stacks of copies, so I had loads of time to brood.

Or I did—until Maria walked in with work of her own. "Hey," she said with a faint smile.

"Hey." We might not be besties, but at least she'd been kind of sticking up for me with Sharon.

"You need the other copier?" She motioned to the other behemoth just behind me.

"Nope," I told her, and moved to give her more room. "Just have to make another thousand of these packets."

With a grimace, Maria slid her backpack off and held up a sheaf papers. "I just have to make forty of these."

"Cool."

Look at that. We were being all polite. Maria was taller than I was. Had that lean build to go with it. She also had shorter, much darker hair and the kind of skin tone that always looked sun-kissed. We joked about it in junior high. She didn't need to tan, all she had to do was look at the sun twice a day. Whereas I needed sunscreen and had to actively work at it, or I'd burn.

Arms folded, I leaned against my copier, keeping an eye on the collated and stapled packs as they came out. It had to cycle through the pages again and again to make the packets. At least the machine did all the work, it was just dreadfully dull.

We were the only two in the resource room. When Maria got the other copier running, the dueling machine noises created a godawful hum.

"Hey, Frankie?"

Oh. Please let's not talk anymore. We'd been doing so well.

Twisting a little, I glanced at her. "Yep?"

"I'm sorry about the Instagram thing."

Of all the things she could have said, that wasn't what I expected. "Okay." What else was I supposed to say? I lifted my shoulders. "Not like any of it was a lie, right?" Maybe not that.

Smiling faintly, Maria matched my pose with her arms folded. Neither of us wanted to be vulnerable in this conversation. But she was the one who approached me. "Yes and no. Sharon's…look, I'm not going to make excuses. When Jake asked me to help out with her, I made him meet me to talk about it. I mean, if it was so important to him, then he should be able to do it face to face, right?"

The ground seemed uneven and a little treacherous, but I already knew about their meeting and the fact Maria hadn't done anything.

"I was kind of bitchy about it—because it let me stick it to Jake." Maria winced. "While I think he deserves whatever he gets, you didn't."

"Thanks," I said slowly. "I think."

With a huff of laughter, Maria dropped her folded arms and raked a hand through her shorter hair. "Yeah, that didn't sound good either. This is so fucking awkward."

"Little bit," I admitted. "Look, Maria…I didn't try to steal Jake from you."

"I know you didn't," she said. "But I did try to take him from you."

I raised my eyebrows.

"We all did. We all knew they had crushes on you, and it didn't stop a single one of us." That kind of went with what I'd overheard from her and Sharon in the bathroom. "Anyway, I should have tried a little harder. Just—look, be careful of Sharon. She's not usually vindictive."

"Wait, we are talking about the same girl who TP'd Mr. Blaisdell's yard after he gave her a C in Texas History, right?"

That had been seventh grade, but still.

Eyes rounding, Maria laughed. "Oh my god, I forgot about that."

I lifted my shoulders. "Just saying."

"True. I want her to back off on you. But Jake's a dick."

I frowned. "You're entitled to your opinion." I got it. The guys hadn't always been that great to the girls they dated. Trust me, I was aware, but at the same time... "Just do me a favor? Remember he's my friend, too."

Her mouth tightened a little, and she nodded once. Then frowned. "Wait… you consider me a friend?"

I shrugged. "We used to be. I get that we haven't been, and you've got your things and I've got mine. But I prefer to not bad mouth others."

"Sometimes I think you're too damn nice," she said flatly. "You should stand up for yourself more."

"Well, like I said, you're entitled to your opinion."

Maria actually smirked at that. "At the risk of sounding like a hypocrite… I have missed you."

"I've missed you guys, too." It wasn't hard to admit it. "I've missed a lot of things. But we all made choices. For what it's worth, I'm sorry you got hurt."

No, I was not sorry her and Jake didn't work out. Call me selfish, but I *liked* having Jake.

"Thanks," she said. "I'm sorry you did, too."

Her copier was done, but mine kept humming along. Maybe I should have left it at that. I mean, we'd reached a kind of peaceful accord, yeah? But Sharon's words to Maria in the bathroom surfaced with a vengeance. If she just told Jake…

"You okay?" I asked as she gathered her copies out. Though her back was to me, her shoulders stiffened. Not a lot, but enough I could tell.

"I'm fine," she lied in that airy kind of tone you use when you want to change the subject.

Let it go. Let it go.

But I ignored that litany. We had been friends once. "You sure?" I pressed one more time. "I meant it when I said we were friends once. If something's going on…"

The brief pause worried me, but she straightened her copies and pulled out the originals before she faced me. "Did Jake tell you why we broke up?"

"No."

"Oh." That seemed to surprise her. "I thought they told you everything."

"Sometimes," I admitted. "But that's kind of personal."

She laughed a little hollowly. "Yeah, personal. Look, I'm fine, Frankie. Thanks for asking. Take care of you, and seriously, watch your back with Sharon. Hopefully she gets over this, but with Bubba on the Homecoming committee now, she's probably going to get worse."

Yay?

I was there for another ten minutes after she left, turning that over in my head. Why did she and Jake break up, besides Jake wanted to break up? Maria hadn't wanted as much. He said it was over before school started, but the note talked about the last hurrah of summer, which was just days before we were all back together.

When the last copy was done, I stacked it in the boxes and rolled it over to the slot for my teacher. She'd either get it, or I'd be back here tomorrow to grab it.

I fired off a text to Jake.

Me

Had to do copies in resource room.
I'll meet you at G's.

Jake

I'll meet you halfway.

A part of me wanted to roll my eyes. I could walk on my own. The guys had been overprotective and great. I had to admit, being valued had a lot of merit. Despite the 'meet me halfway' part, Jake caught me as I made it to the end of the resource hall after the bell rang.

"Did you cut class early?"

"Nope," he said, snagging my backpack and slinging an arm around my shoulders as we flowed through the sea of humanity. "Just said I had to hit the bathroom." He grinned.

He totally cut class early. I gave him a poke. "Thanks."

"Happy to help." He smelled great.

G was waiting for us with a pair of quizzes though, and I wasn't alone in groaning.

"Remind me again why I wanted to do all these AP classes?" Dramatic? Sure. But a little on the serious side, too.

"Because it's where all the cool kids are," G teased us as he put the tests down. "You will have thirty minutes once you open the packets to complete the reading and Q&A sections. That will leave you another twenty-five to do the short essay."

"That's cold, Mr. G," Jake protested.

"It is, isn't it?" He grinned. "C'mon, let's see you two show me what you got."

With shared looks of commiseration, Jake and I dug in. The nice part, G didn't make us sit away from each other. Even if we were testing—he was right there next to me.

Yeah. Okay. That was sappy.

But it still made me smile while I took the test.

The last bell was a relief, but I felt pretty good about the test. G promised to have our scores the next day. After a quick stop at my locker to swap out books and so Jake could see there was no note waiting for me, we headed out.

"So, good day? Bad day?" he asked as he pushed open the door for me. Since he already had my backpack, I should've been doing that, but he got there first.

"It was all right. Nothing—particularly bad, I guess, except Ian's stuck doing the Homecoming committee."

"Thank fuck he talked to you." Relief seemed to roll off Jake.

"He texted," I corrected him. "Briefly, we were both in class—do you mind if I ask about your session?" I wasn't really sure if I should ask. It was definitely personal.

"It was fine," he said with a wave of his hand. "What do you mean he just texted?"

"We didn't have time to talk in math class, we had a test. Then you were there, and he just went the other way." That hurt. Almost more than when he'd left Saturday morning.

Jake scowled.

"He said he would talk to you today."

"Day's not over," I reminded him as we made our way out to the parking lot. Unsurprisingly, Coop was already leaning against the side of Jake's SUV, Archie idling next to it, and Ian…Ian stood there holding his helmet.

"I can kick his ass if you want," Jake offered, and even if he said it cheerfully, I rather doubted he was kidding.

"I'd really rather you didn't."

He made a face. "Fine."

"Hey," Coop called out as we got closer. "Is it weird that I found it weird there was no message or anything on his car when I got here?"

Archie rolled his eyes. "You are the king of weird."

"Nah, maybe the jackass of it," Jake tossed back, and Coop flipped him off. The relaxed manner brought a smile to my lips, and I fought to hang onto it as I tracked my gaze to Ian's. He gave me a hesitant smile as he shifted the helmet in his hand.

Jake clasped my hand abruptly, and I squeezed his fingers. I was all right, we were still all friends, right?

"Hey," I said to Ian.

"Hey…"

"We're swinging by Frankie's and my place for suits, then out to Archie's right?" Coop said before Ian could continue.

"That's the plan," Archie said. "I called Jeremy. No sign of Edward. Jere's getting food and drinks sorted out for us. He also promised to distract and warn us if Edward shows up. So we've got you covered there."

The sun warmed away some of the chill as I cut a look to Ian. He moved the helmet back and forth between his hands.

"I'll run you two home for that, and Bubba can follow Archie out, and we'll meet you two there."

"Actually," Ian said. "Do you mind if I give Frankie a ride?" Though he was asking them, he focused on me. "The guys can take your backpack. We'll get your stuff…maybe talk?"

The offer should have relieved me, but I was suddenly clammy and my stomach knotted with nerves.

"Maybe we wait for the heavy discussions?" Archie suggested. "We're supposed to be celebrating Frankie's success, not pissing on her day further."

I winced at the description.

"I wasn't asking you, Archie. You may be rich, but you don't own everything, and you really don't own her."

"Never I said I did," Arch retaliated. "I also didn't bail."

"And on that note…" Coop stepped between them, focusing on me. "Frankie, what do you want to do?"

Jake's hand had tightened on mine. "You don't have to," he said.

I sighed, fighting was the last thing I wanted. "I know I don't have to. I want to…" Relief crawled across Ian's expression.

Frowning, Archie straightened. "Then you be damn careful with her on that bike."

"Do you mind keeping my bag to bring to Archie's?" I asked Jake rather than feed more fuel to the fire. At my question, Jake dragged his gaze off Ian to me, and he nodded.

"Of course I don't mind," he said. "We're going to be right behind you anyway."

True.

I squeezed his hand and let go. For a second, I thought he wasn't going to let me go, but then he did.

Ian held out the helmet to me as I crossed to him, and I accepted it. Suddenly aware of three gazes focused on us, I pasted on a smile. "Ready when you are."

He nodded. "Thanks," he murmured, and then motioned to his bike. I tried not to glance at the others, even as the sound of slamming car doors echoed as I waited for Ian to climb on the bike first.

Once he put on his helmet, I tugged on my own and tightened the chinstrap before I climbed on behind him. I was a little wary of putting my arms around him, so I settled for putting my hands on his hips and hooking my fingers in his belt loops.

The engine rumbled to life, and I stole a look at Jake's SUV. He and Coop were arguing in the front seat, and a sigh rolled out of me.

What were *they* fighting about?

Archie was behind the wheel of his car, and when he caught me looking, he blew a kiss.

"Ready?" Ian said over his shoulder.

"Yes," I assured him, and tightened my grip as he rolled forward. Even with the long line of cars to get out of the lot, Ian went around most of them and slipped away.

Oh, Jake would be annoyed. Hard to follow us if he was stuck trying to get out behind the other vehicles. The wind brushed against us as we zipped onto the road and then made it before the light changed. Something in me just relaxed as I leaned into him and followed the lean of his body when he took the corners.

It was over all too soon, and we were pulling into the apartment lot. I tightened my grip. Somehow, I'd managed to go from holding his hips to wrapping my arms around him. Even as I spotted my car, I didn't see any sign of Mom's.

Ian swung his bike in to park next to me and then waited for me to hop off. Reluctantly, I slid free and tugged the helmet off. After shutting the bike down, he took the helmet from my hands and hung it next to his.

"You want me to wait down here or go up with you?"

"Hard to talk to me if you stay down here."

He nodded, and then raked a hand through his hair. It had gotten a little longish now that I stared at it. Had it been for a while? Or was it just a change in the last couple of days?

Not that two days was some huge amount of time. God, I was being ridiculous. I didn't see any of them for weeks at a time this summer.

And you were miserable then... The snide little voice in the back of my head didn't help.

"You have a point," he said. "Lead the way?"

Awkward didn't begin to describe it. I pivoted and dug my hand into my pocket for my keys. My bracelet bounced against my wrist as I headed for the stone steps leading up to the back door. Ian was right behind me as I held my breath and unlocked the door.

Please don't be home. Please don't be home.

The sooner I fed the cats and grabbed my stuff, the sooner I could be out of here.

Silence greeted me, followed by a yowling complaint as Tiddles raced into the kitchen. Relief flooded me as I blew out a breath. Ian shot me a look.

"You all right?"

"Yeah," I said. "Just didn't want Mom to be here."

Understanding kindled in his expression. "You want me to feed the cats while you grab your suit?"

"I can do it." What I wanted… "What happened on Saturday?" I opened the pantry to grab the canned cat food out while I asked. Maybe I was being a bit of a coward, but… "We were out here, you were making coffee. It seemed fine, and then you went back to my room, and you and Jake were arguing, and then you left."

I cracked the can open.

"After you said you didn't…after you said you'd still take me to Homecoming, but we'd be friends nothing else."

A muscle twitched under my eye. The words came out, but they still lacked cohesion.

"What did I do wrong?"

I dumped the food into the bowls as Tory and Tabby joined Tiddles in their yowling.

"You didn't do anything wrong," he said quietly.

Discarding the used can into the recycling, I stole a look at him. His expression was pained and tense. He did not look like he agreed with what he said.

"Okay. So what happened?"

Ian rubbed the back of his neck. "We all spent the night."

"I was here," I told him. "I was really glad all of you were, too. Friday evening… it sucked." That whole dinner had been a nightmare. "If not for Archie…"

"Yeah, if not for Archie," Ian muttered.

"What does that mean?"

"It means…" He sucked in a breath. "Frankie, I adore you. You know that, right?"

Folding my arms, I lifted my shoulders. Considering how rigidly he held himself and the tightness in his expression, I wasn't so sure I did. "I know you said we're friends, best friends. I know you've said how much you missed me this summer, too. You asked me to Homecoming. I thought we were close, but I'm kind of wondering, and maybe that's not fair to you."

"No, it's totally fair. I was kind of a dick."

Well, on that we agreed.

He pressed his hands to the side of his head, then dropped them as he straightened and faced me. "We're fucking around with your life, and we shouldn't be."

Of all the things I thought he would say. *That* hadn't even been on a back-up list.

"What the hell does that mean?"

"It means, Archie had no business having sex with you. It means Jake should have kept it in his pants, but no, not Jake. He's always got to push things, and not Archie because he always has to be first or grab what he wants. Doesn't matter what it is."

He touched his tongue to his teeth and took a couple of steps toward me.

"You have never dated. Not once. You have…fuck, Frankie, you're our best friend, and we did our best to keep the rest of that crap from touching you. Liking you? That's never been a problem. We all like you. Too much sometimes, but we do. And it was safe when you didn't want us."

I stared at him. "It's not safe now that I do?"

"No," he said simply. "You're catching hell from girls we…girls we fucked over. Right, wrong, or indifferent, we did. Now they're taking it out on you. Archie took you from zero to sixty."

"Okay, you need to stop talking about me having sex with Archie like it's something he did to me and I'm poor Penelope Pitstop who didn't have a say. He gave me every opportunity to say no, not that it's any of your business. And yes, I made out with Jake before that and I *liked* it. I made out with Coop, too. Right there on that sofa. When I had sex with Archie, I did it because *I* wanted to. I did it because *I* said yes. No one made *me* do anything—"

"Sweetheart, that's my point. We know how to get girls to *say* yes," he shouted, and then raised his hands and took a step back. "That's what we do. That's what we did all summer."

My stomach bottomed out, and I stared at him. "Excuse me?"

"Getting girls to say yes, it was a game. A game we could all do, and we got really good at it." He dropped his head and then shook it. "And I'm not saying you're the game, Frankie. Because God knows, you're the fucking best prize there is. Sooner or later? You have to pick one of us, and I don't know that you'll ever be able to, and that's going to tear you up. They need to think about *that* where you're concerned, and not just about how good it feels to be wanted by you."

Chapter Five
THE SONG HAS NO TITLE

"The prize," I said slowly, and I wasn't sure whether to laugh or to smack him. "Did you just seriously call me the prize?"

"I know how it sounds," Ian bit off the words, a grimace straining his expression. His beautiful blue eyes were sharp and pained.

"I don't think you do." Spinning on my heel, I headed for my bedroom. We'd come here for my suit, and apparently, so Ian could tell me I was too stupid to date.

Got it.

"Frankie," he said with a sigh as he followed. "I'm not saying this to hurt you."

"Could have fooled me." I jerked open the drawer and shoved aside a wrap to pull out the two-piece I'd gotten. Ian stood a couple of feet in the door, but he'd stopped talking.

Instead, he stared at my bed briefly. The disheveled covers. Jake's t-shirt was over the back of my desk chair. He hadn't taken it with him, and I could probably use it to sleep in tonight if I wanted.

Pulling his attention from the bed, Ian focused on me. "I'm worried about you," he said quietly.

"You don't have to," I promised him. "You've made it very clear that you don't want to 'date' or to put me in the position of having to 'choose,' particularly since you're all masters at making girls say yes. You can have anyone you want. Apparently, I'm just the ditz who falls for every line."

"That's not what I said," he challenged.

"No, that's pretty much what you said and you implied."

"Fuck," he said, vehemence punching up the word. "Frankie, I don't think you're a ditz. I think you're perfect."

"Then why don't you believe me?" And why were you pulling away? But the last question seemed glued to my tongue.

"I never said I didn't believe you. I know…look, I know you agreed. But I also know them." He scrubbed a hand over his face. "I can't make decisions for them. I can't pull them back from what they've already done. I want you to be happy…"

"Weirdly, I was pretty happy Saturday morning, even after all the crap. Then you just left. You decided that I didn't get to have any say in it. That I couldn't be trusted with my own agency. Wow…it's kind of don't date Frankie all over again. Only instead of warning off other guys, you're taking you away from me."

"I must be shit at explaining this, because I'm not leaving you," Ian insisted. "Am I trying to protect you? *Yes*. Do I think they pushed you too fast? *Hell yes*."

"What's too fast?" I asked.

"You know what I mean."

"No," I challenged, narrowing the gap between us. This was the guy who sent me recordings of him singing so I could go to sleep when I was crampy and hurting and stuck here with bad meatloaf. This was the same guy who gave me my first real kiss. This was *Ian*. "I don't know what you mean. What's too fast?"

"You wanted to date," he said slowly.

"I'm aware of what I wanted. I was there."

A faint smile quirked his lips. "Fair. We all want to date you."

Well, that was some improvement. "Except now you don't."

"No, I do," he insisted. "Maybe more than is fair to you. There's a reason I want to take you to Homecoming. To make it a great night for you. It's why I wanted to ask you. To give you that memory, but also to treat you *right*."

All right, now I was confused. "You want to date me, but you don't want to date me. I'm confused, which is it?"

Confused.

Irritated.

Irked.

Annoyed.

Vexed.

Pissed off was right around the corner.

"You deserve to be treated better…to be precious. To be given the opportunity to get to know us as more than just the guys who want to get in your pants."

"I didn't meet you five minutes ago. I didn't go out with Archie on day one and have sex with him. Holy shit, Ian—where is all of this coming from?" Because this didn't make sense. "You got mad at Archie because we had sex."

"I know. You asked me why I hit him, and I told you he understood why."

"But you still haven't told me. Is it because of this game you used to play? Are you still playing this game?"

"No."

"And I was never part of the game?"

"No. Never."

"You don't want to date me, because you want to treat me better than the game and what Archie, Jake, and Coop are doing…"

"You've had sex with Coop?" He jerked a little.

"Not that it's any of your business at the moment, but no—we made out. He kisses me…a lot." Some of the tension bled out of my shoulders. "He's…he's Coop. Just like you're Ian. No one kisses me like him. No one kisses me like any of you." I really didn't know how to make this clearer to him. "Did I ever picture myself dating all of you? No. I could barely imagine dating one of you. I never realized you guys had a thing for me. I wasn't making that up."

Some of the tautness in his expression eased, and he lifted a hand to cup my cheek. "I know you didn't," he promised. "I do know. The day you told us you wanted to date, that you were seeing Mathieu, and that you wanted those experiences—Frankie, that was a great day. Then you kissed me in the pool… and everything was so clear. You always got me. You got me on a level even the guys don't always get me. You never forget my music."

"I wouldn't. That's a part of you, and maybe I get you, but sometimes you confuse the hell out of me." Like right now.

"Then I look at everything that's happened since then…not just the guys, but the thing with Rachel and the flowers, the shit the girls are pulling, the secret notes, the fact that someone vandalized your car—and I won't bring up your mom, but…"

"Yeah. You know a lot of that isn't your fault."

"Except I don't think you've done anything to anyone to make them hate you like that. Even Sharon doesn't hate you for anything other than I like you a hell of a lot more than I ever liked her." He stroked his thumb over my cheekbone. The same one my mother had bruised. It had faded a lot, but it was still tender, or maybe the memory of it ached.

Leaning into the touch, I stepped forward. I still had my bikini fisted in my hand. "Ian…" I licked my lips. "What you guys did over the summer…how it affects the others, the girls you dated. I can't control that. I can't control their feelings. I can't control anyone's feelings except my own. Are things a little crazy right now? Yes. They are. But there are *good* things, too. *Really* good things."

Studying him, I looked for some sign. He said he wanted to date me but not. He liked me more than the other girls. Hot. Cold. Yes. No.

"I'm not going to make this a thing," I said finally. "If you don't want to date me…"

"I do want you," he said simply, like it should be crystal clear no matter what he kept telling me. "But that's not what you need."

"Why don't you let me decide what I need?" Seriously.

"Because I care too much to let you tear yourself apart."

Impossible. Stubborn. Sweetheart. Asshole.

The last two words crashed into each other. Assheart?

Sweethole? Yeah, maybe not that one.

A laugh burst out of me. Inappropriate? Probably. "It really is a good thing you're pretty," I told him, and then pushed up on my toes and kissed him. He gripped both of my biceps, but he didn't push me away, and I didn't press to deepen the kiss.

If he didn't want to *date*, then I guess I had to *understand*.

Didn't mean I had to take it lying down either. When his lips parted, I pulled back. Heat had already swept through me, and my lips tingled. His grip on my arms tightened for a beat.

"That's one," I told him.

"One what?"

"I'll give you three more. If you're still out after because you want out… then I'll understand." No, I wouldn't. I'd be hurt. But I was a big girl. Dating was harder than I expected. Better than I expected. More terrible than I expected. "I won't make decisions for you. I think I'll even trust you to handle working so closely with Sharon and Patty. Since you can make them say yes so easily."

He flinched on the last comment.

Did that make me bitchy?

"But we need to go. Because the guys are waiting." My phone had started buzzing a few minutes earlier, but I'd been ignoring it. It took everything I had to paste on a smile. My mother did stuff like this. Blow hot and cold. The best thing to do was humor it until it passed.

He opened his mouth, but I didn't wait for him to finish the thought. We needed to go. Because if we stayed here, I'd either end up crying or begging him to change his mind—and I absolutely refused to do either.

If he was telling me he needed out for him, I'd hate it, but I'd do my damnedest to understand. Having him tell me he wanted out because I was too stupid to make my own decisions stung a lot.

Outside, Jake and Coop stood next to Jake's SUV, and Ian let out a sigh when he saw them. Honestly, so did I. Probably not for the same reasons. "Hey," I said. Look at me smile. "You guys didn't have to wait."

Jake glanced from Ian to me, then back. "Sure we did. Wanted to make sure everything was all right. We good now?"

"Sure." I still had my bikini in my hand. "Actually, I'm gonna put this in my backpack, okay?"

Coop frowned. Don't ask, I mentally pleaded. Just don't ask.

I glanced at my watch. It was later than I thought. "We should get going. Poor Archie is waiting."

"Yeah," Coop said slowly as he moved aside so I could open the backdoor. My backpack was on the seat, and I set the bikini on top of it.

Jake and Ian were staring at each other.

If I made this a thing, there was going to be a fight. I didn't want them fighting. Being understanding sucked. Then again, I wasn't the only stubborn person I knew. I got it, Ian wanted to do what he thought was best.

I didn't like it. But I could pretend. Maybe he'd get it through his thick skull.

He had three more kisses to figure it out.

That was the deal I made with myself.

Done, I closed the door and gave Coop a pat on the shoulder. "I'm with Ian. Try to keep up."

I tried not to let the surprise on Ian's face when I said that get to me. He and Jake finally stopped staring at each other as Ian passed me the helmet. "You sure?"

"Do us both a favor," I said quietly, and tugged the helmet on. "If I say it, I'm probably sure. So you don't have to verify every statement in triplicate. Particularly when you're going to decide what I need without consultation anyway."

Definitely came out bitchy. His eyes shuttered, and then he tugged his own helmet on before throwing his leg over the bike. I waited until I had the strap in place before I climbed on behind him.

We really needed to go before my mother showed up. Wrapping my arms around Ian, I clasped them together over his abdomen. He touched my hands once. The clasping gesture settled some of the chaos bouncing in my system. As he accelerated toward the road, I was very aware of the yellow SUV following us. I was still in shorts. Maybe I should have changed into jeans, but I closed my eyes and focused on the breeze as we turned out.

For the first time, I was really glad the bike prevented us from talking. Not even the ride home from the party had felt this awkward.

What was I doing?

Was I being a real friend because I would rather preserve the relationship, even if it hurt to be rejected?

Was I being bitchy because I'd made some comments, and despite his protests, I didn't really believe him?

Weren't these the exact problems I'd feared when we started dating in the first place?

Around and around my thoughts raced. When Ian accelerated and the rush of warm wind hit my face, I sighed. There was a thrill on the back of this bike. I loved riding it.

Were we going to take the bike to Homecoming? The mental image of trying to climb on it in my dress and whatever heels I ended up getting—had I mentioned I wasn't a fan of heels? But I'd get them. That dress needed the right kind of shoes, and Converse weren't it.

Combat boots would be funny.

Oh—motorcycle boots. I bet I could pull that off.

Cheryl would have kittens. Rachel would laugh.

I didn't think the guys would care.

I was still giggling when we turned into Archie's driveway. The gate swung open. Someone had been watching for us, so we barely slowed before Ian skimmed around it. I was just climbing off the bike and still chortling to myself as Jake and Coop pulled up next to us.

Ian twisted to look at me while he shut off the bike. A grin twisted his lips. "What's so funny?"

"I was thinking about going to Homecoming on the bike."

His eyebrows climbed.

"Not a chance in a hell," Jake called as he slammed the driver's side door.

"Yeah, Frankie," Coop said as he opened the backdoor to grab my bikini and both of our backpacks. "That dress leaves you far too bare for the bike. Seriously, not a good idea."

Ian glanced at them, then back at me as I shrugged. "I dunno. It would be different," I told him. "Then I thought about heels, and that I wobble in them anyway, so I could do motorcycle boots. It would be cute, right?"

The skeptical looks I got from two of them made me laugh harder, but it was Coop who shook his head. "Nope. I saw you in that dress. I want to see the rest of your legs. With the heels. It will be hot as hell."

I rolled my eyes. "Buzzkill."

"Not my fault you looked fantastic. Course, I liked you in that first one you put on, too." He grinned. "We still need an excuse to go back and get that one."

"Dream on," I told him, and passed my helmet to Ian, who watched us with a bemused look before I grabbed my bikini and backpack.

"Oh," Coop called as I headed for the front door. "I intend to."

I'd barely lifted my hand to knock when Jeremy opened it. The man ran a tight ship, and he was actually one of my favorite people. "Hello, Miss Frankie. Mr. Coop. Do come in."

"Hey, Jeremy," I greeted him.

He smiled. "Mr. Archie is already out by the pool, he said for you to go up and use his room to change. The gentlemen can use the adjoining guest bedroom. Food is also waiting."

"You're the best."

"I try." He wore a fond smile. "If you'd like to give me your backpacks, I can take those out for you."

Normally, I'd just hold onto mine 'cause that seemed like an imposition, but I was going to dive into this afternoon and evening with the best mood I could muster.

"Thank you," I said as I surrendered the backpack. It wasn't until Coop and I were on the stairs though that I realized Jake and Ian weren't right behind us.

"They're coming," Coop said, putting his hand at the small of my back.

"Please tell me they weren't fighting."

"I dunno," he admitted as he nudged me along, and we headed up the stairs toward Archie's wing. It didn't matter that we'd been coming to this house for years. The size of it never failed to kind of awe me. Archie had his own wing, entertainment room, guest rooms, and even an office in addition to his bedroom.

I loved my space in the apartment, but it was contained to my bedroom. If I had all of this?

At Archie's room, I paused at the open door to glance back at the stairs. Still no Ian or Jake.

"Hey," Coop said softly, pulling my attention to him. "You really all right? You and Bubba talked?"

I shrugged. "We talked."

"That doesn't sound promising." Worry filled his gray-green eyes.

"It is what it is. Tonight, we're celebrating, right?"

He searched my face, but I pasted on my smile and lifted my chin.

"Yeah," he said slowly. "We are. But you don't have to pretend with me. Ever."

That made me smile for real. "I want to have a good time tonight. I want to not be—angsty Frankie, and her awful no good bad decision bagel days."

The corners of his eyes crinkled, and he chuckled. "Bad decision bagel days?"

"Well, it sure feels like that lately. But Ian's talking to me, so that's something. I got the scholarship, and that's awesome. And…I'm here with my best friends."

"Okay," Coop whispered after a long moment, then wrapped his hand around my nape and pressed his forehead to mine. "We're going to celebrate. Talk college apps. Plan homework. See you in that hot bikini. Play in the pool. Have fun. Maybe not necessarily in that order."

"I like that plan. Even the homework stuff."

"Of course you do, you're an overachiever and a workaholic."

I made a face and pinched him. He stole a kiss and then danced away from my jabbing fingers.

"Go get changed," he said. "I'll see you in five."

He headed to the room next door, and I glanced at the stairs. Still no Ian or Jake.

Shaking my head, I slipped into Archie's room and closed the door. There was something comforting about being in there. I crossed over and dropped my bikini on the bed before I sat on the edge and pulled off my shoes.

Archie wasn't messy. In general, he picked up after himself—I'd seen him do it. Though, there were times he just tossed things, too. I would imagine the maids—there were two of them who came in to clean the house three times a week—definitely made passes through here.

Having a maid was weird. Having a Jeremy was cool, but someone who actively cleaned up after you? Eh. Even Mom didn't do that. I stood and pulled out my phone. There was no message from Mom on the screen.

So far, so good. I put it in do not disturb and dropped it on the comforter before undoing my shorts.

A whisper of air brushed my neck a second before hands settled on my hips. Heart slamming against my ribs, I swallowed a scream as Archie leaned close to me and whispered, "Boo." As it was, I jerked my elbow back and got him in the stomach. He oofed and then laughed.

"Oh my god, you asshole," I yelled as I pivoted. He had both hands over his stomach, grimace-laughing.

"Thank you for not hitting me in the balls," he grunted, but his eyes danced. "And sorry, you were lost in thought and so damn delicious looking, even when you didn't notice me in the bathroom door."

I groaned.

A knock on the connecting door preceded the jiggling of the handle. "You okay in there?" Coop called.

"I'm fine," I answered. "Archie left a big jerk in the middle of the floor."

"Wounded," the guy in question chuckled. "So wounded." He swiped at an imaginary tear and then grinned harder when I flipped him off.

"Jerk."

"Sometimes," he agreed, just like he had earlier. "Sometimes." He tipped his head to the side. Dressed only in his swim trunks, he looked positively edible. "Please don't stop changing on my account."

"You sure you're all right?" Coop asked again, his tone exceptionally dry. "And I thought the big jerk was down by the pool."

"You thought wrong!"

"Ha," Coop bellowed. "You snuck in there to startle Frankie."

"Lies," Archie answered with a smirk. "All lies."

We could be up here all day at this rate, so I stripped off my shirt, then my bra and reached for the bikini top. Archie gave me two thumbs up before he reached out a hand. When I smacked his fingers, he cracked up all over again.

"Lookie, no touchie," I scolded, and that just set him off in another fit.

When I slid out of Jake's boxers, I kept my gaze on him, and it was delightful to see the heat in his eyes. Even more, the pout when I pulled on the bikini bottoms.

"Fuck, I'm giving you a pair of mine." He crossed over to his dresser and opened it. Then he pulled out a pair of dark boxers and held them up. "You have a preference on color?"

I laughed. "You're making it weird."

"Says the girl who wore another guy's boxers and turned me on by standing in my room in them."

"You weren't supposed to see them," I pointed out, though I was a little warm from the way he kept raking his gaze over me.

"Getting girls to say yes, it was a game. A game we could all do and we got really good at it."

Ian's words whispered in my ear, and I straightened, turning away long enough to fold up my clothes.

"Hey," Archie said. "I was just teasing."

"I know." The words would probably sound a lot more convincing if that little niggle of doubt wasn't doing a version of a stomp dance on my good mood. "You pick out the boxers, but I'm not telling you when I'm going to wear them."

"Oh, that's cold," he said slowly. "And a little mean."

"Take it or leave it," I offered before reclaiming my phone and meeting his gaze. See, I didn't always say yes.

"I'll definitely take it." He pulled out a dark blue pair that he'd worn on our first night together. "These." When he dangled them, I had to take a couple of steps to get them from him. Even expecting it, I still laughed when he tugged me closer and then wrapped an arm around me a heartbeat before he kissed me.

The light nip of his teeth stung my lower lip before he laved his tongue over it, and I sighed against his mouth. Coop knocked and said, "You've hogged her long enough. Let's go, it's time to share Frankie."

Archie groaned against my mouth, even as a light shiver skated up my spine. We dragged the kiss out for another ten seconds, and I wasn't the only one panting when he lifted his head.

"Better. Ready to be shared?"

That sounded so much dirtier when he said it.

"And if I'm not?" I challenged.

He squinted. "I could be totally convinced. Really, wouldn't even take much. We can just keep the doors locked."

I laughed. "No, we can't." I patted his chest as I took possession of his boxers. I set them with my clothes and headed for the door. "We're celebrating."

"Right," he exhaled. "Celebration. Put a little swing in those hips because the party in my pants is all about celebrating you."

I groaned and stared at him.

"Too much?" He gave me a cheesy grin, and a real laugh bubbled up through me.

They were idiots sometimes. All of them.

But they were my idiots.

"Maybe a little." I held my thumb and forefinger together, and he winked. There was no mistaking the pleasure in his eyes when I laughed. Archie was worried about me, and he was trying to cheer me up.

It worked.

"Heading out," I called to Coop.

Archie covered my hand on the doorknob, and we wrestled it open together, laughing to find Jake and Ian had finally made it up the stairs. Jake raked an appreciative gaze over me and smiled, but Ian's expression shuttered as he glanced from me to Archie behind me.

"It's about time you slowpokes got up here," I said, refusing to be embarrassed, even if my face heated.

All the air seemed to be sucked out of the hall as we stood there in that awkward frozen tableau.

"Finally," Coop declared as he left the guest room. "I thought I was going to have to *Mission: Impossible* my way in there to get you two out." He squeezed right past Jake and Ian to sling an arm around my shoulders and tugged me out into the hall. "Move it or lose it, guys!" he called back as we headed for the stairs with Archie right next to us.

It wasn't until we were outside in the heat that the shiver hit me. No way Coop missed it this close to me, but I bumped his hip and slipped away before I dropped my phone and bracelet on the table, then I raced forward and dove into the pool.

We were going to have fun tonight, dammit.

Bad decision bagel or not.

Chapter Six
ARE YOU FOR REAL?

JAKE

"Not a chance in hell'?" Bubba quoted my words back at me as Coop disappeared inside with Frankie. "Really?"

"Her? In a dress that's thinner than cotton while on your bike to go to Homecoming? Yeah, that definitely falls in no chance in hell." I dragged my backpack out of the back and then locked the car.

"You think I'm going to take her on the bike?" Bubba stared at me, his expression tight. To be honest, we hadn't said much to each other the last couple of days.

"I don't know what you're going to do. I didn't expect you to take off on Frankie or bail on me, so what do I know?"

"Apparently enough to make decisions for her." The barest edge of hostility frosted the words.

"I don't let my friends do stupid shit," I told him bluntly. "I tried to stop you on Saturday, too. But you wouldn't listen. Now…she thinks you're out.

While she puts on a great show, it's eating away at her. Personally, I think she has enough problems, she doesn't need any more."

The only thing keeping me from punching him—particularly after he had to bail on lunch to hang out with Sharon and the kill-me-now club—was Frankie. It would ruin her day. We were here to celebrate that killer scholarship.

I didn't know a more deserving person. I came clean about my own scholarship, and she'd been thrilled for me. When I'd admitted I'd worried about the fact she hadn't gotten it, she'd laughed at me and called me sweet.

Yeah, I was sweet. On her.

The fact that I got to spend the whole night with her pretty much made all the crap parts of the week worth it. Even the anger management—wasn't that a joke?

When Bubba continued to be silent, I shrugged. "We better get moving…"

"You know what the problem is," he said, and I sighed as I dropped my chin. Facing away from him, I seriously debated just continuing to walk.

"No," I answered. "But I'm sure you're going to tell me."

"We're pretending the summer didn't happen."

"Excuse me?" I pivoted to face him.

"You heard me." He'd dragged his own bag out of the saddlebags on the bike and slung it over his shoulder. The sun beat down on us, but right now, I didn't care about the heat so much. "We made a lot of bad calls, and we're pretending it doesn't matter because now she likes us. I know how damn desperate I was to even have her talk to me again."

"We screwed up with Frankie." I could admit that much. "We should have been up front with her. Maybe a little more blunt." If I'd had half an inkling of what it would be like to really kiss her? I'd have long since just done that. "But the summer has nothing to do with her."

"It has everything to do with her, Jake," Bubba exhaled. "Now you and Arch… you just had to get her into bed. Did you even slow down for a second before you fucked her to think about whether it would be good for her?"

"Be really careful, Bubba," I warned him as aggravation raced over my skin like an angry rash. "Nobody gets to talk about her like that."

"Like what? Another notch you and Archie punch into your belts to make a point?" Bubba glared at me. "She'd never dated, and in less than a week, Archie has her in bed and you…tell me you didn't get damn close? You were pissed that Archie got there first? Or were you just pissed at the points you lost?"

"Say it again," I dared him as I dropped the backpack and narrowed the space. "I fucking dare you to say that again. Your face won't be so pretty for the game."

"See, I don't know if this is just your natural state or if you really do care…"

"Where the fuck is that coming from? Do I really care about Frankie? Fuck you, Bubba. I know I care. I know I care enough that I'm not putting her on the spot or making her feel bad that she likes all of us. I'm not going to punish her for not just picking me."

His eyes shuttered, and he gave a little jerk like I'd actually hit him. Good. He deserved a solid fist to the jaw.

"What is going on with you?"

Bubba sighed and then shoved a hand through his hair.

"Dude, I'm not playing with you right now," I pushed on. "'Cause you plan to keep this shit up, just leave. Cut the cord and let one of us take her to Homecoming. Don't jerk her around like she's some puppet for you to play with."

He turned that glare on me, anger flaring in his eyes. "I'm not playing with her. I *care* about her. I care about her more than I do me or scratching some damn itch. She's worth a hell of a lot more than a score card or a pickup line that will make them agree."

"No shit. So what is wrong with you?" Out of all of us, I expected Archie to play the power games—not Bubba.

"I'm worried about her."

"So are we."

"The crap with her mom, the stuff at school—we still don't know who did that to her car."

"Yes and yes, how does shoving her away help with all of that?"

"Because Rachel was right."

Now there were words I never wanted to hear. Rachel Manning had a thing for my girl, and all other competition thoughts aside—Rachel could be a real bitch on wheels when she put her mind to it. Nobody fucked with Rachel. Not if they didn't want to be eaten alive.

"About Frankie needing a friend?" Because Rachel had said other shit to her, some of it in those notes—and didn't that just burn that Rachel was the one to give Frankie those words of encouragement and thought that should have come from us—and more at the party the weekend before last.

"Yeah," Bubba said. "We're supposed to be her best friends, but…we haven't really been good at that part. All we've done is make it worse. You guys…look, Jake, I get it. You saw an opportunity, and you took it. But did it ever occur to you how she was going to cope with it later?"

"Cope with what? The sex?" Because if he was implying I forced her, I really was going to relocate his jaw.

"Yes. Frankie's not one of the other girls who didn't care as long as they got off."

"No shit." Why the hell he had to keep bringing up some of those… "Bubba, no one was lied to. If Frankie said stop, I would have stopped." I did stop. Not that it was any of his business. That first night she and I made out after I slept over. The first time I got to really touch her and she'd touched me.

'Course, after she put her mouth on me, I don't think anything could ever compare again. All the heat in my body drained south just at the idea.

"Stop lumping her in with everyone else. She isn't them, and they could never be her." The game had been fun, stupid maybe, but fun. And it had been a way to drown out the noise. None of us had been happy with her cutting us off, but it wasn't about dating Frankie—at least, not then. We hadn't stood a chance then, at least we hadn't thought we did. "You and I both know none of us ever thought we had a chance with her." Sometimes spoken, often left unsaid, was the fact we'd all been hung up on Frankie, and she didn't look at us the same way until now.

I wasn't going to make excuses.

"And that's done now." We hadn't marked a point in weeks.

"Then why the rush?" Bubba asked.

Was he for real? "What rush? I've been into Frankie for years. This didn't feel like a rush, so much as finally having a chance to show her how I feel."

"You're right, it has been years—for you, for me, for them. We're supposed to be her best friends. But we sucked. Then we hurt her. Now you're setting her up to be hurt again. To have to choose between us…I can't do that. I'm not leaving her, but I am going to be good. I'm going to be her *friend* and not just the guy who wants to get between her legs."

"Good. You're going to be the *good* guy?" I pinched the bridge of my nose and started laughing. "Okay, you go hang out with your ex and plan Homecoming. That sounds great."

"Not my idea," Bubba argued. "Don't be an ass."

"You first," I retaliated. "Being a good guy means not making her feel like crap."

"I talked to her."

"And?"

"And, none of your business. We butt out of each other's dates."

"Except you're not dating, and I definitely am. You can be the friend, I'm definitely the boyfriend."

"*A* boyfriend," Bubba corrected. "One of…not the only one. I just told you I'm not leaving."

"No, you're going to be her *good* friend. Like I said, boyfriend," I continued, and tapped my chest. "Which means now I'm telling you. Get your shit together, Bubba, before you damage what you could have irreparably. Then again…if you're out, you're out. I'm not gonna fight for you, if you can't be bothered."

I hated it. It had been the five of us for years. It felt wrong to have him step back. Not leaving wasn't the same as being in. Not leaving wasn't the same as continuing to date.

"Can you make it sound less like I'm a villain? I'm just trying to be a good guy. The guy she needs."

I snorted. Whatever, man. He wanted to be the good guy, and that made me what? The bad one? Fine. Whatever. "I get it. Good boys go to heaven." I clapped him on the shoulder before picking up my backpack. "Bad boys take her to heaven. Keep being good, man. She'll get there with or without you."

Then I headed in the house.

"You are such a jackass," Bubba muttered, and I grinned.

Yes, yes I was. But at least I knew what I wanted and who I wanted. I could be her friend and her boyfriend. I wanted it all.

COOP

Jealousy didn't look good on anyone, and Bubba was so jealous, he could spit. The fact he wouldn't actually label it jealousy didn't change the facts. I got it, I really did. I understood when he tried to explain to me he felt like an ass and that we were taking advantage of Frankie.

But understanding it didn't mean I agreed. We weren't taking advantage of her. When she bumped my hip and darted away, I had to swallow a sigh. Even the lightest touch left me panting like I was getting my first erection all over again. Sometimes I wondered, was she for real?

Just looking at Frankie was enough to make me want her. But it was more than that. Frankie was this fixed point in my life. We'd been in each other's back pockets since before I realized girls were supposed to be icky.

She never achieved that status with me. Other girls? Sure. But not Frankie. She was my best friend. Then Jake came along, and he was all right, but I lived closer. When Bubba joined the mix, it was cool, and Archie. They each brought a different dynamic, but I liked having a big friend group.

The simple truth was, I liked her more. I liked seeing her every day. I liked it when she rolled her eyes at me. I liked it when she teased me.

I fucking loved it when she spoke French.

When she dove into the water though, I had to resist the urge to dive in right after her. Particularly because Archie stared at her the same way I was, and the asshole had been in his room while she changed in there.

Like I said, jealousy wasn't a good look on anyone, and I was damn jealous of Archie at the immediate moment. Considering I knew exactly where Jake was last night, all night.

"Are you planning to get in the pool?" she called. "Or just stare like a pair of doofuses?"

The comment pulled me out of my reverie, and Archie let out a laugh as he strolled forward. Like me, he was dressed in swim trunks only, and he dove right in the pool. I hesitated, but only because I needed to get my mind on other things like…

Yeah, that wasn't working, the only thing I could see was her, and I didn't want to think about math formulas or baseball stats.

Not that I knew any stats.

Fuck.

Here was hoping the water was cold.

I hit it at speed. The water, while cooler than the temperature outside, wasn't cold. Frankie's laughter was my only warning before she wrapped her arms around my shoulders and twisted. I pivoted, catching her legs for balance and then got a face full of water from Archie.

Oh. It was on. I shoved Frankie up and back. She twisted as she dove back into the water, and I started flinging water at Archie before having to fend

Frankie off, too.

"Two against one!" I complained in between bouts of laughter. The water was flying fast and furious.

"Aww," Frankie said. "I'll help!"

She vanished under water, and I couldn't see where she went as I kept fending off Archie. Then he yelped, and I cracked up as she tugged his leg and dunked him.

When she would have shot away, he caught her leg and hauled her backward, and then lifted and tossed her. She emerged giggling, and I had to grin. There had been so much crap the last few weeks, I'd almost forgotten how good it was just to laugh with her.

Damned if I didn't love her laughter.

She darted around me when Archie went for her again, and I blocked happily. We ended up wrestling, and both of us got dunked for our trouble. When I came back up for air, she was leaning against the side of the pool, grinning.

"Cannonball!" served as Jake's announcement before he landed in the deep end with a terrific splash. The wave was impressive.

"Oh, I can beat that," Archie announced as he climbed out. I pushed away from the center and swam over to Frankie in time to catch Archie's demonstration.

He definitely made a bigger splash.

She snickered, and I grinned.

"Five bucks says Jake does it again," she told me.

"No takers," I countered and pointed. Jake was already climbing out of the pool. Her deep green eyes brightened as Archie let out an "Oh shit" a half-second before Jake hit the water not a foot from him, and he got nailed with the splash.

"Ten points!" Frankie called.

"But the Russian judge takes off at least one for artistic style," Bubba called as he finally came out of the house. What the hell had taken him so long? I hadn't seen any bruises on either of them when they came upstairs, but you could have cut the tension on Jake and Bubba with a knife.

Then Jake hit the pool almost a full five minutes before Bubba?

The smile lighting up Frankie when Bubba played along made me wistful. It really had been a while since she totally relaxed. Who could blame her? It had been a shit few weeks, despite how much I loved the fact she was interested in dating.

Dating.

Making out.

Kissing.

The kissing was good.

"Fuck the Russian judge," Jake called out as he swam toward us.

She snickered, and I had to laugh, too. This was what it used to be like. The five of us playing, teasing, giving each other hell, even before Frankie wanted to date. Sometimes we'd had girls over, but they hadn't really mattered when Frankie was here.

That should have been my first clue.

Jake caught her arm, but she clasped my hand so when Jake pulled her away from the side, I ended up following. Bubba dove in the far side, no cannonballs, and Archie yelled something.

"Up," Jake said as he ducked under the water, and then Frankie let out a gasp and a laugh as he rose up with her suddenly perched on his shoulders. "Coop, you wanna base for Arch or the other way around?"

Oh, hell.

Bubba cut through the water to us. "I can do it," he said as he came up. "Arch or Coop, whichever."

Jake smirked and the look that passed between them wasn't friendly.

"C'mon Coop," Bubba invited, and I rolled my eyes.

"All right." I waited for Bubba to duck into the water, and then I was on his shoulders and going up.

"Hey," Archie said. "What about me?"

"You gotta be the ref!" Frankie said. "And throw us some noodles!"

"Fine." He let out an aggrieved sigh, but I didn't miss the way his expression shifted at her smile, or the fact that Jake was currently stroking her thigh with his thumb.

"Okay, first one to topple the other wins," I suggested before anyone else could add some ridiculous rules to the competition. Jake and Archie were both overachievers, but at the moment, I was more worried about the animosity between Jake and Bubba.

Archie passed us the foam noodles, and then it was on. Frankie wielded hers like a champion, laughing as I batted hers back. Bubba and Jake kept moving, and we were heading for the deeper end of the pool.

I half-expected the shove when it came, but Bubba recovered, and I managed to hold onto my balance. Frankie's expression tightened briefly. Yeah, I wasn't the only one who saw it. She bopped me and then flicked her eyes at the pool and made a wavery motion.

She wanted to throw the match. I didn't blame her, but I could take the dive. The guys lunged at each other, and I bopped her and she went sideways, and if I hadn't been watching for it, I would have missed it. Instead of just sliding off Jake, she hooked her legs under his arms and pulled him with her.

They both came up laughing, and I had about two seconds before Bubba dumped me backwards.

Eh, all fair.

No more water battles, instead Frankie hooked her arms around the noodle and floated, head tipped back. Archie dove back in and we all sorta wound down a little.

"We still need to talk homework," Frankie said after a while.

"Yes!" Archie lifted a fist, and I laughed. "She didn't make it an hour. I win."

Frankie snorted and kicked water in his direction.

"Yeah, no one took that bet," Jake reminded him. Nor would we. Frankie was too damn determined and driven to get the right grades to get into the right college and get out of that apartment and life with her mom.

I couldn't blame her.

"All right," I said, grabbing the edge of her noodle closest to me and tugging her. "Everyone out, and we can get food while we talk the academic stuff, and then we go back to celebrating."

"I have homework," she reminded me, then gave me a hug and a kiss. It was just the barest of brushes, but the stupid grin on my face had to give me away. 'Course, she grinned wider, and there wasn't anything wrong with that.

"If I help, do I get a kiss, too?" Archie teased as he held a hand out to her. He'd already gotten out of the pool.

"You can have one whether you help or not," she said as she let him pull her up. Like she had with me, it was a light kiss, a bare brush, and it still sent a shiver down my spine. Not as hot as when she and Jake had been intent on devouring each other, or as hot as when she came alive in my arms, but I didn't mind watching.

'Course, she also leaned into Archie and laughed when he blew a raspberry against her throat. That was how Archie Standish, dude with more money than all four of our families put together, always delighted her. He had the capability of being a dork.

"You coming?" Frankie asked as she headed toward the table where the towels and the food waited in the shade.

"Yep." Couldn't keep me away.

Bubba and Jake glared at each other. When I whistled, they both looked at me. Yeah. Let's not piss on Frankie's day. "C'mon, time to eat and to plan. You snooze, you lose."

ARCHIE

Yeah, that bikini looked fantastic on her. It had more coverage than the string one she'd borrowed here, but it wasn't the skin so much as the way it fit Frankie.

Or maybe it was the way Frankie moved. She had a smile on her face, her eyes lit up, and she seemed genuinely happy. Whatever Bubba said to her, hopefully it fixed that stupidity.

We had enough bullshit going on without him suddenly getting cold feet. Then again, if he wanted to bow out, fine. Less competition. I wasn't too worried about it at the moment. We all got time with her, and I knew I meant something to her.

I was the one she'd called when she needed to get away from her mom. While I wasn't fond of the tie, the idiot affair Edward was having with her mother added another bond. 'Course, it also meant I needed to make sure Edward didn't do anything stupid.

Just thinking about him was enough to sour my mood. As far as Jeremy knew, Edward was in New York. Apparently, he and Ms. Curtis had scampered off there late on Friday. Things didn't go well at dinner—and by well, I meant I shut that shit down because the hell I was going to let them browbeat Frankie into going along with this farce. Seriously, Edward had done some shitty things, but fucking around with Frankie's mom? That was low, even for him.

Usually he went for the single, childless chicks. Maybe I should figure out a way to convince him to take Frankie's mom to New York permanently. They could live in the apartment on the Upper East Side, far, far away from us.

Frankie shot me a look as she squeezed the water out of her hair. The openness in her expression tugged at me. I'd seen her kicked, wrecked, wounded, and hurt enough in the last few days. I never wanted to see it again.

Her smile faded, and she frowned, then mouthed, "You okay?" without saying the words aloud.

Shit, I shook off the melancholy and gave her a quick grin and a thumbs up. "Was thinking about Thursday," I lied. "We still need to decide what we're doing for Coop's birthday."

"Good call," she complimented me. "Actually, I'm gonna rinse the chlorine off real quick." She snagged a towel and headed for the outdoor shower.

Bubba grunted as he bumped me on his way past.

"Are you two going to be pissing on each other all evening?" Coop asked as he slung a towel around his neck. He wasn't looking at me, but at Jake and Bubba. Yeah, I'd noticed that, too. I was also ignoring it. Jake had a temper. Bubba was biting off his nose to spite his face.

But tonight wasn't about them…

"We're not," Jake said abruptly. "At least I'm not. He made his call. Friends it is."

Bubba sighed. "You know, fuck you, Jake. I'm done trying to explain it to you."

I glanced at him. "Explain what?"

"Why I'd rather take this slower than the warp speed the two of you are moving at. Why she deserves a hell of a lot better than to just be another point."

"She's not a point," I gritted out between my teeth, even as I cut my gaze between Bubba and her. She was on the far side of the patio where the outdoor shower was, standing under the water. "She's never been a *point*. That game is done. I'm not playing it anymore."

Frankie had *never* been a game.

"We're not going to talk about it here," I said hurriedly. "Do you understand me? She has enough shit to deal with, and that ended before school started."

Technically, the last time we called points had been the last blowout of the summer. The day all those fucking pictures were taken. But after we got back to school and Frankie, I had zero interest in pursuing the rest.

Patty and I had broken up before that party. She thought it changed things. I told her it didn't.

Frankie had changed everything.

"Cut it out," Coop said softly as Frankie stepped out from the water and used the towel to start drying off. "Gonna go rinse off, I suggest the rest of you do the same and everyone cool down."

"Agreed," I said with a nod. "Tonight's about Frankie, and Jeremy got us ice cream cake for her, so let's eat, get the homework planning out of the way, and get back to partying."

If nothing else, that seemed to decide them. They dialed back on the glares, and we all took our turns rinsing off. There were sandwiches in cold pans, chips, and sodas. So even if it took us an hour to get to the food because we'd been romping, it was still chilled and ready to go. Jeremy had loaded us up with everything.

The man was a gift.

Frankie curled up into a chair between me and Coop with Jake and Bubba across from us. She had her laptop open, and I pulled out a tablet and booted it up in between bites. Jake and Bubba killed three sandwiches each.

Were they even making eating a contest?

"So," Frankie said. "What are we doing after planning and homework?"

All the things I'd like to do required the guys getting the hell out of here, so I settled for, "It's your party. Whatever you want to do."

The moment her eyes lit up, I knew I was screwed.

"Mini golf?"

Coop laughed, and then Jake did, and even Bubba cracked up.

Yeah. For that smile? "Sure," I said. "Mini golf it is. But we've got ice cream cake, too."

"Yes!" She clapped her hands and then flipped open her notebook. "Who's going first?"

It took us all of fifteen minutes to nail down the schedule for the week—Frankie would still go over to Bubba's on Tuesday for Calculus and whatever, but she said she would drive herself. Ouch, slapped by a simple comment, and Bubba knew it.

Wednesday she had work, but Thursday we had all day. "That's Coop's call," she said. "It's his birthday."

So we all looked at him. When he left tonight, he was taking a sedan with him. The insurance was ready to go, and Jeremy had added him to the coverage.

It could come out of my allowance until Coop could afford to pay for it. No one brought it up to Frankie. It was going to be Coop's surprise.

My part in it was not for public consumption. We all had pride. The look on his face when I told him earlier to just say he managed to get it for his birthday had been worth it.

Maybe I could give it to him outright. That would really even the playing field.

"Nothing like being on the spot to go absolutely blank," Coop admitted. "But we could drive up toward Arlington. Go to Six Flags for the day."

We could. It was a hike. Lots of rides.

"Then back here later," Coop said with a quick look at me, then the others. "I'd kind of like to just take Frankie out for dinner."

"Damn, thrown over for a chick," Jake drawled. "But since that chick is Frankie…" He laughed when she threw a chip at him.

"We'll play it by ear, but yeah, your birthday," I said. "Friday is the game, and Frankie's with me…"

It was funny, we were doing homework planning in this mess, but we also made sure we could account for dating time. I'd bet even dollars that Jake would be at Frankie's after work on Wednesday, especially if her mom was still out of town.

I'd get us a hotel for Friday if I had to. The more we kept her away from them, the better.

"Are we good on projects, since all we're doing is date planning?"

"Damn," Coop said, clutching his chest. "She's caught on to our cunning plan."

"It wasn't much of a plan," Bubba said drily.

"Or that cunning," Frankie teased. "But I do want to talk college."

You know what… "So do I, applications open on Friday."

For everyone planning on early admission, the sooner we got them in, the better. That scholarship put Frankie over the moon, but I wanted to put Frankie in Harvard, thousands of miles from her mother and the bitches at school.

Not to mention, whichever asshole vandalized her car. College was a first step in that plan.

"Yeah, I'm ready to record that audition tomorrow," Bubba said, focusing on Frankie. "If you're still willing to help."

Audition?

Frankie's smile grew. "Of course, I'll help."

I narrowed my eyes at the exchange. Wasn't he on the shit list?

"What audition?" Jake asked.

"Yeah," Coop glanced between them. "Spill."

"It's a secret," Frankie said.

"Not much of a secret if you're talking about it right here," I protested, and she put a hand on my arm.

"Let's start with essays. Do you guys actually need them for MIT? And are you going to apply to Harvard, too? You know, for real?"

I'd told Muriel I was. I covered her hand with mine. "Damn straight I'm applying."

"Whatever we do," Jake said. "Once we know where we're going, we'll nail down the place to live."

"It has to take cats," Coop added, and Bubba gave a firm nod to that.

Frankie blinked, then looked at all of us, and I raised my brows. "We're not leaving them behind." Especially not after what her mother said about getting rid of them. I hadn't been kidding about moving in with Frankie if I had to. Jeremy could free up the money for me. I'd pay her rent.

She wasn't losing her cats or her place.

Fuck the bad meatloaf.

Her laugh and little squeal of delight were worth it, and we each got a hug. Even Bubba. The look on his face when she wrapped her arms around him…

Idiot needed to get his head out of his ass. I liked the guy, but I wasn't waiting around for him.

"What actual homework do we have then?" Coop said. "Because if you want to get mini golf in, we need to eat, get the work done, then get changed and get out of here."

"Actually," Frankie said, perching on the arm of Bubba's chair. "I got most of mine done at school. So I'll go change, while you guys get caught up."

Sneaky.

I liked it.

As soon as she was in the house and the door was closed though, I looked at Bubba. "Get it together and figure it out. Because if you screw this up for any of us—"

"Especially yourself," Jake tossed in there.

I nodded. "It won't end well for anyone, *especially* Frankie."

"She's really my only concern," was all Bubba said.

I really hoped he meant that.

"Good. Then we won't have a problem."

Chapter Seven
SONGS TO LOSE AND LOVE BY

Mini golf rocked. We'd all gone back to Archie's after for ice cream cake, and to be honest, I was both floating and exhausted. Ian's behavior left me in a tangle of confusion. We weren't dating, but he wasn't leaving. During golf, he'd been reserved but very present. The other guys played and ribbed, but the comments between them grew a little more abrasive and cutting as the evening dragged on.

As determined as I'd been to have fun, it grew more difficult each time one of the guys gave me a hug or a kiss or a teasing remark, and Ian's gaze would level at us. After we'd had ice cream cake and Jake offered to take me home rather than ride with Ian, I leapt at the offer. The speed at which I said yes got me a long look, and honestly, I hadn't cared.

Ian made me tired. Coop didn't ride with us, and Archie said he'd make sure he got home later. They were still playing on the Xbox. It wasn't until I was in Jake's SUV that I even gave a thought to the fact I'd blown Mom off.

"You okay?" Jake asked as he turned in the driveway to leave.

"Yeah," I answered, not really wanting to dwell on anything that brought down the evening, even if I already was. "Just tired." It was almost ten. "But I had a really good time."

His grin warmed me right up. "Good, I'm glad. You deserved to have a good time."

I laughed. "Is it weird that having fun felt weird?"

"Yes," he said. "But it also felt a little bit like old times out there tonight. I hadn't realized how much I missed all of us being us, even if Ian's being a dick."

"He's not a being a dick," I argued, even if I kind of agreed. I'd braided my hair when I went to get dressed, and it was mostly dry now after the evening, but I still needed to actually wash it when I got home.

"Yeah, he is," Jake said, then rubbed my thigh. "But I'll shut up about it."

"Sorry," I told him, covering his hand. "You don't have to. I mean, it's not like you aren't entitled to an opinion."

"Cool, then in my opinion, he's being a dick."

Laughing, I shook my head.

"What about you?" he asked quietly when we had to stop for a light.

"What about me what?"

"What do you think about him?"

"I don't know what to think," I admitted. "I'm not going to twist anyone's arm, and he has a right to his opinions, too. I just…"

"You just?"

"I just don't know what I did wrong."

"You didn't do a damn thing wrong, baby girl," Jake assured me as he gave my thigh a squeeze. "This is him. He'll figure it out. Even if I have to drop kick him."

"Don't fight, okay? You guys were scowling at each other off and on all night."

"He's pissing me off," Jake said, then sighed. "But I'll try, okay?"

That was a lot for Jake. "Thank you. Try to remember he's your friend, too. This can't be easy for anyone, and I'm being pretty selfish…"

"First," Jake said, holding up a finger. "No, you're not. Not a single one of us didn't know the score when we asked you out."

Technically...

"And second, anything worth it is never easy. We've had easy, Frankie. We had skating by and doing whatever we wanted. I wouldn't trade this with you now for anything."

Heat crawled over my face. I didn't want to think about what having easy meant, or at least, not think about it too closely. "You know, technically, Ian asked me out first."

"I know he did, baby girl. He slipped in there ahead of all of us..."

"He kissed me first, too."

Jake pursed his lips but said nothing until he pulled into the apartment complex and parked. Mom's car wasn't in her slot, and relief sagged through me. 'Course, it hadn't been there before... Worried, I searched the lot, but I didn't see any fancy cars like the BMW.

"Frankie..." Jake pulled my attention back to him, and I met his steady gaze. "Whether Bubba was your first kiss, or Coop met you first, or Archie got you in bed first—"

"Well...technically..."

He grinned. "Fine, technically that was me, but he was the first full intercourse you had."

"Yes." My face had to be on fire, yet at the same time, I didn't look away from him.

"The fact is, we've all been your firsts in some ways. That doesn't mean we get more..." He hesitated a beat, before he continued, "... say in what you do or don't do. Bubba knew you were going out with us when he did the ask. He wanted Homecoming to be his first real date with you, and that's weeks away and that was his choice."

I licked my lips. "I know. Now he isn't sure he wants to date because he thinks I need a friend more."

"What do you think?"

"I think I want to date him, but I don't want to force him to do something he doesn't want to do. That isn't right either. I like…I like all of us, even if it's different. I don't want to have to choose." Even if I was going to have to at some point—I dreaded that nebulous day.

"Is he asking you to?" The intensity in Jake's gaze trapped me. "Is that what Bubba wants?"

"That's not what he asked me…" No, he'd explained about their points game. Glancing down at my hands, I bit my upper lip.

"You can tell me anything, baby girl. I mean it. If you don't want to tell me, I'll shut up." He grimaced. "I won't like it, but I'll shut up."

I laughed. "No you won't." I sighed. "You push me, and you're too blunt to dance around the topic."

"For you, I could try."

"No, I've always liked that you won't let me ignore things, even when I want to."

It was hard to admit that. His expression gentled in the faint light cast by the dashboard. When he cupped my chin and brushed his thumb against my lower lip, he said, "You know, I'm going to remember that the next time you snap at me when I call you on pushing us away or not telling me something. You like it when I push. Got it. I can totally do that, too."

Laughing, I leaned forward, and he met me halfway. The kiss was gentle and sweet. The gentle stroke of his tongue requested entrance, and I opened to him. When he settled his hand against my breast, I groaned, or maybe that was him. The weight of his fingers tugging at a nipple through the fabric sent languid heat spilling through me.

"God, I want to ask to come up and stay tonight," Jake admitted in between kisses. "But I have to make an appearance at home, or Mom will get testy."

"Wednesday?"

"Absolutely. Even if your mom is here. Maybe even definitely if your mom is here. You shouldn't have to deal with her."

Unfortunately, life wasn't that kind. Another kiss, and I leaned back. "Thank you, Jake."

"For?"

"Just for being you." I covered his hand on my breast. "I'll think about you when I curl up with my pillow." It would still smell like him.

"Fuck," he groaned, and leaned his head back. "Maybe I can text my mom…"

"Don't," I said. "We don't want her to get mad at you, and it's probably better we both get sleep because I doubt we would if you spent the night."

"Not for a while, no," he said with a smile. "And don't think I haven't noticed you didn't really answer my question about what Bubba said."

"I know, but I'm not sure I'm ready to talk about that with you yet. It feels personal." It also included all of them and would likely start another fight. Maybe Ian didn't need my protection, he'd certainly not acted like it this evening, but we were all friends, and all of those connections were important to me.

"Okay, baby girl. I'll let you off the hook—but if that changes, you can tell me anything. I promise."

"That goes for you, too, you know." And while I'd like nothing more than to just sit here and make out for another half hour or more, he needed to go home and I needed to go inside. Shouldering my backpack, I smiled at him through the open door. "I'll see you tomorrow?"

"Yes you will. I'll text when I get home, but I'm going to wait until you're inside. Text me if she's there, okay?"

The ball of tension in my gut unraveled. "I will."

I blew him another kiss before I closed the door. Once inside the apartment, I found it mostly dark and silent. Only the single light I'd left on in the kitchen burned.

Carefully, I made my way to Mom's door and listened. Tiddles came trotting up the hallway, yowling his disdain. Okay. The cats were out. I texted

Jake that all was well and I was alone.

Jake

Good deal. Talk to you when I get home.

In my bedroom, I put my backpack down and checked my other messages. Nothing from the guys, but then I hadn't expected any. I'd spent the whole evening with them.

Nothing from Mom, either.

Well, maybe I wasn't the only one who didn't show up for her ordered appearance. My mom was not shy about letting me know when I'd pissed her off. Tory attacked my feet from under the bed as I tugged off my shoes.

I debated sending a text to the guys individually, but I was tired, and if I started chatting, we might be up for another hour. I really needed a shower and for Jake to let me know he was home, so I sent a message to the group chat that I was home and grabbing a shower, and that I'd probably crash right after that.

There was a litany of good nights and sweet dreams from Archie and Coop. But nothing from Ian.

Making a face, I dropped the phone on the bed and headed to the bathroom. It took me fifteen minutes to shower, wash my hair, and shave. One problem with dating, I had to keep up with the shaving. The guys hadn't said anything, but it was the principle of the thing.

Hair blow-dried, teeth brushed, and pajamas on, I padded back to my room and dumped my dirty clothes in the laundry basket. I'd rinsed out the suit and left it hanging in the bathroom to dry.

Smothering a yawn, I checked my phone.

Jake

Home. Saw your message. Sweet dreams, baby girl. Wish I was there.

I grinned.

A second message also waited.

Ian

I'm sorry if I spoiled your evening. I really didn't want that. I get that I'm confusing you, and I don't want that either. Maybe we can talk more tomorrow? Sleep well, Frankie. I miss my muse.

His muse?

Me

We can definitely talk. I don't like this distance either. I don't like how it's making me feel.

I debated whether to hit send on that, then added another line or three.

Me

I really like you, Ian. I hate the idea that you don't trust me to decide what I want. Or who I want.

I almost added *I need you* and then backed that up before I hit send. I did need them. I needed all of them. But that was a step too far, considering how much crap spilling around me kept splashing onto them. Need implied a lot more. Particularly after admitting I'd missed them.

Ian

I trust you. I get that probably isn't coming across. I just don't know how much I trust the guys.

Me

They're your friends.

Ian

I know. Maybe that's why. I know them, F. I know them better than you think.

Me

What does that mean?

His response wasn't immediate, and I took the time to climb into bed and shut off the lights. The cats immediately pounced, each one looking for their spot. The fact that Tiddles settled right on my chest and started purring made me smile.

This was another reason I loved my cats. They were always willing to cuddle, and they didn't let me down. Mom could stand to take a few lessons.

Ian

It means when we're all together and you're not there, we're not always the same guys you know.

Well, that wasn't ominous or anything.

Me

Are they still your friends?

It was another long moment before he answered, but the three little dots told me he was typing.

Something.

For a while.

Maybe Ian was like me, writing something then erasing it because it was too much.

My eyes were getting heavier, but I wanted to know why yes or no was such a hard thing to type.

Ian

They are.

Well, that was pithy.

I chewed on my lower lip.

Yeah. I sighed and closed my eyes. It wasn't a no, but it wasn't a yes. Okay. "That's it," I said aloud. "No more chasing. I want him to want me, but I'm not going to beg for it. We're all mostly adults…" Well, technically Ian was the only adult, but Coop was getting there, and we were all turning eighteen— them this year and me in spring of next year. "Leave it, Frankie. If he wants you, he'll figure it out."

If he didn't or if he couldn't…well, maybe I shouldn't be going to Homecoming with him.

That thought made my stomach hurt.

I totally didn't switch the phone over to the songs he sent me, nor did I put them on repeat before I put the phone on a charger. I didn't roll over on my side, and I definitely didn't lie there thinking about how I could have handled it differently and how it was going to feel if Ian was well and truly out.

Because after tonight? If I was still dating the other three and not him, I didn't see him hanging around much. Even if he wanted to, I didn't know if the guys would want him there.

That part?

That sucked.

His songs? They had just enough love, loss, and longing in them to make me ache.

Another message blinked on the screen.

Ian

I care, Frankie. I know it doesn't feel like I do. But I do care.

No, I didn't have the wherewithal to respond to that, so I just swiped up to close the message and then burrowed against the pillow. It wasn't curling up next to Jake, but it still smelled like him.

Morning came, and I was not in the mood for it. Sleep had been elusive as hell all night. Just when I'd start to go to sleep, I'd jerk awake. I kept replaying my conversations with Ian. Then the conversations with Jake, Coop, and Archie.

Maybe what we needed to do was all sit down and talk. I'd talked to them individually, and maybe that was a problem. Then again, we did talk about dates and stuff when we were altogether.

Well, not really.

We talked about who was doing what when. We parceled out the time to make sure I got to see everyone. Sometimes I saw Jake more than Archie, but I got to see Coop almost every day, and we hadn't gotten to have a real date yet.

Ugh. Around and around, the thoughts raced on a gerbil wheel to nowhere. But every time I circled back, I realized, no, we had never sat down—all five of us—and discussed what we were doing.

Dread curled in the pit of my stomach.

Should I? Would that be asking for a massive problem?

Ian already had issues. Would this just make it worse? Or would it be what we needed to do? If I hadn't unloaded on them that Saturday night about dating…

We'd probably not be dating at the moment.

I played out the debate in my head while I got dressed for school, fed the cats, cleaned out the litter box, and jogged down to check the mail that I'd been forgetting to check.

It was a stuffed box. I hurried back and sorted through the massive stack. There were some bills, most of which were autopays, I was pretty sure. Then there were envelopes addressed to the parents of, more college stuff, and three letters to me.

I separated those out and then carried the ones for Mom to her room. I kept the "To the Parents of"—she never wanted to read them anyway unless they were something important. Even if she hadn't been home the night before, I knocked on the door anyway and waited.

When no sound was forthcoming, I let myself in.

The bed was a mess of rumpled sheets and blankets.

Gag.

Averting my eyes, I went to put the mail on the stack—that she hadn't looked at. At least not based on the height of it.

Fuck.

I flipped through the mail real fast, because if we missed something, it would suck if something got shut off. Without a doubt, it would be my fault. I pulled out five envelopes that had no return addresses or any sign of what they were.

I left everything I recognized or at least knew was not an issue. Then I got the hell out of her room. The longer I was in there the more it smelled a little musky, a little like foreign cologne, and a lot like sex.

Things I did *not* need nor want to imagine.

Shoving the mail in my backpack, I added the letters for me. I didn't have time to look at them now. Archie would be here any minute, which meant Coop should be knocking…

The rap on the backdoor made me laugh.

"Right now," I murmured to myself before slinging the backpack over my shoulder and heading for the door. Bracing for it, I opened the door and grinned.

Coop wore the biggest smile, and he had a hand resting on each side of the doorframe. "No escaping the good morning kiss for you," he intoned in the most comical voice.

A giggle eddied up, and I clasped my hands to my chest as I retreated a step. "Oh no, whatever shall I do?"

Waggling his eyebrows, Coop stalked inside—still grinning like a loon, mind you—and continued in his horrible accent, "Surrender, and I'll go easy on you."

The snort escaped before I could stop it. "Eep." I waved my hands like I had no idea what to do, and Coop shoved the door closed right before he tugged me forward by the backpack strap. He slid it right off and then kissed me as I opened my mouth to protest.

Well, playfully protest anyway. Wrapping my arms around his neck, I fought the smile, even as he locked his lips on mine. It was hard not to laugh as everything in me tingled. He locked his arms around me in a firm grip. Guess I won out over the backpack. Not that I was complaining as he licked against my tongue and slid his hands down to cup my ass.

The first hard suck against my tongue had me sighing. Coop tasted a little bit like a strawberry smoothie that he'd probably had for breakfast. He smelled freshly showered, and he was hot everywhere. When he nipped at my lower lip, tugging on it gently before he lifted his head, I shuddered.

"I surrender," I whispered, and his eyes lit up. The soft gray-green of them reminded me of a stormy sky in spring, when the tornado sirens could blare up at any moment. "What will you do with me?"

"I think I'm going to kiss you again," he whispered. "Just to be certain."

My heart did a little twist as he made good on his words. This kiss was much slower, far more nuzzling, and had my toes curling as I slid a hand onto his hair. The soft curls slid through my fingers, and my pulse rabbited. The languid heat exploded into a conflagration, and I was burning up.

He gripped my ass as he lifted me, pressing me right up against the fridge. It was like he loved pushing me against things, and the bump of his hips to mine had me groaning.

Panting when he let up this time, I licked my lips. "Good morning." The words came out far shakier than I wished, but Coop's pupils were huge, and his chest rose and fell with the swift, shallow breaths he released.

"Hey, beautiful," he whispered. "How are you?"

"So much better right now." It was true. The bad night of tossing and turning faded, the frantic thoughts quieted, and the worry diminished. This was Coop, and he always had a knack for making things better.

"Good," he said, then nipped my lower lip again before laving it to make it better. Who knew having someone else lick my lips would be such a fucking turn-on? The distinct pressure of his erection against me promised I wasn't the only one getting excited. "I wish it was Thursday."

"Yeah?" I teased. "What's so special about Thursday?"

Chuckling, he massaged my ass, and I swore all the heat in my body pooled between my legs. Crap, I was going to have damp panties, and there wasn't a thing I could do about it right this second.

"If it was Thursday, I could keep you right here and kiss you until we both melt. Birthday boy privileges."

"Ahh," I said. "I've been wondering what you wanted for your birthday."

"I have everything I want right here," he said, then he gave me another soft kiss before easing his grip and taking a deep breath. "And I really don't want to let you go, but I have a surprise I want to share with you."

"You mean that good morning kiss wasn't a surprise?"

Waggling his eyebrows, Coop asked, "Were you surprised?"

I tilted my head, trying to tamp down the very real lust surging in my veins. The little voice in the back of my head that whispered it wouldn't be so bad to skip school for once was gaining volume.

"No," I said softly. "I pretty much knew you were going to start my day off beautifully."

The red flushing his cheeks charmed me. I slid my hands down to rest against his chest.

"You do make things better for me. Even when I'm not looking for it or expecting it."

"Glad to hear it," he whispered. Then he brushed some my hair from my face and tucked it behind my ear. "I'm crazy about you, Frankie."

Excitement and trepidation did a mad dance through my system. Too much. The intensity in his eyes, the fact he was still holding me, and my body's exceptionally visceral and vocal response to him held me hostage. Too much. "You could have stopped at I'm crazy," I teased.

Coop laughed. "You're right," he teased. "While it might be true," he continued, moving his hands to my hips. Then he lifted a hand to trace his finger against my lips where I caught it lightly in my teeth, and his pupils flared. It was impossible not to stare at him. "I adore you."

The soft declaration bowled me over, even if I'd always known Coop cared. Coop, who always put an arm around me. Who curled up with me for years, whether I was reading or we were watching movies. Coop, who always seemed to know when I needed a pick me up or just needed someone to sit there and say it would be all right.

"Then I'm a really lucky girl," I admitted. "Because you're pretty cool yourself, Coop Brennen."

One more kiss, and he pulled away entirely with a groan. "Okay, beautiful, out the door before I abandon my surprise and work on convincing you that today is our senior skip day."

Oh, he wouldn't have to work hard at that, but I bit those words back before they could break free. He snagged my backpack and opened the door. When I went for the trash sack, he nudged me over and took that too.

"I can carry stuff," I told him.

"Absolutely, and when I'm not here, I know you exercise it constantly. But I am here, and I want to do this for you."

"Fine," I said with a flounce, and that pulled another laugh from him. I locked up and then followed him out to the parking lot. There was no sign of Archie yet, and I glanced at my watch. That was weird. He was usually here by now.

Coop tossed the bag in the dumpster, then headed toward me and wrapped an arm around my waist. "So," he said. "About that surprise."

He guided me over to a car—a *Lexus*—parked next to mine.

"Surprise."

I stared at it for a beat, then at Coop as he held up a set of keys and hit the auto unlock.

"You got a car?"

He grinned. "I got a car."

Mind. Blown.

I threw myself at him and gave him a hug. "Oh, I'm so happy for you! Oh my god, Coop. It's a Lexus. Did your dad finally stop acting like a horse's ass and do something cool for you?"

"Nope," he said, still beaming. "Archie did. The guy is a rock star, Frankie, and he got me a car so I'd have wheels to take you out."

If I'd thought my mind had been blown before, I was stunned now.

"Pretty cool, huh?"

Archie got him a car?

That was…awesome. It went above and beyond in the realm of friendship.

"I'm really hoping you don't mind, but I want to take you to school for a change," Coop continued. "My girl should be the first passenger in this car."

His girl.

I bit my lip.

"I would love to be the first passenger in your car," I said, and I wasn't sure what thrilled me more—how happy Coop was to have a car, or the fact that Archie had done something so damn nice for his *friend*.

That settled it.

All five of us were talking.

I wasn't going to destroy this friendship between all of us.

Not ever.

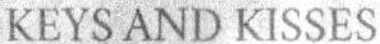

Chapter Eight

THE WAY WE USED TO BE

IAN

The five a.m. alarm went off, but it didn't jerk me awake. Hard to wake someone up if they aren't asleep. Fuck, I was tired. Rolling over, I hit the floor and started the morning routine. Whether we were in training or not, everyday—well, most days—I did one hundred push-ups followed by one hundred sit-ups.

On mornings I didn't have to be at practice early, I ran. Today, I had practice. We had to get these plays right, or we weren't going to take that game on Friday. Losing Jake from the line-up hurt more than anyone wanted to admit.

Or maybe it was just getting on my nerves. I totally get why he beat jackass's face in, but he led with his fists and his heart. We were just lucky he wasn't out for the rest of the season. Every pump of my arms didn't help my wrestling with that fact, because I really did get it. I even respected why he'd done it.

The shit Frankie had been taking was unreal. Part of the reason I wanted to take a step back. But I wanted *all* of us to do it. They weren't listening. We'd gone from all of us dating her to two of us already having sex with her, and I hadn't missed the looks on Coop's face. He bided his time.

Then what? We made it even worse for her because sex muddied the waters.

After I hit a hundred push-ups and no answers, I rolled onto my back and began the sit-ups. I hated the fact she was hurting. I hated even more that I seemed to be the one hurting her.

The words from her text message the night before had been permanently etched into my brain. *I really like you, Ian. I hate the idea that you don't trust me to decide what I want. Or who I want.*

She wasn't the problem. I got it. She liked all of us. Did I particularly like the fact that Archie nailed her as fast as humanly possible?

No.

Did I like that Jake was all over her and had spent the night with her first? No. Not even close.

Coop wasn't much better. The day he told her he was in, he'd also said the same thing to me.

"You don't get it." Coop told me. "It's been me and Frankie since before kindergarten. No way in hell am I not throwing my hat in the ring."

"You don't think that's not going to confuse her more?" I'd asked her out first. They hadn't until I did. But I asked her first. They weren't slowing down. And it was turning into this game of one-upmanship even if they claimed it wasn't.

"Nope," Coop said. "She thought no one was interested. I trust you guys with her. But I'm not stepping aside."

Maybe that was the problem. I panted, trying to catch my breath after that last sit-up. Forearms on my knees, I stared at one of the four photos in my room. It was all five of us from the summer between sophomore and junior years. We'd all started dating that year. But it was still the five of us for everything.

Even for our dates. We'd bring girls with us, but we always made sure Frankie was there because Frankie was one of us.

That was the last time I remember when we were all just us. Archie went through girls like they were tissue paper. At one point, he'd had a thing for girls that started with the letter M. He always swore it wasn't on purpose, but Frankie was the only one who kept track of them.

I swore, I called Melissa 'Michelle' like fifteen times before she demanded to know who that was. Unfortunately, she was the girl who landed between Michelle with two Ls and Michele with one.

Jake was almost as bad, but he didn't date anyone long-term. Archie managed a week. Two weeks was his max before junior year, and even then… they didn't last much longer. Jake was more first and second date then he was done. The chances of a third date were virtually nil.

One could argue that was all of us.

Dragging myself up, I hit the shower. I needed to move my ass.

Coop was the only one who got into relationships, and that guy couldn't seem to help himself. He was so fucking thoughtful, girls wanted to confide in him. Then he'd be stuck. Right up until he was done, and then he just ended it as abruptly as it began. Frankie though? They were thick as thieves, they always had been. At least 'til last summer.

A laugh broke out of me as I ducked my head under the water. It was still a little on the coolish side, and it helped with the morning wood that showed up every time even the vaguest thought of Frankie crossed my mind.

Not that it diminished much of the need. The day she'd straddled my legs in the pool and then brushed her lips against mine, I'd gone instantly hard. The kiss that followed cemented it.

I seemed to be living in a permanent state of need.

Not that the shower was doing a damn thing about it. A flash of Frankie's green eyes as she'd laughed the night before danced across my mind, even as the feeling of her arms wrapping around me from behind sent another bolt of lust right to my balls.

Right hand on my erection, I braced my left against the wall and focused on what it felt like to kiss her and how it felt like when she held onto me. She always smelled so great—even when she complained about smelling like hamburgers after work. Frankie always smelled like Frankie.

It was hardly my first time jerking off in the shower, and definitely not the first time I jerked off to the thought of her. The first slow stroke of my hand from base to tip sent a very pleasant tingling through my balls and up my spine. Eyes closed, all I had to do was imagine pressing my lips to her throat as I stroked slowly. It took very little to stiffen to the point of painful. Wanting her? No, that had never been a problem.

The first time I jacked off, I'd been thinking about Frankie. Well, her breasts specifically. We'd all been wrestling, and she'd ended up smashed against me, and I had a handful of boob. It didn't hit me until later just how soft and fucking fabulous that had been.

If all I wanted was a pure physical relationship? I'd probably be just like Archie and Jake. But I wanted more than that. Frankie saw me—she saw me when no one else did. Not even the guys. She never forgot the music.

The rasp of her voice when she said my name lit me up. I'd been Bubba to all of them forever. The only other people who called me Ian were my parents. But when Frankie said it? Fuck, that had felt good. The way she'd bite her lower lip when she concentrated on something always pulled me. There was an effortlessness to being around her that I craved.

We didn't have to be anyone other than ourselves.

Or we used to only have to be us.

Somewhere…that changed.

Pushing my cock through the damp cradle of my palm, I wished like hell it was her. The image of her sprawled on my bed, naked and sweet, open and vulnerable, a temptation and revelation in one beautifully strong package had me groaning as my hips jerked with the orgasm I pulled out.

Fuck. I leaned my head against the tile and sighed.

Wanting her was definitely *not* the problem.

Pushing away, I finished my shower.

Five minutes later, dressed in play gear, hair combed, and my change of clothes stuff stuffed into my duffle, I headed downstairs. I had just enough time for food before I had to leave for school.

"Good morning, Ian," Dad said from where he waited at the kitchen table.

Crap.

I'd really hoped to avoid this morning's discussion surely generated by Mom asking me last night if Frankie would be coming by today.

"Morning, Dad. Not a lot of time to talk, got to get to practice." I had been planning cereal. For now, I dropped a Pop-Tart in the toaster. Too much sugar and I'd be regretting it at lunch, but at the moment, I didn't care.

"I know, but I wanted to remind you about this afternoon."

Turning, I stared at him. "Dad, Frankie and I are friends."

"You're taking her to Homecoming, Ian. That makes you a lot more than friends."

"Maybe, but right now, we're just friends. She's important to me."

"She's troubled," Dad said quietly, folding his hands together. Everything about him was relaxed and solemn. "After last week—the incident with Jake, the bullying…the photographs."

I made myself not look away. The sheer level of Dad's disappointment over my presence in those photos had lain like a pall over the house. We hadn't told Mom. Dad didn't see the point in upsetting her, and he expected me to do better.

"Dad, she's Frankie. Is her mom a raging bitch for treating her so badly? Yes." I didn't give a damn that he scowled at my language. "But she's still Frankie."

"I agree, but that's the point, Ian. Frankie's clearly got issues because of her mother's treatment. Son—abuse comes in a lot of forms. I know you didn't want to listen to me this weekend, but I took you to that hospital for a reason."

Yeah. To show me what troubled youth looked like. As if I didn't know. "I spent the night at her place," I reminded him. "Me and the other guys. After everything that went down with her mother and Archie's dad—we didn't want her to have to be alone. Especially if they showed up there."

"I understand. I also understand it's very easy to get swept up in the feelings of needing to save her."

"We're friends, I'm going to look out for her. Someone has to…"

My father sighed. "It's easy to get sucked in and to make their problems yours."

"Just stop," I told him, and bit into the first Pop-Tart. As hot as it was, it burned the roof of my mouth, but I didn't care. "I'm not going to take advantage of her. You made your point about her mother's emotional unavailability and her need for approval and closeness."

It all sounded like a lot of crap, but Dad had made a compelling argument.

"Ian, I didn't tell you this to upset you but to protect both of you. You want to make her feel better, but there's every chance she's looking for emotional validation through intimacy because she has been so deprived. What I wish… is that I'd realized how bad it was. Her mother's always been…distant with us. Good for a quick call, but not close. I just always put it down to she was busy."

"Well, so did most of us." Except Coop. Coop always said there was something off about her mom. I only noticed the absences. More and more, the woman was gone on her trips. Maybe this year it just stood out because Frankie had cut all of us off and she'd been there alone.

That just sent another swell of guilt through me.

"I told her I wanted to be friends, okay? She's dating the other guys, and that's good. But she and I are going to be friends. I'll look out for her. Take her to Homecoming, try to keep the crap from Sharon and the others from coming down on her. Happy?" I took another bite. Dad had hammered on this point. That

Frankie was in a vulnerable place, and I got it. He wasn't wrong.

Just—now I had to be the bad guy.

"No," Dad said quietly. "I'm not. But I do want to talk to her about trying to get into some therapy."

"That's never going to happen." I didn't even have to try and pretend. "She doesn't want to talk about this stuff. She barely wants to talk about it with us." Actually, she didn't want to talk to us about it at all. But her mother had left her little choice.

"So I gathered from the conversation I had with the student advocate. My next step is to talk to her mother myself."

"Dad…"

I glanced at the clock. I had to hurry up and eat.

"Look, you do that, and it's just going to blow back on her."

"Your mother wants to call child protective services—"

"Frankie's seventeen. She's going to be eighteen in a few months. You guys do that, and they take her away, she loses her cats, her home, and maybe they even pull her out of the school, and then she loses us. You *can't* do that."

"I understand the concern. CPS isn't ideal. Nor is leaving her in that situation…"

Fuck. "Dad, I know you want to fix this. But when I talked to you about what was going on, I did it because I trusted you to listen to me."

"Ian, I'm not just doing this because of what we talked about, but because of what I saw myself when that issue with the post happened last week. Jake's lashing out because he feels like he couldn't protect his mother, and he refuses to not protect Frankie. That's going to get dangerous if this keeps escalating. You throw in the issues at Archie's home now and how does that not create a conflict for them both? But beyond *all* of that, neglect is a serious issue."

"So is isolation. The only thing reporting this does is punish *Frankie*, and I think she's suffered enough. Between us, we can look after her. We can give her a place to go. We can keep her safe."

Dad pinched the bridge of his nose, then shook his head. "I don't think the answer is anywhere as neat as you're trying to make it."

"I also don't think it's found in tearing her away from all of us."

As it was, Archie had already volunteered to move in with her if her mom and his dad were serious about moving them out of that apartment. Fuck—why couldn't her mom have waited?

A few more months, and none of this would be Frankie's problem.

"Has Frankie ever mentioned her father?"

I stuffed the last of the Pop-Tart in my mouth to avoid that answer. Mouthing through crumbs, "Don't know, gotta go," I diverted for the door.

Every inch of me regretted confessing to Dad when I got home on Saturday about why I was upset. I'd woken up and seen Frankie all snuggled between Coop and Jake, and it ate away it me.

It shouldn't have, but it had.

Then…then I told Jake that I didn't think I could do this. Not if they were all going to keep pushing the lines until they'd erased them. Archie had never been with a girl long-term, not even Patty counted. Because it was Patty who pursued him, Archie just let her hang out.

This, though?

No, it had gone on for weeks and showed every sign of intensifying. Jake, too. Coop? Not even a question. So where did that leave me? And then Dad had to point out all the ways this was just another sign of how bad Frankie's situation was.

That had been the last thing I intended or wanted to hear. Frankie *needed* us. But more, I needed her.

I stored my gear in the saddlebags, then pulled on my helmet. I almost left her helmet here. Hers, because no one else had been on this bike with me, and I hadn't picked up the second helmet for anyone else either.

She didn't want to ride with me. I got that it was my punishment for pulling away. Fine, I deserved it for confusing the issue. Didn't make it sting any less. I just couldn't tell her what Dad thought. She did not need that kind of negativity in her life.

Even if he was right, and the more I thought about it, the more I thought he might be. Frankie's mom was a bitch. There was no two ways about it. I snagged her helmet and secured it to my bike. Maybe she'd change her mind.

I was talking to her today and straightening this out. I didn't want her to think I didn't care. But I also don't want the four of us to be the reason she has any more trouble than we'd already created.

The points thing with the guys…when they figured out I told her, they were all going to lose their minds. I slid onto the bike and started it up. Walking it back toward the street, I focused on what I could control.

The points thing had been a stupid idea. Even knowing that, I had to admit we'd had a blast doing it. It hadn't seemed like it was hurting anyone or anything. But the reactions from Sharon and the others?

I was pretty sure we had hurt them.

They were taking that hurt out on Frankie.

The ride to school was quiet. Not a lot of traffic this early, and the parking lot was a ghost town except for the other players.

Jake was waiting, leaning against his SUV when I pulled in. I had to park a few slots over, because most of this was paid per the spot and I'd paid for mine before the school year. I just hadn't used it when I could park next to Frankie. But we weren't letting her drive to school.

When the hell had this all turned into such a cluster fuck? If nothing else, the assignment as the liaison to stupid Homecoming committee might let me make some semblance of peace with Sharon and get her off Frankie's case.

"Hey, man," Jake said as he walked over to meet me. Unlike me, he was dressed for school. He didn't have to deal with actual practice while riding the bench. "You look like crap."

"Thanks," I said, shouldering my duffle and backpack before we headed toward the stadium. "You look fresh as a daisy."

Jake snorted. "What's up?"

"Being a dick is hard," I said. "Or hadn't you heard?"

"Then stop being a dick," was his stellar advice. "Not even sure what the hell set you off in the first place, and you're being less than clear in your statements."

"It's hard to talk about," I admitted. I'd talked to one person beyond my dad about all of this, and it was Coop. I didn't know what I'd expected when I just unloaded on him, but his listening quietly before he agreed 'it was a shit result to me losing it even for a minute' hadn't been it.

Then he'd told me he agreed with my dad—at least about Frankie being abused. "Comes in all shapes and sizes, Bubba," Coop said. "Her mom is abusive as fuck emotionally. Thinking about it, I don't think I've ever seen her mom even hug her."

If that wasn't weird enough. There were all the other pieces. I didn't have the right to mess up her life, she had enough complications. But I couldn't say— *hey, Frankie, my dad thinks you're emotionally compromised, and me dating you is doing more harm than good. Friends, right?*

"Try me," Jake offered as we reached the gates and let ourselves in. More of the team was arriving behind us. Mitch was already there along with a few others. He nodded to us, but no smile or greeting. While not antisocial, he was definitely not friendly. Jake ignored him though and nudged me.

"Not here," I told him. There were way too many ears here.

"Sure, and then it's not in school, and not at lunch, and not after school, not on text, and not on the phone. At some point, you either tell me you aren't talking to me about this and man up, or you just open your fucking mouth. I can't help if I don't get it."

Well, he wasn't wrong. I cut across the field to the locker room, and Jake was right behind me. I just needed to store the bags and grab my gear for practice.

Inside, it was empty, and I double-checked the showers.

"Watch the door," I told him as I started pulling it on.

"I'm watching," Jake promised, arms folded as he leaned against the lockers. "What's going on?"

"I fucked up," I told him.

"You did not let that skank get to you at that meeting, right?" Jake demanded, and I blinked as I stared at him.

"What?"

"Sharon?" He gave me a look like I was stupid.

"No, I didn't let her get to me. Hell, no. Even if I never talked to Frankie again…" The idea made me want to puke. "I wouldn't go out with Sharon again. Period."

"Good." He relaxed a fraction. Though I was pretty sure if I'd given any other answer, he'd have pounded me. Overprotective of Frankie? Most definitely.

"I wouldn't do that to Frankie," I said. "I'm not that much of a dick."

"Even better."

He wouldn't think so in a minute.

"I was a little screwed up when I left on Saturday."

"I remember."

"I talked to my dad."

Jake winced. "Your dad's pretty cool."

"Yeah, he is, but he was already worried about Frankie." And in as few terms as possible, I told him what my dad had said and what happened when we went up to Dallas and how my dad was worried about her and now…well, so was I.

"Shit," Jake said, leaning his head back against the locker and staring at me. "I get it. Sure. Her mom's a raging cunt who deserves to be slapped into next year. But walking away from Frankie is akin to calling CPS—you're just punishing her because she doesn't know what she did wrong."

That thought crushed me.

"Jake, what if we screw this up? What if we make it worse?"

"We won't."

"You don't know that," I said.

"Yeah, I do. Because she's Frankie. She's a part of us." The door shoved inward, and we both shut up. I locked up and headed out with Jake hot on my heels. At the edge of the field, away from the others, he added, "And none of us are gonna let the others hurt her. I won't let you hurt her anymore."

"What does that mean?" I pivoted to face him.

"I mean get your shit together and figure it out. She deserves better than this, and you're way better than this. You got jealous. It's going to happen. We all do it. But we get over it, and we put her first."

"You're the most possessive guy I know, and you don't care that she's seeing all of us?"

"As long as it's us, I don't. No one else." Jake spread his hands. "But keep it up, and it won't be okay with me that you're a part of us. Fix this, Bubba. Even if telling her about what your dad said sucks, talk to her and give her a chance to talk to you. God—man, she is so worth it."

Yeah. She was. But…

"I told her about the points."

All of the friendliness in Jake's expression dried up. "What?"

"I told her about them, because that's on us. You say we're the right people to look after her and protect her. But we did that."

Yeah, should have seen that fist coming.

Fuck, that hurt.

Chapter Nine
EVERYTHING CHANGES

Our phones blew up before we even made it into the parking lot at the school. Coop had been almost giddy driving the Lexus—seriously, Archie got him a Lexus?—and his good mood proved contagious. We laughed and sang along with the music.

I'd always been the one with the car out of the two of us. While Coop hardly complained about being wheel-less, an unmistakable sense of freedom populated the interior of the car. His grin remained a fierce and visceral thing. Half-twisted in the seat, I stretched a hand over to rest on his shoulder while I savored his expressions.

Happiness looked good on him.

Curling my fingers against his nape, I grinned when he shot me a look. "Hey…" The music in the car lowered. Controls on the steering wheel rocked. My car didn't have that. Lots of amenities my car didn't have, not that I was complaining.

"Hey."

Our phones buzzed again and he quirked a brow. "You going to check that? It could be Arch or one of the guys."

"I know," I admitted. "But I'm enjoying seeing you so happy."

Red tipped his ears. I wouldn't even have noticed but I stroked my fingers through his hair and back down to his nape. "I'm being a dork, aren't I?"

I laughed. "I am so the wrong person to ask that of. I'm always a dork."

"No you're not," he said, almost a little too vehemently. "You're the coolest, ever."

Yeah. I snorted. Thankfully, he couldn't hold onto his fierceness, and his smile reappeared.

"You're the coolest to me."

Now our phones buzzed in tandem, and I groaned. We were almost to school, so I brushed my fingers against his nape once more before pulling my hand away and facing forward again. Coop caught my hand though and pulled it over to his thigh, where he held it as he waited for the last light. We were less than a half-block from where we'd pull into the school parking lot.

"Thanks for being my first passenger," he said.

"You're welcome." It seemed like a little thing, then again, I remembered what it was like getting behind the wheel of the car when it was finally all mine and not just borrowing Mom's. Part of the reason I resented the need to keep my car off campus. That car was my lifeline to escape. Now I had to rely on the guys—or walk.

Not that I couldn't rely on them, but I craved my own independence. I wanted to hang with them because I wanted to, not because I had to. It might be a thin line, but I stuck to it.

"I'm really happy for you," I told him, then gave a dramatic sigh. "No idea how I top this for your birthday."

"I'm going to tell you a secret," he said as he slowed for the turn. But he didn't finish until we were pulling into the lot and he headed for where I usually parked. "You've got everyone beat just being you."

Heat pounded to my face not just from the words, but the low-tone he spoke in. After he slotted the car into a space, he put it in park and then covered my hand with his.

"You know you're my favorite person, right?"

I glanced down to our hands then back at him. "You're definitely one of mine."

"Good." Then he sighed as he drifted his gaze to my lips then back up. "Now the sucky part of the day."

"School's not great, but it's not that bad."

"It is when I can't kiss you."

My face burned, but I didn't look away.

"You're also really gorgeous when you—" Our phones buzzed again. "For the love of all that's holy and not," he muttered, and grabbed his phone from the cup holder. "What?"

The look on his face had me reaching for mine.

"What?" I repeated his question, but the texts from Archie said it all. My good mood fled, and my heart sank.

Jake and Ian got into a fight.

Not just a little fight.

But a brawl.

They were both in the office. Archie had other details.

This was Jake's second fighting offense in as many weeks.

There was no way he wasn't getting suspended.

"Did I do this?" I asked, staring at the message.

"No," Coop said, his voice firm. "You didn't. This is them, Frankie. Not you."

I sent a text to Archie that we were there and heading inside. We needed to know where he was.

"Then why does this feel like my fault?" I asked, even as we grabbed our backpacks. Before I could slide out of the car, Coop caught my hand again and tugged.

"Listen to me," he said, his gray-green eyes calm. "You are not responsible for our behavior." When I would have opened my mouth to respond, he squeezed my hand and shook his head. "Ah-ah. No. You are responsible for one person and one person only—you. What we do? Me? Archie? Bubba? Jake? That's on us."

I wanted to believe that.

"Ian's upset right now."

"So are you. I don't see you starting fights."

An inadvertent laugh slipped out. "Maybe you haven't been looking closely enough."

For his part, Coop snorted. "Frankie, this isn't your fault."

"But this is what worries me about dating all of you."

"I know, and that is why I'm telling you…" He cupped my cheek with his free hand. "Whatever went down between Jake and Bubba? That's on them. Jake's got a temper."

Did he ever.

"Bubba…Bubba might be the golden boy, but there's repressed rage there."

I frowned.

"Just—none of us are perfect."

"No shit," I said, some of the guilt eating like acid though me cooling at the comment. "I never thought you were. I'm definitely not."

"Ha," Coop said. "That's where you're wrong, though I guess in being wrong, you diminish your perfection but only a little."

Half-groaning and laughing, I turned my face and pressed a kiss to his palm. "Nobody's perfect. That's what makes us so interesting."

His pupils flared, and he stroked his thumb over my lower lip. "That good morning kiss is never enough, you know."

"I do."

"You're going to Bubba's tonight."

"I'm supposed to." Who knew what was happening after this morning? "And we should probably…"

"We will. Text me when you head home?"

The question pulled at me. "Save a kiss for me?"

"I'll save every kiss you want," he promised. We lingered like that, trapped in the raw honesty in his answer. He wanted more, and Jake's soft promise that no way Coop was going to wait echoed back at me.

No. I didn't want him to have to wait either.

"Time to go," I whispered.

"Yeah," he said. "Arch's waiting."

"And coffee." At the comment, Coop flashed me another swift grin.

"The fastest way to your heart."

"Ha."

The soft beep-beep of his car alarm engaging echoed as a pair of hands clapped. Turning away from Coop, I met Sharon's bland stare. Patty stood not a foot behind her. "Thanks for the performance," Sharon said as she held up the phone. "Though I have to wonder why anyone would be fighting over scraps of *your* time."

Coop let out a little sound, but I caught his arm and didn't look away from Sharon. "You know what?"

"I know everyone is going to see what a slut you are," she said with a smirk as she tapped on her phone.

"Your jealousy is showing."

Patty snapped her gaze up and Sharon scowled.

"I know," I told her as I started forward, slinging my backpack on and keeping it casual. I actually used to feel sorry for her. But not anymore. I paused close enough to see her phone screen and the Snapchat she had open. Before I said, "I'm sure you still have biggest bitch in school all locked up."

When she gawked, I smiled.

"See you."

Then I marched inside with Coop hot on my heels. Inside, I was shaking like a leaf. But fuck Sharon.

Seriously.

Just fuck her.

"That," Coop said as he slung an arm around my shoulders, "was epic. You just achieved like—seriously—mega levels of hotness. Be my friend? Please?" He leaned into me on the last.

I rolled my eyes, laughing. "You said that when I punched John in kindergarten."

"I did, and when you socked Felicia MacNamara."

Ugh. I laughed, head back. "I forgot about her."

"I didn't. You had a wicked right hook, even when you were five."

Despite the banter, I couldn't quite shake the trembling on the inside. But hell if I would show it. Not with there already being an issue. Archie sat at our table, drumming the fingers of one hand until he caught sight of us.

"Finally," he said as we got there, and he shoved my iced coffee over to me. At the pinched worry around his eyes, what little humor I'd cobbled together fled.

"What do we know?" Coop asked as he dragged a chair out for me and caught my backpack.

"Thanks."

"Anytime," he said, flashing me a smile.

"Just—Bubba and Jake got into it when they hit the field this morning."

"Jake's on the bench still," Coop said, and I frowned.

"Yeah, I literally only know what the rest of the team and that dick Mitch was bitching about when he got in here." He nodded past us to where Mitch sat with Cheryl. Rachel wasn't at their table, but that didn't mean anything. "Bubba and Jake came out of the locker room. They looked pretty intense, then Jake sucker punched him and it was on."

I groaned. Of course Jake threw the first punch.

"It's not your fault," Coop reminded me as he bumped my knee. "They're big boys. They can handle it."

"Coop's right," Archie said, meeting my gaze. "This isn't you."

"It's easy to say that, but it's not like you guys fought like this before."

At that, both Coop and Archie both laughed.

"Um, babe," Archie said, dropping his voice. "We fought all the time."

"We fought before Arch and after him," Coop said. "Hell, we argue all the time now."

Since when? I glanced from one to the other. With a wry look, Archie motioned to his face. The black eye was mostly gone, but there was still some faint yellowing from when Ian slugged him.

"It's healthy," Coop said, and thankfully, I wasn't the only one staring at him skeptically. "It is," he continued. "There's such a thing as positive fight culture."

"What?"

"Think about it," Coop said before he swigged down a deep drink of his coffee, and then he leaned in. "A lot of stress comes from biting our tongues. From not saying what's bothering us. Illustration, you didn't talk to us for months because you were pissed about the untouchable thing. Right?"

"Right."

"But if you'd just come at us, and we'd fought about it right then? The internalized resentment, the confusion, and all the *stress* of not fighting about it would have been out in the open. We could resolve the issue, addressing it specifically."

Okay, that made a certain amount of sense. "But how are fights positive?"

"Because we're taught to not say things that are uncomfortable for other people. Um…if I ask you if you're hungry and you're starving, but you don't want to impose, what would you say?"

"I'm hungry," I told him. I didn't play with food, and Archie snickered.

"I think I get it," Archie said. "It's more like when you need help to get your tire changed. Yes, you can do it. It would be easier if someone helped, but you don't want to ask or make someone else feel obligated."

This was true.

"But asking is positive communication," Coop pointed out. "If you're angry, and you sit on that anger, you're hurting yourself. You're also not letting the subject of your anger have a chance to have their say."

"You really have been hitting the books," I said, studying him.

"Yeah well, I've had some good reasons to study psych, and the more I learn, the more I want to know. Besides—didn't it feel good to say that to Sharon earlier?"

"What'd you say?" Archie asked. While Coop described it, I turned the question over in my head. When I glanced at my phone, there were no new messages.

Laughter erupted across the cafeteria. Then it rolled like a wave. Chances were, Sharon's latest, vicious missive was making its way around the student body.

"A little," I admitted when Archie and Coop looked at me. "It felt a little good to not just suck up her crap. In my defense," I continued before they could say anything more, "I used to feel bad for her."

"You never should have," Archie said flatly. "None of them deserve your sympathy."

"They didn't deserve to be score card points either, but we're not all perfect as Coop and I already established."

Stiffness went through both of them, and they jerked like they'd been shot. I went to Instagram first. No post from her there. I hated Snapchat, but I opened it anyway.

Morbidly curious I supposed.

Yep, it wasn't just a photo, but a video of Coop and I still in the car talking. He had his hand on my cheek, and we looked deeply invested in each other. It was kind of humbling to see the naked emotion there. I mean, I got it when he looked at me, but it was different in the video.

Then it cut to the fight between Jake and Ian, and I winced.

Welcome to Frankie Club.

The next clip was worse than the first one. Ian and Jake were literally pounding on each other, and they were on the grass wrestling.

The first rule of Frankie Club is you do not talk about Frankie Club.

The image cut to where I kissed Coop's hand.

The second rule of Frankie Club is you DO NOT talk about Frankie Club.

There was even a video of Archie sitting in the cafeteria alone with their coffee typing on his phone.

The third rule of Frankie Club is if they're fighting, she's probably already tapped them out.

It cut back and forth between me and Coop to Archie alone to Jake and Ian fighting on the field.

Then it was done. More snickering across the cafeteria, and I shook my head.

"Well, at least we look cute in our part of the video." It was about all I could muster on that one. I glanced over to find Coop and Archie glaring daggers at each other, but they jerked their attention to me at my comment. "Why are you two pissed at each other?"

"Someone told you about the points." Archie's tone was flat as he studied me.

"It's not like I thought you guys were monks."

"Who told you?" Coop asked.

"It doesn't matter."

"It kind of does," Archie said.

"Because I know? Or because you didn't want me to know?" Honestly, I was more curious than I was angry. The whole concept was kind of gross. I could make excuses for them, but I wasn't going to. Ian indicated it was a mistake, and he wasn't proud of it. I didn't think any of them were.

"Because…" Coop scrubbed a hand over his face. I guess we'd all pretty much lost any shine of a good mood. "Shit…" He glanced at his phone and then dragged his seat closer and dropped his voice. "Positive fight culture."

I raised my eyebrows and then nodded slowly. "Okay, positive fight culture."

"I'm not proud of it. Though—admittedly, it was a lot of fun in the beginning, and we're pretty competitive." Coop winced and then met my gaze. "I'm sorry."

"Why are you sorry?"

"Because it doesn't say much about us as people."

"It says it's the past," Archie argued. "It didn't have anything to do with Frankie. That's why we agreed it would stay there."

"It's not going to," Coop said. "Let's face it, we've apparently pissed off enough people that it's all going to get aired. So better we're the ones telling her."

Kind of what I said when I asked if there was anything else I needed to know.

"I don't want you to know it," Archie said, his lips compressing. "I can be a real bastard. I learned from the best. I don't like that part of myself."

"You're never that way with me," I said.

"Because you're the exception," he said with a sigh. "You've always been the exception. I hate that you know. I don't want you to look at me differently."

"I don't want to look at you differently either," I said slowly. "But I already look you differently—not because of that. I'm still… I'll be honest, I don't get it. But the party pictures are making more sense now."

Archie winced. "Frankie…"

"It's okay, I mean…it's not really okay. But you don't owe *me* any apologies. What you guys did or didn't do—it's not about me. If you did it because I shut you out, then…that sucks, but it's still not about me." It wasn't denial so much as… "I want to think that you're not doing that with me."

"No," Coop said sharply, and Archie glared.

"Hell no. I told you—"

"I'm the exception. Then…" I lifted my shoulders in a bit of a shrug. "Okay." I glanced at my phone again. "Maybe you guys owe apologies to other people. I'm not saying you should make them. But maybe you should think about that. Sticking our heads in the sand and pretending the bad stuff didn't happen doesn't work."

It hadn't for a long time.

"The bell's gonna ring." I looked at Coop. "Text me if you hear from them? Chances are they're going to talk to you guys first."

"Yeah, of course," Coop said, but his troubled expression deepened. "Frankie, you are important. You're more than the exception. You've always been the rule. I got a little stupid when you weren't around…but you're right. That's not on you, and it's not about you. It's us."

I gave him a little smile. "Not sure I'm a fan of positive fight culture."

Ian and Jake's coffees were still there, but Archie picked them up and then tossed them before he grabbed his bag.

"I'll see you later," Coop said as we headed off.

"Bubba told you," Archie said softly.

"Does it matter?"

"In this instance?" he said. "Yeah, it does."

Ian wasn't in math.

I had to walk myself between classes because I told Coop and Archie they weren't going to race back and forth all over the school. They didn't like it, but they listened.

I ran into Sharon twice.

She didn't say a word.

Good.

Coop hadn't heard from them by AP lit.

We met up with Archie for lunch. He'd heard nothing either.

I spent most of my study hall trying to get homework done. My heart wasn't in it, but it needed to be finished.

There was a note from Rachel in my locker that I grabbed before seventh.

> *Hey,*
>
> *Just reminding you that not everyone is an asshole. Hard to tell around here sometimes. I almost texted you like ten times, but I figure—you know where I am now. Let me know if you need me to be the pushy friend or not. I totally got you covered there. Chin up, girl, and fuck Sharon. I'm totally going to mess up her day sometime this week. Stay tuned. It's going to be a riot.*
>
> *R.*

The note cracked me up, and I fired off a text to her.

Me

> I'm totally fine with the pushy friend.

She got back three thumbs up, a laughing face, a mad face, and more thumbs up.

Rachel

> Dude. I so have you covered.

Me

> Can't wait—and just so you know. It's a 2-way street. If you need me...

Rachel

> I could be cheesy, but I get it. I'll call. Thanks. CUsoon

The only real good news I got in G's class was my test score on that second test was a hell of a lot higher. He didn't comment on Jake's absence, and

I didn't ask. I used the time for homework and checking my phone. Arch and Coop had kept up a running chatter, more than usual. Pretty sure they were as worried as I was. I'd given in to temptation and sent texts to both Jake and Ian, but neither had answered.

That didn't mean anything.

Or at least, I hoped it didn't.

After class, I headed out, and it was weird to be leaving school without Jake right there. Coop met me at the door, and Archie was there, too. "Nothing?" I asked.

They both shook their heads.

"Okay, I'm going home if one of you will take me…and oh shit. Archie, I forgot with all of that. You're awesome."

"Well, thank you for noticing," he said, his expression bemused. "But what did I do?"

"Coop's car. That's very awesome."

He shot a glance at Coop and raised his brows. "You told her?"

"Yep," Coop said as we fell into step. "Because she's right man, you're friggin' awesome."

"Here I was trying to not make it about me."

"S'okay," I told him as I looped our arms, Coop on one side and Archie on the other. "It's not."

They both laughed, then Archie clutched at his chest with his free hand. "Wounded."

"You'll live."

"Anyway," Coop said as we neared the Lexus. "What were you saying?" Archie had followed us all the way to it when his car was out in the other lot.

"Take me home, and I'm going to get changed and drive over to Ian's. Harder to blow me off if I'm at the door."

"Want me to go to Jake's?" Archie asked before I could even suggest it.

"Would you?" That had been next.

"Not a problem," he said, then squeezed my hand before fixing Coop with a look. "Drive carefully with her. I'll text if I find anything out."

It didn't take long after we got home—and Coop gave me a very thorough kiss in the front seat of the car, because it needed to be christened with a kiss, right?—for me to take care of the cats, get changed, and check the mail.

Crap, I still had mail in my backpack. Making a mental note to check it later, I headed out. Mom was still MIA, and for once, I really was glad. Not sure what it said about me as her daughter that I didn't really want to see her.

The drive to Ian's seemed to take forever and was over in an instant. The garage door was shut, and there were no cars in the driveway. I was a little later than we normally got here. His parents had a date night on Tuesdays, so maybe they were already gone.

Blowing out a breath, I knocked and then got my phone ready to send him a text.

When the door opened, I was not prepared to see the swollen wreck of his face. Black eye, busted lip, and scraped chin.

"Ian…" I exhaled, and he braced his hand on the doorframe—his knuckles were scraped and bruised, too.

"Hey," he said with a wince. "I didn't think you'd still be coming over."

"Why not?"

"You know—" He motioned to his face.

"Really? You think because you got into a fight, suddenly I'm just going to cut and run? I'm not the one who decided I couldn't handle the dating part."

He flinched.

"And we're supposed to still be friends, or did I misunderstand that part, too?"

Honestly, maybe he didn't deserve me being pissed at the moment. Or maybe he did. Either way…

"I've been texting you, and you said nothing. Not a word. Not you. Not Jake."

He dipped his chin. "Jake got arrested."

My stomach bottomed out.

"What?"

Chapter Ten

WE THREE

(MY TEMPER, MY FUTURE, AND ME)

JAKE

My jaw ached. So did my knuckles. Pretty sure my bruises had bruises. Bubba had a wicked left hook and a worse right one. I'd gotten in a lot of blows, too. A click sounded when I ground my teeth together. Fuck, my jaw hurt. The corner of my lips was puffy, too. Every time I moved my mouth, even a little, the taste of blood touched my tongue.

I sat in a small room at the local police station. Not a place I ever thought I would find myself. On the upside, I wasn't handcuffed. On the downside, I'd been here for hours.

As far as I knew, I hadn't been charged—yet. At least, that was what the officers who picked me up from the school and brought me in had said. The handoff between the SROs and the police could have been embarrassing.

Except, I'd been too pissed. Pissed at the coach because he'd called the

SROs. Pissed at Bubba because he was a jerk who'd told Frankie one of the worst possible things about us in addition to being a dumbass. Pissed at myself because all I'd seen was red.

My temper.

Mom had been on my ass for the last few years, "Jake, you have got to learn to control that temper. I get it. Things make you mad. But you have to be in charge of you."

Welp, that was a big fat negative.

My inability to control my temper had me here. If they pressed charges, I had no idea what that meant. I wasn't eighteen, but that was a formality. It was a couple of months away. I did know better than to answer anything without an attorney. Hence why they had to call my mother. I wanted to call Frankie or at least let her know, but the only option they'd given me was using their phones. She was in class, and I wasn't leaving this as a voice mail.

"Hey, Frankie. Don't freak out. I busted Bubba's face 'cause he's a jackass. I'm at the police station. Can you pick up my homework for me?"

Worst of all, my phone was in my backpack, which I hadn't been allowed to have. They'd gotten Mom's number from the school. I was sure the school had called her, and if they hadn't, the cops here had.

That was why I was now sitting in this boring ass room with literally nothing to do but stare at the ugly ass institutional walls painted this cream color and wait.

Homework.

The door opened, and one of the cops who'd brought me in was there. "Need a Coke or something, kid?"

My face was killing me.

"Maybe an ice pack?"

The officer wore a look of sympathy. "They had the nurse look at you, right? Before we got there?"

"Yeah," I told him. "She did. Said it was probably going to hurt more later."

Great advice.

"I'll grab you an ice pack. I'd give you some Tylenol, but you're not eighteen."

And laws were kind of stupid. "Yeah, it's fine. I'll live. But I would like a Coke, thanks."

The man frowned. "I could get you a sandwich, or something. You've been here a while." No shit.

"I'd appreciate it. Have you guys reached my mom?"

The officer, I couldn't remember his name, glanced back at the bullpen behind him, then back at me. "Yeah, she was at work. She said her boss wouldn't let her leave early twice. But she'll be here after."

Right.

I couldn't blame her. "That's cool. Thanks."

"You're welcome. I'll be back in a few." Then he closed the door after him as he left.

Slumping back in the chair, I stared at the ceiling. Mom had to leave for a few hours the week before. She needed her job. It wasn't like I was going anywhere.

Shame itched at the back of my shoulders. She was going to be pretty fucking disappointed in me. It wasn't that long before the cop came back.

Gregson. His badge read Gregson. He left the door open, which was nice because the air in here wasn't that great and it was warm, but the cooler air from the open door helped.

"Coke," he said setting down a pair of cans. "Sandwiches." Two plastic boxes—one said turkey and swiss, and the other said chicken salad. "They aren't fancy. The machine down there doesn't have great stuff, but it's edible, and they stock the sandwiches everyday."

"Not complaining," I told him. "Thanks."

The ice pack he set down last. "Just crack that when you're ready, and it will get cold."

Instead of leaving though, the guy stood there as I tore open the sandwich container. My stomach had been gnawing on my backbone for hours. I pulled out the first triangle of the turkey and swiss and took a bite of it. Lettuce and mayo didn't add much more than some texture, but I'd take it.

Folding his arms, the officer—Gregson—studied me.

"Take a picture," I suggested. "It'll last longer."

The older man smiled faintly. "I knew your father."

Oh. That killed any humor I had, and I took another bite of my sandwich. Bully for him. I knew my dad, too. "He won't be showing up. He's still in Germany."

"Ah," Gregson said slowly. "Well, I wanted to tell you I put in a word for you."

I paused. "Why?" Maybe I shouldn't look a gift horse in the mouth, but I didn't know this guy.

"Like I said, I know your dad. Go ahead and eat. Soon as your mom gets here, they'll want to start the questioning. Okay?" Gregson moved back to the door.

"Yep." I took another bite as he closed it behind him, leaving me alone once more.

Not that there was much to question. I was pretty sure that some of the guys got that fight on video. There was a solid chance Frankie already knew, and I hated it. I hated that she had to find out like that. I hated that she was going through her day, and I wasn't there. Who the hell was walking her between classes? Arch and Coop couldn't be everywhere.

What if…?

Suddenly, my appetite faded. If I'd not lost my temper or at least not landed that first punch, I wouldn't be here right now, I'd be with Frankie. Instead…I popped open the can of Coke and grimaced as it burned the cut inside my mouth when I took a drink. Cracking the ice pack, I shook it until it began to grow frigid and then put it against my bruised face.

It was going to be a long ass day.

Mom wasn't the first one to show up, though. Joe—Bubba's dad—came in about an hour after Gregson brought me the sandwiches. I could see him outside in the bullpen talking to another cop—this one was in a suit and not a uniform. Though they glanced at the room where I waited, they made no move to come in here.

Joe was a good guy, and I wanted to say it surprised me he'd show up, considering it was Bubba I had the fight with, but I wasn't. Joe was that guy. He'd been there when my dad wasn't.

Guilt ate at me. Bubba and I had been close since we tried out and made football together. We'd always been friends, but the team drilled working together into us. I'd always thought it was easier for him and me, because we'd been buds before.

Thought that same team spirit would help with all of us dating Frankie. It had helped while we were all crushing on her and still being her friend. Bubba's parents were part of that. My mom loved Bubba, too. She liked all my friends, even Archie.

Though she did tell me once that Archie was too young to be that much of a snob, but at least he was polite about it. I started to grin, then stopped when my mouth hurt.

It kind of sucked how all of this went down. I didn't get what was going on in Bubba's head. Fine, he felt guilty about the points. It was a shit thing to do. The points had never been about anything except us. We didn't use them to lord it over anyone.

So why the fuck would he tell Frankie about it? What did that accomplish but give her one more thing to feel bad about? To feel like we'd lied to her?

The worst part…I had. She didn't deserve that. Frankie asked me if there was anything about the summer she needed to know, and I'd told her no.

We all had.

Then he does this.

Fuck.

I was going to die in this room. The Cokes and the sandwich had been great, but now I needed to piss like a racehorse, and it was… I leaned to check the clock on the wall. After four.

The day had dragged past, but school was letting out now, and I was here and it was Tuesday. Would she go over to his place for homework? Had she been texting me?

No way she didn't know about the fight.

Rather than dance around on the seat, I stood up, and everything ached as I stretched. My bruises had bruises, and I swore they stiffened in the time I'd sat in here. I opened the door, and Joe stood as soon as he saw me, as did the cop he was talking to.

"Mr. Benton, you need to remain in there until your mother comes."

"I know," I told him. "But can I hit the bathroom?"

Joe frowned when he saw my face. "Jake, has someone taken a look at you?"

"The nurse at school. I'm fine," I assured him. "Bubba and I have done worse on the football field." Technically, we'd never done it this bad. But we'd had our share of scrapes over the years.

"Morgan," the cop in the suit said, and another uniformed officer came over. "Take Mr. Benton to the facilities."

Great. I got a babysitter. Hopefully, the guy didn't mind if I held my own junk.

"I'm waiting for your mom, too, Jake. I'll be here," Joe promised. He'd come through for me before, and he was here now. I wanted to ask about Bubba, but I bit my tongue. Not sure I should ask in front of the cops.

"Thanks, Joe."

He nodded and then slowly sat back down as I followed 'Morgan' to the bathroom. Thankfully, he just stood by the door. I did my business, then washed my hands. I got a good look in the mirror. Yeah, Bubba cracked me good.

That was definitely going to leave a mark.

Well, at least grad pics had been done over the summer. I didn't smile. Smiling hurt.

Back to my little room I went, and I'd almost dozed off when I caught sight of my mom.

She wasn't alone. Archie was with her and another guy. Didn't know the guy.

Huh.

We locked gazes, and he lifted his chin in greeting. Then he glanced back at the conversation briefly and asked something. When he motioned to my door, I figured the question was could he come talk to me.

No. That wasn't the question. The guy with them headed for the room while Archie and my mom continued to talk to the cop with Joe.

Okay. This officially just got weird.

The door opened, and the man stepped in and left it open. "Mr. Benton, I'm Roger Wittaker. Mr. Standish requested I come down here to represent you, but you are not being charged. If you'd like to grab your things, we'll get you out of here."

"I'm not?" Then why the fuck had I been stuck here all day?

"No," the man said. "Your things?"

"I don't have them." I tossed the empty sandwich containers and the dead ice pack into the trash can as I stood. "They kept my backpack and stuff when they put me in here."

"Then we'll get those returned to you." He waited until I closed the distance before he turned to walk over to where Mom, Archie, and Joe were.

"Hey," Arch said when I got there. "I can give you a ride to your car when we're done."

"Thanks."

Mom twisted and pinned me with a look. "Don't," she said when I opened my mouth, so I snapped it closed and nodded. Then she focused on the cop again. "Now, please explain to me if he's not being charged, why you kept him here all day. I was called this morning, but I couldn't leave work."

"Ma'am—"

"Mrs. Benton will do." Damn, Mom. That frosty tone kept my spine rigid, and Archie straightened next to me. Mom didn't get mad. She got disappointed. At the moment, that sounded pretty damn mad.

The cop nodded. "Mrs. Benton, after the incident at the school, he was turned over to my officers by the SROs because it was considered an assault. Mr. Rhys—the younger one—declined to press any charges. The coach, who reported the incident, has since recanted his insistence that charges be filed."

Shock rippled through me, and I cut a look to Joe. The older man gave me a quiet nod.

"In that time, we were waiting to question your son because he wisely invoked his right to counsel and to have you here." The compliment and tone weren't doing anything to relax Mom's stance.

"He's not under arrest?"

"No ma'—Mrs. Benton. At this point, while he was in our custody for the day, he is not being charged. There won't be a record. I can't speak to what the school will do, but he's free to go."

"Excellent," Mr. Wittaker interceded smoothly. "If we could collect Mr. Benton's things and let him assure us that everything is in order, we'll go."

It was an awkward few minutes, but I got my backpack, everything was there—including my phone with messages from everyone and Frankie. I stuffed the phone in my pocket. I needed to answer Frankie as soon as I got out of here.

Fuck, it was six. It was like I'd been trapped in a bubble where time lost meaning. Slinging the strap over my shoulder, I said, "It's all here."

"Mr. Benton," the cop said before I could walk away. Should have known I wouldn't get off that easily. "You got lucky. You keep this up, that luck is going to run out. I'm glad you've got good friends and a support structure. You might consider them the next time something like this happens and refrain from solving issues with your fists."

Yeah. Great advice. "Yes, sir." I'd get right on it. Not that the cop wanted to hear all of that. No, just like Dad and every other uniform I'd ever known. They wanted to hear two syllables.

"Let's go, Jacob."

Oh. I was dead. Mom never called me Jacob.

We left in a group, Archie falling into step next to me as Joe moved forward to walk with my mom. The attorney waited for all of us, then he followed.

"Is she all right?" I asked quietly.

"She's worried," Archie said. "None of us knew about the arrest until she got to Bubba's."

"Is she still there?"

"I don't know. I just know she called me as soon as Bubba told her. I was already at your place waiting for you, then I called Wittaker. Coop went to get your sisters so your Mom could come straight here."

"Thanks, man," I bumped his shoulder.

"No problem, you look like crap, you know."

"Bubba looks worse." But I said that lower and didn't brag. As if she sensed the comment, Mom glanced at me. "I'm so getting my ass kicked."

"Yeah, I love you like a brother. But you are on your own with your mom."

I laughed. Fuck that hurt. But damn, that was funny. "Yeah, I get it. If you talk to her before I can, tell her I'll call as soon as possible, and that I'm fine."

Arch gave me a skeptical look. "You do not look fine."

"Then tell her I said I was fine."

He rolled his eyes. "Yup."

We were in the parking lot when Mom wheeled around. "Jacob Elijah Benton."

Fuck, she trotted out all three names.

"What the hell were you thinking?"

"Alicia—"

"Don't," Mom said to Joe, and he raised his hands. "This time, Jacob answers me. What were you thinking?"

"I was thinking Bubba was being an asshole."

She sighed, and Joe looked pained.

"I get that I…I probably shouldn't have punched him." Damn it had felt good. "But after that—we had some issues that needed to be worked out."

Joe's eyebrows climbed to his hairline, but he didn't comment.

"He's your friend, Jake," Mom said, easing back on my name. "Your friend. And you both do…" She waved her hand up and down at me. "This."

"Looks a lot worse than it feels." Total lie, but I'd given Mom enough grief. "I'm sorry they called you and had to drag you down here."

"And?" She stared at me.

"And I'm sorry I started a fight." Not really, but again, it was what she needed to hear. "Am I suspended?"

"I don't know," she admitted, and glanced at Joe.

He shook his head. "I don't know either. You're going to have to talk to Diane tomorrow, in all likelihood, and I wouldn't be surprised if they suspend you. I'm more worried about the team."

I didn't give two flying fucks about the team. Which was weird. I used to love it, but it was because it was fun and I was competitive, but right now, it seemed more a burden than anything. I didn't need it.

"Well, Coach already has me riding a bench."

Mom rubbed her face. "You know I should ground you."

"Okay." I'd hate it, but again, she had enough grief from me.

"Why are you being so agreeable?"

"Because I already pissed on your day, Mom," I told her. "You didn't deserve this, and it's not your fault. So if you need to ground me, I'll do it. If the school needs to suspend me, I'll suck it up." If I have to miss Frankie, I'd talk to her on the phone every second I got. Maybe she could come over.

"Mrs. Benton?" Archie said, and Mom focused on him. "I know it's none of my business. But—we fight. The four of us. The five of us, really. We have arguments and disagreements. Sometimes they get heated. This one just got a little rowdy."

"Rowdy," Mom said. "That's a word for it."

"I know, I guess what I'm trying to say is they basically put Jake in a timeout all day. That place was pretty dreary. If it were me…I'd be damn sure to never get stuck somewhere like that again. Lesson learned."

"If it were you." There was almost a hint of amusement in Mom's voice.

"Yes."

She shook her head. "I need to talk to Joe, and Becca texted that she and your sisters are home. You can thank Coop for that." When she stared at me for a long moment, some shame crept through me.

"I'm really sorry, Mom. I'll do better."

With an exasperated smile, she gave me a hug and then leaned back to study my face. "You really look terrible."

"It'll heal, and it really doesn't feel that bad."

She pressed a kiss to my cheek. "Go on with Archie, I know you want to go find Frankie." The last few words were soft. "Don't scare her with that face."

I laughed and fuck, that hurt, but she smiled.

"And I'm not going to tell your father."

"Thanks, Mom." I meant that about seeing Frankie and her hug. I didn't give a damn if she told Dad. What would he do? Lecture me via Skype? That was what mute was for. "I'll try not to be late."

"Hmm…tomorrow we'll deal with the school."

Mr. Wittaker shook Archie's hand, and then Mom headed for her car. Joe lingered behind, and then he focused on Archie and me.

"Thanks for coming down, Joe," I said.

"You're welcome," he said. "Ian won't tell me what the fight was about."

Okay.

"You're probably not going to tell me either."

Archie and I both stayed mute.

Joe nodded once, then folded his arms. "Boys, whatever is going on with all of you—and yes, I am aware of some of it—you need to find a way to resolve it without fighting. You've all been friends for too long, and you're not doing Frankie any favors."

Bubba had mentioned he'd talked to his dad about Frankie. While Archie frowned, he didn't say or ask anything. I just nodded. "I get that, sir, I do."

"I hope so," he said with a sigh. "And Jake…you and Ian should talk. I mean really talk and not with your fists."

Didn't really see that happening, but… "Is he all right? I didn't see him after the nurse."

Mostly because they separated us. I'd meant it when I said he got the worst of it.

"Looks a bit like you, definitely in a worse mood, and his mother was not as understanding as yours."

I didn't laugh, but it was kind of funny.

"There's a chance he'll be riding the bench with you," Joe continued. "So maybe you two will have some real time to talk."

Yep, and maybe monkeys named Bob would fly out of my ass.

"Be good, boys," he said. "Remember what I said about Frankie."

No sooner had Joe climbed into his car and pulled away did Archie round on me. "What the hell was that about Frankie?"

"I'm fucking starving, and my face hurts. Feed me and get me to my car, and I'll tell you."

He jerked his thumb toward the Ferrari before heading toward it. "Should I call Coop?"

Probably.

Fuck.

What I wanted was to go find Frankie, but we needed to figure this out.

"Yeah, we should probably loop him in since Bubba told her about the damn points thing."

"Oh yeah," Archie said as he slid in the car. "We know."

"What?"

I twisted to look at him before I reached for the seatbelt.

"She told us. Took it way better than we deserve," he told me before he started the engine. "Way better."

Well, that was something.

"But I still want to hear this, and then the three of us are going to have a heart to heart with Bubba."

We needed to do that, too.

"Because right now?" Archie told me as he backed out of the spot. "I'm done with this shit."

"Ditto," I said, and pulled out my phone.

I fired off a text to Frankie.

Her response made me grin for real, and I didn't even care that it pulled at my lip. Head back against the seat, I blew out a breath as Archie told his car to call Coop.

We had to sort this out, because Archie was right. I was done with this shit, too.

Chapter Eleven
CRYIN' WON'T HELP

"**S**o what happened?" Rachel asked as we wandered through the dense and crowded shop. Coat Rack was everything Marsha promised. Between the vintage clothes, accessories, and more, there was barely room to stand, much less walk. We had to squeeze our way through, but it was like digging for treasure.

Right now, I desperately needed the distraction, even if it was for Homecoming. The fact that Rachel hadn't even questioned the why of it and shown up when I asked helped, too.

"He told me Jake had been arrested after the fight." Ian had looked like crap. The bruises were pretty bad. Not a little bad, but very bad. Worse had been the look in his eyes. "When I got past the initial disbelief, I asked him what happened…"

"You knew the fight happened," Rachel observed, then paused to pull a dress out from the overstuffed rack, and I braced some of the items back so she could free it. When she held it up to herself, I stared at it skeptically. It looked like something a grandmother might wear to a funeral. "I could do things with this."

"Burn it?" At my suggestion, she grinned.

"You never know, anyway…you knew the fight happened."

I shrugged. "Yes, I knew they fought. Hard to miss with Bitchy McBitcherson's video this morning."

Pressing a hand to her chest, Rachel swooned. "Damn, it does my heart good to hear you talk smack."

"Shut up," I grunted, and gave her a light shove, even if I was grinning. We pressed through and came to a whole display of gold jewelry pieces, bangles, necklaces, rings, earrings…so much glitter and gold.

"Uh huh, spill, you're killing me with the anticipation. What did the great golden one say when you asked?"

I rolled my eyes at the description. "Be nice."

"I am being nice, I didn't call him the football dickhead."

My mouth twitched as a giggle-snort escaped. "True." When she pinched me, I yanked my arm away. "All right, all right." Where to start? "We went out by the pool, he's not supposed to have guests, but he said he figured his mom would make an exception. Apparently, he's in a lot of trouble with his parents because of the fight." His parents hadn't been there, so that might have been an excuse, too.

"Sucks to be him."

Kind of did. He was eighteen and likely grounded, but he said he deserved it, so maybe that was on him. I don't know anymore. Bit by bit, I told Rachel a little of what happened over the last few days, beginning with Ian leaving Saturday morning after telling me he didn't think he could do this but we could still be friends.

The whole time I spoke, I kept my attention on the jewelry. Coming to the shop had been half an excuse to talk to Rachel on neutral ground, and half because I actually did need something to go with my dress.

If I even ended up going to Homecoming at this rate.

When I reached the part where Ian told me about the points, she grimaced. "Yeah, I knew that." At my askance look, she lifted her shoulders. "Everyone knew it."

The note about did I know who they'd done that summer made a lot more sense.

"Sorry," she muttered. "Go on."

"Anyway, he told me Jake wanted to know what was going on with him, so he told him, and Jake was sticking up for me and telling Ian he needed to talk to me, just lay it out there and find a solution." For which I could kiss Jake because dammit, that was what I wanted, too. I hated this awkward distance between me and Ian, and I hated it even more that he and the guys are struggling. "I mean, it was bad enough the night Ian punched Archie."

"Party night. Good times. Tell me rich boy deserved it."

"Rachel…"

"I'm still being nice, you just happen to like the douche bags more than I do, and frankly, I don't think one of them deserves you. But I'm definitely biased, so I will do my best here. Okay?" She crossed her eyes and made a face at me, and I shook my head. I didn't know what to do with her sometimes.

"Moving on," I said, because while Ian and Jake seemed to think Archie deserved it, I personally did not. "Ian's convinced I don't know what's good for me."

"Oh, he's sounding better to me…"

"Like I can't make my own decisions about what I want."

"Never mind. Not so much."

Rolling my eyes, I tried to focus. The conversation had been uncomfortable because he'd avoided looking me in the eye for a lot of it. Right up until he got to the part I needed to know. "The fight started because Ian told Jake he'd told me about the points."

"That would explain why Jake threw the first punch," Rachel mused. "The question I have is, was he more pissed that you knew about their dirty laundry or pissed because 'Ian,'" she said with air quotes, "telling you broke some kind of bro code."

That was food for thought. "Maybe both. Jake's really protective."

"And in other news," Rachel held up a box of a necklace and earring set like it was a microphone. "Water is wet." Sobering, she put the box back. "What did you do?"

"I asked him if the problem lay with me dating Coop, Jake, and Archie. Or if he just didn't want to date me."

Pivoting to face me, Rachel studied me. "And he said…?"

"He didn't know."

"You should plug your ears. No seriously—because I'm about to not be nice."

"Rach—"

"Nope. He doesn't fucking know?" She spread her arms. "Those were not difficult questions."

"But they are complicated ones."

"Frankie," she said, gripping my biceps. "Do you want to date all four of them?"

"Yes."

"Do you still want to date just three of them if one is out?"

"Yes but…"

"But what?"

I couldn't look anywhere else. "It won't be the same. It's been the five of us since freshman year."

"It was the four of you before that, and the three of you before that, and what? You and Coop before that. So you can only add, not subtract?"

Ouch.

"I'm not trying to be a bitch."

"If you never have to try," I said dryly as I hung the necklace back up.

Rachel hugged me. "There. That right there."

"What?" I extracted myself and stared at her.

"That bite in your words, that's what you've been missing for months. If I hadn't told you about their asinine plan, maybe you would still be right there kicking them in the ass, and they wouldn't have tripped over their own toys. But you carry the water for all of them. I know part of it is who you are, but the other part is very much they are used to looking at you as their barometer for whether something is okay. Clearly, they suck at it on their own."

Head back, I groaned. "This isn't helping me."

"Because I can't help you, and neither can they. You have to decide what you want."

"I did."

She paused, then glanced around before she focused on me again. "What did you decide?"

"Ian said he didn't know. Then—the whole we can still be friends and he would still take me to Homecoming and…" I waved my hand at the jewelry. "Part of why I'm here. Marsha and Cheryl are both insisting I need accessories."

"You do, and we'll get them. Go on."

"But I don't want 'I don't know.'"

Rachel said nothing.

"And I don't want them fighting."

The silence grew deeper, if that was even a thing.

"So I told him I didn't want to go to Homecoming. I was releasing him from his obligation and his ask. That, if we were friends, then we were friends, but we were officially not dating. I broke up with him. Two weeks…three weeks. Seems like forever and no time at all." I blinked furiously. The only reason I'd come out and called Rachel was Archie and Coop said they were working to get Jake. There was literally nothing else I could do, and I had to get my own head figured out.

If Jake ended up charged…I didn't know what would happen next.

"What did he say?" The soft question reminded me Rachel was there, just as I spotted a really pretty necklace with several layers and it had charms on it. Charms like my bracelet.

I lifted it down carefully. "He didn't say anything."

"Nothing?" Disbelief populated the word.

"I left." I lifted my shoulders. "He needs to figure out him. If dating me or not knowing if he can or any part of that is the issue, then he needs to figure that out first. I don't know how to do the other." Even with my inconsistent and mercurial mother, and her waxing and waning affections. It took every ounce of my energy to keep up with her, and I didn't even want to do that anymore.

She was my mom, but the more she was away, the more I wanted her to stay gone. What did that say about me?

"Wow." No smart remarks. No cutting comment. "You okay?"

"I don't know. It's weird because I never realized they all had things for me. I'd always nursed little crushes on them. I mean—they were my best friends. They were my rocks." If I couldn't count on my mom, I could count on them, and then… "And even before we started dating, when they asked, and I said I was worried it was going to change everything. This is what I was afraid of."

Rachel sighed. "That necklace, these earrings, and these bangles." She plucked two things off the shelf and pressed them in my hand. "Come on. Buy those, and we're going for ice cream."

"I don't…"

"You do and you can." She turned me by the shoulders and marched me through the squeeze until we found the register. All together, it didn't cost more than a few dollars.

Outside, the humidity smacked us in the face, and she pointed to her car. "Ride or follow?"

"Follow," I said almost automatically. I'd been jammed out of my car so much lately. I didn't want to not have it.

"Okay…we're going to—" She broke off when my phone buzzed.

After digging it out of my pocket, I stared at the message on the screen and let out breath.

Jake

> I'm all right. No charges. With Arch and getting food. You ok?

For the first time since I heard about the fight, I could take a deep breath. It didn't even bother me that Rachel read the message over my shoulder.

"He's okay."

"Yeah," I exhaled. "Archie went to help and yeah, he's okay."

"Cool, tell possessive dickhead you're having a girl's night, and you'll kiss his boo boos later. Don't tell him about Bubba or the rest of it. If he just got out and texted you first, he's worried about you. You need to figure this out before you see him." All really practical, if colorful, advice. Jake had enough to worry about.

Me

> You have no idea how happy that makes me. Girl's night with Rachel. No dickheads allowed (her rule, not mine). Will txt when done.

"Nice," she chuckled. Then with a glance at Rachel, I shifted to keep my screen private and added.

Me

> No mom. Sleep over is available.

I hit send before I could chicken out. I wanted to see him badly. Not just because he tried to talk to Ian for me and not just because of the fight, but all of it really. As crazy as all of this had gotten, Jake hadn't wavered. Nor had Archie or Coop. Or maybe they had, and it just hadn't escalated to me, I don't know.

I really didn't want to think about it.

"Ice cream?"

Rachel gave me an encouraging smile. "You got it."

Once in the car, I sent texts to Archie and Coop, just googly-eyed smiley faces. I added that I was with Rachel, and I'd text them later.

I got back a gag face from Archie, and a wide-eyed one from Coop. I could almost picture their faces, and I laughed. They were okay, and Jake wasn't in jail. The day was almost fifty percent better. I almost tabbed to Ian, then stopped myself.

Instead of going to a place to sit down, we hit the grocery store. I picked out some double-chocolate chocolate chip, then grabbed a bag of yogurt covered pretzels and another bag of chocolate covered donut snacks. Rachel didn't say a word, even if all she picked out was some mint chocolate chip and a bottle of Magic Shell. We grabbed a thing of plastic spoons, too.

After, I followed Rachel out to the lake this time, and she parked off near one of the picnic areas. The sun was setting, the breeze off the lake was cooler, and the whole area was empty, our cars were the only two in the lot.

"Okay," she announced, peeling open the ice cream tub. "Back to shit for brains."

I didn't even try to correct her this time. Honestly, it was easier to think about it all if I didn't think of their names. Ian had been Bubba forever, but Ian for only a few weeks, and I missed him already.

"You broke up with him."

With a nod, I dug into my own ice cream. "Seemed the thing to do. He couldn't seem to decide what he wanted, and he was miserable. I don't want to make anyone miserable."

"Yeah, I don't care about him right now," Rachel said, pointing at me with her spoon. "How do you feel?"

I laughed, but there was no humor in it. I tore open the yogurt-covered pretzels and used one to dig out another bite of ice cream.

"I say this as someone who thinks you're amazing—I fucking envy you your metabolism."

"Sorry," I said, though I wasn't really. "I tend to eat my feelings."

"Truth. You can eat and talk though."

I shrugged. "I don't know how I feel. It's all been so messy. At the same time…" I took another spoonful of the ice cream. "I don't know how to do this. The first guy I ever dated was Mathieu, and that was all of one and a half dates, one of which was me cooking in my kitchen, and then the guys were all asking me out, and I didn't feel about him the way I do them."

"How do you feel about them?"

That was the ten thousand dollar question. "They're my best friends. I miss them when they're not around. They're the first people I talk to in the morning and the last ones at night…" I adored them. "Not talking to them over the summer was like carving out a piece of myself, and it was lonely as hell."

Sighing, I closed my eyes.

"I don't mean to dump all of this on you."

"Dump away," Rachel said without an ounce of sarcasm. "I meant it when I said you needed a friend. This right here…" She motioned to the ice cream and the snacks. "This is what friends do. You're so locked in your head all the time. They're the only people you talk to, and your feelings for them are complicated—are you supposed to talk to rich boy if shit for brains upsets you, or with dickhead and asshat?"

"Really?"

"Hey, I'm doing my best. My point is that when you start dating—friends isn't always so easy to go back to. What happened when you guys fought in the past?"

"Is it rude to ask if this has ever happened to you?"

"Nope," Rachel said before taking a mouthful of ice cream. "I've dated, sure. Never four people at once—that's hot, by the way—and never dudes. First, gross. Second, everyone says girls are the emotional ones, but we're just emotionally different."

"I don't know, Coop's got really great emotional availability." I think that was the word. "He always seems to know what to say."

"To you," Rachel added. "He knows you. He's available to you. That whole cradle to grave thing you two have going on, it works for you. But back to me for a sec so I can answer your question. I dated a girl in junior year. You might remember her, Hannah?"

I frowned. "Tall, dark hair, glasses…had an accent?"

"She was from New England. Her parents moved down here when her dad got transferred. Anyway. She was a senior, good looking, funny as hell, and damn could she kiss." Rachel paused, a slow smile creasing her lips.

The depth of warmth and affection on her face pulled a smile to my lips. It was weird to see Rachel happy. The fact it was weird? Yeah, that said something. Maybe I wasn't the only one who needed a friend.

"Anyway, we hooked up like day three of junior year. I don't to this day know what she saw in me, but it was awesome. She was my first, not that you asked." She let out a little sigh, then seemed to shake herself. "But we were never friends. I didn't realize that until right around Christmas when she was gone for three weeks. Didn't call, didn't text, didn't email, and when she came back, it was like, pick up right where we left off and I'm all—wait, you ghost me, and suddenly, we're still dating?"

Another dollop of ice cream, and she stared out into the growing darkness. The sun had long since sunk on the horizon, but the lights scattered around the area left us with some illumination and fortunately attracted all the bugs away from us.

"She didn't get why I'd be upset. Told me I was being ridiculous. She'd been away with family. But now she was back and wanted to see me. The thing was…we did date and make out and do all that fun stuff, but it was different. It was like not seeing her all those weeks showed me what we didn't have when we were together. She was hot. She could kiss like a goddess, and the things she could do with her tongue…"

"Might be TMI," I suggested, and Rachel threw me a wicked grin.

"If it's TMI, remind me to have a chat with your boys about what they are or aren't doing with their tongues."

Oh. My. God.

Pretty sure my face caught on fire, and I went icy hot and then laughter bubbled up. Putting a hand over my mouth I said, "They do great things with their tongues. Leave them alone."

Rachel threw her head back laughing and gave me a fist bump. I was still giggling, embarrassed and amused. Taking another bite of my ice cream, I tried to glare at her, but she kept laughing.

Finally, after wiping some tears from her eyes, she said with a big grin on her face, "Anyway… Hannah and I didn't work out. The more I realized it was just sex and just kissing and just a little bit of fun…the more I realized I wanted something else. I also had a crush on this other girl who does not go to our school. Her name was Reese. She and I had been friends for a long time. You know, the kind you can call up and whether it's been two minutes or two months, you just pick right up where you left off?"

"Yeah." I had that with the guys. After the summer, and when Coop decided he wasn't letting me wander away, and they all made a concerted effort. It hadn't been hard at all, even as I struggled with everything else, I wanted it to work.

"Reese was—a lot of work. She's more bi than lesbian. That's okay. I'm not that picky. I'm not bi, but I don't mind it." She waved her hand before scraping down to the last bit of the pint. "We could talk about anything and everything. We did. It was—everything Hannah and I couldn't be. Reese and I were great, except she started liking this other guy and liked him a lot."

"Oh, Rach…"

She shrugged. "No, it was all right. At least she told me, you know? I didn't find out. She just said she really liked him, and she wanted to go out with him, he'd asked her. And did I mind? You know, I really did mind. I didn't want to share. I didn't want to compete. So, I told her if she wanted to date him, it was okay with me. We could go back to being friends. I didn't want to be the person making her stay where she didn't want to be or hold her back."

That I got. Reaching across the table, I clasped her hand. "I'm sorry."

"You know the break up wasn't the hard part—it was talking to her after that sucked. Remember how I said we could talk about anything? Two minutes or two months?" At my nod, she squeezed my hand. "That went away. It was just awkward as fuck, and eventually, I stopped calling her and she stopped calling me. I see her now and again, but…it's not the same."

"That was right before the spring dance."

"Yep, and then in my great and profound wisdom, I decided that you should know why no one asked. I suppose I could have kicked a puppy. That might have been kinder."

Now I rolled my eyes. "Regretting telling me already?"

"Regretting that sometimes I am too blunt and too harsh. That I say what I think, and it doesn't always work out. Then, I think about biting my tongue, and I don't." She had the last spoonful of her ice cream. "Because it hurts."

I chuckled.

"So after that long story, my only advice is that—you might not be able to go back to how it was. You've changed. They've changed. How you see each other and the potential you see…it's always going to be there."

My shoulders sagged, and I bit into another yogurt-covered pretzel dipped in the leftover melt of the ice cream.

"Then again, you five are weird," Rachel offered. "Maybe you can figure it out."

"I'm worried because the guys are fighting now, and I don't want them to fight over me. They were plotting to get rid of Mathieu when they just thought I was dating him, and then…I asked them what would happen if they wanted to get rid of each other. All I wanted was to date and do the things all the other girls were doing." To be a real teen instead the girl with the flakey mom who sleeps around and has had to look after myself for years. "Did I mess all this up?"

"I think yes, and I think no."

I stared at her for a beat. "Well, thank you for clearing that up for me."

"What I mean is," Rachel said making a face. "That maybe you haven't handled it the best, but you told them how you felt. You've been honest since the beginning, right?"

I nodded. "We even kind of plan date nights and stuff when we're all together, so everyone knows when I'm going out with one of the others…"

Rule number two.

That was what Jake meant. They knew when I was out with one of them, and they weren't supposed to interfere.

Ugh. They made *rules*? I wasn't sure if that was cute or irritating.

Or maybe just thoughtful.

"Then, I think you did that right. I think you have to be true to you. You have to ask yourself, are you dating all of them as a unit or individually? And do you want to continue if one or more of them doesn't?"

The thought of losing one of them made me want to cry, and I'd broken up with Ian. Me. I'd taken that decision out of his hands. The thought of losing all of them?

No. That was just too damn bleak.

"You don't have to decide right now," Rachel said. "Just something to think about."

"Yeah."

We both sighed.

"Well…are you dating anyone now?" I asked.

She grinned. "No. But I have my eye on someone—not you. I know. I'm not your type. So we have very clear boundaries."

I laughed. "I thought you didn't like boundaries."

"Never have been a fan," she agreed.

We sat out there for another hour, talking about everything and nothing. By the time we cleaned up our trash and headed back to the cars, I felt—while not better—at least a little less stressed.

When she offered a hug, I returned it. "Thank you."

"Anytime," she whispered. "I've got your back."

Then she was in her car, and I was in mine.

My phone had been very quiet since I texted the guys earlier. I sent a text to Jake that I was heading home, and I hadn't even put the phone down when he replied.

Jake

OMW

Thirty minutes later, I'd just changed into PJs when the knock hit my door. The cats were put out with me for having been gone for so long, but I ignored them as I hurried to answer.

Jake surged inside as soon as I opened it, and I wrapped around him tightly. "Oh, your face…"

"Trust me," he said. "I don't even feel it." Then he was kissing me, and we had to get the door closed and locked.

Even being careful, it was hard not to put my hands on something bruised on him as we made it to my room and stripped out of our clothes. We needed to talk, and we would.

But right now, I didn't need words, and neither did Jake.

Chapter Twelve

WE MIGHT AS WELL BE STRANGERS

ARCHIE

My place. 30 minutes. No excuses.

No one argued with the text. Now, sitting around the outdoor table overlooking the pool with food spread out in front of us, no one said a word. The only one actually eating was Jake, he had torn right through one burger and into the second before he began to slow.

Coop sipped his soda and watched him eat with his eyebrows raised. No missing the concern there—or the fact Coop had taken the chair next to Bubba's. The fact that I could barely look at Bubba without getting pissed off didn't bode well for this conversation.

Still, we needed to have it.

Now, maybe more than ever.

Cracking open a beer, I took a long drink and gave them all another minute. Personally, I didn't want Jake to be responsible for choking. The only good part of this particular moment, Frankie was somewhere else having a girl's night with Rachel.

I couldn't stand the bitch, but she'd been nice to Frankie. Maybe too nice. But right this moment, Frankie needed nice. One thing going for Rachel, none of us had dated her.

Yay.

"Look," Bubba said, breaking the silence as he leaned forward. Jake stilled and laser focused on him so hard, I braced. If he launched at Bubba over this table, it was going to be hell to separate them. Like Jake, Bubba's face was a mass of bruises. His right eye was a pitch perfect black and purple bruise that looked like it hurt.

Call me petty, but I didn't mind that part. Mine had only just faded from where Bubba slugged me, but it was still tender. What bugged me was they'd beaten the shit out of each other. Not like we hadn't had our share of scraps over the years. This was different.

This was fighting over Frankie.

For real fighting.

"You're all pissed at me," Bubba said after a protracted silence.

"Great revelation," Jake retorted, his tone dry. "Did it take you all day to get there?"

The two glared at each other. "Fuck you, Jake."

"Right back at you."

"Stop," Coop said, his quiet voice slicing between them as both looked at Coop. Our peacemaker. Frankie called him zen, and I used to tease him he was Valium. He had a way of going with the flow and sanding down the rough edges. It was a mistake to think his laid-back demeanor meant he didn't care or didn't lose his temper.

Cause he sure as hell did, especially where it concerned Frankie. Jake might be overly protective, and Bubba the golden child and solid backup. I had my own plays, but Coop? No one ever saw him coming.

"If you want to whip those dicks out, I'll go get the tape measure. Otherwise, knock it off." The mild tone didn't match the cool look in his eyes. "But we've all had a shit day, some more that others." He flicked a look at Jake before he lifted his soda. "So keep it civil and remember *why* we're here."

Bubba sighed. "I told her, okay? I told her about the points."

"She told us," I said with a shrug I definitely didn't feel. "What I want to know is *why* you told her. What the hell did you think that would accomplish? It's not like you were the innocent choirboy we dragged into the game, Bubba. You were right there with us. Every. Step. Of. The. Way." The last five words came out with a punch of breath as I wrestled with my own temper.

Suddenly, I wanted to punch him in his perfect teeth. Bubba had the good family. The perfect school record. The jock status. And he'd asked her to Homecoming while the rest of us scrambled around with our dicks in our hands. Then he tells her something that couldn't do anything other than *hurt* her.

Maybe I should have cracked open the liquor cabinet. Jeremy wasn't a fan of when I got into it. The beer, he could overlook. The occasional bottle of wine, he didn't mind. But the hard liquor? Not on his watch. Not usually.

"No, I brought Sharon into the game."

"She wasn't the only one you brought, either. If you want, I can get the playbook with the specifics." I still had the damn thing. The little side bets we'd placed. The scores we'd kept. It started as a joke, a half-assed thing while I was in the hospital right at the top of summer. The emergency appy had fucking sucked.

The idea though? It had been funny.

Then it had been fun. A little dirty. A little challenging.

Worth the laughs to fill the hours because there was a Frankie-shaped hole in our lives.

We'd tagged different girls with different equations for scoring points. That last party…

I shook my head. Yeah, that last party had been a race to the finish line in more ways than one, and I'd half-forgotten it by the next morning and shoved it all the way out of my mind the minute Frankie had arrived in the cafeteria.

Everything clicked, back where it belonged, and I didn't need the game. Didn't care about it. Yesterday's news.

Only it wasn't…

Not anymore.

"No, Arch, I know who I brought in. I can list every BJ I got and every girl I got out of her clothes before you did, too." Or Jake. Or Coop.

That was the point.

Last man got the fewest points.

"Why did you tell her?" Jake rasped. "You told me what your dad said, about how she seemed abused…"

Fuck her mom. That opened a whole other avenue for my temper. Fuck her. Fuck Edward.

For that matter, fuck Muriel, too.

Selfish assholes. Every. Single. One.

"…so why tell her that? She's already getting shit from the Bitch Pack. Her mother is…a fucking piece of work, and no offense, Arch, but your dad can go suck a dick."

"Agreed," I said, and held the beer bottle out. He tapped his drink to mine before he took a swig. One beer, he'd said. His face hurt, and he was having one beer. But his phone was on the table in front of him. As soon as Frankie texted, he was out of here. He'd made that clear, and he wanted to be sober to drive.

Bubba sighed. "I told her because we keep lying to her. All of us. I don't want to be that guy. I told her because you guys were going after her the same way you did Maria… Patty… Ch—"

"First," Jake interrupted. "Fuck you. We did not treat her like a goddamn point. Ever. Second, fuck you twice for thinking we would…"

I put a hand on his shoulder because violence lashed every word, but Bubba didn't back down from it.

"Sure, except I asked her to Homecoming first because I knew what you assholes would do, so…guess that made me an asshole, too."

"And telling her, what? That makes you not an asshole?" Jake dared him.

"No," Bubba sighed, and shook his head. "It makes me worse."

"Bubba," Coop said before Jake or I could say anything else. "What did you hope to accomplish? Break all of us up? Look better to her? Sink all of us? What?"

That was a damn good question. Bubba stared at Coop. "We talked about this."

"Yeah," Coop said, his tone still mild and relaxed. "We did. They didn't. I think they need to hear it. Because on the surface, it looks like you wanted to stab all of us in the back because you were jealous."

Coop was not wrong.

"I don—" Bubba edited himself with a grimace, then drained his soda before he shoved his chair back and stood. There was no mistaking the wince as he turned away, then dropped his can in the recycle bin before pulling out another cold one. "I wanted a clean slate. I wanted her to know the whole score—no pun intended—because I don't think she understands all of this."

"All of what?" I asked. "Us? Sex? Dating? Life?"

Turning, Bubba faced me and focused on me. Fine. Bring it. "You fucked her, Arch."

"I was there," I said without an ounce of repentance in me. "You're not going to make me feel bad for that." It had been beautiful. It still was. I couldn't wait to be with her again. Most of the girls had bored the shit out of me.

Frankie was not most girls.

"So did Jake."

"Careful, Bubba, Coop's right—your jealousy is showing." He crumpled the paper that had wrapped his burger and shoved it in the bag before he took another swig of beer.

When he looked at Coop, I waited to see where the hell he was going with this. "You came close—I'm pretty sure, even if you won't admit it."

"None of your business," Coop said easily. "Just like what she does with Jake and Arch isn't your business."

"It's about her."

"Yes, Bubba," Coop told him evenly. "It is about her. The only one making it a competition right now is you, because you seem to be acting like a sore loser."

Damn. That barb struck.

"You know that's not what I'm talking about…"

"Then stop beating around the damn bush," I snapped. "I fucked her. Jake fucked her. Coop's dying to fuck her, and if you weren't so busy lying to yourself and being pissed at us, you'd admit you want to fuck her, too. But you *didn't* because you wanted to do things a certain way, and none of us played by a rule you didn't bother to add to the list."

Not that I ever would have. The sheer fact she'd said yes to me had been one of the most blissful moments in my life. I'd wanted her from day one. I'd settled for not pursuing it when she never seemed interested. But she was damn precious to me, and he wasn't going to turn this into some ugly thing.

Gripping the back of the chair, Bubba met my glare. "Then I'll stop beating around the bush. How does this end?" He looked at us in turn. "Seriously, how does it end? We all sleep with her. We all keep dating her. Then graduation comes and what? We move to college together and keep doing this? What happens when she picks? Or worse—just isn't interested anymore and meets someone else?"

Rage flashed through me at the idea. No fucking way was anyone *else* moving in on Frankie. "That's not happening."

"You can't know that," Bubba said. "You can't. We didn't even know she wanted to date until she met the French guy."

"We never asked her directly either," Coop said. "We all just assumed."

Wasn't that a kick in the nuts 'cause Coop wasn't wrong about that. In my defense, I didn't have moves in 9th grade. Spending all that time with her—I thought she got it. Then she just never responded the way I would have expected.

"We made sure no one else asked her either," Jake said quietly. "We were the assholes, Bubba. We were. When she finally admitted what she wanted, yes, I leapt. So did you. So did Archie. Coop was a little slow…"

"Hey," Coop protested, and for a moment, some of the tension cracked and I almost smiled as Bubba huffed a laugh.

"You leapt *first*," Jake pointed out. "She didn't know how to tell us, and we apparently sucked at letting her know how we felt. But was there a doubt in your mind?" He locked gazes with Bubba, their matching bruises giving them both a gruesome kind of focus. "Did you really think you were the only one who cared about her?"

Not wanted to fuck her. But cared.

"Because you're not," Jake continued. "You never have been. I've been half in love with her since the fourth grade."

Holy shit. The whole table went still, and I wasn't the only one staring at Jake.

"Yes, I'm damn aware of what I just said," he continued without looking away from Bubba. "I've been in love with her almost as long. Longer than you or Arch has been around. I wouldn't have looked twice at another girl, if I'd thought there was a hope in hell she'd ever look at me the way she looks at me right now."

Bubba looked away first, dropping his chin to his chest and staring down at his hands as he gripped the back of his empty chair. "How does it end, then? You let her date everyone until you steal her away?"

"I don't care."

I shifted in my chair and looked at him, and I wasn't alone. Coop leaned forward. "What?"

"I don't care how it ends," Jake said, lifting his beer as he looked from Bubba to Coop and then finally to me. "I don't care that you were her first. I care only that you made it good for her. I don't care that Coop wants her." He looked at Coop. "I think it's hot when you kiss her." Finally, he went back to Bubba. "I don't even care that you asked her to Homecoming, or that you sang to her in the cafeteria. I care that it put that dopey smile on her face. I care that we have right now. Tomorrow. The day after that. I'm going to make every single one of them worth it. The only thing I care about is that she's happy. That *we* make her happy? Fine."

Holy shit twice.

Staring at Jake, Bubba blinked hard. "Just like that?"

"Just like that," Jake said easily. "I won't let any of you hurt her. Ever. You wanna talk shit about her or fuck with her, I'm going to fuck you up." He gestured with his nearly empty beer bottle at Bubba. "Pure and simple. We made those rules for a reason, Bubba. The points thing—it was a stupid fucking game we got off on, but it meant nothing. Telling her? That means we hurt her. Fine, I'll take my lumps for that, but it should have been something we all agreed on to tell her, not you trying to sabotage us."

"I swear," Bubba said. "I wasn't trying to sabotage you…" He dragged the chair out. "This has all gotten so fucking confusing. I want her like I want my next breath, but…I don't want to fight with you guys. I don't want to hurt her. Dad said…" He swallowed.

"Your dad said what?" I demanded. Jake had filled me in on some of it.

"He said that Frankie's showing a lot of classic signs for emotional and physical abuse," Coop supplied. "The need for hugs, the fact that she's never once rejected us for putting an arm around her. A desperate need for approval and that standing up for herself is hard, especially if we push back. It takes a lot of courage for her to do that. Her mom…her mom's never been the best. But she's gotten worse, and now I know for a fact she's hitting her. I used to suspect, but Friday clinched it."

Friday—when Frankie showed up with the red mark on her face.

"Dad's worried that she doesn't have the emotional security to wrestle with all of this and that we're going to tear her apart," Bubba admitted. "He didn't say it quite like that, but on Saturday, after I left, when…after I woke up and realized she was curled up sound asleep between Coop and Jake, and I wanted to punch both your heads in because it should be me up there…I went with Dad to Dallas. I was—I am a little messed up about all of this."

No surprise flickered on Coop's face. So he really had known. Bubba had told him.

"While we were there, we went to this center where they have groups for teens in abusive situations. We sat in the back and listened to their stories as they shared them… a lot of stuff just clicked. Then there was this one girl…" Bubba's gaze took on a distant look. "She talked about the day she tried to kill herself. Because she thought no one cared. Broke up with the only guy she thought did and…I can't stand the thought of it being Frankie, and I hate myself a little bit right now because I'm not as fine with all of this as I thought I was."

"Have you asked yourself why?" Coop asked quietly, and I drained my beer. Rising, I left them in silence as I went for another. This really was a hard liquor night.

Fuck, the idea of Frankie being so despondent or alone she wanted to kill herself? Fuck no.

"Because the day I kissed her in our pool," Bubba said quietly. "She was so surprised and then so delighted. It was everything I thought it would be…but she said she'd never, and I didn't want to rush her. Rush us. Rush anything. I wanted to savor it. The time. Every other time, it's been…"

"A quick fuck," I admitted. "Get in, get out, tap that, move on."

Bubba grimaced. "She's not that."

"No," Jake told him. "She's so much more."

"Then you guys…" Bubba rubbed a hand over his face and winced. I almost winced in sympathy. 'Cause fuck that looked like it hurt. "You guys just went for it. There she was all sandwiched between you two, and I'm asking myself—what the fuck am I doing? I'm just going to end up making this worse. When she chooses…"

"Stop obsessing about that," I told him.

"I have to," Bubba said. "She showed up at the house today, after school. It's Tuesday, and even after everything, she still came over."

Jake straightened. "And?"

"And I told her you got arrested, and then I told her why we fought." Misery hung all over him. "She asked me if the problem was the fact she was dating all of you too, or if I just didn't want to date her."

I popped the lid off the bottle of cold beer and sighed. "I'm almost fucking afraid to ask what you said."

"I told her I didn't know."

Coop leaned his head back and stared at the sky. Some of the patience on him seemed to just drain away as his jaw tightened.

I pulled my phone out and reopened that message from her. There was nothing in it that indicated she was upset. Nothing.

"For what it's worth, she broke up with me."

It wasn't worth much. Because… Crap, that changed things.

Jake stared at him. "Broke up with you?"

"Yeah, said she didn't want me to take her to Homecoming, I was released from that obligation…it was never an obligation."

"She doesn't know that," Jake told him quietly with a hell of a lot more sympathy than I wanted to feel, and at the same time…

"You have to fix this," I told him, and I wasn't sure who was more surprised because Bubba straightened and turned to look at me. Jake stared at me a beat, and I met his gaze. "He has to fix this. If he's out—all that does is create strain, and she's not going to be happy."

Frankie needed all of us.

"It's been the five of us," I reminded him. "Since ninth grade. It's been all five of us."

"Guys…"

"Shut up," Coop said before Bubba could continue, and I wasn't the only one shooting him a startled look. "Archie is right. You have to fix this. If you pushed her so hard she had to let you go, she probably feels like it's her fault. That's the one thing that terrified her when we started this…"

Dammit. I tipped the bottle up and took a long drink. After the bomb fell with Edward and her mom, that day after the epically crappy party—she'd said that. What happened when we turned on each other?

She'd said it to me and to Jake. What happened when we decided one of the others had to go, and we'd got there today. This crap with Bubba had to stop.

"You have to fix it," Jake said finally, and Coop motioned to him to continue. "I hate that you told her that shit. I hate that you've made her feel bad about herself." Each sentence landed like a blow, but he held Bubba's full attention. "I hate even more that because I couldn't control my temper, I wasn't there for her today and apparently you weren't either."

Bubba flinched.

No. She'd been on her own for parts of the day. I was definitely not a fan, not after the other crap.

"So you have to fix this," Jake said. "But only if you really want to be in. Because if you don't, or this jealousy crap keeps up—then stay out. Leave her alone. Let us fix it. She doesn't need another yo-yo in her life."

On that… "Agreed," I said. "As much as I want this to work, Bubba," I told him. "Jake's right. You're either in or you're out."

"She already broke up with me."

"Then you go after her," Coop said. "You let her know she's worth it. You put her first. I'll help…but only if I think you mean it."

"And there isn't another chance after this one," Jake continued as if the rest of us hadn't said a word. "I want her happy. This…" He motioned to his face, then to Bubba's. "Not going to make her happy."

"I don't even know where to start," Bubba said.

"Do you know the answer to her question *now*?" I asked. "Because if you don't—then this is pointless."

At some point, my fury had drained away. Maybe if Frankie had been pissed at us or seemed really hurt about the points, it would be different. We'd still let her down. I couldn't change the past. I could only focus on the future—on what I would do and how I would treat her.

Jake was right about one thing. "You have to know, or you should leave her alone. She wanted a good senior year, and I'm thinking it's been shit so far. One way or another, she's getting Homecoming and it's going to be the best night possible."

"Agreed," Coop said. "If you need time to think about it, Bubba, think fast. Because trust once lost is almost impossible to rebuild."

"Almost," Bubba said, and Coop nodded. "But not completely."

"Anything's possible, just some are more possible than others."

"I don't want to hate you guys." That was good. "I do want her. I want her to be happy." The misery rolled off of him in great sheets now. "I fucked this up."

"Huge," Jake said flatly, and his phone buzzed.

I was close enough to see the message.

Frankie was on her way home. He shoved his chair back and stood.

"I gotta go. She wants to see me, and I want to see her. Yes, I'm spending the night. No, you fuckers don't get to say a word." He pinned Bubba with a look. "Figure it out and get ready to grovel. If I think you're serious…" He made a face. "For Frankie, I'll help. But it's her call."

Then he was gone, not waiting for a response from any of us. Turning back to the table, I met Bubba's narrowed gaze. "What?"

"You don't care that she texted him and that he's going over there to spend the night, again?"

Did I care? I shrugged and took a page out of Jake's book. Who knew the guy could be so smooth? "Sure I care. I care that she's not alone. I care that she's asking for what she needs. Would I love to be the one? Hell yes. But I also know she cares about me. I know she wants me, too. So… I'm good."

When he turned to Coop, I waited, and Coop grinned. "I only care that I don't get to see them make out. Jake's not wrong, it really is hot."

I laughed. It came out a deep chuckle, and Bubba shook his head. "We're nuts."

"Maybe," I said. "Maybe not. So what's it going to be, Bubba? You in? Or you out?"

I really hoped he made the right choice. Because if we went from five to four, it would take a hell of an adjustment and there would be a Bubba-shaped hole in our lives.

If summer was any indication? I really didn't want to figure out how that worked.

Chapter Thirteen

DEAR FUTURE SELF

Life had tough bits, easy bits, and then the complicated bits in between. The easy bits? You had to eat, sleep, pay taxes, and under a certain age, you had to go to school. Yeah, going to school didn't seem easy, but it was an easy decision.

Go to school.

Do the homework.

Get good grades.

Graduate.

Get the fuck out of here.

All straightforward and easy to define chunks, even if the experience itself fell on the tough end of the scale. The decision whether to stay or to go was easy. I had to go. So I went.

The tougher parts? The complicated ones? Everything else. Friendships. Dating. Kissing. Arguing. Crying. Fighting. Confiding. Those were definitely complicated. Difficult, but not impossible. Challenging, but also rewarding. Even the arguing.

Yes, I said it.

Even the arguing.

Breaking up? That hurt. It had hurt Ian when I said it, and it hurt me the next day, even after waking up with Jake right there. He hadn't asked me about Ian, and I hadn't told him. His face looked as bad as Ian's had. It looked even worse in the morning.

"Don't worry, baby girl," he teased me. "I'll get pretty for you again."

I groaned and then kissed his nose, his chin, and the one undamaged corner of his mouth. Guilt gnawed on me a little. I wanted to smother Jake in care, but I'd resisted it with Ian the night before. He'd looked like hell, but if I'd given into the urge—no. He had to figure him out.

"Hey," Jake murmured, cupping my face. "It's going to be okay, I promise."

"You're not in jail," I said, leaning into his touch. "That's an amazing thing."

"Agreed."

"But you and Ian…"

"Will take care of itself," he said, then tugged me in for a kiss. "We didn't really talk about the fight."

"He told me most of it."

"I know." My surprise must have shown, because he gave me a half-smile. "I talked to him last night."

"Oh."

"Yeah, the four of us had a long talk."

I almost didn't want to ask.

Jake caught one of my curls and rolled it around his finger. "He told us you broke up with him."

Glancing down at his chest, I considered making an excuse to go take a shower. But we had another fifteen minutes before we needed to move, and I liked being tucked up against him. "Yeah," I said, then pressed a kiss to the bruise on his pec. We hadn't talked the night before. I'd meant it when I said we hadn't needed the words.

Now, I wasn't sure what the words should be.

"You all right?"

I glanced up at him and gave him a smile. "I will be. Right now, I'm more worried about you."

"Nothing to worry about," he murmured, then tapped my nose. "Promise."

"Can you go to school today?"

"Well, they didn't tell me I couldn't. I talked to Mom again on my way here; she didn't say anything about it. So, for now, I'll assume yes."

That had my stomach fluttering.

"Worst case scenario, even if I'm suspended, I'll be back to pick you up after school and make sure you get home."

"Coop has a car you know."

"Don't care," he said, the undamaged corner tipping upward as he smiled. "If I can't be with you in school, you can be damn sure I'm going to grab every other minute."

A soft laugh escaped me. Try as I might, I couldn't deny the possessiveness in his voice wrapped around me like a security blanket. Snuggling carefully, I pressed a kiss to his throat as he traced his fingers along my shoulder. "Here's me hoping you can be there. Yesterday sucked."

"Yeah," he said. "It did. I missed you."

I smiled. "I missed you, too."

"Frankie?"

"Hmm."

"You can talk to me about anything, okay?"

"Right back atcha."

"Do you want me to talk to you about the points thing?" The directness in the question didn't shy away from what Ian had told me.

"You mean, besides was that the reason you punched him?"

"Yes," he answered. "To both. Yes, it was why I punched him. Yes, if you want to ask me anything. I won't lie about it."

Settling my chin on my arm folded across his chest, I stared up at him, and he met my gaze evenly. "I only have one question."

"Okay, hit me." No hesitation, not even a wince.

"I'd really rather not, I actually think I could hurt you at the moment."

He chuckled and wrapped his hand on my nape before dragging me in for a kiss. "You remain, adorably, the worst."

I snorted and grinned.

"Now ask your question."

"Are the points why you and Maria broke up?"

He sighed. "Yes and no."

"Well, that just cleared it right up for me." I crossed my eyes, but he massaged the back of my neck, and I let out a little sigh. That felt really good.

"Yes," he continued. "Miss Impatience, she found out about the points and was well and truly humiliated." He didn't sound proud of the fact. "Particularly when she assumed that the points were the only reason I was dating her."

"But they weren't?"

"No. They were part of it, I won't lie. But at one point, I thought she was cool. Easy enough to be around. When she found out about the points, we fought. Well…she fought. I just didn't care enough to explain it."

"Or apologize?" It was a guess.

He nodded slowly.

"She was—pretty pissed."

"I can imagine," I said with a sigh.

"Look, baby girl. I'm not a perfect guy, and to be perfectly frank, I was a jackass to her. She didn't deserve it. The day I went to see her about the photos Sharon put up, I told her I was sorry."

I studied him. "She didn't believe you."

"No," he admitted. "She was pretty sure I was only apologizing because I wanted her help."

"Which you were."

He grimaced. "Yes."

As hard and as ugly as it was, he didn't hesitate to own any of it.

"You said you had stuff on them." Apparently I had two questions.

"I did."

"Photos or points?"

"Both."

I groaned.

"Please don't hate me," Jake asked in a soft voice, and I pressed my face to his throat.

"I don't hate you," I promised him. Was I disappointed? Yeah. Did I feel bad for the girls in question? Hell yes. But…no, no buts. I couldn't excuse it.

"But you're sad now."

"It's…it was a terrible thing, Jake." Lifting my head, I started to sit up, but he kept me caged close. "Tell me you see that."

"It was bad she found out about it. That—shouldn't have happened."

"It was bad that you guys *did it*. Just finding out about it doesn't make something bad."

"I disagree."

Raising my brows, I tugged to sit up, and he let me this time. I didn't go far, and I didn't drag the sheet up. Which might have been a mistake, since he fixed his gaze on my breasts until I cleared my throat.

The sheepish grin he wore was equal parts exasperating and cute. Intent on not getting distracted, I had to ask, "Why do you disagree?"

"Because our game was for us. The points, the numbers—it was to entertain us. It didn't inform how we treated them or even why were dating them." He must have seen the contradiction to his earlier statement. "Mostly. Look. I get that it hurt her feelings and humiliated her. Another reason she shouldn't have known, another reason we didn't advertise it. If she never found out, then it wouldn't have hurt her."

Folding my arms, I studied him. "If you had never found out about Mathieu and I kept seeing him behind your backs and somehow managed to keep it a secret, would that have been fine as long as you didn't know?"

Straddling his waist, I was very aware of his cock resting between my legs. Even half-hard, it teased at my labia, but I tried not to focus on it. For his part, Jake didn't stir. He seemed very focused on me and listening.

His expression hardened at the question, and his eyes chilled. "Goddammit, Frankie."

He lifted an arm to cover his eyes and then lifted it almost immediately. Guilt swamped me.

"Goddammit," he said again. "I'd have hated that."

"Sorry," I told him. "I've found that the truth hurts a lot more than I think it should these days."

Setting his hands on my hips, he surged up so we were breast to chest. "Just…I need you to be all right with me. To not hate me for it. I'll…I'll find a way to apologize to her and mean it."

"Okay."

Surprise flickered in his gaze. "That's it? Just okay?"

"Like I said, you didn't do it to me. As much as I wish you hadn't done it to anyone, I'm not the one who has to forgive you. I will say if it ever happens again, I can't be friends with you." I couldn't. This lapse? This lapse I would forgive from my side because we all screwed up.

"Never," he promised with a kiss. "Ever." Another kiss. "Again." Kiss. "I promise." Kiss. "I mean it." Kiss.

I laughed a little, then kissed him gently before he wrapped me up in a tight hug and I closed my eyes. "Thank you for being honest with me."

"Not easy," he whispered. "I mean, it used to always be easy. I could tell you anything and now…now I never want you to disappear on me again. I'm terrified of doing the one thing you can't take anymore, and you vanish."

"I promised to not ghost you again," I reminded him. "That if something was wrong, I would talk to you." His bunched shoulders relaxed. "But I need that same promise from you. If anything…Ian couldn't tell me why he was so unhappy, and I feel like I let him down somewhere. That's…that's why I broke up with him."

"You broke up with him because you feel like you let him down?" Jake pulled back some and cupped my face as we locked gazes.

"Because of the indecision and the confusion. It was hurting him and you two…"

"We'll fix this," he promised.

"Jake, you can't fix this. I adore you for wanting to, but you can't. I needed to put me first, and as selfish as I felt about wanting to date all of you—I don't know how I'm going back to being just friends with him, but I have to try. He's still Ian. I'll get there, I just might need some time."

"Baby girl, you have all the time you need," Jake said, his eyes solemn and intense. "Except now."

I raised my eyebrows.

"I really have to pee," he admitted, and I burst out laughing. Tumbling sideways off of him, I grinned as he ran his hand up my thigh. "You're also adorably the best, you know that, right?"

"I think what you mean is goofy."

"Nope," he said, then slapped a hand against my ass. The jolt went all the way through my system. "I mean adorably the best and the worst in every perfect way."

The compliment might have been silly, but the intensity in his eyes and the liquid heat simmering in his voice seemed to strip me bare and wrap around me like a hug. In the same breath, the connection fulfilled something I craved and confused me. The weight of it blanketed me, and I didn't know what to do with that emotion.

Somehow, I landed on, "You're a weirdo."

Shoving off the bed, he gave my ass another slap, and this time, I couldn't mistake the heat for anything other than want. I shivered as he grinned at me, split lip and all. "That, too."

As much as I'd have liked to shrug off the day, we had school. Coop showed up by the time we were getting breakfast, and my cereal was on hold while I got my good morning kiss. Then he turned me around, breathless, and Jake kissed me again. I was pretty sure they were intent on melting my brain before the day got started. Only, Coop never backed off. Jake kissed me while my back was pressed against Coop's chest, releasing me only to spin me back to Coop, and then holy hell.

Burning up and panting when Coop lifted his head, I forgot what I'd been doing before this started. "You know," Coop told me. "That just gets hotter every time we do it."

Jake wrapped his arms around me from the back, and I leaned into him as Coop drew a finger down my cheek.

"I wish it was tomorrow," he admitted.

"For a birthday kiss?" I asked.

He grinned. "Well, that too. But I was thinking the no school part and heading up to Six Flags for a day away from everything. Just us being us."

My smile didn't falter, but in the craziness of all of it, I'd forgotten about that part of the plan. A whole day of us. Which meant Ian, too.

I could handle it. I firmed my smile. It was Coop's birthday. I would handle anything to make it a good day.

He tilted his head when I gave him a gentle push and wiggled out from between them. I still had to finish my breakfast. The fact that the two of them shared a long look wasn't lost on me, but Jake and I had covered a lot of uncomfortable territory that morning. I'd skip the rest.

Besides, I was getting low on groceries. I needed to hit a store this week. After making sure the cats had water and dry food, we locked up and headed out. I rode with Jake, but Coop claimed bringing me home after school.

At school, Jake was the one pulling all the looks when we came in. Ian was at the table with Arch and the coffee. I settled in the chair next to Archie while Jake dragged out the chair next to me.

The conversation was awkward. Made more so by the number of eyes pointed in our direction. When Ian asked me about calculus, I was proud of my answer. I kept it pretty straightforward and neutral, and even offered him my notes, but I just slid them across the table. I didn't hand them off.

Maybe it was the bruising on his face, or maybe he just felt like crap in general, but every time our gazes clashed, I swore he looked in pain.

Rachel said she and her friend had never been able to go back. There had to be a way to make it work. Thankfully, we had to split up for class.

The reprieve was brief.

Archie didn't say much as we walked to calculus, distracted by some project he was now behind on. I told him to go on, I could make it on my own. Of course, he didn't take me up on the offer.

I kind of figured.

Math class promised to be a blast, but Ian just gave me a small smile when I took the same seat I'd taken since the beginning of the year—the one right next to him.

"Hey," I said, smile firmly in place.

"Hey." He tried. I'll give him that. He did try to smile, but if anything, his face looked worse today than it had yesterday. Guilt stabbed at me again.

"You doing okay?"

"Yeah," he said. "Just tired."

I nodded. The silence stretched out. "Ready for Friday?"

"Yep."

I'd never been so grateful for a pop quiz in my life as when the teacher passed out those calculus tests.

Never.

After class was over, he fell into step with me. "Frankie…"

I glanced at him, but he stared down the hall and went mute. Following his gaze, it wasn't hard to miss what captured his attention. Sharon had her phone up and pointed right at us.

Fuck. That.

Ian and I were friends? Fine. This was what I did for my friends.

"Excuse me," I said, and diverted away to walk straight down the hall at her. No way she wasn't pointing that camera at us, because she jerked her head up at my approach.

Her eyes narrowed, and I smiled.

"I'm ready for my close-up," I told her, and then lifted my middle finger. "Just in case you wanted a real message for your next little puff piece."

A scattering of giggles went up around us, and Sharon lowered her phone the rest of the way. "You really think you're funny."

"Oh, honey, I'm not the one obsessed by me and every step I take."

A little woo went up around us, and red flushed Sharon's cheeks. "You know, sooner or later, they're going to figure out you aren't worth it."

"Maybe," I agreed. "If that day comes, I guess I'll look to you for all your experience with it and what I really shouldn't do after."

Dead silence filled the air, and tears welled up in Sharon's eyes, but the hate in them was hard to miss.

Yeah. It was a lot like kicking a puppy. If it were a vicious little bitch who'd bitten me a few times already.

"Let me know if you need any more clips," I told her with a little wave, and pivoted to head back to where Ian stood just a few steps behind me. He stared at me, a little wide-eyed, then at Sharon, then back to me. "French is this way," I told him and tapped his biceps as I passed him.

A step before the door to French, Ian caught my arm. "Frankie?"

"Yes?"

"That was pretty kickass." The warmth in his voice sent a shiver all the way up my spine. Bad Frankie. Just friends. Keep it just friends.

I grinned. "Well, a friend told me that I used to do that, and maybe I needed to be doing it a little more. See you later."

In the classroom, I settled into the chair, heart racing and palms sweating. I barely heard a word of the French, and thankfully, it was all stuff we'd studied before.

Did you know there was a tense in French that actually makes everyone groan in despair?

Yep, Madame reminded us that began the following week. Subjunctive tenses, here we come.

Ugh.

By lit, I'd chilled out some. Some.

Then the texts came in.

Jake and Ian had to meet with the principal and the coach at lunch.

My stomach bottomed out.

Archie and Coop still insisted we go out anyway. We needed to eat, they reasoned, and there was nothing to do at school but sit and pace and worry.

They spent the whole lunch hour talking about Coop's birthday, and try as I much as I wanted, I couldn't generate the enthusiasm. Not when Archie wanted to give me a high five after they heard about Sharon, or when Coop asked me to tell him what I wanted to do for his birthday in French.

Faking it all the way, I fought to keep it upbeat. But I checked my phone a dozen times. So did they.

The only topic that didn't come up was me breaking up with Ian. Since Jake knew and he said they'd all talked, I assumed they knew, too.

If they didn't bring it up, I didn't want to talk about it.

At school, Archie caught my arm as Coop headed off to class.

"You all right?"

"I'm great," I told him, and he stared at me steadily. Had I turned transparent at some point? I used to be able to do this without them noticing.

Jake saw through it sometimes. Well, so did Coop.

Fine, they all did. But they didn't always call me on it.

"I know you're worried about Jake and Bubba. Whatever it turns out to be, we'll figure it out, okay?"

I nodded.

"And, Frankie?"

"Do you want to come over tonight?" I asked abruptly. "I know Jake usually comes over on Wednesdays, but…maybe you want to? Or I could go over there?"

He blinked. "Whatever you want, babe. Seriously."

"I'd like to…I'll talk to Jake, but…we haven't really had any us time, and tomorrow is everyone." And I really had to get myself in a place where I could deal with Ian being there.

"No problem," he murmured, slinging an arm around my shoulder. "Let me know, and we'll make it happen, okay?"

I smiled. "Thanks."

"Never have to thank me."

Jake didn't make it to Study Hall. There was no word from them. Most of my distractions didn't work, so I settled for texting back and forth with Archie and Coop.

Both of whom scolded me for not studying.

I checked in with Rachel too, and thanked her for listening the night before.

She sent me back a thumbs up and then a link to an Instagram post.

It showed me flipping off Sharon and Sharon's shocked face with the word *schooled* in the caption.

That got all the heart eyes from Rachel, and I giggled.

It helped.

When Jake arrived at AP Euro, I damn near said to hell with our lack of PDA rule and hugged him. G gave him a long look, then asked how he was feeling.

"I'm good, Mr. G. Real good. Looks way worse than it is."

"Uh huh. You two fine to handle studying on your own? I have tests to go grade."

We agreed readily, and he left us to it. As soon as he was out of the room, I twisted to face him. "What happened?"

"We met with Coach and the principal. We're not suspended, but there are no more strikes. If I get in another fight, I'm suspended for a week. He didn't say expelled, but you could hear him thinking it loud."

I winced.

"Bubba's in the same boat—only now, he's also riding the bench with me."

Oh shit.

"Yeah," Jake said with a shrug. "He also has to see Diane…and that's why I wasn't in study hall. They took us straight from lunch to her office, where he and I have to sit down and talk about our feelings at least once a week for the next couple of weeks, so we can learn to manage our disagreements more positively."

I gagged, and Jake laughed.

"It wasn't so bad."

"No?"

He shook his head. "Bubba and I are…well, we're friends, and we have been for a long time."

"I know that."

"So, probably a good idea if we learn to get a grip on some things. Not be so competitive." He locked gazes with me. "Put our jealousy and envy in perspective."

Frowning, I glanced down. Ian's jealousy. "Are you jealous?"

"Me?" Jake said, grinning. "Nope."

"Not even a little?"

He shook his head. "Told those knuckleheads that last night. I meant it when I said I wanted you—wanted to see you—date you. Make out with you. I don't mind if you're seeing them. Just them though, no one else."

"Like I have *time* for anyone else."

He grinned again. "Good. Also—Bubba told me about Sharon."

Heat rushed to my face. Seriously, they were talking about me. Wasn't that weird?

It all felt so weird.

"I wish I'd seen it."

"I kind of felt like I was kicking a dog."

"A rabid one," Jake pointed out. "And you didn't start it. But I'm proud of you."

That really shouldn't have made me as warm and fuzzy as it did. "Jake… I know the last couple of Wednesdays you've come over, but do you mind if I see Archie tonight?"

"Not at all. Not that I won't miss you terribly and be waiting for my good morning kiss on Thursday. Let me tell you, I think Coop is on to something with that. But you've been with me the last couple of nights, and all of us were there Friday…" He winced at the reminder.

"It's okay. I have to learn to deal with it right. We gotta make it normal. Cause Ian's still our friend."

Jake stared at me steadily, and then he lifted my hand. After kissing my palm, he said, "You can do anything. And yes, see Arch tonight if that's what you want. We have all day tomorrow—though you should probably pay special attention to Coop. Birthday boy and all that."

"Yeah," I told him, fighting a small smile and a surge of affection for how easy he was making this. "Because we should set a precedent with your birthday and Archie's still to come."

"That would be good, too," Jake said, almost too innocently. As our smiles faded, Jake tucked a strand of my hair behind an ear. "You know it's going to be all right, yes?"

"I want it to be."

"Then it will be." The confidence there was mind-blowing. Battered and bruised, lip still puffy, he remained upbeat. "I promise."

"Don't make promises you can't keep," I warned him. "We can't control everyone."

"No, we can't," Jake agreed. "But there's lots we can do and I will do."

After class, he walked me out to where Coop waited before giving me a scorching look that suggested all the things he'd like to do but couldn't. Then he was off to meet Ian to sit on the bench for practice. Coop got me home and got a few more kisses in to end his seventeenth year—or so he claimed—before I pushed him out the door so I could get ready for work.

I was almost ready to leave when Mom and 'Eddie' got home.

Life had tough bits, easy bits, and then the complicated bits in between. School had been a lot easier than I expected. The complicated bits with Ian had been tough, but we'd muddled through. The really tough bits…coming face to face with my mom—the cheater—and her very much married boyfriend/fiancé.

"Don't look so forlorn," Mom told me as she breezed in. "I'm just here to pack some things. Eddie and I found a place."

Wait.

What?

I pivoted to where she'd disappeared, but she'd closed the door, leaving me with the boyfriend.

Ugh.

Turning, I faced him. It was hard to look at him. Not just because he was having sex with my mom—seriously I *never* want to think about that, bad meatloaf, bad meatloaf, bad *meatloaf.* No, the problem here was he looked like Archie.

Too much like him.

Wearing the same faint smirk Archie used when he anticipated delivering uncomfortable news to someone he wanted to knock down a peg, 'Eddie' said, "I think your mom is trying to take your wishes to heart. But I would like you to reconsider."

"Funny, if she was taking my wishes to heart, she'd dump you before she gets hurt." You know, that just kind of popped out.

The faint smirk vanished, and he frowned at me. "Do you hate me that much, Frankie?"

"I don't hate you at all, Mr. Standish." I wasn't calling him 'Eddie.' It wasn't happening. "You're married. You're one of my best friends' dads…"

"Well, we both know Archie is a lot more than just your friend," he said, folding his arms and giving me a stern look. "If you want to call it like it is, then I see no reason to not be as blunt with you."

"Fine, he's more than a friend, it doesn't change the fact that you're cheating, and you're the reason my mother is a cheater." My mother, who seemed to want to live any life except the one we had.

"The heart wants what it wants."

"Does the heart plan on getting a divorce, or is it just taking a vacation?" Yep. That was me. "Because whatever happens, Mr. Standish, if you break her heart, I will find a way to get you back."

He raised his eyebrows.

Maybe my mom deserved it. But she was still my mom.

"Maybe your mother is right," he said after a moment. "Maybe you are never going to support her in this."

"Nope," I said firmly. "I'm not. I'm definitely not on Team Bad Meatloaf."

Confusion clouded his expression.

"I have to go to work. Don't lock my cats up. Don't touch them. Are you planning to stay here tonight?"

"No," he said. "We have plans…and I'm going to have my secretary send over the address for the new place and a key. You are welcome."

Wait. "New place?" They'd said something earlier.

"You were right about moving your mother into the house. It's where Muriel still lives. Archie wouldn't enjoy it. So I got your mother and I a different place. There's room for you."

They were serious.

"Or you can stay here." He looked at me expectantly. "But you're always welcome with us, and I was serious about the car. It's already purchased for you. Your mother told me about your plans for Harvard. I could help with that…"

My jaw locked for a moment, but I shot a look at the clock. "I have to go. My shift starts soon."

He didn't move, and it was like a standoff. If I wanted to get to the back door, I had to squeeze past him.

Fuck that.

Not calling goodbye to Mom, I pivoted and went out the front. It was a longer walk to the car. I didn't care.

So, she was going off with Eddie to live in a new place.

Fine.

When I got back tonight, I was parking in the fucking carport.

In the car, I did my best to ignore my shaking hands as I turned it on.

Work.

Work, and then I could see Archie.

That was the plan.

Fix You

Archie

You know, Bubba, part of fixing this is showing up.

Bubba

I know. Be there soon Mom and Dad wanted to talk to me.

Coop

That can't be good.

Bubba

Technically still grounded.

Jake

Technically, you're 18.

Archie

Point

Bubba

Home. Then I'll be there.

Coop

K. Arch and I are here.

Jake

Practice just got out. How is she?

Coop

She looks good.

Archie

Real good. Hey J...

Jake

Yup?

Archie

She talk to you about 2night?

Jake

Yep. All good.

Coop

What about tonight?

Jake

OMW

Later...

Coop

Problems

Bubba

Dad's on a tear.

Coop

Your dad is so chill. Define tear.

Bubba

We're talking relationships.

Coop

Ahh...

Bubba

Told him I wanted to meet everyone over there.

Coop

ETA?

Bubba

15 – 20, I hope.

Coop

The grounding a problem?

Bubba

No. He's talking CPS again.

Coop

See if you can stall that. Something else is up.

Bubba

Trying.

Still Later…

Bubba

She hates me

Coop

She doesn't

Jake

Can't really blame her, can you?

Bubba

Thanks.

Coop

Guys

Jake

NP.

Bubba

She barely looked at me.

Jake

Dude, you said 'hey' and that was it.

Coop

She smiled.

Jake

Besides, you deserve it.

Bubba

What happened to helping?

Coop

Guys...

Jake

Did you make a decision?

Coop

Seriously?

Bubba

I think I should stay home tomorrow.

Jake

It's Coop's b-day. Don't be a dick.

Coop

sigh

Jake

Sorry man, just keeping it real.

Archie

B. You're going. J. Leave it alone.
C. Tell them to shut up. Going DND.
Don't need us. Pls. Edward and her
mom were here earlier.

Coop

Shit.

Bubba

Is she okay?

Jake

Probably not.

Bubba

She didn't say anything earlier?

Coop

No, she wouldn't though.

Jake

Yeah, she sits on it all.

Bubba

Dammit. Can she catch a break?

Jake

Yes. You would be a good start.

Jake

I'm knocking out hw and the sisters
are being annoying. Later.

Coop

Ltr.

Later...

Bubba

U know I care.

Coop

Yes, I do.

Bubba

How do you reconcile it?

Coop

Nothing to reconcile.

Bubba

...

Coop

Dude, the only one who can answer is you. Frankie is worth it to me. She always has been. J has the right idea. If we end up all breaking up or only some of us... we adjust. I'd rather remember what we had than regret never trying.

Bubba

I'll talk to her tomorrow.

Coop

About that...

Bubba

Right, your b-day.

Coop

Yeah, just be you. Don't overplay it.

Bubba

Easy for you to say.

Coop

Ha.

Bubba

What?

Coop

Everyone thinks I never worry. You're wrong. I'm always worried. Tomorrow, just relax. We're gonna have fun.

Bubba

Happy early birthday

Coop

Thanks. See you tomorrow...

Chapter Fourteen
PICTURES OF YOU

Archie was there when I got home, waiting with take out from the Japanese steakhouse he'd taken me to for dinner and his overnight bag. That meant he was also there when I found the door to my mother's bedroom open, for the first time in ever.

I told him about the parents' earlier visit before I went to work as I studied the room. Mom's half-empty closet and the partially open drawers told me when she said she'd come by to pack up a few things, she meant packing to move out.

The stack of mail had been cleared off. Some of the knickknacks that she'd had most of my life and I'd never been allowed to touch were also gone. The bed had been stripped down to the mattress—that was something—and even her bookshelf had been emptied.

The most telling piece? Tory sat in the middle of her bed, looking like a queen.

Aware of Archie's presence at my back, I pushed the door inward to her bathroom.

Everything was gone. Cosmetics, hair products, everything.

It was a mess and needed to be cleaned, but anything and everything she used regularly had been removed.

"Frankie…"

"Well," I said, blowing out a breath. "I guess they were serious."

When he wrapped his arms around me, I leaned back against him. "We're going to figure this out," he promised. "I can get some people over here and clean this all out whenever you're ready."

Clean all of this out?

"You don't think she's coming back."

"At the moment," he admitted. "I'd be more worried if she did. Especially about you."

Staring at her bedroom, I tried to work out what I was feeling. Particularly when I stared at the one photo she'd left behind. It was on the far side of the bed, on the other nightstand. It was me and Mom at Scarborough Faire. We'd gone there a few years back…like forever ago. She'd woken me up early one morning.

Vivacious in her excitement, she'd rushed me to get dressed, and then we'd driven for over two hours to get there, making it just in time for the opening. Inside, she spent a small fortune on outfits for the day, and we spent it as roaming elves. It had been—magical.

She'd left that photo behind.

Guess my not being supportive really sucked for her.

I let Archie pull me from the room. We ate in the kitchen and made a fuss out of the cats. I didn't have to look to see her favorite coffee mugs were gone. Little things were missing from the kitchen. A magnet she'd liked. A picture that used to hang over the stove that said *Live. Laugh. Love.* The irony had never been lost on me.

She'd been a terrible cook, but we always managed.

"Hey," Archie murmured, sliding his fingers through mine and giving my hand a squeeze. "Talk to me?"

"Just…I don't believe she packed and left. That she waited to do this on a night I was supposed to be at work." I should believe it, but somehow, I couldn't wrap my mind around it. "If they'd gotten here five minutes later, I wouldn't have seen them at all."

His expression tightened. "You're going to be okay," he said. "We'll figure out the bills and make sure the rent is covered."

"Your dad already told me he was going to have his secretary email me the address, and that I was more than welcome to move in with them."

Not that I had any intention of taking him up on that offer.

"Edward likes to staff out his problems, family ones included."

"You know, I told him if he broke her heart, I'd find a way to get even with him." I blinked back tears. "Why do I care so much about what happens to her when she doesn't seem to care about me?"

"Because she's your mom," Archie said roughly. "Muriel's a stone-cold bitch most of the time, but she's still my mom, and Edward's still a dick for treating her badly. We can't help it, but want them to pick us…to be better."

"Wow, we really won the lottery with parents, didn't we?"

Pressing my hand to his lips, he kissed it. "I got two shitty ones to your one, though. I guess I win."

"Except now you have to share one of them with me," I pointed out, and Archie let out a harsh chuckle.

"Of all the things I'd share with you, babe, Edward is definitely not one I would have picked."

A huff of a laugh escaped. "You know…I never told her about my scholarship."

"Well, it's none of her business," he said bluntly. "Not anymore." Drumming the fingers of his free hand against the table, he frowned. "Have you ever considered getting emancipated?"

"Emancipated?"

"Yeah, as an Emancipated Minor, you don't have to rely on her for anything. There's still a ton of stuff you're going to need from her, but the emancipation could help…"

Panic clawed at my insides. "Student loans."

"What?"

"We had to fill out all that FASFA stuff, she was supposed to cosign my loans, as the parent."

"Don't worry about it," Archie told me.

I sagged in the chair.

"Frankie, I mean it. Don't worry about it. I'll call Mr. Wittaker tomorrow."

"Who's Mr. Wittaker?"

"Family attorney. I called him in for Jake, I can call him for you. We'll figure out what we need to do to get you emancipated. Then your mom has no control over anything anymore."

But she'd really moved out… "You know she isn't the devil."

He studied me for a long moment. "Never said she was."

"I mean...she can be distant, and she can be hyper focused elsewhere." His mouth tightened at that description, but he didn't contradict me. "But she's also the same mom who would wake me up some mornings and we'd just take a road trip. You weren't here, but when I was in fifth grade, she took me to Colorado the week of my birthday. No reason, just woke up one morning and said, get in the car. Let's go. I saw snow for the first time…real snow. It *snowed* on my birthday, and it was awesome."

I'd almost forgotten that.

"One time she came home, she'd gotten a raise at work and she bought that laptop I use. It was a random day, but it was sitting on my bed with a bow on the top. Just because."

The corner of his mouth tipped up, but his eyes held no smile as he released my hand and brushed away the tears on my cheeks.

"She's not totally terrible."

"Frankie, you can still love your mom, even if you can't stand her." The soft understanding in those words left my eyes hot with tears. "When I was little, my grandmother told me that family is something you build. Relations are something you maintain. But the thing she stressed the most was that just because you love something, doesn't mean it's good for you. It's okay to say no to what isn't good for you."

My mother wasn't good for me.

The distance between us had been expanding for months. Years really. When was the last time we had a spontaneous trip? A moment of levity and impulse?

"I guess I get leaving, I don't get how she does it without actually telling me, or how she does it without taking that picture in her room. She loved that picture. Or at least, she used to."

When Archie pulled me out of the chair and wrapped his arms around me, I hid my face against his shirt and cried. I didn't even want to cry. First Ian. Now my mom.

Neither should be a surprise.

I mean, I broke up with Ian. I made that choice.

I told Mom I wouldn't support the thing with Mr. Standish. Another choice.

Didn't quite explain why it all hurt so damn much. I had no idea how long Archie just sat there with me curled up in his lap crying, but eventually, the sobs gave way to hiccups. My eyes hurt. My nose was runny. My throat was sore. Not giving me any teasing or grief, he eased me onto my own chair before he got me water, then he disappeared only to return with a cold, damp washcloth.

His smile was gentle the whole time he wiped my face, and then he told me to sit still while he cleaned up the remains of our dinner. Only when he was done—and he checked the cats' food and water—did he double-check both doors were locked before he tugged me back to my room.

Archie stripped down to his boxers and then he helped me out of most of my clothes. Most, because once I was down to panties, he tugged his t-shirt over my head. "Come on," he told me before tugging me over to the bed. Curled up together, he dragged the blankets over us. It didn't take long before all the cats found a spot.

Then he opened his phone and tabbed over to the photos and a folder called Frankie.

"Holy crap…"

"You said she loved that photo," he told me. "I bet you loved it, too."

I did.

"So, confession time…and if it's a little stalkery, apologies in advance, but I've been saving these for years and I keep adding to them."

He tabbed the folder open, and one of the first pictures came from the other night when we'd been celebrating my scholarship. I was sitting on Jake's shoulders in the pool, soaking wet and laughing. The next shot was me studying at school—

"Archie, I'm chewing on my hair." It was a terrible habit. One I thought I'd stopped.

"You do that sometimes," he sounded practically indulgent. "It's adorable."

I groaned.

There were so many more pictures. Some I'd known he'd taken, like the ones from our date. Others—including one of me sleeping—I hadn't known. Scrolling back through them was like taking a trip through time over the last four years we'd known each other.

"This one," Archie said as we reached middle. "This one is one of my favorites."

I had on a red baseball cap, my hair was in a messy ponytail, my ratted jeans were on, and I was wearing a white crop-top. You couldn't see my face really, since my head was down.

"Why is it your favorite?"

"Cause you… I'd just come from a really shitty fight with Muriel and Edward. I was in a terrible mood, and I didn't want to be at school or dealing with any of their crap. You walked over, popping your gum, and said, 'Who did you kill, and what do we need to hide the body?'"

Realization bubbled up in me. As much as my eyes ached and I was still sniffling, I laughed. "You gave me the worst look and said, 'Think you could handle a hard time?'"

The corner of his mouth kicked up. "You stood up, fixed your hat as you said, 'I can take you, Standish. Bring it on.' You know what, I totally believed you, and I started laughing. Killed all that anger in me with one smart ass remark." He pressed a kiss to my temple. "You made my world better. I made you say it again, and you did the exact same thing, and this is the picture I took."

A little bewildered and a lot flattered, I twisted and gave him a real kiss. The phone slid away as he cupped my face. The heat of his palm coupled with the tenderness in the kiss had me chasing his tongue almost playfully as he rolled onto his back and tugged me over him.

The gentle skate of his fingers over my hips to his shirt had me lifting up and breaking the kiss. I tugged the shirt up and off, and dropped back to meet his kiss as he massaged my breasts. We seemed to be in a state of hurry up and wait. I couldn't get enough of his kiss as he seemed intent on devouring me. Even then, I was running my hands over him everywhere I could touch.

When he dragged his mouth away from mine, I groaned, but he urged me a little higher and then latched onto one of my nipples. The electric sensation zinged right through me. Long pulls coupled with little bites had me squirming. Then he kissed and nipped a path to my neglected nipple. I stretched between us and teased his cock through the fabric of his tented boxers.

Dipping my hand beneath the waistband, I closed my fingers around the hot, silky taut skin, and he let out a low groan as I began to stroke him slowly.

A minute later, I was flat on back and he had my panties off. His boxers followed, and he pressed my leg up so he could tease my pussy with a kiss and a lick that had me bucking. It felt good, but I wanted more. When he speared two fingers into me, I groaned.

"Archie…"

"Shh, babe, just making sure." When he crooked his fingers inside of me, the tension redoubled. "Never going to hurt you."

They treated me like porcelain, and then he sucked against my clit and I came. It chased all the other thoughts away except for the need to ride the feelings he provoked.

When he slid away from me, I wanted to complain. Then he was back and rolling the condom on. Easing onto the bed, he lay on his back, and he reached a hand out to me. "Come ride me?" The request sent a shudder through my overstimulated system, and I scrambled up to straddle him.

Mouths locked together, I hummed against his lips as his hand and mine wrapped around his cock and drew it back and forth against my pussy. His soft moan as we positioned him and I began to descend to take him in sent another lance of electricity down my spine.

Inch by inch, I dropped until I'd taken him all the way in, and then we both sighed. "I love this," I admitted in between kisses.

"Yeah?"

"Oh yeah," I closed my eyes as I pumped my hips a couple of times, the shallow thrusts lifting me up only to grind back down. "The feeling of you stretching inside of me…" Seriously, I did. It was one thing to get myself off, but I didn't think I'd ever get tired of when he—or Jake, for that matter—pushed into me. "It's…those first few moments, it's so big and it feels like I'll split open."

Eyes open, I met his gaze as he settled his hands on my hips, and I began to move. Palms braced against his shoulders, I began to roll my hips, deepening the motions of rising and falling as he met my every downward thrust.

The play of emotions across his face captivated me.

"Then you're there…and it feels so good."

We found our rhythm, and I stopped trying to describe it as I dug my fingers in. At his urging, I went faster. This was different and sublime in the same moment. The tension coiled tighter and tighter. His fingers bit into my hips, and his expression grew more taut. When he dragged his hand up my side as he sat up, I met his kiss and we writhed against each other.

So close. The tension ratcheted higher, and then it burst. Everything clenched and fluttered as I cried out against his lips. He gave another couple of thrusts and then let out his own groan, shuddering as he gripped me to him.

Panting, we clung to each other. "And I really like that part, too." The admission pulled laughter from him, and then we were both giggling.

"Just like it, huh?" Archie teased as he pinched my ass, and I laughed.

"I like a lot of things about you."

"Yeah?" He brushed my hair back and gave me a light kiss.

"Yeah. I'm sorry…I'm sorry you have to keep picking me up lately."

"I'm not," he promised. "I'm sorry crap keeps happening, but I am definitely not sorry about being there for you."

"No matter what happens," I said as I brushed a stray cat hair off his cheek. Deliciously rumpled, he looked utterly kissable. I gave into the temptation and kissed him as lightly as he had me. "Stepsiblings or not, I'm still going to date you."

His soft chuckle rolled over me. "Good."

Eventually, I eased away, and he made his way to the bathroom and got rid of the condom. Flopping back on the bed, I stared up at the ceiling. This wasn't entirely how I planned to spend this evening.

Well…the sex had definitely been on the list of things I'd like to do, but the whole emotional dump thing.

"Stop it," Archie said as he slid back into the bed and rolled next to me lie sideways, head propped against his hand. "You're worrying. No more worrying while we're naked."

I chuckled. "Is that going to be rule number three?"

"Nope. Rule number nine or maybe ten. Still, valid." He settled a hand against one of my breasts. "Naked worrying is forbidden."

"Okay." I could try that. "Thank you for coming tonight."

"Oh, babe, I'll come every time I'm with you." He waggled his brows at me, and I laughed.

"Oh my god, that was so cheesy."

I don't know when we finally fell asleep, but the laughter helped. The cuddling helped. Curling up against him with the cats finally venturing back after they'd fled our sexual athletics helped.

Waking up to his erection snuggled against my ass and his kisses on my throat as he massaged my breasts was pretty damn nice, too. We were spent and panting when the first text messages started hitting, and Archie gave a little hip thrust as I continued to flutter around him.

"I don't want to move," he complained.

When I would have stretched for my phone, he pulled me back and buried his face against my hair.

"I don't want you to move either."

Laughing, I flexed my ass against him, and he groaned again.

"Give me twenty minutes, and we can repeat both of your favorite parts again."

That did it, I descended into giggles all over again. Despite his grunt of protest, the pressure of his smile against my skin made me grin wider. Eventually, I rolled over to get the phone, and it was Coop.

Coop

Knock knock, sleeping beauty. Kick Arch out of bed and come let me in so I can have my good morning kiss.

Coop

Better idea. Send Arch to let me in, and I'll meet you in bed for my good morning kiss.

Coop

Wake up!!!! It's my birthday!!

Archie glanced at the message, then at me. "Stay here." Then he was off the bed, snagging his boxers as he went. A minute later, the front door opened, and I heard Coop's whoop.

A minute later, he leaned around the bedroom door, one hand over his eyes. "Is it safe?"

"It's your birthday, and I guess a kiss in my birthday suit is as good a plan as any."

Fingers parting, he peeked at me and then laughed. "You're still under the covers."

Setting my phone down, I grinned. My body was still humming from Archie, but at the flash of hunger in Coop's eyes, the tension settled like a knot in my belly.

"Showering," Archie called. "Don't do anything I wouldn't." The bathroom door thumped closed.

Coop stared at me until I held out a hand. "C'mere, birthday boy."

He crossed the room like a shot, and it was like we were kids again, only very much not as he bounced onto the bed once before rolling right on top of me. I barely had a chance to open my mouth before he was kissing me.

It was like every other good morning kiss, if they'd been dialed up to Texas scorcher in July. I forgot how to breathe as he deepened the kiss. When his hands skated over my breasts, I groaned, and then he was kissing a path down my throat, and when he sucked one nipple against his teeth, I let out a little cry.

Lifting his head, he grinned at me. "You're so gorgeous."

"I have bed head." Worse. I had sexed up bed head.

"I don't care," he murmured. "You're beautiful. Your lips are swollen…" He drew his finger over my lower lip. "Your breasts are really gorgeous, even your nipples look redder and swollen." I bit back a groan as he sucked against the other one. "Archie take good care of you?"

A shudder shifted through me at the question. "What?"

Another smile quirked his lips. "Did Archie take good care of you?"

Was he really asking me…?

He kissed me again, and I gasped against his mouth as he skimmed his hands beneath the blanket, and then he eased his fingers between my legs. Fuck, I arched at the contact. I was more than a little sensitive.

After nibbling my lower lip, Coop smiled against my mouth. "Definitely feels like he took care of you." Slanting his mouth over mine, I wasn't prepared for the stroke of his fingers against my clit. The pressure turned insistent, and this foreign mewling noise escaped me as he chased my orgasm with a kind of deliberate focus I hadn't expected.

It burst through me, leaving me straining against him as he swallowed every cry with his kiss. Slowly, he eased his hand away as the aftershocks shuddered through me. If I'd thought I was sensitive before, I was almost sore now.

"Fuck," Archie said, and Coop lifted his head. Archie stared at us with an almost dumbfounded look on his face. Hair still damp from the shower, he had a towel around his hips, and it wasn't doing much to hide the fact he had an erection again. "You weren't kidding when you said it was hot."

"Nope," Coop told him cheerfully. "It's pretty fucking awesome huh?"

Heat scorched my cheeks, and I grabbed a pillow. "Oh my god."

"Awww, it's okay," Coop said, tugging the pillow away. "You're beautiful when you lose it, I promise. And I love how you sound and feel."

"Yeah," Archie said with a sigh. "That's one of the awesome parts."

Oh, I was pretty much on fire with them talking like that. Coop nuzzled my jaw with a kiss. "Thank you," he said softly. "I loved my birthday present."

"But I didn't do anything for you."

"Oh, yes you did," he said, a supremely satisfied smile on his face. "You let me see you and kiss you. Good morning kisses are the best. Birthday good morning kisses are even better." Then he gave me another long, thorough kiss, and Archie let out a groan.

"Fuck me, I'm getting changed before I blow off this whole going to the amusement park thing."

Oh. That sent a curl through my tummy, and Coop laughed against my mouth. "My birthday, my rules."

"Yes, Coop," I said, even as Archie echoed me, and Coop grinned before pressing a kiss to my nose.

"Have you fed the cats yet?"

"Nope, we kind of overslept." And they'd let me.

"Okay, you go shower, and I'll take care of it for you."

"You don't—"

He pressed a finger to my lips to quiet me. "I want to. Now go. Birthday boy rules, remember?" He winked, and I let out a soft chuckle.

"Sir, yes, sir."

"Better."

Then he rolled to the side as I slid out of the bed. Awareness of both of their gazes eating me up had me pausing for a moment, and I met Archie's gaze and then Coop's. They both grinned at me.

The blush had my face burning, but their smiles…

"I'm going to shower."

"Okay," Coop said. "I'm just waiting to watch you walk away. I love watching your ass in just about everything, and I have a feeling it's even better in nothing."

That was even cheesier than Archie's line earlier, and at the same time, it sent a flush of pleasure through me.

"Well, I'll be sure to put a little sway in my step," I teased. It was his birthday, after all. Instead of snagging my clothes to take with me, I just headed out of the room, hips swaying as promised.

Two wolf whistles followed me, and then I cracked up. Their laughter followed, and I was still grinning when I got into the bathroom and shut the door. It was already warm and steamy from Archie's shower, or maybe that was just me.

As I ducked under the water, it hit me. I'd just come apart in Archie's arms, and not twenty minutes later, Coop made me come again and Archie had watched some of it.

Wow.

Chapter Fifteen

DON'T TAKE ME FOR GRANTED

COOP

The minute the shower came on, I rolled off the bed that smelled like sex and Frankie to stare at Archie. Thankfully, he'd covered his naked ass and had his shorts halfway on.

"Why was she crying?"

The red-rimmed eyes would have been a tip-off, but there was just a bit of swelling also around her eyes and the faintest tear tracks on her face. The minute I'd seen them, all I wanted to do was chase away whatever pain put them there.

Didn't think it was Archie, she'd been damn near boneless before I kissed her, and wet and warm…fuck, she'd been warm and soft. My cock was going to have a zipper imprint against it if I didn't get my own hard-on under control. Having her come apart for me would never get old. It had been a couple of weeks.

I wasn't in a hurry—we had time, and I planned to savor it. Part of why I understood where Bubba was coming from. Unlike him, I had no hang-ups about

Archie or Jake being far more enthusiastic partners. As long as she had a good time, it was fine with me.

But the crying?

Hell no.

"Fuck," Archie said, buttoning his shorts before he ran a hand through his damp hair. He glanced at the door and listened. "We gotta feed the cats."

"Right." I stood, and Tiddles streaked out of the room. I swore those little furballs had sixth sense. They hadn't followed Frankie.

Or maybe they just understood English.

Whatever.

I had the can open and three excited cats at my feet as I said, "Well? Why was she crying?" It had to be her mother. We hadn't heard from Archie or Frankie after he said he was going DND.

"Edward moved her out."

Wait. "What? He moved…" The reality of it crashed in on me. "Her *mother* moved out?"

I couldn't stand the woman. There had always been something sketchy about her. Even when my mother told me to show her respect, 'cause you know, adult and all that, I'd done my best to avoid her and still be there for Frankie. Considering how crappy she treated Frankie? I wasn't all that sorry to hear she'd moved out, except…

"What the fuck is Frankie supposed to do?"

"Pretty sure it's a play to make her move in with them," Archie said as he folded his arms. Leaning back, he glanced toward the hall leading to the bathroom. The shower was still on. "Edward pushed the car thing again. Told her he'd have his assistant get her the address. They packed up her mom's things while she was at work. There's not even a note."

"What a bitch."

"My thoughts exactly."

"But Frankie is already working her ass off…"

"Don't worry about this place. I'm going by the office and paying the rent for the rest of the school year. Stay or go, whatever she wants, she's not losing her apartment."

Sometimes, it was easy to forget that Archie was loaded, and then he said things like that.

"If her mom comes back?"

"I'm considering getting the locks changed, too. But I might need to ease her into that. This really fucking hurt her." The dislike in his voice was so thick, I could damn near feel it pulsate.

"Dude, I don't get it. How does a mom do that? I mean…I have issues with my dad, but he still does what he can. Even if what he can ain't much." Which was true. Jake had a hate on for his dad. Bubba lucked out as far as all of us were concerned, and while Mr. Rhys was getting kind of intrusive, it was hard to fault him—Frankie was in trouble.

"You know, I'm not even going to try and figure her out. Psych is your thing." Archie leaned his head back against the wall, and I got the coffee started. No matter what else we did today, I wanted Frankie caffeinated. A caffeinated Frankie was a happy Frankie.

"If I ever go for my doctorate, maybe I'll use her as a case study." As jokes went, it fell flat.

"I just want her to stay away. I know it hurts Frankie that she left like that, but the in and out and the toxic nature of the relationship isn't good for her either."

"She's still seventeen." She was the youngest of all of us. Her birthday was months off.

"Yep, I'm going to send a message to the attorney about seeing if we can file to get her emancipated. Then she will legally be able to sign all her own stuff. But…let's focus on your birthday today."

"You already have a plan."

The water cut off in the other room, and Archie nodded firmly. "I have a plan. The first part of that plan is it's your birthday. Let the fun and mayhem begin."

Mayhem.

"Maybe let's skip that last part," I called as Archie headed back to the bedroom to finish getting dressed.

When I opened the fridge to look at breakfast possibilities, I glared. It was getting low on a lot of things.

Ugh. I hated her mother.

Putting hate out into the universe was just a bad idea, so I disliked her mother intensely, and I was with Archie—if she wanted to sever ties, make it permanent.

But Frankie didn't have any other family that I knew of. Not family she talked about.

There had been a grandmother. When we were kids, like even before we met Jake, she'd come to visit. Frankie had been super-excited about it. When my grandmother used to visit, or Sis and I went to her place, we always came back with presents and stories.

Looking back, it was easy to see why Frankie would have been excited. But she'd also said something weird, something I hadn't ever thought of…

"I didn't even know I *had* a grandmother."

How does a kid not know? Knowing what I do about her narcissist of a mom? I totally get it now. As for her dad?

"Hey," Frankie said, pulling me out of my thoughts, and I had to grin. She looked delightful with her damp hair, rosy cheeks from the shower, and dressed in a pair of slim shorts and a tank top.

Man, I almost didn't want to go to Six Flags. But we all needed it. We needed to get away from this place, from the crap going down here, and just go be somewhere no one knew all of us. Hold her hand, kiss her when we felt like it, and have fun.

That was what I wanted for my birthday. "Hey," I said, and wrapped my arms around her when she curled into me. She fit perfectly right up against me, and I loved being able to hug her. Honestly, there wasn't much a Frankie hug couldn't fix. "Feel better?"

"I was feeling pretty good before," she teased, and I grinned. "Though you seem to be a little on the stiff side."

"Oh, I'm a lot on the stiff side." The sweet weight of her pressed against me just reminded me all over again of how hard I was for her. It wasn't difficult, every time I kissed her, I got a boner. Sometimes when I was just talking to her. Wanting Frankie was a lot like breathing—vital to my existence.

Tipping her head back, she studied me, and I dropped a kiss on her lips. The traces of tears were gone from her cheeks, and her eyes weren't so red. They were still a little swollen though.

"Still up for going out on my b-day?" It was a little juvenile to use my birthday to get my way, but I hadn't been kidding when I said we all needed a break. Her more than the rest of us. She had a crapton of shit landing on her shoulders, and it kept raining down. Unfortunately, our shit kept hitting her, too.

"Yep," she said, pressing a kiss to my jaw. "Right after I have coffee."

"Oh, absolutely." After giving her a gentle squeeze, I turned her around toward the coffee pot. "Already brewed for you."

The grounds had been low though. We might need to make a grocery run before we came back.

"Jake's on his way," Archie said as he wandered back in, shirt tucked in and phone in his hand. "And he's bringing donuts. I said we might stop somewhere on the way and get real breakfast."

Sounded good to me.

"Are we leaving when Jake gets here and eating in the car? Or eating here?" Frankie didn't look at us as she asked the question, she'd poured coffee for all three of us though. I slanted a look at Archie. The last time I talked to Bubba, I told him to just show up and relax.

Archie shook his head once.

So no, he hadn't heard from him either.

I shrugged. We couldn't make him figure it out, we could just try to be supportive. It seemed to bug him that Frankie was keeping her distance, and maybe, just maybe, he was waking up.

We were halfway through the coffee when Jake got there. Damn, I winced for him. The bruises looked worse today. They had gone this Technicolor shade, though the angry green at the edges said they might be healing.

Out of curiosity, I watched Archie instead of Jake and Frankie when she gave him a good morning kiss. It was funny, Jake was kind of a noisy kisser. Not obnoxious, but he made no pretense about going all in. It was heavy, it was wet, and there was just the faintest hint of sucking noises. Course, the fact that Frankie let out this little moaning sigh every time he kissed her didn't hurt.

She didn't do that with me, it was a little different with me. The sound was more of a groaning purr. Trust me, I wasn't complaining. She and Archie hadn't made out in front of me. So I couldn't really say what they sounded like, but that swollen, just fucked look she had this morning when I arrived confirmed he definitely knew what he was doing.

Head tilted, Archie watched them, coffee cup paused halfway to his mouth, and I had to grin as I took a sip of mine. When he walked in on me getting Frankie off—my birthday present to me, thank you very much—for a split second after he'd said *'Fuck,'* I couldn't lie, I'd worried.

The word had bounced around in my head like a tornado-warning siren had gone off. Were we about to be hit by a storm, or would it evaporate up into the air without ever hitting the ground? But the wonder in his eyes and his admission that it had been hot punctured the balloon of fear before it could even achieve lift off.

And if his current expression was any indication, then he found Frankie kissing Jake to be every bit as hot as I did, and I was more than okay with that.

"Yo, Jake," I called, giving Archie a beat to get it together 'cause his shorts were not the best for disguising the fact he had a hard-on. Hell, I had one, but mine wasn't going anywhere anytime soon.

My hand was not enough anymore, and that was okay. I wanted Frankie. Bubba was right about one real facet of his hesitation and idiocy. We had been pushing her a lot the last three—four weeks? Hell had it really only been that long?

I'd loved Frankie Curtis since the day she knocked me on my ass in kindergarten.

No, four weeks was nothing compared to thirteen years.

"I'm busy," Jake grunted as Frankie laughed, and then he kissed the sound right out of her. Yep. Noisy damn kisser. Still, I was grinning.

"I can see that, but Frankie needs to eat, and to eat, she has to breathe. If you keep that up, we're all going to have to do another round of morning kisses and we're never getting out of here."

For his part, Jake just flipped me off and dragged Frankie closer. Bruises and a busted lip weren't slowing him down any. Archie chose that moment to crack up. Shoulders shaking, he seemed to stare into his coffee cup, but the chuckling snorts kept coming.

Dragging his head upward, Jake stared at him and Frankie twisted. My near smile died a rapid death, because for one fragile moment, genuine fear flashed in Frankie's eyes, and then she relaxed when Archie looked at them, still chuckling.

"Yeah, okay—new rule. If we have to go somewhere, no making out for anyone that leaves us all with painful boners."

Looping his arms around Frankie, Jake dragged her back against his chest. Not that it was a fight. She leaned right into him. "Yeah, I'm going to go with a big fat negative on that, Arch. We don't get to do kisses at school, that means when we're somewhere we can, we do. Capiche?"

At her giggles and flushed cheeks, I relaxed. "Agreed, also, come on, share her. Birthday boy here."

"Fine," Jake grumbled, but he flashed me a grin. "Happy birthday."

"Thanks." I chuckled, but Frankie gave me a playful look before she wrapped her arms around me. "I already got the best present right here."

"Damn. Definitely beats my car," Archie said almost sorrowfully.

Then we were all laughing again. Frankie's lips were definitely swollen and getting a work out today, so I gave her a bare brush of a kiss and murmured, "Go eat. We should get on the road soon."

"Yes," Jake said. "And we need a plan."

Archie made more coffee while we divvied out the donuts, and Jake brought up the map on his phone. That we were taking his SUV was a foregone conclusion. It was just bigger. Course, it was just the four of us, so we could probably take my Lexus.

Seriously, if that just didn't make me grin. Take my car. Granted, it had been a gift, and I hadn't earned it. I wanted to pay Archie for it, and he'd flat out told me no when he handed me the notice of the pink slip being transferred into my name.

"It's a gift. Pure and simple."

"It's a really *expensive* gift."

Mom had been aghast when she'd seen it, but Archie remained adamant.

"It's a gift for you, it's your birthday. Look, I get it, it's expensive. That's not why I'm giving you a car. I want you to have the same freedom we all do. You take care of Frankie, too. You always play it cool and nothing ever ruffles you—so pay it forward."

That had shut me up.

Under the pre-text of looking up the park times and ticket prices, I dug out my phone. No messages from Bubba.

As tempted as I was to text him and tell him to get his ass in gear, the next move really had to be his. He'd fucked up with Frankie. Instead of talking to us about what was going on and maybe getting some clarity, he'd gone straight to her and messed with her head.

The fact it had left them both confused and hurting bugged me. Archie and Jake were just pissed with him. Jake because he couldn't stand anything that stood the chance of hurting Frankie, especially if it was one of us. Legit. The first fight I ever saw him get into was over Frankie. Kind of fit, most of the fights I saw him wade into involved her in some way.

Archie was good with her in other ways, but he had a kind of code. It was a little weird, but it had been there from the first day we met him. Literally the first question he asked when Frankie was out of earshot was which of us was dating her.

At the time, the answer was no one.

Obviously.

He'd grinned and asked if we minded. Jake grumbled. Bubba had frowned. But I'd only shrugged. I didn't think he would get anywhere.

But the next ten months were fun to watch. And along the way, Archie became a damn good friend, to all of us but especially to Frankie, and even if she'd remained oblivious, he'd never gotten mad at her. Frustrated? Sure, but never angry.

That right there made him a good fit.

"Think that works?" Jake asked. "If we leave in the next fifteen minutes, we can make it by the time they open. That includes grabbing breakfast on the way, but probably drive-thru. Since you and Frankie have a date tonight, what time do you want to be back here?"

I glanced at Frankie. "Between five and six, the cats need to be fed."

Her grin had me puffing my chest out.

"I pay attention," I reminded her.

"You always do," she murmured, and real pleasure rushed through me. I could be a pushy bastard where she was concerned. I hated when she closed everyone out. I really hated it when she blamed herself for things that were definitely not under her control, or downplayed when something really bothered her. So yes, I paid attention.

So did she.

When I coiled one of her curls around my finger and gave it a tug, she rolled her eyes and all was right in my world. "Gonna ponytail or braid this?"

I hated when she put it up, but it wasn't my hair.

"What do you want?" The question startled me, and she grinned.

"I like it down."

"Then down it is…not like we're riding with the windows open."

I grinned.

"Yep," Archie said, and I glanced over to find him offering a five-dollar bill to Jake. Despite the bruises on his face, Jake just laughed as he took the five and slid it into his own wallet.

"I don't even want to know," Frankie declared as she rose and grabbed the coffee cups. After rinsing them out, she added, "I'm going to pee and wash up, then we can go when you guys are ready."

None of us said anything as she left the room, and as soon as the bathroom door closed, I looked at them. "Spill."

"Jake bet me five dollars that Frankie was going to be all 'yes, Coop' today."

"She always says yes to the birthday boy, dumbass. She's done that for years, it's *why* she showed up at Bubba's birthday party."

True. She had. We went almost all summer never seeing her, and she made the dumbest excuses to me to avoid fighting with me. But she had come to Bubba's party.

"Cool," I said.

They both snorted and laughed. We were cleaned up and ready to go. Not one of us brought up Bubba, but since I wasn't the only one who looked at my phone, I knew they were just as aware of it as I was.

Jake checked the front door, and then we all headed out the back and waited for her as she locked up. I don't know which of us saw him first, though it would have been hard to miss him. Bubba stood next to his bike, which he'd parked right next to Jake's SUV.

Poor bastard. He looked awkward as hell holding his helmet, and the silence stretched out uncomfortably.

C'mon, man... I was practically willing him to get it together.

"Sorry I'm late," he said, then twisted to open his saddle bag. "Had to stop to pick this up."

'This' was a plastic bag wrapped item. We'd reached him by then, and he held it out to me. Peeling the plastic back, I started to laugh. "Seriously?"

"Hey, you're the weirdo who likes that game."

It was an old school castle game. The thing had the singularly most annoying narrator known to man, and yes, I'd freaking loved this game. My copy died forever ago on a computer that went belly up. This was a classic repackaging.

"Thanks," I told him, and he clasped hand before giving me a nod.

"No problem. Ordered it a few weeks back, wasn't sure it would come in in time, but it was there. Just had to wait for the store to open."

"Let me just go put this in my car," I said. "You made it in time. We're just heading out."

"Hey, glad we didn't leave you behind," Jake told him. "You can ride shotgun."

That wasn't going to help him get closer to Frankie, but she'd drifted back a little, and the smile she had on was nothing like she'd had inside. That clinched it for me. Jake was right.

Frankie wasn't up for this today. Bubba had created this distance, so he could suffer with it for a while. But she also needed to know he wasn't running away.

At least if he had decided. He said he had, said he wanted to try.

Here was hoping he did.

Frankie rode in the back, sandwiched between me and Archie. I wasn't complaining. She was holding both of our hands. Jake played music for a while, then turned it down when Archie brought up rides. Bit-by-bit, the conversation dodged out of uncomfortable territory and toward something fun.

Roller coasters.

Frankie hated them.

"But I'll go," she offered.

"You don't have to," I assured her.

"It's your birthday."

"Yeah," Jake said from the front. "It's your birthday."

It was my turn to roll my eyes. "Doesn't mean she has to torture herself."

"Who knows," she said, elbowing me. "Maybe it will be fun." The impudent note in her voice and the first flash of a real smile had me dropping a kiss on her lips.

"Fine, we'll try the kiddie coasters, and if you don't freak out, we can try something else."

Her indignant denial of freaking out set everyone off laughing—even Bubba. I hadn't missed the look on his face, and man, I was sorry he was on the outside looking in at the moment, but he made that bed.

We grabbed drive-thru as promised, and Frankie got three of the hash browns—her favorite—and a breakfast sandwich. I gave her my extra hash browns when she was still hungry.

When we reached the park, we had like five minutes to spare, which was good. We all needed a bathroom break.

After, with tickets bought, we headed inside and the best part—we were just five kids in the throng of people heading into the amusement park. It wasn't super busy, but we didn't know any of these people.

Frankie clasped my hand. She shared an ice cream cone with Jake. Archie kissed her when he got her up on one of the rides. I laughed my ass off when after she'd proved her mettle on the kiddy coasters, we went on the big one. She screamed through the whole thing.

Admittedly, I was a little deaf, but her eyes were sparkling, and we got off and got back in line and did it again. The thing about having her hair loose, after the rides and whipping upside down, it had gotten bouncier and curlier. She didn't care, she was having fun.

We dropped too much money on competing to win her a toy. None of us would leave the shoot shack until we got something. Jake finally landed one, and then Archie did. Not enough points for what we wanted, so Bubba and I raced to get the last one, and we nailed it at the same time.

"The bear," I said. Birthday boy privileges. It was a psychotic looking bear in psychedelic colors with eyes that looked a little helter skelter. Half the reason we even noticed the place was Frankie staring at it as we walked past. When I handed it to her, she grinned and gave me a kiss.

"Hey, it was a team effort here," Archie protested, and she gave him a kiss. Then Jake, and she paused at Bubba. The tension suddenly ratcheted up, but she settled for pressing a quick kiss to his uninjured cheek.

"Thank you," she said, withdrawing and hugging the bear. "Now I expect a present on everyone else's birthdays, too."

The comment amused, and I laughed along with everyone else, but damn, I felt for Bubba. She'd missed the way the hope flashed up in his eyes and then disintegrated when she retreated.

Thankfully, he kept it cool, and we hit a couple more rides before it was getting time to head back. We could have hung out the rest of the day and that would have been fun, too.

I'd had a blast. My best friends and our girl? Yeah. Great birthday.

Date with Frankie tonight? Without the fashion show and Cheryl?

Even better.

On the way back out to the SUV, I wrapped an arm around her, and she leaned into me.

I was never going to take this for granted. Not even a little.

I'd meant it when I said I wasn't going to regret what I missed out on. We had way too much to enjoy.

"Good birthday?" she asked me as we lagged behind the others, and I grinned.

"Smile for me?" I asked. When she grinned, I winked. "See, there, it's the best."

Then she laughed, proving my point.

Chapter Sixteen

IT'S HIS BIRTHDAY!

The day at the park had been alternately wonderful and heartbreaking. Anytime I caught myself stealing looks at Ian, he'd seemed miserable. What used to be as easy as breathing—talking—had become a nail-biting affair. I didn't want to mislead him or make him feel self-conscious. At the same time, it was exhausting to straddle that line. Jake and Archie helped to keep it upbeat, and I focused on Coop.

The kitchen make-out following Coop's one hell of a morning kiss and fingering me right into another orgasm that morning, and all of that on the heels of the night and morning with Archie had left me loose and lax. A state I could barely comprehend, considering my mother's abandonment.

On the ride back, I settled my head against Coop's shoulder while Archie played the fingers of my right hand. Once again, Ian had taken the shotgun position. No one said anything, he just headed there while Archie held the door open for me to climb in.

Awareness of being watched hit me, and I caught Jake's gaze in the rearview mirror. I gave him a tired smile, and the corners of his eyes crinkled.

Some of the worry faded, but it didn't erase fully. A yawn stole over me, and I pressed my cheek into Coop's shirt.

He smelled like sunshine and the sticky sweet snow cones we'd had after the wild ride on the roller coasters. They'd scared the crap out of me, but I'd had fun, too. Especially after his smile when I asked to go again. The guys weren't really talking, and the music wasn't too loud. Between that and the steady hum of the car, I dozed right off.

Coop nudged me awake when we were back in the lot of the apartments. Everyone slid out of the car, pee breaks were required after that drive. I led them all up to my place, even Ian.

Mine.

That nervous twitch in my gut redoubled as I considered the fact that Mom had moved out.

Was she still paying the rent? Or was that the plan? Wait until I was evicted and had nowhere else to go?

I'd sleep in my car first. But that wasn't good for the cats. One thought crashed into another. The stress of worrying about Ian while trying to enjoy Coop's day left me wrung out. The cats were very vocal once we were inside.

The guys jostled jokingly as they raced for the bathroom. From the sudden laughter and playful curses, Jake had slid in there first. It wasn't the first time today the four of them had found rapport again. The tension was there, sure. But their friendships seemed to be relatively intact, and as envious as I was for their ease in adjusting to my breakup with Ian, I wish I could do the same.

As much as I needed to pee myself, I waited and got the cats fed. You'd think they never got to eat the way they attacked the wet food when I put it down.

I should have made a cake or something for Coop's birthday. It wasn't that late, I still could.

"Dude, are you doing your nails or something?" Archie called, and I grinned. Jake was making them wait.

Ian's huff of laughter had my smile fading, and I turned to the fridge. I had a cake mix in the pantry, but…no eggs, and milk that was perilously low if not expired, and what leftovers were in there weren't edible. I'd pretty much eaten most of what could be devoured from the perishables.

Long-formed habit, I ate those first, or they just spoiled and wasted money. Not wasting money had been beaten into me young. Closing it, I checked the freezer.

Mom had never transferred that grocery shopping money. I guess the dinner had soured her appetite for that. I couldn't really call and complain, could I? There was some chicken, a dead pair of frost-burned pork chops, and a bag of tilapia. Ugh.

Birthday dinner and cake, and I had nothing.

Okay, first things first, I needed to get the guys moving and then I'd head to the grocery store. I had money in savings and in my checking account. Maybe Marsha would give me an extra shift to make up the difference.

Unable to put it off any longer, I made it to the hall in time for Jake to come out and Archie to push in before Coop or Ian could. Laughter and grumbling filled the air, but the guys looked far from upset.

"Hey, baby girl," Jake murmured as he gave me a hug. It was an easy gesture, and he pressed his forehead to mine lightly. Those pale blue eyes always saw too much, and he searched my gaze now. "You okay?"

"No," I told him honestly. I could have lied, but Jake tended to push and prod. Coop would just power right past it with a simple bullshit. Jake dragged it out of me. So, I didn't bother with the subterfuge, no matter how mild. "But I will be."

I had no other choice.

The corners of his mouth curved, and then he pressed a kiss to forehead. It was gentle, earnest, and very affectionate. "Yes," he promised against my skin. "You will. I have your back, you know that, right?"

Rising on my tiptoes, I hugged him tightly and closed my eyes. "I do," I answered in the same hushed voice. I felt more than saw his smile against my ear.

"Have fun tonight, okay?"

I chuckled. "We will."

He gave me another kiss, this one even lighter as his lips brushed mine before he said, "I'm out, guys. Don't be stupid."

Coop snorted, but Archie's voice muffled as he called his goodbye. As Jake moved, my gaze snagged on Ian's. He jerked his attention away, as if I'd busted him for staring.

"Yeah," Ian said. "I'm going, too. Have a great birthday, man." He clapped Coop on the shoulder, and I moved to press against the wall so he could pass me. When he paused in front of me, I wasn't sure what I expected him to say, but "See you tomorrow?" wasn't it.

"Yep. It's a school day, I'll be in the cafeteria getting my coffee infusion." It came out flip and easy, neither of which I experienced. He stared a beat longer. For a moment, I thought he would say something else, but he compressed his lips and gave me a nod before turning to where Jake waited in the living room.

Jake had definitely waited, and while he wasn't staring at us, I was under no illusions about whether he'd been waiting to see what happened. Despite the strained awkwardness lingering between them, Jake and Ian left together.

I sagged against the wall as the backdoor closed. Then Archie was out of the bathroom, and he and Coop shared a look. Then Coop gave me a quick smile. "You need it?"

"Go ahead," I told him, and waved him on.

Archie strolled toward me, his expression concerned but gentle. "You really okay?" Had he heard Jake asking me? Maybe. Though he'd been murmuring. Or maybe I just looked as bad as I felt. Archie had been there last night when I burst into tears. He'd held me while I cried, and then he'd made me smile again.

"Nope." I told him the same thing I'd told Jake. "But I will be."

"Damn straight." He cupped my face and pressed a kiss to my lips before he pressed one to my forehead. "You need me, you know where I am."

I wanted to tell him I would always need him. I needed all of them. But that was a big declaration, and if my life had taught me nothing, it had taught me I had to stand on my own two feet. "I do." Covering his hands with mine, I raised my brows. "You know that goes for you, too, right?"

He grinned. "Thank you. I will definitely call. If it weren't Coop's birthday, your phone would ring the minute I was out the door."

I laughed. Not just because it was funny, but because there was so much emotion there. He wasn't kidding. "I'll see you tomorrow," I promised.

"I'll be in the cafeteria with your coffee, babe." He winked and then gave me another kiss. "I'm out, Coop. Happy birthday!"

The bathroom door opened. "Thanks, Arch…see you tomorrow."

Then there was just us, and Coop raised his eyebrows. "You're doing the happy pee pee dance."

The dry comment made me giggle snort, even as I flipped him off. Chuckling, he backed off to let me in the bathroom.

Ten minutes later, washed up and changed, we headed for my car. "I'm serious, Frankie. I can order food for us," he offered.

"So can I," I said with an exasperated grin to try and soften the snap that almost escaped. "But it's your birthday, and I want to make you dinner and a cake, and I'm the world's worst friend because I didn't get you anything."

"I don't a need a present," he told me flatly. "I'm getting to be with you, and that's the best gift there is."

The moment elongated as we stared at each other over the roof of my car. Then the corner of his mouth kicked a little higher, and a laugh escaped mine. Giggles assaulted us as his smile deepened.

"Too bad we can't buy wine to go with all that cheese," I deadpanned once we were in the car, and he braced his hand on my seat.

"Ha ha," he said with a grin. "Yuck it up."

At the grocery store, Coop and I debated the list. He nixed the birthday cake idea and pointed out cupcakes in the bakery. There were some obnoxious ones with blue frosting. It would totally turn our tongues and teeth blue. But the puppy dog expression in his gray-green eyes had me saying yes. We got four. Then we went in search of staples that I needed. When I tried to go for food for his dinner, he kept redirecting us elsewhere. Like me, Coop knew how to shop a sale and we never missed the rack in the back with clearance items. So what if part of the bread was smooshed, it was a steal at fifty cents.

The deli was the next stop, and I figured out his plan. They had deals on the barbecue whole chickens, pre-cooked and ready to go that included a pair of sides for free if you buy the whole thing. One of those would feed me for the next few days, even after we had dinner.

"Chicken?" He grinned.

Eyeing him, I made a promise. On Coop's next birthday? I was going to make him a huge meal and a perfect cake. "Sounds good."

The only real problem we ran into was when we got to the register. He'd wanted to pay for my groceries, but I beat him to the punch. A fact he sulked about on the way to the car with the bags.

"Coop, it's my food. I should be the one paying for it. Besides, I'm also the one with a job."

"I got a job," he dropped in casually as we stowed the groceries in the backseat. It was way too hot in the trunk.

"Since when?"

He gave me a smirk and just climbed in the passenger seat. Slamming the door closed, I dove into the driver's seat and started the car.

"Since when?" I repeated. When had he gotten a job and why hadn't he told me?

"Since I got the car," he admitted, smiling. "I'm delivering food. It's not glamorous, and sometimes I don't make much in tips, but it's still money, and in the evenings I'm not with you or the guys, I'm going to keep it up. I needed to get back to saving money for school, too."

"That's awesome," I told him. I never thought about delivering food with the car. I had Mason's, but it might be a way to pick up some extra money. An apartment on my own was really going to cut into my savings account.

"Yeah?" That hesitant shyness was Coop to his core. He was so laid back about everything, except those things he might be uncertain about. A job that he'd just managed to acquire with his brand-new car?

"Yeah." I leaned over and kissed him. When he cupped my chin and nudged my mouth a little wider to deepen it, I sighed against his mouth. The fact we were making out in the grocery store parking lot surfaced, but then Coop tilted his head and sucked my tongue against his teeth, and I didn't give a damn where we were.

My body was humming by the time he lifted his head, and I was thankful for the air conditioning because it had gotten warm in here. With gentle fingers, he traced my cheek then the outline of my lips.

"I really want to say something cheesy and deep right now," he told me. "But all I got is damn, I like kissing you."

I grinned. "I'll take damn, I like kissing you, because damn—I like kissing you, too. You've been making me crazy with all those wild kisses and then leaving or dragging me off to school."

"Yeah?" His expression ranged from tender to smug. "I wanted to make sure you remembered me."

"I'm not likely to forget you."

He chuckled. "Good. I'll tell you a secret though." When he crooked his finger, I leaned in closer and braced a hand on his thigh. Lips against my ear, he whispered, "I think about those kisses every time I rub one out. Nothing compares to the real thing though."

A shiver went all the way through me. "Now all I can see is kissing you while you do that."

His laughter choked off, and his pupils expanded. "Damn…never made it a spectator sport before."

"Then it's a good thing I'm really not into those." It was fun to watch him strain for something to say as his mouth opened and then closed.

Rendering Coop speechless had happened maybe five times in all the years I'd known him. I grinned. Touching my tongue to my fingertip, I drew a point in the air and made a sizzling sound.

That set him off laughing all over again. "Yeah, yeah. You definitely win that one."

We laughed and teased all the way back to the apartment. Between us, we got the groceries in and put away, then turned dinner into a picnic in the living room, even if we had to fend off the cats while we ate our chicken, potato salad, and the hot rolls—though admittedly, they weren't that hot now—he'd picked for his sides.

"Okay," I admitted after slurping down more chicken. "This was an awesome idea." Hungrier than I realized, I devoured it. We hadn't worried about cutting it neatly, since the meat practically fell off the bones. My fingers were a mess though, when I went to suck some of the barbecue sauce off my fingertips, Coop caught my hand and sucked the digits into his mouth.

The flutter in my stomach intensified as he stroked each fingertip with his tongue, as if to be absolutely certain not a drop escaped him. Biting my lip, I locked gazes with him. The first real pull of suction against my fingers evoked an answering tug in my system.

"That's so not sanitary," I whispered.

Coop chuckled against my fingers. Then freed them before plundering my mouth with a kiss. I could taste his potato salad, but he went after me like he wanted to lap up any trace of the sauce lingering. When he let me up for air, I almost whimpered.

"Now it's totally sanitary," he teased, and I grinned. From scorching heat to delighted amusement, it was a delicate seesaw of feeling, and Coop's easy grin and playful manner gave me something to latch onto. When he offered me a bite of chicken, I sucked his fingers into my mouth too and returned the favor.

His answering groan and twinkling eyes were worth it. All those kisses had been leading up to today, of that I had no doubt. But I wasn't going to push. I was having way too much fun just playing with him.

"Do you remember Tommy Monaghan?" I asked after we'd cleaned up the remains. So much for the chicken lasting the rest of the week, we'd eaten it down to the bones and killed most of the potato salad. There were still a couple of rolls, but I doubted they'd last much longer.

"Dark haired kid…second grade?"

"First."

"Yeah. Sorta." Then he made a face. "Why?"

"Just… I remember he asked me to marry him in kindergarten, and you punched him in the nose."

"No, I didn't," Coop said, swinging around to eye me. "*You* did."

"Oh." Huh. "Then why did I hit him in first grade?"

"Cause he told you that he was marrying you anyway."

I rolled my eyes, and Coop wrapped an arm around my waist and tugged me to him. "Why are we worried about people you beat up in kindergarten and first grade?"

"I beat up exactly two people."

"It was more like five."

"Two."

The corners of his lips twitched. "Two or five, my question is the same."

"I dunno, I was thinking about your birthdays and how we've spent some of them. For some reason, I keep thinking about when I punched him."

"Oh. Fifth grade."

Good grief, how many times had I punched this guy? "I don't remember that…"

"'Cause Jake beat him up right after you hit him."

Oh.

Shit.

"When he stole the cupcakes I snuck to school to give you on your birthday. He got them out of my locker."

That punk. I'd never been so furious. I'd worked hard to get those to school without Coop seeing them. I'd brought three. One for me, one for Coop, and one for Jake.

Coop grinned, then nuzzled the corner of my mouth. "I remember," he soothed. "Then you used your lunch money and got me an ice cream sandwich rather than food."

"And you and Jake split your food with me so I'd eat, and then you broke up the ice cream sandwich into three pieces."

"Hey, what's a birthday if I can't share?" He didn't wait for me to answer before he kissed me again. Every kiss with Coop started at a simmer and ramped up to four-alarm blaze. Every. Single. One.

We were both panting when he lifted his head. "I'm not asking to spend the night," he said quietly. "No pr—"

I touched his lips with my finger. "You don't pressure me, Coop. You drive me crazy. You wind me up. You turn me inside out sometimes. But you don't pressure me. Even when you corner me in the laundry room so I'll talk to you because you're worried about me."

His eyes gentled, and he kissed my finger. "I do worry about you. You've been my best friend forever, Frankie."

"Ditto." That was why all of this scared me. "Ian couldn't…"

"I'm not Bubba," he told me before I could form the whole thought. "I'm me. I know you're with Archie and with Jake. If you couldn't tell today, it didn't bother me at all…maybe a little envy that I didn't get to slide into that bed with you all naked and warm and wet…"

My stomach went taut at the description.

"But I fucking love how hot it is when you kiss them." Heat swarmed my face at his description. "Even hotter when I think about getting you all revved up for them."

Oh my god.

I tilted my head back, and he nipped kisses along my throat. "You totally did that…that Friday before I went out with Archie, when you kissed me."

The soft huffs of his breath as he laughed against my skin sent tingles radiating everywhere. "Then my evil plan worked."

I giggled. "You are so not an evil genius."

Head up, he waggled his eyebrows. "But would an evil genius really look like an evil genius?"

"I didn't say you didn't look like one," I retorted, then pinched him, and he gave a little jump before lifting me up with his arms around my waist. My feet dangled as he walked, but kept my arms around him.

"Then what did you mean?"

"I said you're not one. You're too nice."

"Ha," he snorted the sound and kept walking right through the living room. The cats were darting out of the way. "Too nice. I get you all hot and bothered thinking about me before you make out with them, and I'm too nice?" The dare in his eyes made me grin.

"Well…" I tipped my head to the side. "You have a point."

"Thank you. Evil genius should be rewarded," he murmured before he closed his mouth on mine. In my room, he twisted and fell back on the bed. We were so lucky we didn't knock our heads together, but it still managed to set me off giggling. His answering laughter made it hard to keep kissing, but when he didn't abandon the attempt, neither did I.

Sitting up, I straddled him, and he slid his hands under my shirt, just resting his palms against my skin.

"Nothing has to happen tonight," he told me. The fact that he had a very thick erection and I was sitting right on it kind of suggested his interest was otherwise. "I just wanted to spend my birthday with you. This isn't a ploy to get you into bed."

"What if I want something to happen?"

His eyes softened as did his smile, and he began to trace his thumbs in little circles against my skin. "Depends on what it is you want to happen." The glint in his eyes was an invitation to play.

"Truth or dare?"

Surprise followed by glee danced across his shifting expression. A chance to make me answer questions? Coop loved to pry things out of me. He was a bigger gossip in some ways than the girls at school. Only Coop didn't pass on what he learned, he just collected it. We all talked to him because he was just that good at listening.

"Or we could pull out that old dart board, and the first to a hundred gets to give the other a blowjob."

His pupils swelled at the offer, and so did his cock. "Okay, dirty talking Frankie is something I never thought I'd get to hear. And I'm in no way taking your insult to my ability to hit a dartboard into consideration. You'll win, no problem, and then I do."

I laughed, and he slid his hands higher, and when they brushed my bra, I reached behind me and unsnapped it. Coop didn't move as I worked one strap out from under the shirt and off my arm, then the other, and pulled the whole thing free and tossed it across the room.

"Well then," he exhaled. "Truth or Dare?"

Coop either wanted me to take a dare so he could tease me some more or truth so he could get more dirty talk. Still…either way, it was like he said, a win for us. Running my tongue over my lower lip, I pretended to debate it for a moment.

"Dare."

Chuckling, he slid his fingers down to my shorts and flicked the button free. "I dare you to take off your shorts…"

Rolling my eyes, I said, "Like that's hard." But before I could move, he clasped my hips.

"Without getting off me," he continued. "You didn't let me finish."

Huh. I glanced down at him, then my shorts. "All right." This would take a lot of squirming, but from the way he was grinning, he seemed to be looking forward to it.

After unzipping my shorts, I leaned forward so I could rest my chest against his. He helped balance me as I began to roll my hips from side to side, tugging my shorts down and then working down my legs. Every slow grinding pressed me tighter against his groin and teased my breasts against his chest at the same time.

The friction from his shirt and mine teased my skin. By the time I finally kicked the shorts off and sat up to straddle him again, Coop's face was flushed and his breathing much shallower.

"Fuck. Me."

I couldn't help it. I pressed one hand over his hammering heart. "It's my turn."

He closed his eyes and groaned. "Okay…I'm ready."

"Truth or dare," I whispered, and I had to be honest, I didn't know which one I wanted him to pick either.

Chapter Seventeen

CAN'T STOP THIS THING WE'VE STARTED

"**T**ruth," he said after a significant pause. I must have looked disappointed because he added, "I'll take dare next time, I promise."

Chuckling, I rested my hands on his thighs as I leaned back. The motion stretched me out, but with my knees on either side of him and the stiffness of his cock pressing upward, I didn't want to hurt him either by putting too much pressure on him.

He followed my every movement with a half-sleepy look, but he wasn't tired. No, not even a little bit. The way he'd track his gaze from my lips to my chest then back up to my eyes again was doing all sorts of happy things to my system. Coop liked looking at me, and right now, I was definitely enjoying him doing it, too.

What did I want to know…oh. Focusing on him, I squinted a little to study his expressions. I was pretty sure I'd know if it was the truth or not. "Did you or did you not lop off the heads of my Barbies in second grade so you could do a brain transplant with one of your action figures?"

His eyes widened. "Seriously?" The last syllable of that question came out on half-broken note. "You're bringing that up? Now?"

Oh, he didn't want to answer. Folding my arms, I nodded once. "You said truth. I want the truth." Because he'd always squirmed out of it and said I must have misplaced them.

But I'd found their severed heads near the dumpster.

I didn't misplace their heads.

He groaned. "Frankie…"

"Ah-ah. Truth!"

"Fine," he said, spreading his palms and raising his hands in a gesture of surrender. "I did *borrow* them. I thought I could switch the heads out and put them back, and then you would have much cooler Barbies."

I snorted.

"Unfortunately, the heads of my figures wouldn't work, so I tried to put the doll heads back on and…" He grimaced. "You remember Ginger?"

The yappy poodle he'd had for years before she passed away right before high school? Of course, I remembered Ginger. She was cute. "Are you trying to tell me your dog ate my dolls?"

"Well…yeah." He gave me a hopeful look. "She was fast, and she stole them when I went to get gummy worms."

"You doll slayer."

He grinned. "Technically, I'm a doll decapitator. Ginger took the bodies."

"No body, no crime?" I asked, and he grinned.

"Something like that. But I'll get you two new Barbies. I promise." He slid his hands back against my hips. "Just don't throw me over for second grade me's vain attempt to do something cool for you."

Snickering, I touched a finger to his nose. "If I can get over you stealing my ice cream, I think we can survive the doll-pocalypse."

"I didn't steal your ice cream." He danced his fingers along my sides, tickling as he rolled me over onto my back, and I squirmed to get away even as

I laughed.

He let up when I swatted him. "You know…that's what got us into all of this."

"The doll-pocalypse?" He blinked at me, and some of the hair fell down over his eyes. He hadn't had a haircut in a while, and the sandy-blond cut comically down to give the illusion that he only had one eyebrow lifted.

"No, dork. You tickling me." My breath still came in little wheezing puffs, and he frowned for a beat and then began to grin.

"Hey, you're right. Then I messed up your shirt." He hung his head a little and rained little kisses all over my face. "I'm sorry. I'm sorry. I'm sorry."

"I'm not."

Hovering over me, he tilted his head. "No?"

"Nope. Because if you hadn't made me mad, and we hadn't had that fight. Then the guys being here…I might have never unloaded why I was upset." That would have sucked.

Granted, the last few weeks hadn't been easy. Not even by any vivid stretch of the imagination. As bad as they'd been in places, I didn't regret them. They'd have been so much worse without the guys.

So. Much. Worse.

"You know," Coop said slowly. "I'm not going to disagree with that." Then he rubbed his nose to mine gently. "I'm not sorry anymore."

I grinned and combed my fingers through his hair. "It's your turn," I reminded him.

"Truth or dare?" he whispered.

Running my tongue along my lower lip, I had to know. "You really want me to say dare, don't you?"

He chuckled. "I'm good with either, Frankie. Both are fun—even if someone asks questions about elementary school."

I laughed. "Well, I did one dare, so I'm going with truth this time." There.

"Ah, revenge for my avoiding a dare, I see how you are." He nipped a kiss to my chin, then another along my jaw, before he reached my ear. The soft tug of his lips and the gentle scrape of his teeth sent need sizzling through my system all over again. I wiggled a little to get my legs apart so he was more cradled between them.

He stilled until I stopped moving, and then he whispered, "Is there any part of your body that's off-limits?"

Surprise flickered through me. That was kind of a weird question.

"Um…" I shook my head. "Nope. I don't think so."

"Really?" His smile grew more delighted, and I raised my brows. "Why?"

"Just curious." But he looked enormously pleased. Another kiss. "Your turn."

Running my hands down his back, I mirrored his earlier move and eased them under his t-shirt. The first brush of my fingers against the sinewy layer of muscle there had him giving me a lazier smile.

"Let me save you a dare," he said, pushing up with his arms, then holding himself up with one before he tugged his shirt up, and over. When he descended again, it was all hot, bare skin, and I clenched my thighs to his hips. "Before you ask," he stared at me steadily, his gaze fixed to mine. "Dare."

A thrill skated through me, even as he settled his chest to mine. What did I want?

Everything.

I pretty much wanted everything. Maybe I was being greedy. Really, no maybe about it. Still…

"Cat got your tongue?" Coop asked, but kissed me as soon as I opened my mouth to reply. He chased my tongue lightly with his, and then when I dared follow it back to his mouth, he sucked against it again, and the hard pull sent liquid heat unfurling everywhere. "No," he murmured, letting up for a split-second. "I have your tongue."

Another kiss, and he had his hand in my hair, tilting my head so our mouths were slanted. The slow grind of his hips pushed the heavy weight of his erection right against my panties. Digging my fingers into his back, I slid them down to his shorts. Why did he have so many clothes on?

"Uh-uh," he whispered, catching one of my hands and pulling it away. "You still haven't given me my dare."

Then the ass locked his lips around one of my nipples, right through the tank top. The liquid heat ignited, and I dug my fingers into his hair as my back arched. Pinned to the bed, I couldn't move him, but I really didn't want to.

"What?" he asked, a sly grin on his face as he glanced up. Then he locked that hot mouth on my neglected nipple, and the only sound I let out was a moan.

A dare.

I needed to give him a dare. When I pressed up with my hips, he gripped one and eased me back down. The last time we'd done this, he'd gotten off in his pants.

That would not do…

The hard suction kept scrambling my brains, and I shuddered when he slid his free hand under my shirt to toy with the other nipple, massaging my breast and then giving it a little twist and pull that was just at the edge of painful.

"Did you say something?" The shit-eating grin he wore now made me laugh, even as heat swept through me.

"I dare you to keep it up," I said, fighting for every breath to get the words out.

"Which it?" The gleam in his eyes said he knew damn well what I was daring him to do, but he asked anyway. "This?" He bit the nipple through the shirt, just sharp enough for me to feel his teeth, then sucked on it until I was writhing. "Or this?" The tug of his fingers on my other nipple teased right at the edge of pain again.

My little moan became a longer one, and I didn't care if I was noisy. I had a hand in his hand and another on his back. And I stroked everywhere I could reach.

"Or maybe this?" He did that roll with his hips that ground him against my pussy, and I wanted to cry.

"Yes," I told him.

He grinned, laughter eddying under his words. "Which one, beautiful?"

Somehow, I got an arm between us, and I had his shorts open and slid my hand right around his cock. The hot, silken shaft almost pulsed under the contact.

"Fuck," Coop exhaled, and his taunting of my body slowed as he locked his gaze on mine. "That it?"

The corner of my mouth ticked upward. "Only if you want to." My voice came out a lot rougher than I expected, but Coop's whole demeanor shifted, and then he was kissing me, and I didn't need a verbal response. His whole body shuddered from my stroke. Each time I slid my hand up to the crown, he thrust his hips.

Dampness leaked from the tip, and it eased the passage. He thrust his tongue against mine in time to the glide of his hips, and then he planted his hands on either side of me and arched until he could pull away fully.

"Hey." I pouted. An honest-to-god pout. "I was playing with that."

"Uh huh," he said, then he was up and hooked his fingers under my shirt. "Off."

That morning when he'd given me the good morning kiss in bed had been one thing. Then he'd worked his fingers against my clit and teased me until I came. It didn't seem to matter that I'd gotten off once that day.

Nope. I wanted more.

I wanted Coop.

Scooting backward, I lifted the shirt up and off. The heat of his gaze scorched me as he watched, and then he grinned. "Panties too. Off."

"Hey now, bossy," I argued, even if I had a hard time not smiling. "It was my dare, you're the one who's supposed to keep it up."

Clasping my legs, he hauled me forward over the bed, and I flopped onto my back, laughing as he gripped the panties and yanked them right down. "Don't mind at all doing it myself," he informed me, and then he just stopped and stared. His shorts hung off his hips, his cock jutting out, red, swollen and thick.

Holy shit, it was thicker than I'd imagined. Dragging my gaze upward, I studied him. Coop's whole posture had gone rigid, and he ran his thumb back and forth across his lower lip.

I'd seen that look on his face before. He was laying out the plan for what he wanted to do. I was the subject of said plan. My nipples tightened, and I bit my lip as I let my legs spread just a little wider.

When he flicked his gaze up to mine, he wore a delighted little smirk. "Happy birthday to me."

I groaned. The comment ruptured some of the raw tension and relaxed the tiny flare of unease and embarrassment that stealthed in when I wasn't looking. This was Coop.

My Coop.

I didn't have anything to worry about.

"I really don't know whether I want to eat you out, or just slide into that pretty pink pussy that I've imagined for far longer than should be normal."

A shudder worked its way up my spine.

"Or ask you to wrap your lips around me, because they're swollen and puffy from kissing, and you already look like I've had you, even if I haven't… then there's that gorgeous ass."

As charmed as I was by the rockiness in his voice as he verbalized his debate, I couldn't help but be turned on by all of it. Except… "What about my ass?"

"I really want to play with it," he told me so earnestly that I blinked.

"Like…" I glanced at his cock and then up to him, and he nodded.

"You said no part was off-limits."

Well, I had but…

"We'll go slow," he promised, his rough tone dipping soothingly. "Not tonight. Too many other ways I want to do this. Fuck, Frankie… I'm going to sink into you and blow my load, I know it."

"It's your birthday," I told him, and held out a hand. Seriously, this was Coop. "We have time to do everything."

His eyes lit up, and then he dug into his pocket. His wallet and a small strip of condoms hit the nightstand. Then he shucked off his shorts and damn, he was so nice to look at. I wanted to devour him with my gaze, even as my palms itched to get my hands on him.

"Truth or dare, Beautiful." He reached for a condom and pulled it open as I watched.

Licking my lips, I frowned. "It's still your dare."

"No, I'm going to do my dare…" He pinned me with a look as he began to work the condom over his cock. "Truth or dare."

I was pretty sure I'd begun to blush everywhere, but this game and conversation while we were just a foot or so apart and butt-assed naked took on a whole new level.

"Truth."

"How wet are you?"

Considering he could see me clearly, I wouldn't think that was a question he needed answered. Then again, that night Archie and I teased each other before our date…

That had been so damn embarrassing when I'd done it then, and I had no idea what came over me. But right now? I knew exactly what I wanted or, I should say, who.

Sliding my hand down chest, I skated it over my abdomen and then slipped it against my pussy. He tracked every movement with his gaze. Emboldened by the way he laser-focused on me, I spread the lips wide and then teased a circle around my clit. The sensation eddied up to add another band of tension. One more slow circuit, I dipped lower and press a finger inside to coat it with moisture and then withdrew it.

His mouth rounded before he dropped a harsh little, "Fuck."

"Very…want to see?" When I held up my hand, he staggered forward a couple of steps and then locked his mouth around my fingers and sucked on them.

My mind blanked as everything turned to sensation. He ran my fingers against his teeth and then slowly released them before he motioned with his chin. "Scoot up more, Beautiful."

I shifted even as he crawled up me, dropping kisses along the way. One right inside my thigh, and then he nudged my clit with nose.

"I'll be back," he murmured, before kissing upward.

"Coop," I gasped as he grazed his teeth to the underside of one breast. "Did you just talk to my…?"

"To *my* pussy?" he corrected with a soft bite of my nipple, never looking away from me. "Yes, I did. She and I are about to have a very personal connection, and I believe in treating every part of you right."

Laughter swelled through me. It was both dorky and sweet and so utterly him… Then his mouth was on mine, and the soft push of his cock teased my entrance.

"Truth," I murmured between the kisses. "Or dare."

He laughed as he began to press forward. The thickness seemed more somehow, and he gave little shallow thrusts, working his way in. When he urged my thigh higher, I went loose. He could maneuver me wherever he wanted. I'd stretch, I knew I would, but oh—the glide of him pushing inside narrowed the whole world.

"Truth," he groaned. Beads of sweat gathered along his brow, and I licked at his lips until he kissed me again. Tongues tangling, I slid my hands down to his ass and gave into an urge I'd had for a while. Cupping one hand against each cheek, I gave his butt a squeeze, and he pushed as I pulled forward. He sank all the way to the hilt, and I dropped my head back.

'Cause the sensation was intense. Coop's gray-green eyes seemed almost black as he stared down at me. The lights were on, we were on top of the covers, there were no secrets, and I could feel him deep inside where every muscle had begun to flutter at the intrusion.

With a kiss to my throat, he studied me even as our breath came in these loud, little pants. Line crossed. No turning back from it. Never even occurred to me to hesitate. Not this time.

Not with Coop.

I adored all of them so much, and this…

"What do you want from me?" It wasn't what I meant to ask. I'd planned to tease him. Ask him about some stupid painting thing we did at school that we planned to give to our moms. It had never made it home. Not that I really cared, but it had been funny.

That was what came out.

I ached from the feel of him, even as I grew more used to him. I shifted my other thigh to pull it higher, to wrap my legs around him, and his face went strained.

"Everything," he assured me, and eased back almost as slowly as he'd pressed into me. The slow drag lit me up, but nowhere near as much when compared to when he pushed back in. Focusing grew hazier as I squeezed his ass, pushing up to meet him when he drew out the next time.

"Truth or dare." He gritted the words out, and I laughed.

His muscles went tauter as I flexed around him and sweat slicked the contact. I was burning up, and we'd barely moved. Oh, I wanted him to…

"Truth," I gasped out the word, and then he kissed me as he pumped his hips, each thrust seemed to push him deeper, or maybe it was the angle as I kept arching up to meet him.

He dug his hand against my hip and then hooked a thigh to push my leg higher. The stretch burned a bit, and then he snapped his hips forward and my whole body jolted.

"Can I have everything with you?" The question had me shuddering even as he increased the pace. The slide of his chest against mine sent fresh frissons of need to braid around the tension pulled so tight, it was going to cut me in half.

"Yes." He could have whatever he wanted with me, and then he kissed me, and the words stopped. It was just his body thrumming into mine, and mine spiraling as we clawed and pulled. The tension expanded suddenly, breaking with a wave that had me keening even as I cried against his mouth. The soft grunts as his pace increased just drove me harder, and then it all splintered.

When he stiffened against me, I forced my eyes open. His face was a rictus of pleasured agony, and he sank down, panting against my ear. Eyes closed, I tipped my head back, boneless beneath his weight. I loved every inch of where he pressed me into the mattress.

How long we lay there trying to catch our breath, I had no idea, but my eyes were getting heavy. Then he kissed the column of my throat. Another tender brush to my lips as he stroked my hair back. I tried to open my eyes wider, but he murmured a shushing sound.

Then, "I'll be right back."

The absence of him had me shifting restlessly, but then he was back, and the lights went out just before he slid into the bed behind me and pulled me against his chest, the big spoon to my little spoon.

"Thank you," he whispered against my ear. "That was…"

Never caught that last word. The next time I woke, he pressed his cock against my entrance, my thigh up as he teased me from behind. My body was already lax and soft as he cupped my breast. "Please," he asked, nuzzling kisses against my ear.

A little laugh escaped. "How long have you been waiting to wake me up?"

"Fifteen minutes," he murmured almost mournfully. "But I wanted you here for this." I slipped a hand down and eased him forward. His soft sigh as he sank into me echoed in my own head.

There was no rush, just a series of lazy thrusts as he worked his way deeper. I couldn't do anything at this angle but feel, and oh, it felt good.

It seemed to go on and on, ramping just a little higher with each stroke, the climb so gradual that when he brushed his fingers against my clit, I wasn't prepared for the wave to burst so suddenly.

I clamped down on him, and his answering groan preceded the three or four hard thrusts before he squeezed me and then pinched around my clit just lightly, which only set me off again.

This time when he left me, I didn't move. I slipped right into a dreamless sleep.

But Coop was still there when Tiddles woke me in the morning. His arms around me, his cock heavy and ready against my ass. A little laugh escaped me, but he hadn't moved. Pushing the cat away, I twisted carefully, and Coop flopped on his back.

He had said he wanted everything.

Hopefully, he wouldn't mind a little happy wake up call, because I was damn curious and a little sore. Trailing my fingers down his chest, I followed them with my lips. It took some time, nuzzling around his thighs, teasing the tip just lightly before he shifted and said, "That feels fucking amazing."

What had he said the night before? "Good, I wanted you awake for this." Then I swallowed around the tip and began to work my hand at the base. It took some practice swipes and swallows, but I found a rhythm.

My only regret was it was too dark to see his face when he came. But his grip on my hair never pulled or forced, he didn't try to guide me. After, he dragged me up for a kiss and didn't seem to care about anything else.

"Best birthday ever," he whispered, and I snuggled him. We had to move soon, the cats needed breakfast, we had applications to submit, and we both had school.

But right now, it was just us, and while it hadn't been my birthday, it almost felt like it was.

An hour later, showered and dressed for school, I was halfway through a bowl of cereal when Coop let himself in the front door. He'd run home to grab his own shower and change.

"Mom said morning, by the way," he called as he went to put the key back.

Standing in the kitchen doorway, I said, "Keep the key, and please tell me your mom said that after you showered and not when you still smelled like sex?"

Because wow, had we smelled like sex. I'd even changed the bed sheets out for an older, cleaner pair 'cause after the last few days—yeah, I was going to have to get more if we were all going to be here. Laundry was once a week.

"After," he promised, then held up the key. "Are you sure?"

"Yes," I told him. "I'm sure." It wasn't like Mom was going to need it. She had her own key. "And I like the idea that you have it."

With care, he added it to his own keyring. "I'll take good care of it."

Not even a doubt in my mind.

"You ready?" He checked his watch. "Apps open in five minutes."

My nerves took off, but I nodded, even if I wasn't. "Yep. Laptop's set up. You have yours?"

He'd pulled his out and followed me into the bedroom. He grinned at the bed before he flopped down while I sat at the desk.

It could be weeks before we heard anything. The nerves weren't necessary.

Didn't quell the panic though as the clock ticked over and I reloaded the application page to see it ready for me to fill out.

"Hey, Frankie," Coop said, and I glanced at him. "Knock 'em dead. You got this."

Thank god he believed it, because that confidence boosted me. I smiled. "You too. They'd be idiots to turn down someone as awesome as you."

He winked. While the nerves didn't vanish, they did abate some.

College applications, here we come.

The Lonesome Road

Archie

Muriel's in town. I'm keeping an eye on her tonight.

Jake

I can go over again.

Coop

Aren't you working?

Jake

Yep. But I'll cut it so I'm there with take out when she gets off.

Coop

Sounds good. I'm going to work late, lemme know if it changes.

Bubba

I can go, if you guys can't.

Jake

You planning on sleeping over?

Archie

Maybe not the best idea B. She's still a little raw.

Bubba

I've tried talking to her.

Coop

You need more than 'hey.'

Archie

Sing her another song.

Jake

Or try an actual apology. But I got it tonight.

Later...

Coop

I'm picking up the supplies tomorrow.

Jake

You know everything we need?

Coop

Yeah, looked it up on YouTube.

Jake

LOL. Sry. Just funny.

Archie

Can't be that hard.

Coop

Dude, I dare you to watch the video and tell me that.

Jake

LOL My mom said she'd help.

Archie

I still think we can just buy one.

Jake

I'm with Coop on this.

Coop

We make it, it's special.

Archie

We buy it, it's still special

Jake

Suck it up

Coop

Come on, it'll be fun.

Archie

Fine, send me the damn video. If I can build a robot, how hard can a mum be?

Still later…

Bubba

You got a minute?

Coop

Just waiting to pick up this last order. It's late, dude.

Bubba

Yep. Earlier… you guys are making her mum for Homecoming?

Coop

That's the plan

Bubba

Is one of you taking her?

Coop

All of us are.

Bubba

What?

Coop

We're not playing swap the date. But she wants the whole high school dance experience. Getting a limo and going. All of us. It'll be a group thing.

Bubba

…

Coop

You should come.

Bubba

How does that work?

Coop

It doesn't unless you try.

Bubba

How is she? I barely get to talk to her and I'm worried.

Coop

It's been almost a week since her mom moved out and the shrew hasn't said a word to her. How do you think she is?

Bubba

I haven't told my dad.

Coop

Good. Don't. We're rotating who stays so she isn't alone.

Bubba

Archie said he covered her rent.

Coop

Yeah, he's gonna tell her that after Homecoming.

Bubba

I'll be there for Homecoming. Should I get myself there or join you guys in the limo?

Coop

Excellent. I'd say limo, BUT we'll talk to the guys first. I want Frankie comfortable.

Later...

Archie

Hey F. Got a sec?

Jake

She's in the shower.

Bubba

Thanks

Jake

Everything okay?

Bubba

Hope so.

Jake

Cool. Crashing soon.

Bubba

Friday's gonna be a bitch.

Jake

LOL at least we're both playing

Bubba

Coach didn't have much of a choice.

Jake

No complaints here. 3 weeks out is enough for me.

Later...

Frankie

Hey, sorry, was in the shower

Ian

That's what Jake said.

Frankie

What's up?

Ian

Think you could listen to a song?

Frankie

...

...

...

Ian

It's okay if you can't.

Frankie

... I can listen. I've always listened.

Jake

It might be tmrw, is that cool?

Ian

When you can.

Frankie

Got it. Is it for audition?

Ian

No, I sent those already. You saved me with those. This is for you.

Frankie

...

...

...

Ian

Night, F. Sleep well.

Chapter Eighteen
WHAT ARE YOU WILLING TO LOSE?

"So," Rachel said, ignoring the guys as she dragged a chair over and slid into the narrow space between me and Coop. "Tomorrow… we need a plan."

With a roll of his eyes, Coop scooted over, and I grinned. Jake stared at Rachel like she'd sprouted a second head, but Archie just groaned and sank down in his own chair. None of them really liked Rachel and they wouldn't pretend otherwise, but they also hadn't been complaining about her at all over the last few days as she made excuses to drop by our table most mornings.

Ian didn't react either way; he just took a drink of his coffee and studied us. He'd been stealing looks at me since Jake, Coop, and I got here. What he hadn't asked was had I listened to the song he sent me the night before.

For now, I focused on Rachel. "I have a plan. Marsha made an appointment for me to get my hair and makeup done."

"And I got us mani/pedis lined up," Cheryl announced as she dragged a chair over to join us. With a sigh, Jake kicked his chair out and moved over to sit on the other side of the table next to Ian.

"What time are we picking you up?" Cheryl said. "And you should bring your dress and everything, we'll all get ready together, and then Bubba can pick you up. Wait…you got a limo, right? If not, I'm sure Mitch won't mind, and then we could all go together…"

Panic flowered in my gut. I hadn't actually told Cheryl that Ian wasn't taking me.

"Actually," Rachel said. "We can't all get ready together. Mani/pedis are in the morning, then Frankie's hair and makeup is later in the day, and we're going to a different place."

"Aww," Cheryl pouted, but I could have kissed Rachel, and she winked at me. "Well, Rach, who are you taking? Or are they taking you? You could double with us?"

"I'd sooner drink drain cleaner than ride with Mitch," Rachel told her. "Besides, I'll pick my own date up, thanks."

With a real pout, Cheryl propped her chin on her fist. "Fine, what about after party?" She scanned the guys and fixed on Ian. "What are yours and Frankie's post dance plans?"

The silence hit the table like a lead balloon, not that Cheryl noticed. For his part, Ian shrugged and said, "We made other plans." Relief swarmed me. He could have called out the fact he wasn't taking me. He could have said any number of things.

But he had my back. After Cheryl flicked her fingers at him like she could erase his comment and latched her focus on Jake, I mouthed 'thank you' to him, and he gave me the barest nod.

"What about you Jake? Who are you taking?"

"Going stag," Jake said easily. "We're not making any plans. Just going to do what we feel like doing."

Next to me, Rachel snorted and I elbowed her, so she gave me teasing grin.

"Oh, I hate you all," Cheryl complained, then leaned her head against my shoulder. "You could change his mind right? Or theirs? This is our last Homecoming! The last one we'll celebrate all together. We need to make it memorable."

Guilt clawed at me because it fell right in line with my desire to do all the things senior year. Not that my version of all the things had gone anywhere in the vicinity of what I'd hoped for. In fact, if there were a GPS program for what I'd wanted the year to be, I was pretty sure it rerouted to some alternate routes without letting me know ahead of time.

A flick of a look toward Archie, then Coop, and finally Jake and Ian earned me three slight headshakes and one faintly worried look. Then again, Coop only gave me the head's up this morning that Ian wanted to ride with us. But he and Jake both said it was up to me. Considering they probably ran it by Archie—a part of me would die to be a fly on the wall of those conversations, even if the rest of me would likely die if I was a fly on the wall—I appreciated the fact they solicited my input.

"We'll see," I told Cheryl finally, and Archie made a choking noise.

"Don't die, asshat, you'll ruin our weekend plans," Rachel deadpanned. "Well, not mine."

Flipping her off, Archie took another drink of his coffee. "Are we almost done with the estrogen portion of the morning? We want our Frankie back."

"You boys get her every damn day, you need to learn to share." Rachel smirked, then nudged me. "I'll text you the mani/pedi time and place. Why don't you meet us so someone can't hold you hostage?"

"I'm not going to hold her hostage," Cheryl argued. "I just want to do it all right. And you two should get to the dance early so we can get pictures, too. Not just the couple pictures, but all of us girls."

"We'll get pictures," I promised. "Whether we're early or not, unless you think Mitch isn't going to let you get off the dance floor."

Cheryl grinned. "Maybe I won't let him get off the dance floor, think about that!" Despite her protests, she rose and followed Rachel, pausing to say,

"Don't be late!"

Behind her, Rachel made a face, and I laughed.

"So," Coop said idly. "What time are the mani/pedis? When do you have to get your hair and makeup done?" When I glanced at him, mischief danced in his eyes. "Because we need to make sure we do all the pictures, the before, the during, the after…"

Snagging one of the donut holes from the bag, I threw it at him, and he caught it with a grin. "Thank you."

Archie chuckled. "Though that's a good point, what time will you be done with hair and makeup?" Then he made a face. "It's like it's contagious."

"We'll get you a training bra," Jake told him. "We already scheduled the car to pick us up at Frankie's at six-thirty. Don't be a shit."

I laughed because Archie flicked a donut hole at Jake this time, and he caught it easily, then popped it in his mouth and chewed with a smirk. Over the last week, his and Ian's bruises had gone through a riot of shades, they were still pretty green and yellow in places, but the worst of it had begun to fade.

They'd also done two more "meetings" with Diane, and Jake said it was going well. For that, I was glad. All of us talked more—well, I talked more with Archie about our parents and the fact that he had a locksmith come change the locks on the apartment. He gave me a new set of keys, and then I divided them up—one for him, Coop, and for Jake. There was an extra that he'd probably meant for Ian, or maybe just so I had a spare. I stored it—for now.

While I hadn't talked to Ian about the song, I'd listened to it while I went through the mail in my backpack. Coop had collected the mail the day before, and it reminded me of the letters I'd stuffed in there.

Two of them had just been standard college recruiting letters. The third one had been different. It was an offer, handwritten note included, to visit NYU and to apply. I was considered a great candidate apparently. The recruiter included the schools at the university he thought I'd enjoy and asked me to call if I'd like to schedule a visit.

NYU hadn't been on my list. Coop had brought it up. I hadn't told the guys about it yet. Archie also made calls and got me an appointment with his attorney. He'd taken me to see him right after school on Tuesday, so I'd had to let Ian know I couldn't hang out with him that evening.

While that relieved me of the awkwardness of trying to talk out this "just friends" state we were in, it had been hard to miss his disappointment. Mr. Wittaker was an attorney for Archie's family. The potential for conflict of interest had given him pause, but as far as I knew, Mom hadn't married Mr. Standish yet. They couldn't—thankfully—get married legally. My issue was with her, not Mr. Standish—legally. I had plenty of issues with Archie's dad, and so did he.

After consideration, Mr. Wittaker asked me to detail how often my mother had been absent in the last twelve months, and it was easier to remember when she was home versus when she wasn't. Then he asked me a lot of hard questions, including questions about my job, rent, bills, and how did I expect to make ends meet. I told him everything, including the fact I had a scholarship. That I'd applied for others, and I had plans for college. I'd submitted my application to five schools, but only one was my top pick.

After all of that, he agreed to represent me. I signed the paperwork, and Archie gave him a check Jeremy had written for the retainer. It was a few more zeroes than I was comfortable with.

We argued all the way back to my place about it, but eventually, I agreed. Mr. Wittaker had told me the process could take a while, and that I needed to be prepared I could hit eighteen before it happened. Well, if it did, I'd still be free. The other concern was technically, her moving out constituted abandonment, and that could raise some red flags with Child Protective Services. At seventeen, it wasn't likely they'd try to force me into the system, but we also couldn't discount it.

So, I had Mr. Wittaker's cell number as well as his office phone. I was to call him if *anything* came up. In the meanwhile, he also wanted a full accounting of any bills I had to pay, even if it was just groceries.

Since submitting my college apps ate up nearly a grand in application fees, he wanted those records, too.

"Hey," Archie bumped my foot with his, and I blinked to find all four of them staring at me. "You good?"

"I'm good," I assured him. "Just got a lot on my mind. Two tests today, and the big game tonight."

"You do not have to come," Jake told me.

"Yes, I do," I said. "I'll sit there and have hot dogs and nachos while Coop and Archie give me all wrong answers on what's happening on the field. It'll be a blast."

"You don't even like football," Jake said.

"I like you."

He grinned, and Coop chuckled. "Ha, she got you there."

"Yes, she does."

"I like you, too," I reminded Ian when he'd begun to bore holes in the table with his stare. At the faint surprise on his face, I shifted my attention back to Jake. "Besides, it's an important game for you guys."

"It's a really unimportant game," Jake countered. "We're not going to make State unless we pull a miracle out of our butts. That said, you wanna show up and root for us, I'm all for it. Just don't get too bored."

"She won't," Archie said, and tossed me the last donut hole. I actually managed to catch this one with my mouth, and they all cheered. It only took four years. But hey, a girl's gotta have some skills, right?

"Ugh," Coop said as he sat forward, and his chair thumped. "Incoming."

I glanced over my shoulder, tracking Sharon and Patty's ballistic approach. Well, maybe not ballistic. Sharon had avoided me all week, and by avoided, I meant if I was in the bathroom, she turned around and left as soon as she saw me.

Good times.

"Bubba," Patty said after dismissing me with a look. I didn't really care. Sharon's eyes narrowed on me briefly, and then she fixed her attention on Bubba.

"What?" he asked, his tone dead neutral.

"We need to have one more meeting for the parade tomorrow—"

"Nope."

"I wasn't asking you," Patty said. "I'm telling you. One last meeting to go over everything…"

"I got that, and I'm still saying nope. I have two big tests today and a game tonight. I'm not spending my lunch hour listening to you two haggle over whether a float should pause for two seconds or five as they first come out, or if the band should alternate their pace, or if we should redecorate the car when the decorations are already done. If you want to do that—knock yourselves out. I did what Coach asked, and I've got other things to do."

"So," Jake said, slinging an arm over Ian's shoulders. "You two can move along now. Buh bye."

Patty's whole expression tightened. "You do realize this is our very last Homecoming…"

"Can't get here soon enough so it's over and done with," Ian muttered, and switched his attention to me. A frown tightened his brow. "I didn't mean it like that."

"I know." Despite the rest of it, that I did know. He'd meant it when he asked me. The care he'd taken with the ask revealed that, even if nothing else did. Maybe we weren't going as a date anymore, but that part I had no trouble believing. He just wanted to be out of the planning committee, and since they'd met at lunch every single day this week, I couldn't blame him.

Sharon almost vibrated with the urge to say something, but I just waited and sipped my coffee. With a scoff, she pivoted on her heel and marched away.

"If this goes wrong, I'm not at all averse to throwing you under the bus," Patty stated coolly. "This parade is important to everyone."

"Sounds like a plan," Ian told her, and then she threw her hands up and followed after Sharon.

"Wow," Coop said. "It's about time you cut the cord there, Bubba."

"Yeah, bite me," Ian said, rubbing his face and then wincing as if he'd half-forgotten the still fading bruises. "I couldn't take another minute of those discussions. I could feel my brain cells dying."

A giggle escaped me as Archie snorted, and even Coop started laughing.

"Well," Jake said with genuine sympathy. "Let's hope that's the end of your brain damage."

They shared a look that I didn't try to interpret as I gathered my stuff. The bell would ring any minute. I was ready for Friday to be over, and we'd barely gotten started.

The guys still walked me between classes, even Ian. He walked me to French every day after calculus. Only today, he kept brushing my arm with his. Part of it might be the test we'd just had. I had a headache after it just from the sheer number of problems.

"You okay?" I asked when he bumped me for the third time. He wasn't a careless kind of guy, so either he wasn't paying attention or he wanted my attention.

Which ever it was, we were almost to French.

"Did Coop talk to you?"

"He talks to me everyday." About a lot of things.

"About Homecoming tomorrow."

Ah. Whether I minded if Ian rode with us. One thing that had stood out in all of this, the guys had their own opinions, but they weren't trying to get me to agree or disagree. Ultimately, Archie said as he summed it up, the final decision was mine.

We were all going together. No "official" date, but unofficially, they were all going to be the date. We'd even do a group picture.

A part of me wanted to tell Ian no, he should come separately. That had been what he wanted, after all. To not make me choose. Yet, here I was, having to choose.

Friends.

We were friends.

"Of course you can," I told him lightly. "The guys know all the details. But, it's our last Homecoming so—yeah, I'm okay if you ride with us. We should go." It had always been the five of us, and if the guys could hold onto their friendship with Ian, I had to encourage it. I didn't want to lose him either, even if it was all so strained now.

"You sure?" He paused us a couple of feet from the door and tugged me over to the lockers. The warmth of his fingers on my arm sent a shiver through me. "It's okay to tell me no."

I snorted. "Thanks for your permission, I know it's okay. You also said we're going to be friends."

He winced and then let me go. "I really cannot seem to not stick my foot in my mouth where you're concerned." The frustration in his voice pulled a reluctant smile from me.

"Well, at least you know you're flexible."

Chuckling, he grinned at me. "Thank you for that mental image."

"You're welcome. Now go away, I have class and so do you."

His grin widened a fraction, and one of the rocks in my gut eased off. It was probably the most normal conversation we'd had since he'd walked out of my apartment two weeks earlier.

I let Coop know when I got to lit, and he studied me for a beat before he said, "Okay."

The weirdest part about the shifting dynamics between all of us, my relationship with Coop seemed the least affected. I mean, don't get me wrong, he was a hell of a kisser and I adored making out with him. When he spent the night, which he'd done twice since his birthday, he proved to have a hedonistic side I'd never expected. Yet, we were always laughing and teasing.

At the end of the day, he was still Coop. Jake and Archie were in their own ways very possessive. Archie had a tendency to just take over and try to solve a problem, Jake got protective. While they'd always been like that, it magnified now.

Honestly, I was grateful for all of them. I hadn't spoken to Mom since she left, and I didn't want to. As he'd stated, Archie's dad had his assistant send me their new address and the details on the fancy new car he'd purchased.

They'd even enclosed attached photos of the car and what would be my room.

I deleted the email. Then undeleted it.

When I deleted it a third time, Archie had forwarded it to himself and then said, "Now delete it. I have a copy for the attorney, and you don't need to stare at it."

His mom was back in town, too.

Fun. I would just avoid his place for a while, and he was spending a lot of time at mine. The guys had actually asked me if I wanted them to empty out the furniture in Mom's room.

It had only been a week.

There was still a chance she would come back. Were she and Archie's dad really gonna keep this going?

One of our tests was in lit and it was another essay, so I dragged my mind to the present and focused on it. By the time our hour was up, my brain was mush.

"Food," Coop said. "Caffeine. Maybe a sledgehammer to hit myself with."

Chuckling, I slid my backpack on. "It might feel good after that."

"Agreed."

"You two are hilarious," Ms. Fajardo called, and we both grinned at her. "But may I borrow you for a minute, Frankie?"

Coop followed me up there as the room emptied of kids heading to lunch.

"Frankie, Coop," Ms. Fajardo told him lightly. "You can wait for her in the hall."

"It's okay," I told him and her for that matter. "I don't mind if he hears."

"Well, then you can tell him after. Off with you, Mister."

With a roll of his eyes, Coop rubbed my arm. "I'll be outside the door, and I'll text the guys. Pizza for lunch?"

"Works for me." At the moment, I'd eat just about anything. Hamburgers included. I was starving. I'd worked late last night 'cause of a rush and the fact that I had Saturday off. I needed to figure out a way to work in more hours.

As soon as the door closed, Ms. Fajardo beckoned me over to her desk. "All right, I'll make this quick, but…I have an opportunity I think you would be perfect for…"

"Me?"

"Yes," she said, and then turned her monitor so I could read the screen. The website for Compass Reach was on the screen. "Do you know about this program?"

"Never heard of it."

"For the last twenty-five years, they've been providing first generation, college-bound high school students with an intensive experience that focuses on skill development and personal growth with the goal of preparing them for college, career and civic life. Students don't apply, they're nominated. I spoke to Madame and to Ms. Costgrove…"

"Ms. Costgrove?" She'd been my humanities teacher for two years.

"Yes, we all agreed you were the best candidate and the one most likely to benefit, so we all nominated you and Mr. Fulton, the assistant principal sponsored the nomination."

"Wow…thank you." I wasn't quite sure what to do with this. "When do we find out?"

"Well, they'll notify us of the exact grant right before winter break, but you're a finalist, so you're in."

Wait. What?

"If you accept, you're increasing your workload. You'll have interactive seminars all through the spring, one day a week. We'll work it out so you will be technically studying off-campus on those days. Once the spring is over, you'll qualify for one of their paid summer internships at a law firm or a non-profit or even a government agency."

Dazed, I stared at her. "But I'm not studying law. Or…government." Well I was, but only the requirement.

"No, but you're a gifted linguist and translators are always in demand. You're very savvy and you're a skilled writer. You can learn the other stuff, but this type of internship is also going to reflect well on your college applications, and I got the notice of your apps going in and I'm writing my recommendations this weekend."

My stomach bottomed out as my heart slammed against my ribs. This was a lot.

"I plan on mentioning you're a finalist in this."

"Wow… I still don't know what to say."

"You don't have say anything, I'm thrilled for you. The only thing you're going to need is to get your mother to sign permission for you to attend the seminars so we can adjust your schedule and everything else is covered. There's no expense."

She was so utterly thrilled for me, I couldn't wreck it, even as she put a nail in the coffin of the plan. Mr. Wittaker said it could take months to sort out the emancipation. If I wanted to do this, I'd have to ask Mom or give it up.

"Tell you what, I know this is a crazy weekend. So you think about it, I'll send copies of this over to your school email. Read up and then talk to me next week with your questions, okay?"

"Sure… Thank you, Ms. Farjardo."

Her smile grew. "You're very welcome, Frankie. You're a talented student and I can't wait to see what you do."

It was an amazing opportunity. But at least one day a week? I'd be doubling up my workload, and I'd have to compensate with my hours at Mason's, not to mention the guys. Coop was waiting for me when I came out, and he studied me.

"Good news? Bad news?"

"I don't know what to do with it news," I admitted. On one level, it was awesome, and on another, it was gut wrenching. Without Mom's approval, I'd have to turn it down, disappointing my teachers who'd done this for me.

"Tell me?" Coop invited as we headed down to the doors for the parking lot.

I did, even if I had to repeat it when we got to the car.

The stunned look he wore matched how I felt. "That's really awesome, but your mom has to sign off on it?"

"Yeah," I admitted. I could ask her. What was the worst thing she'd say? No? "But I don't want to ask her."

"We'll figure something out," Coop said with such firm and steady faith, I almost believed him.

"Or maybe we won't."

"Nope," he said. "We will. You watch."

I laughed. He grinned.

"Much better," he said. "Chin up, keep smiling. We've got this."

No, we didn't. But I had him, and the others were already in Jake's SUV waiting, even if Archie was hanging out of the back passenger side window like a corpse.

"He died of hunger," Ian explained in a dry tone as we got close, and I chuckled again.

I had all of them.

Well…most anyway.

Chapter Nineteen
THE HEART BRINGS YOU BACK

Awareness drifted in as warmth settled in behind me and wrapped an arm around my middle. The light press of a kiss below my ear made me smile.

"Morning," I mumbled, and Coop chuckled.

"Morning, go back to sleep." He dragged the covers up, and I yawned. Even tucked securely against him, I tried to rouse. "I fed the cats, they're happy."

Oh, then I didn't have to.

"Shut up," Jake mumbled, and reached past me to thump Coop. "She was asleep."

"Jerk," Coop mumbled, and I opened my eyes in time to see Jake smirking.

"You're only saying that because you're hiding behind her." Then his gaze dipped to mine, and he brushed my cheek with a finger. "Shh, he's right—go back to sleep. We don't have to be anywhere for hours."

There was homework. Chores. Work…

Oh, wait, I didn't have work today. I burrowed again and pressed a hand against Jake's chest. Somehow, we'd all piled onto the bed and slept after watching the worst movie I'd ever seen.

"I'm glad you won your game," I mumbled. "That was a very good catch thingy before you slid home."

Coop pressed his face against my hair, as if that would muffle his laughter.

"Thanks, baby girl. Thanks for being a cheerleader."

I snorted. Though, I had worn one of Jake's old football jerseys and painted school colors on my cheeks. Archie and Coop had found it hilarious. Then they fed me plenty of hot dogs and nachos while they made up stories about alien invaders and the resistance to fill in my knowledge gaps about the game.

"You're not going back to sleep, are you?"

When I cracked my eyes open, Jake had rolled onto his side and studied me. Between the stubble, the disheveled hair, bruises, and pillow wrinkles on his cheek, he seemed the perfectly rumpled rogue. I liked it—well, everything except the bruises. With care, I traced my fingers against the green discoloration still marring his cheek.

"Stop worrying about it," he murmured. "It's fine."

"I just hate the idea that you and Ian were fighting." I didn't like it when Jake was in any fight.

"Well, not a fan, but if he's gonna be a dumbass then he gets what gets." Dragging his thumb across my lower lip, he said, "Don't worry about it, baby girl. Today is all about the dance."

I snorted and shifted, but Coop tightened his arm around my middle. "What happened to going back to sleep?" Despite the hint of grumpiness in his words, no trace of it echoed in his voice.

"Well," I offered. "I'm not getting up."

"Good." The word echoed from both of them, and I laughed. It was barely light outside. We had time.

"I don't have to be at the nail place until ten, I think, or ten-thirty." It was on my phone. Rachel had made the reservations and sent me the address. Her running interference for me with Cheryl helped. "What are you guys going to do today?”

“Shower,” Jake said.

“Shave,” Coop tacked on.

“Probably get something to eat,” Jake continued.

“Then you know, maybe watch a game before we have to go put on the suits.”

“Guy spa day.” The smirk on Jake’s face grew. “Gotta get all pretty for our girl.”

A snicker escaped. “Are you guys going to braid each other’s hair and do your nails?”

“Fuck no,” Jake said with a snort. “Probably tell dirty jokes and then compete to see who gets to ask you for the first dance.”

“Oh, damn,” Coop said, thrusting out his fist. “Rock-Paper-Scissors? We decide now, we have the fifty-fifty on that, and Archie and Bubba have to wait.”

Amusement filled Jake’s eyes as he lifted his fist. “I like this plan.”

“It is kind of cheating,” I pointed out, and received a matching pair of “So?” for my trouble.

Wiggling a little, I rolled onto my back and then watched as they rocked their fists three times, and Coop did rock but Jake did scissors.

“Dammit,” Jake said with a scowl. “You *always* do paper.”

“I know,” Coop said smugly. “That’s why I did rock. I get the first dance.”

Laughter swelled up in me. “It’s fine, Jake gets the second.”

“Then Archie and Bubba can fight it out for third,” Coop suggested before settling his hand on my stomach.

“Nope,” Jake said. “Archie gets the third dance, and if Bubba wants one, he can ask.”

Coop sighed, but another one of those wordless conversations seemed to pass through them.

“Guys?” At my question, they both focused on me. “What’s going on?”

“With what?” The too innocent look didn’t fool me.

"Coop."

He sighed, then flicked a look at Jake. "You told Bubba you didn't mind if he rode with us tonight."

"I did…is that a problem?" They had left it to me, right?

"No," Jake said softly. "It's not a problem. But neither of us want you to feel like you have to do something. The thing with Bubba is…"

"Messy," Coop supplied. "You haven't really talked about it."

I shrugged. "What is there to talk about?" If we were going to talk about this, I needed to get up. Before I could do more than shift, Jake pressed a hand to my shoulder.

"Hey, it's us. We get it. Bubba was an idiot. Then you broke up with him."

"I know," I said, trying not to snap. "I was there." Then my mother moved out. I'd had a great week. Just when I thought it was as bad as it was going to get, something else happened. I didn't want to even look forward to Homecoming, despite the guys' attempts to make it awesome. They were doing everything right, but my luck seemed to wax and wane between wow, they all like me and it feels good to be with them, to wow, my mom and everyone else hates me and my life was imploding around me.

Not really a win-win.

"Frankie," Coop said, rising on his elbow so he could meet my gaze. "Whether you want to talk about it or not—and yes, I'd prefer you not sit on the things hurting you anymore." The knowing look in his eyes was hard to avoid. "You also have a lot of crap you've been dealing with. Our job is to make it easier, period."

"That means," Jake said, picking up the thread. "We aren't letting anyone do anything you don't want to do. Bubba's my friend—our friend—no lie. He can be your friend and you can be his, whatever you want. But you don't have to do a damn thing you don't want to do."

"So, if you're uncomfortable," Coop tacked on. "Then you tell him no, and we're one hundred percent on your side."

It was terrifically sweet, and my eyes burned a little. "He's your friend, too."

"He is," Jake said with a nod. "You're more."

A shiver worked its way along my spine.

"Dance with him. Don't dance with him. Take a picture. Talk to him. Whatever you want, but if you don't, then no one is making you." For a minute, he lifted his gaze from me to focus on Coop. "No one."

"Agreed," Coop said after a few seconds. That came out a little more reluctant than his earlier statement.

"But you don't agree," I called him on it, and Coop caught my hand and pulled it up to kiss.

"Yes, I do. I just…I feel for Bubba. Doesn't mean I don't think he was an idiot. 'Cause trust me, I told him he needed to get his head out of his ass. At the same time, he's human. He screwed up. At the heart of it, I know it's because he cares about you."

"He just has a really shitty way of showing it," Jake argued. "And we're done with that pressuring."

"He's not pressuring me," I scolded Jake. This time when I tried to sit up, neither of them stopped me. Leaning back against the headboard, I stared at my room. "I don't know what I feel about Ian. It's…a lot harder to just be his friend than I thought it would be."

"Give yourself time," Jake suggested.

"Rachel said the same thing."

"Woah," Coop twisted as he sat up. "You talked to Rachel about this?"

"Yeah…some of it, anyway. Last week, after I broke up with him and then on Sunday when she and I went to get coffee after work." I'd been a little late getting home.

"How much did you tell her?" Worry filled Jake's eyes.

"A lot, but I trust her," I told them both. "She's not going to throw it out like gossip for consumption. She's been—pretty awesome, actually." From Mr.

Thorns, my mysterious admirer, to Rachel, my friend. It had been an interesting transformation considering our previous love/hate relationship.

Coop and Jake looked at each other again.

"Stop it." It was kind of funny, but I really was beginning to recognize the look for 'protect Frankie' they shared periodically. While it used to be annoying, it was becoming kind of endearing, if a little frustrating. "Rachel figured it out before I did that you guys all liked me. She also figured out that I was having trouble with it."

"In all fairness, baby girl, everyone knew before you did." Jake spread his hands like what was he going to do.

I settled for flipping him off, and he grinned. "My point," I continued, "is she's my friend, someone I can talk to, and it helps."

"You can talk to us, you know," Coop reminded me. A note of reproach crept into his tone, and hurt flashed in his eyes.

"Of course I can," I told him. "Don't be a dork."

He straightened.

"Seriously, I know I can talk to you guys. But the thing is...it's hard to talk to you about each other." I chewed at my lower lip. "It was different before. If Archie said something stupid, or Coop was driving me nuts with his mothering…"

He opened his mouth to protest but shut up as Jake shook his head once.

"Or even if I wanted to smack you for being so possessive and acting like a jerk to anyone who wanted to talk to me when you were there." The last bit I directed at Jake. Who for his part, just shrugged. "It was different when we were just friends."

"We're still friends," Coop said.

"But we're also more," Jake conceded. "You need a friend."

Coop groaned. "That friend has to be Rachel?"

"Well, at the moment, yes. One, because I like Rachel. She's sharp, acerbic, insightful—and she doesn't judge me." Right now, that was really important. "She's been on my side when the other crap happened. She did the whole flowers thing because she wanted me to have something to smile about." I'd really enjoyed the roses.

"The flowers you wanted to be from us," Jake grunted.

"Yes. Two, Rachel's on my side, at least where the other girls are concerned." She'd clapped back at Patty, snarked at Sharon, and pretty much given hell to anyone looking at me sideways. "Three, she was there for me at the party after everything went sideways."

Coop sighed, but he didn't argue the point.

"Four, she has a thing for you," Jake pointed out.

"Yes and no," I corrected. "She kind of hoped I'd be into girls, but even if I'm not, she still thought I could use a friend, and I think she needs one, too. Though, honestly she's surrounded by other girls so maybe not. Maybe I'm just the lucky one. But there's another big point in her favor."

"That is?" Coop asked, skeptical.

"In no world has she had sex with any of you or been a part of your points game."

They both winced, then Jake sighed. "Fine, you win."

I laughed. "It's not about winning or losing, I promise. I'm—coping with the whole points thing. But it's kind of nice to know someone who hasn't wanted to be right where I am now."

"I get that," Coop said slowly. "Sorta. 'Course, the fact she's someone who wants to be where we are…kind of shoe on the other foot."

"But I never had sex with her," I countered, and he raised his hands. "Guys, I adore you. I do, and you've been rocks through all of this. But you're also friends too, and those friendships are important to me." It was why I didn't complain that Jake and Ian seemed to be working at mending fences. "But if I'm unhappy, and I complain about not understanding Ian, or why he…why he would tell me one thing and act a completely different way. Why I had to break up with him because I don't have the bandwidth for the push/pull game, and I won't be the person who makes him miserable, and at the same time, I don't know how I can be his friend when…" When I'd wanted more. "I just sound like a selfish bitch, and why should I be complaining when I have all of you?"

"First of all," Jake said, sliding an arm under my legs and lifting me until he plopped me on his lap and my legs were across Coop's. "You're not a selfish bitch, and never say that again. Clear?" The snap in his voice matched the irritation flaring in his eyes. "You are *not* any kind of bitch. If you think I'll let you say what I'd break some other asshole's jaw for saying, you're wrong."

When I turned wide eyes on Coop, he gave me a wry smile. "What he said, only with slightly less violence."

"You'd punch any asshole who called her a bitch."

"I would," Coop agreed. "But not with the kind of ferocity you would. That's why you're the guy who beats people up, and I'm the diplomat."

A giggle-snort escaped, and they both grinned at me. Sobering, Jake continued, "As for the rest of it, baby girl. You made your feelings clear about not wanting to screw up our friendships, but that's not all on you."

"No," Coop said slowly. "That's on us. Me. Archie. Jake. Bubba. If we can't talk to each other or you, there's an issue. We all know, we're all being honest here, and if we can't or if one of us can't, it's not just you they're going to hurt."

"But hurting you is a no-fly zone," Jake said firmly. "If you need a friend to bitch to about all of us, then go for it. If you need that, I'm never going to say no. I might be a little jealous." The admission made him grimace. "I like being the guy you can say anything to, no matter how blunt."

"And I'm the guy who listens," Coop said. "Just like Archie likes being the one who swoops in to fix stuff."

Jake grunted. "He really likes fixing everything."

Like getting Coop a car or changing the locks on my apartment.

"The point is, beautiful," Coop circled back around. "If Bubba hurt you, we do want to know. Part of being boyfriends is protecting our girl."

Boyfriends.

Licking my lips, I tried not to focus too much on the shivery goodness that being called their girl evoked. Instead, I said, "Mathieu called you guys my boyfriends from the very beginning. I thought he was crazy…but he saw it, too."

Boyfriends. Multiple.

"Okay, so maybe Frenchy had one redeeming quality," Jake grunted. Coop grinned, amusement and affection twined in his smile. In some ways, the whole conversation was both bizarre and utterly normal.

Just like waking up to both of them. There hadn't been any sex the night before—making out, yes—but no sex. We'd all been tired after the game, especially Jake. We'd gone out for food and to celebrate, then Archie and Ian had gone to their own homes while Jake and Coop came back here.

"I like this," I told them.

"Good," Coop said, then narrowed the distance and kissed me. I tried not to breathe out 'cause morning breath was totally a thing. Jake tightened his arms around me as Coop toyed at deepening the kiss. Hint of nervous tension wound in my gut. The minute Coop eased up, Jake tilted my head back, and I barely had a second to draw a breath before he kissed me, too. The tension ratcheted higher, and my nipples ached as I fisted his hair with one hand, though Coop slotted his fingers through my other hand, palm to palm as Jake's tongue swirled against mine, and I forgot all about morning breath.

Dragging his head back, Jake said, "Damn." There was stiffness beneath my ass, and the boxers Coop had on did nothing to his own erection. Coop's lower lip was wet like he kept licking it, and Jake dug his fingers into my side.

Dragging his gaze from me to Jake, Coop's expression shifted minutely as his eyebrows raised. A harsh exhale from Jake, and the need shifting in my blood heated.

I wanted…

A door closed beyond my room and apprehension swarmed through me, even as Coop and Jake snapped their attention to my open bedroom door and the hallway beyond.

"You lazy bastards better be dressed…" Archie called. "Frankie, you feel free to stay naked. But I come bearing coffee and breakfast."

Relief swamped me, and they each blew out equally ragged breaths. Disappointment flashed across Coop's face so quickly, I had to wonder if I'd imagined it.

"To be continued, baby girl," Jake said against my ear. "To be continued. Go shower." He lifted me off of him and gave me a swat on the ass. The sting helped with the kaleidoscope of butterflies breaking loose between the tension of a few minutes earlier and Archie's arrival.

At the doorway, I glanced at them both. "We're good, right?"

"Better," Coop assured me.

"Hell yes," Jake said. "Go on, or Archie will threaten to drink your coffee."

"No I won't," Archie said from right behind me, and I gave a little start, laughing as he turned me around and then pinned me to the wall for a kiss. Holy hell.

Every single engine revved at the affection pouring off these guys, and from behind me, came Coop's soft curse and Jake's exhaled *fuck*…

Melting into Archie's hold, I groaned as he eased back. Shivers eddied through me as the want from earlier intensified. "Good morning kisses are definitely the way to go," he said, then pressed another kiss to my nose. "Go shower. Coffee and food will be waiting for you."

I took a good long look at him. He'd showered and shaved from how soft his cheeks were, and his dark brown eyes gleamed. Despite it all, Archie looked happy.

"Everything good with you?" I checked, smoothing my hands over his shirt. He'd gone home because his mother was in town, and he just wanted to keep an eye on her. Apparently, his dad hadn't bothered to inform him of his move, not that Archie was surprised.

'Eddie' was such a dick.

He treated his son like crap.

Muriel didn't seem much better, but Archie wasn't sure what she knew or didn't. Jeremy had been tight-lipped on the subject, but then, Jeremy protected all their secrets. So Archie respected the stance he'd taken, even if he'd complained to me privately.

"She was on the phone with friends. They're planning a cruise so, yes, everything is about to be great." He gave me another kiss. "Soon as she's gone, you and me, slumber party."

I doubted we'd get much sleep at said party, but no complaints from me. I hugged him. "I'll just be a few minutes."

"Take your time," he murmured, giving me a squeeze.

I both wanted the shower and I didn't want to leave them in the same breath. We'd always been close, but they were so far under my skin at this point, I didn't even mind that they'd gone out of their way to try and make sure I wasn't alone.

The rides to school. Walking between classes. Sleepovers. Lock changes. Text messages.

Inside the bathroom, I closed the door.

Sex.

Lots of sex.

The weird part was you'd think as often as I got to have it, I wouldn't actively be sitting there wanting more. But we'd been too tired the night before and now?

I had to go all day.

Closing my eyes, I leaned against the wood and concentrated on taking slow, deep breaths. It was such a long way until tonight.

With that thought in mind, I made it a cold shower.

They sucked.

But it did the trick, at least until I came out and found all three of them in the kitchen, Jake and Coop shirtless as they drank their coffee, and Archie looking like he would be right at home in a magazine.

Yep. Cold shower effort wasted.

"I'm gonna run home and shower there," Coop told me as he gave me a kiss. "Grab some clean clothes, and I'll be back."

"Ha," Jake said. "I brought a bag." He gave me another kiss on his way past.

"Muwhahahaha," Archie intoned rubbing his hands together. "Now I get you all to myself."

I giggled as he rose and pulled out a chair.

"I also brought you a surprise." The first thing was a plate he pulled out of the oven—Jeremy's French toast. Powdered sugar was in a small container and he had heated syrup. "Since you won't come to his French toast, he sent his French toast to you."

Delight curved through me.

Then he set a box down next.

"Archie, what did I say about presents?"

"That you don't need them," he told me as he reclaimed his chair after setting a fork and knife down. "Which is perfectly fine. I want to give them to you, so nyah."

Still, the French toast was amazing, and I sprinkled the powdered sugar on before I flipped open the box.

"Besides, I already gave you this once."

Inside was my charm bracelet, all the new charms in place—including a C and a J added to it and key. That was new. "When did you snitch it?" I'd had it on the night before.

He grinned. "Good night kisses are almost as fun as good morning ones."

Heat scorched my cheeks. At the restaurant, he'd kissed me pretty damn soundly against the car because he had to go. I hadn't even felt him slip the bracelet off.

Guilt stabbed at me.

"Uh uh," he said, lifting it out and snapping it on my wrist when I held it up. "It was a surprise, and Coop and Jake were under orders to distract you."

"Well, *The VelociPastor* definitely did that."

He blinked. "The what now?"

Warmth flooded beneath the delight as I studied the bracelet. The letters surprised me even more than the fact he'd taken it to add the new charms. He'd told Coop he'd have to get his own, but apparently, Archie decided to fix it himself.

They were right, Archie did want to fix everything. Catching his hand, I leaned in and kissed him. Thankfully it was a much more minty kiss following the shower and brushing my teeth.

"It's a movie," I said as I poured the syrup and grinned at him. "About a pastor who turns into a velociraptor and fights criminals and ninjas."

The words bullshit were stamped all over his expression.

"No lie," I promised him. "It was absolutely horrible in every possible wonderful way."

And I had almost as much fun telling Archie about the movie as I had watching it with Jake and Coop.

The whole time, I savored not only the most excellent French toast ever, but also Archie's expression. When Jake wandered back in, he joined me in the retelling that Coop slid in to finish as they all devoured their breakfast burritos.

My new "normal" was all kinds of strange, and right now, I didn't want it any other way.

Chapter Twenty
IF YOU WANT TO BE A GOOD GIRL…

The hot water bubbling around my feet was both weird and relaxing. Next to me, Rachel had her head tilted back and her eyes closed. The scent of roses swirled up from the water. The relaxing rose pedicure was what it was called, and Rachel grinned when she pointed it out to me. The sweet fragrance relaxed me, even if I hadn't seemed that tense when I arrived.

The door jangled as Cheryl rushed in, breathless and flushed. "Sorry, I'm late!" She had her hair stacked up on top of her head in a messy bun, wisps escaping everywhere. Like me and Rachel, she was in shorts and a t-shirt, though she had a gorgeous tan going on. I suppose I wasn't day-glo, but I hadn't spent as much time outside as the rest of them.

Rachel grinned. "Now breathe deep and just relax. We're not hurrying another part of today."

"Pfft," Cheryl said as they set up a chair on the other side of Rachel. "Says you. I still have a hundred and five things to do before tonight."

"A hundred and five?" I leaned forward to look at her. "You have your dress and accessories, you're about to do your nails. Other than hair and makeup, what's next?"

"I can't eat," Cheryl said. "I don't want anything to mess up the lines of the dress. I needed to pack an overnight bag carefully. Didn't want Mom to see it."

Yeah, I wasn't asking.

"I have to pick up a present."

A present?

The lady working on my feet tapped one of my ankles after she'd set up, and I lifted it out of the water. "Why a present?"

"'Cause Mitch went to so much trouble to ask me, and he wants to make tonight special and so do I." She let out a happy little sigh. "I never thought we'd get here after the summer, so I'm just glad he forgave me." She perused the menu and discussed what she wanted done before I could ask what Mitch needed to forgive her for.

And really, it wasn't my business. Considering how much Cheryl overshared, maybe it was better to not ask.

"That's not a hundred and five things," Rachel commented, her voice lazy and relaxed. "You had everything ready last weekend, you're just double-checking and overthinking it. Indulge in the pampering."

The words seemed as much directed at me as Cheryl, and even if they weren't, it was good advice.

The guys had all been at my apartment when I left. It was both weird and not, but they made me promise to take my time and to enjoy this. Archie even offered to drive me to the hair and makeup appointment, but I kind of wanted the time to myself.

Well, not that the time here was to myself. It was kind of nice to just hang out with the girls, no pressure. When a second lady settled in with a dish for me to soak my fingers in, I grinned. My hands were not my best feature. I spent too much time working with them to focus on my nails.

Rachel suggested tips, but I didn't want anything high-maintenance.

Mani/pedis were expensive and an indulgence. Still, I'd picked out a pretty red shade that would match my dress, and while they weren't super long, I had just enough nail for them to shape.

"Rach," Cheryl said. "When do we meet your girl?"

"Tonight," Rachel said. "Stop asking."

"C'mon, it's only fair. You know everything about everyone else, and I don't even know who you asked."

Rachel snorted. "Just because you like taking out full-page ads on your latest and greatest doesn't mean I do."

"Hmmph." Cheryl took a picture of her feet and typed on her phone. "Maybe I just want to make sure she's good enough for you."

A grin tugged at my lips. "And maybe you just want to make sure she has the right dress and accessories," I teased.

"That, too," Cheryl agreed. "Besides, you want us to like her, right?"

"She's my date to Homecoming, Cher. Not my life partner. I don't actually care if you like her or not. I'm the one who is important in that equation." Not even missing a beat, Rachel stretched her leg before slipping her foot back in the water. "You don't care if I like Mitch, right?"

Enough silence greeted that statement for me to slide a look over at Cheryl, who frowned at her phone. "I know you think he's a jerk," she said after a minute. "But you think most guys are."

"I don't just think it," came the reply. "Most of them *are* jerks. Some are just jerkier than others."

"Jerkier," I snorted.

"Oh, you don't want me to get started on you," Rachel wagged a damp finger in my direction. "So sit over there and hush."

The fact she winked took any sting out of it. And she was right, I did not want her to get started on me. Then again, she'd made no bones about her feelings where the guys were concerned. Rachel didn't *hate* them, but she wasn't a fan. That seemed to have more to do with me than them, so I left it alone.

I mimed zipping my lips, careful not to drip on myself. The lady working on my toes had clipped the nails and now shaped them. It was so weird to have anyone doing it, and at the same time, soothing.

The jingle of the bell pulled my eyes open in time to see Maria enter. She flicked a look right at me, and it was the uncertainty on her face that eased the apprehension flaring along my nerves.

"This is a neutral zone," Rachel announced. "Any and all bitchy behavior will be responded to in kind."

Keys in hand, Maria held her hands up. "I just want to get my nails done for tonight."

"Then enter and be pampered." Accompanying her invitation with a magnanimous wave, Rachel grinned. Maria glanced at me again, and I gave her a little shrug.

"It's all roses at the moment."

"You sure?" Even as she asked the question, the staff settled her in the chair next to mine.

"Yeah," I told her. "I'm sure." Maybe I shouldn't be so easy going about it, but I had a whole lot of other problems, and Maria wasn't one of them. We didn't have to make it a problem.

Granted, she and Sharon were still friends, and I wouldn't cross the street to put Sharon out if she was on fire.

Okay, harsh. I would. I just wouldn't like it.

Still, I shook off the wandering thoughts and tried to focus on the fact they were massaging my hands and feet. Every once in a while, they hit a spot and something in my back just unlocked. If they kept this up, I'd be going to sleep, not the dance.

"So…" Maria said quietly. "You and Bubba are going tonight?"

Not a topic I really wanted to tackle, particularly with her, so I said, "He asked."

"It was a gorgeous ask," Cheryl inserted. "I can't believe he sang for you."

He had. The song had taken my breath away. If I were honest, so had the whole scene in the cafeteria. As embarrassing as it had been, it had also been a thrill. He'd wanted to give me a memory, and he'd definitely done that.

"Who are you going with, Maria?" Cheryl asked.

"Just a friend." For her part, Maria glanced at the woman who was now removing the toenail polish for her. "He didn't have anyone to go with, so he asked if I'd help him out."

Ouch.

She shot me a sideways look. "Do you know who Jake is taking?"

Me. But I didn't say that. "Technically, he doesn't have a date. He didn't ask anyone."

He hadn't asked me, so not a lie.

Not sure Maria bought that though, but before she could pursue it further, Rachel changed the subject. They talked about music, the decorations, the theme, and the fact that the parade was in a few hours. It would travel the length of our main street, not that it was very long. But it was an important part of the whole effort.

I had no intentions of attending, even if I was proud of the guys for winning the game the night before.

"What do you mean you're not going?" Cheryl said. "Mitch and the guys will be there. We have to show up."

"I'm not big on parades, and I have plans, so they know I was at the game last night."

"You went to a game?" Maria asked. "I thought you hated football."

"Hate is a strong word. I don't get it, and no matter how many times Jake or Ian try to explain it to me, it still doesn't compute. But I went because it was a big game for them." And the first one they both got to play since Jake got benched. They never complained that I didn't want to go, but they always seemed pleased when I did.

Besides, Archie and Coop were hilarious with their cowboys versus aliens comparisons on the plays and cracked me up.

"It's not that hard," Maria said.

"Maybe not, but it's like a whole other language to me. French is easier," I said with a shrug. They were putting my feet in hot wax; it was really warm and very soothing.

"Besides," Rachel drawled. "Football isn't for everyone. Me, I like hockey. It's nice and vicious, and there's body slams galore."

I snorted.

"I like figure skating," Cheryl admitted then held up a finger to her lips. "Shhh. Football might be the life's blood here, but it's godawful boring."

Maria laughed. "It wouldn't be so bad if ten minutes on the play actually meant ten minutes."

"More like an hour." Though an exaggeration, it wasn't far from the truth.

By the time my nails were painted and my feet had been scrubbed, waxed, and finally massaged before she painted the toes, I was kind of a pile of goo in the chair. This might not have been the best idea if I had to get ready to go out later.

I kind of wanted to go and take a nap, even if I'd been able to sleep in a little that morning. Rachel and I were done first, though Rachel had been done ahead of everyone. She put her barefoot next to mine and snapped a picture of them. Her toenails were done in a rich blue with a little pattern on them but her fingernails were half blue and half black with a little glitter stripe dividing the colors.

"That looks really good," I told her. She'd also gone the tips route.

"Yeah?" Rachel examined them critically. "I wasn't sure, but then I thought why the hell not."

I laughed. "You think that a lot."

"Gets me through the day," she said as we waited to pay. "I like yours, too. Though you could have done the tips if you wanted a longer nail effect."

"Nah," I said, looking at mine. "They're about the right length that I don't break them on everything."

"Fair."

I made sure to add a tip for the lady who did my hands and one for the lady who did my feet. Maria and Cheryl were almost done, but Rachel and I headed outside.

The parade goers were going to be in luck. It was one of those rare, perfect days. Sunny, but not hot. The air was cooler, and the breeze comfortable. The humidity wasn't an issue either.

Maybe whatever Carol did to my hair would last the evening. That would be fun.

"You doing all right, still?" Rachel asked as she leaned against her car. The sun hit her darker brown hair and revealed red highlights.

"I'm good," I said after a long moment. "I thought today would feel weird, you know…"

"Because of the breaking up thing?" She cut a glance toward the front of the nail place, but we were outside.

I nodded. "And it is weird, but not because of that. I mean…I'm nervous, and I'm not."

"Well, glad you have that nailed down." Her chuckle had me shaking my head.

"I mean, we're going all together, so—it'll just be us, the group."

"And Bubba is riding with y'all, too?" She raised some skeptical eyebrows.

"He asked, and Coop and Jake mentioned he wanted to. He also offered to make his own way if I wasn't comfortable with it."

"Aww, so sweet." Her tone suggested anything but… "How much groveling has he done to get back into your good graces?"

"Rach—we're friends. That's what I'm focusing on."

She shook her head. "That boy doesn't want to just be friends with you."

"Well, that was what he said," I reminded her. Before I broke up with him, he was already backing off.

"Well, he's an idiot."

I grinned. "You know, they aren't all bad."

"Nope, I don't know that," she countered. "I don't think any of them are good enough for you, but I'm biased."

"You do realize that by the nature of this conversation, I'm going to have to give your date the stink-eye all evening, especially if I don't think she's good enough."

It was Rachel's turn to laugh. "I'd pay to see you give someone the stink-eye, but that said, you are entitled to your opinion. Just like I'm entitled to mine."

"Good deal."

Cheryl and Maria exited together, though Cheryl remained glued to her phone.

"Cheryl," Rachel said easily, pulling the other girl's attention. "We've discussed walking and texting. You need to see where you're going."

"Ha," Cheryl countered. "I'm just letting Mitch know I'm heading downtown to grab a parade spot, then hair and make-up. He wants me ready early so we can go out to eat first. Especially since Mom is going to want a thousand pictures, especially with the mum she was making me. Not that I plan to eat anything."

"Food might be a good idea. They never serve anything at the dance but drinks." Even then it was bottled water or canned soda.

"If I eat anything, it will give me food baby belly and ruin the lines of my dress. I'd rather starve." Cheryl shot me a grin, then gave me a hug. Okay, I was getting used to Ms. Spontaneity. "Thanks for coming this morning, I can't wait until everyone sees the gorgeous dress you picked out."

"Me too," Rachel said. "I bet you look even better than you did in that picture. Meow."

Eyes rolling, I shook my head. "We'll see. I still haven't seen your dress."

Cheryl's phone buzzed. "Mitch is getting irritated. I gotta go." She gave Rachel a quick hug. Then Maria. "Be good, girls, see you later."

"Why would I want to be good?" Rachel called after her.

With a wave, Cheryl slid into her car, and then she was pulling out.

"What does she see in Mitch?" Maria asked abruptly, and I glanced at her.

I had no idea. Cheryl didn't talk about him much, except that he'd asked her to Homecoming. 'Course, she also said he'd forgiven her for something from the summer.

"Does it matter?" Rachel asked, eyeing Maria.

"Just…" Maria hesitated. "He's not that nice a guy."

"Nope," Rachel said. "Most guys are douche bags. She likes him. I just keep an eye on her to make sure she isn't giving up too much to make him happy. Hopefully, he'll move along again in a few weeks."

"What is wrong with him?" I glanced from one girl to the other. "She seems crazy about him."

"Like Maria said," Rachel pushed off her car. "He's not a nice guy. He's got jealousy issues, for one. Wants stuff he can't have. Anyway, I need to go… I'll keep an eye on Cheryl." Rachel pointed at me. "Don't skip out on tonight. I want to see that dress."

"I won't."

She slid into her car and pulled away, leaving me with Maria.

Rachel didn't want to talk about Mitch and Cheryl. Whether it was out of protectiveness or because she just didn't want to talk about them, I wasn't sure. I checked my phone for the time, I had another half hour before I had to head over to Carol's to do the hair and makeup. I'd thought about going later in the day, but I wasn't planning on doing anything crazy after.

"Frankie?"

Facing Maria, I considered her. A frown tightened her brow, and she'd folded her arms. The color she'd chosen for her nails was the palest pink—it was so pale, it was almost not a color at all.

"Did you talk to Jake?"

Ahh. Had I asked him why they'd broken up? I had asked him. "Yes."

She exhaled. "So, now you know."

I nodded slowly. "For what it's worth, I'm sorry you got hurt."

Maria shrugged. "He didn't lie to me. He didn't make up stories…or lead me on. I could have lived not being a score point, but…" She shrugged. "That wasn't what got to me in the long run."

A part of me said walk away. Just get in my car and go. But the rest of me focused on Maria, who despite everything, had once upon a time also been my friend. "I can imagine."

"No," she said with a faint shake of her head. "You can't. But…" Maria paused, then glanced around before narrowing the distance between us. "Not everything that happened was his fault. I know that…up here." She tapped her head. "But I also know that…the last party, there was something in the drinks. Or maybe just in mine."

I frowned. "You think they roofied you?"

The guys got a little nuts, but they wouldn't do that. Period.

Folding her arms, Maria shivered even in the sun. "Someone did. No…I don't think it was them. But they weren't the only ones at the party. You saw those pictures."

"The ones Sharon posted to point out what a slut I am?"

Maria nodded. "Look, I don't remember a lot of that night. What I do remember was I woke up the next morning with no panties, and I'd definitely had sex."

Heat crawled up the back of my neck.

"At first, I told myself it had to be Jake. I wanted it to be Jake…even after I found Jake asleep with another girl sprawled on top of him downstairs. We'd already broken up, and I don't even know why I went to the party other than to rub it in his face that he couldn't have me anymore. It was stupid."

"Why are you telling me this?" I didn't need the visuals.

"Because I don't think it was Jake. The more I try to piece it together, the more all I see are shadows. I wasn't the first girl roofied this summer. It happened to some of the others, too. Always at one of the parties. We just assumed we got black out drunk. Jake said he got pretty blasted that night—when I asked him about it." Maria shook her head. "Look, the point is—I don't think the guys did it, but they aren't the only ones who were there, and every girl I know who was roofied was on their score cards."

"God, Maria. Are you all right?"

"I'll be fine…I just want to know who. Jake always wore a condom. Always. This guy…he didn't."

Shit.

"I got tested," Maria admitted. "So far so good. That's something."

Was this what Sharon wanted Maria to tell Jake?

"Did you tell Jake what happened?"

"No," she said firmly. "I'd prefer if you didn't tell him either."

"Was Sharon…?"

"No," Maria said with a shake of her head. "She apparently was one of the lucky ones. Cheryl and Patty, not so much."

Cheryl…

Cheryl was one of the score points.

My stomach bottomed out. "Wait…she said Mitch forgave her for the summer. She had to be forgiven for being roofied?"

"Like I said, not a great guy." Maria sighed. "I'm sorry I'm dumping this on you now, but you're seeing one of them. If whoever this dick is wants what they have…you would be next on the list. I want you to be careful."

Heart slamming against my ribs, I wavered between shock, outrage, nausea, and tears. "I'm so sorry it happened to you."

Maria gave me a small smile. "I'll be okay. I told my mom…after I figured it out that it probably wasn't Jake and that…it wasn't that I had too much to drink."

My mother would have slapped me or given me a derogatory remark. The fact the thought popped up unbidden was another reason to swallow back the lump in my throat.

"She's great about it…really great, and I'm talking to someone. Frankie, I know Sharon was an epic bitch to you, and I tried to warn you off Jake, and I know Patty has. Maybe we're selfish, I liked things with Jake before. But it would never be the same, you know?"

No, I didn't, but yeah, I could imagine. "Is there anything I can do?"

"Be careful. Of being around them. And of them."

They weren't going to hurt me. Not like that. They would never. "I know they didn't do it. Maybe I didn't know about the points thing before, and I know they can be dicks."

A faint smile touched Maria's lips. "Yes, they can."

"But they wouldn't hurt someone like that."

"I know you're right, but it's hard. When Jake…called me about the post and I begged Sharon to take it down, it had nothing to do with you."

"No, because…" Oh jeez. I felt awful for her.

"Exactly. But I couldn't tell Jake that, and so I did my best. Jake's…he's crazy about you. I don't know why you've never noticed, but no one could ever compete with you. So make sure they look after you tonight. Okay?"

"Hey…" I narrowed the gap between us. "You, too. If you need me for whatever reason, you call me or come find me. I'll have your back."

When Maria hugged me I returned it. "I'm really sorry, Maria" I murmured against her.

"I've missed you," she replied. The hug was over almost as soon as it began, and she headed to her car.

I really did feel so bad for her. These girls got roofied at their parties, or because of them?

As much as Maria didn't want them to know, Archie and the guys would know who were at those parties. Maybe they'd know who did it. I also had a hard time believing Jeremy wouldn't have done or said something. He tended to keep an eye on things, but they'd been…

...missing me and out of control.

In the car, I checked my phone. The guys were being suspiciously quiet. Then again, they knew I'd be with Rachel, so maybe they were giving me space.

Turning Maria's story over in my head, I sat there for another minute. I wanted to talk to them about it in person, not over the phone, and I had to figure out how to ask without giving Maria away. She'd trusted me with something very personal, I wasn't going to betray that.

Me

> Nails done. Now off to get my hair and face fixed. Gonna grab some drive-thru for lunch. You guys behaving?

Jake

> Hell no. Behaving is highly overrated. Besides, I'm stuck at the parade with Bubba who says hi, btw.

Coop

> Jake hit me with mayo earlier when we made sandwiches. So I've had a facial. Also, Sis wanted to borrow the Black Beauty books, I didn't think you'd mind.

Archie

> Your apartment is in one piece. Coop and I brought his game system over and set it up. I promise, we will not turn your living room into a game room. Much. When do you think you'll be back?

I shook my head.

Me

Sorry about the parade, J. Hi back to B. No, C, I don't mind if she borrows the books. Please tell me mayo didn't get squirted anywhere else. And A, why do I not believe you? Also? I think 2 hours? I'm hoping less. But she has to deal with my hair.

Archie

Because you are as smart as you are sexy. Have fun, babe.

Jake

Baby girl, you always look great. Definitely eat though.

Coop

See, I'm smart, I knew that.

Me

You're all nuts. Driving now...

I set the phone on the other seat and started the car. Weirdly, even with all the crap that happened at school, with the girls, my mom, and the nuttiness with the guys—I still had them. They still had my back.

Who had Maria's back in all of this?

Sharon had been right about one thing, if Maria had told Jake, he would have done something about it. Whether it got them back together or not was irrelevant. Jake protected the people in his life. Chances were he'd kick that guy's ass.

And the guy would damn well deserve it.

I was glad Maria trusted me enough to tell me and cared enough to warn me. But I almost wish I didn't know, because now I had to wonder—who all had been at the party, and who'd done it?

Chapter Twenty-One

WHEN IT ISN'T LIKE IT SHOULD BE

ARCHIE

Hot glue stung like a bitch, but we both kept an eye on the time. "Jake better move it."

"He texted," Coop said from where he was adding the ribbons to the other wheel. Like me, he had a glue gun and hissed periodically when he caught the glue on his fingertips. "They were almost out, but he found red mums for us to match her dress, and a white one for her."

"Good." The video Coop found insisted we could do all kinds of things for the mums and the typical length was to land it somewhere between her waist and her knee with the ribbons. We'd gone with red, white, and purple. The school colors and a little addition. Jake added his football jersey number to a gold football trinket that we were adding, along with trinkets for Homecoming and senior year. Coop had found a cat charm, and I'd picked out one of a couple dancing.

The whole point was to make it senior year special for all the things she'd never done before. It hadn't really occurred to me until we'd started on this that Frankie had never had a mum, and even when we hit Homecoming last year, she hadn't done more than show up for an hour before she left.

Sometimes, I felt like a real asshole. The looping purple ribbon I was doing would edge the mum, then we'd build them all together with mine on top of the ribbons Coop was stringing.

"This thing is gonna weigh a ton," Coop said as he held it up.

I shrugged. "That's why it said to safety pin it and use that to attach it to the dress. We can always take it off if it's too heavy for her. But she gets to have it for the pictures." And our arm garters would all coordinate with hers. Red mums against the purple of our school colors while hers was a white against the purple.

"Yeah," he said, setting the glue gun aside and chasing Tiddles away from swatting at the ribbons. The cats had been all about playing with it. We were both covered in cat hair.

Maybe I could talk Frankie into using the lint roller on me again. The idea had its merits.

"Why are you grinning like that?" Coop asked, and I chuckled.

"Nothing. Just hoping she enjoys the surprise." Because there were some pieces I still wanted to keep to myself.

"Me, too," he admitted. "Though to be honest, I think she will. With everything that's been going on, she doesn't talk about her mom that much."

"She's talked to me some." It wasn't betraying anything. Though I wasn't going to bring up the fact she'd cried or how lost she'd been. The dislike I felt for her mother had only intensified recently. If I could make it so the woman never breathed the same air as Frankie again, I would.

"Good," Coop exhaled the word, and I met his stare. "She needs to talk to someone."

"Don't start on that abused crap." Not that I didn't believe it, because I did… "Not everyone wants to pour their heart out."

Muriel went through therapists like she did designers. Attending when it was in vogue and dropping them when they required she actually do some work. Sometimes, I wondered why she bothered. Then Jeremy would give her a gentle push, and she'd get thoughtful.

It never lasted though.

"It's not crap," Coop said as he added another length of ribbon to the garter mums. He'd lined the colors so they would match hers with just enough, but different enough that people wouldn't totally freak. Prudish hypocritical assholes. "C'mon, Arch. I know you've seen it."

"Fine," I huffed. "It's not crap, but hammering on her for dealing differently than you or Bubba would with whatever emotional deficiencies she's had to cope with her whole life doesn't help anyone."

"Well," he said, pausing to reach for the soda he'd opened earlier. "On that, we can agree."

"Good. I still can't believe he dug a hole so big he fell in it." What kind of idiot did that?

"Well, we all dig our own holes." The other guy shrugged. "We did it when we didn't tell her about the affair. When we warned people off her. Points. I mean, she's had a lot to forgive and get over."

Frowning, I glanced at him. "You think she's run out of second chance cards?" Because, face it, I'd likely screw up again. I wanted to be everything, but my examples for a committed relationship wasn't great. I wanted to protect her. Just like paying the rent on this place so it was secure through graduation. I didn't want any more surprises tearing the carpet out from under her.

"Could we blame her if she did?"

The matter-of-fact nature of the question floored me. "Coop...we're gonna mess up again."

"I know," he said with a sigh. "We just have to do our best to not mess it up."

"Well, with everything from the points to the summer coming back to bite us in the ass..."

"I'm less worried about that than I am the dick who did that to her car." The comment was a blast of cold water in the face.

"We never found out who did that."

"Nope," Coop laid down the third of the garter mums. There was a fourth one, but we'd both been on the fence about whether we should make it for Bubba. Technically, it wasn't a date.

If we wanted to be really technical about it, none of us were taking her for a date, and yet we were all taking her.

"That's why it bothers me," he continued. "Laura wrote the crap on her test. Sharon's been trying to torture her using social media. Some asshat left the notes in her locker."

"But you said not Laura 'cause the writing didn't match."

"Nope. Didn't match Rachel either."

Ugh. I made a face. Rachel. Most of the time, she didn't bother me, but it was weird that she had a thing for my girl and couldn't stand us. Not that she made any pretense of liking us either. "Not sure whether to be happy about that last part."

"Be happy about it," Coop advised. "Frankie likes Rachel, and even if she wouldn't be my first pick, she's been a decent friend to her when we still had our heads up our asses."

"Well some of us still do." Not really what I wanted to hear. "Okay, so who's left that would hate Frankie enough to do that to her car? Or hate us?"

"The list of who hates some of us is longer than others." At his pointed look, I flipped him off. "Maybe it's not hate."

"You think it's jealousy?"

"I think people can be cruel. Frankie never made waves. Most people like her. She's funny, she's smart. She doesn't pigeonhole in any one group."

"You could make that argument for all of us though," I pointed out. "Face it, Jake and Bubba are jocks, you're emo boy, and I'm just a geek."

"You're a rich geek."

I rolled my eyes. "Fine, I'm a rich geek. But the same thing applies. We all have different interests. Jake and I do the engineering thing, Bubba's got his music, you and Frankie have your research and lit—though Jake's arguably more into books and history with her than we are. You also like psych."

"You want to tell me something else I already know?"

I wasn't offended by the challenge. Actually… "Frankie's done nothing but study the last few years, she's pulled back on her extracurriculars."

"She has since she started at Mason's." Coop shrugged. "Part of why she kind of fell out with the other girls. She wasn't doing anything with them, and we hogged the rest of her time."

I stared down at the ribboned circles I'd been decorating. Frankie worked, a lot. Coop had had jobs on and off over the years. Coop had been delivering food since he got his car, but he'd also had part-time gigs. But Frankie worked more than all of us combined.

Money couldn't solve everything, but it could make a person more comfortable. I'd never had to get a job. Not once. As far as I knew, neither had Bubba. He'd done volunteer work, but his parents were comfortable enough.

It wasn't fair.

Of the five of us, Frankie had been working steadily since the day she turned sixteen in our sophomore year. She hadn't even slowed down, heading to Mason's right after school and applying for the job. Almost two years she'd worked there.

"Hey, Arch…"

"What?" I glanced at Coop, who was staring at me.

"You okay?"

"Yeah, I'm fine. Just thinking."

"About?"

"I'll tell you later."

His phone buzzed, and Coop picked it up. "Jake's got the mums, and he's almost here. Said Bubba's following him."

"Yippee."

"I thought we worked things out with him," Coop tested.

"You one hundred percent good with the fact he hurt her?" Because I wasn't. I still hadn't forgiven myself.

"No," Coop admitted. "Jake told her she doesn't have to dance with him tonight either. I feel bad for the guy—doesn't mean he doesn't need to do the work."

"Good." Bad enough the assholes decided on her first dance without me there, but I could always make sure I got the last one. "Fuck…it feels weird that he's on the outside."

"Yep. Feels like we should be helping him."

"But I don't want to." And I didn't. "I told him what I thought. He dug that damn hole and tried to throw all of us in it."

"He meant well."

"They say the road to Hell is paved with good intentions." At the same time, it was true for all of us.

"Look," Coop said as he set the last of the ribboned cardboard circles down. "We don't sabotage him. We're there for him if he needs to talk. We support her. At the end of the day—it's not about what we want."

"No," I agreed. "It's not." But if he couldn't find a way to make things work with Frankie, too…

Huh.

Should it matter if he was out, other than he was still one of our friends? One less person I had to split her time with, and I got that she was dating all of us, but…

But if she did end up choosing, how weird would it be? Worse, how much would it hurt?

Thoughts like that weren't going to get us anywhere.

I wanted to make some grand gesture and say no matter what happened we'd all still be friends. But Bubba was the poster child for how challenging that would be.

Maybe we did need to do more to help right that boat.

We could, but the real question was, should we?

That one didn't have an easy answer.

IAN

Bike parked between Archie's car and Coop's, I slid off and removed my helmet. Jake was already out of the SUV, the mums he'd picked up at the craft store in the bag. They were building a Homecoming mum for her. The fact that they'd all planned it together and the guys were working on it at her apartment while she was out stung.

Not that I didn't deserve it. I accepted the clothes bag from Jake as he passed me my suit and waited while he grabbed his own. We were all getting ready here. Archie had the car picking us up here, and it would drop us off after here.

No hotel rooms. No after party plans.

At least none that anyone had shared and, at the moment, I hadn't wanted to ask.

"Dude," Jake said as he locked his car. "Lighten up. I get it. You're not happy, but today isn't about you anymore. It's about her. We need to keep it upbeat and focus on her having fun."

Yeah. "Just tired," I told him. It wasn't totally a lie. I was tired. Sleep had been elusive, because last night after our little celebratory meal post-game, Frankie had gone home with Jake and Coop, and I'd gone home alone. Dad and Mom had left me a cupcake on the island with a congratulations note.

Dad asked me whether I'd be home tonight after Homecoming. I hadn't told them about the breakup or the fact I wasn't going with Frankie. The way Dad stared at me, I knew exactly what he was thinking. Instead of a straight yes or no, I'd only told him the five of us were going to hang out and we might do a movie after.

I was pretty sure he didn't believe me.

"Bubba…" Jake yanked my attention back to the present. "Where's your head?"

Same place as my heart, but that wasn't what I said. "Just worried about tonight."

Sharon and Patty had been on a tear at the parade. They'd pasted on smiles, but I hadn't missed the cutting looks.

"Look, tonight is going to be great. We're all going. We're all going to have her back. No one is going to do shit." The vehemence in his voice made me smile. Hell, my jaw still ached from his version of handling things. Not that he looked much better.

We were both still sporting some yellow and green in our bruises. "You think she's going to mind we're still beat up in the pictures?"

"They air-brush everything," Jake said with a shrug. "It's hardly the first time we've been bruised or beat up on each other, for that matter."

Also true.

"It's the first time she's not teasing me about it."

Garment bag over his shoulder, Jake met my gaze. "You did it to yourself."

There was no sympathy in his expression.

None.

"Don't you think I know that?" I'd been jealous. I was still jealous. I hated the fact that I was jealous, and at the same time, I hated all of them because they were right where I wanted to be and I didn't want to feel that way.

"No," Jake said softly jerking me out of that spiral. "I don't. I think you're too busy blaming how you feel on everyone else. You let your dad get in your head, and you know, I get it. Joe's a good guy. He cares. But he doesn't know us—you do or you should."

"But he knows…he knows a lot of things, and he's worried."

"Okay, so he gets in your head. Paints an ugly picture. You pull back, you cut her off. How does that help her?"

"I wasn't trying to cut her off." Fuck. I blew out a breath and paced away from him and then turned. Were we really having this conversation in a parking lot? Fine. "I'm crazy about her. I have been forever. I asked her first, because I didn't want you guys to have an in. Not that it stopped you, but I thought the grand gesture would do it, and even that didn't work."

"I know."

That was it. Two simple words. I confessed to being the asshole, and Jake just shrugged it off. "I didn't even realize I was doing it."

"I know that, too."

"Don't be so damn understanding."

"I'm not." Jake shrugged. "She's still my girl. I don't have to understand shit. But I get the impulse. I also had to get over it."

I frowned. "You would take off with her in a heartbeat if she said yes to only you."

"Not a doubt." How did he stay so calm? "But I'm never going to tell her she has to choose. I'm okay with sharing. Sounds weird. Might change down the road. Kind of doubt it."

Disbelief filtered through me. "So, Frankie meets some new guy and she wants to date him too, and that's going to be okay with you?"

"Fuck no," Jake answered, his eyes narrowing. "I told you I was okay with us. No one else."

"How do you get there?"

Some of the irritation in his expression faded. "Because I want to be here."

"Just like that?" Because I wanted to be there, but I wasn't. I had been, briefly and then…

"No, not just like that. You don't think I wasn't envious that you asked her to Homecoming? Or that you put that look on her face?" He lifted his eyebrows. "Did you even see her face when you did the ask?"

There'd been wonder in her eyes. Wonder and tears. That smile. Yeah, I'd seen her face.

"Did you think I wasn't envious when I figured out she'd been with Archie?"

That had pissed me off.

Between that and the fact that they hadn't let up on their stupid ass plan for the French guy…

"You ever ask yourself about why us seeing her bothers you when Frenchy didn't?"

"She didn't care about Frenchy." It wasn't even a question. Jake pointed his forefinger at me, thumb up like he mimed a gun.

"Exactly. But she does care about us. Before dating was on the table, that didn't bother you." He paused a beat, then studied me. "Or did it?"

"No," I said, shaking my head slowly. "I don't think it bothered me. But we all tried to make sure we had our time with her. Tuesdays were my day." If I got nothing else with her, we got to hang out on Tuesdays together, and I used to tell myself it was enough. Even if I had to share her time with the others.

"I told you already, you need to figure this out."

He had.

"And you need to be in a better fucking mood tonight, because if you bring her down, you and me are going to end up in another fight."

I snorted and then kicked at a rock on the blacktop. "I don't want to be jealous, Jake. I don't want to be that guy. I want to make her smile."

"Then focus on making her feel good and don't worry about whether she's paying attention to you right now." For a moment, his expression softened. "Bubba, she cares, okay? She's still hurting over the idea that you suddenly pushed her away."

"She's the one who broke up with me," I pointed out.

"Yeah, because it was something she could control." And that was it in a nutshell. "Can you handle it tonight? 'Cause if not—don't do this to her or to us."

"I'll handle it." Because the thought of not being there or showing up separately was even worse than just being the odd man out. I sucked in a deep breath. "In fact, I'll spring for pizza because I'm starving."

Jake studied me for a long moment. "Good. All right, let's go over a few rules about tonight while we're at it…"

Rules?

I followed him up the stairs to the apartment's back door. When he pulled out a key, I had to swallow the sting of that, too. It was my own damn fault. Maybe if I reminded myself of that enough, it wouldn't burn quite so bad.

"Yeah," Jake said. "Rules. Hey, we're here," he called out as he held the door open for me."

"Good," Archie said. "We're about ready for the mums part of this mess."

"Bubba's buying pizza so throw in your orders. Meat lovers for me."

"Pineapple for Frankie," came Coop and Archie's dual responses. Jake smirked, and I laughed.

"No shit," I said. "She hasn't changed her order in years."

"Just making sure." Coop glanced at us as we walked through to the living room. Two of Frankie's cats perched on the sofa. Tiddles was one and the other had to be Tabby. Tory was the shy one. "Hang your suits up in the bedroom. We put a rack on the door to her closet."

The mum construction was laid out on the table in the living room. The ribbons on Frankie's were numerous along with charms and trinkets. There were three garters made already and a fourth sitting in pieces.

"Rule number one," Jake said as he returned up the hallway. "Coop got first dance, I got second, Archie gets third. You can ask her after that."

Dragging my attention off the mums, I glanced at him.

"What are we doing?" Archie asked.

"Giving Bubba the rules for tonight."

"Ahh…fine, rule number two, there will be no scenes at Homecoming.

We're all going to just have fun."

"That's kind of a rule for all of us," Coop argued. "Not that I object to it, just saying."

"So we're making these rules specifically for Bubba or for all of us?" Archie glanced at me, then at Jake.

Jake shrugged, and I rolled my eyes. Then laughed. "You know what the first rules we had work…"

"No texting on a date, and Sunday nights are Jake's?" Archie raised his brows.

"Eh," Jake said. "The important thing is Frankie has fun. That we all have a good time. No drama. Just partying and dancing. She wants to make memories."

Oh, she'd been making memories the last few weeks. I diverted down the hall to her room and hung my garment bag with the others. The stand was hooked over the door and jutted out like its own clothing rack. The bed was a little disheveled, and there were scattered clothes near her laundry basket.

Frankie tended to be neat, but those were Jake's socks, and the shirt on the back of the chair was one of Coop's.

"Fine," Archie's voice climbed, but I missed whatever he was responding to. "Rule number three, no one disappears with Frankie at the dance."

Wandering back out, I tugged my phone from my pocket to order the pizzas.

"No taking off, or ducking out to make out. We start the evening together, we end the evening together." Archie was hot gluing purple ribbon to the fourth and last of the smaller circle cutouts.

"That's fair," Coop said. "One of us always with her."

"Yeah," Jake said. "Who gets to the restroom with her?"

"Rachel," Coop and Archie said at the same time, and the corners of my lips twitched.

A laugh that had nothing to do with humor worked its way up, but I wouldn't let it out. I plugged in their favorites for pizza and made sure I got

Frankie's too before I paid for it and hit send.

"Fair," Jake said. "Even if I can't stand the bitch."

"Join the club. But she's good for Frankie," Coop said. "And you heard her this morning."

"Yeah, yeah." In the kitchen, Jake opened the fridge. "Want a soda, Bubba?"

"Thanks." Then I glanced at the table where Archie worked, and Coop had begun adding the actual mum to the pieces they'd already made. Frankie's was going to be stunning. "You guys mind if I work on that last one?"

Archie cut a look up at me. "Glue gun's right there. Jump on in."

Stripping off my shoes, I shoved them over to the side and then knelt to get to work.

Jake passed me a soda and said, "You still in for tonight?"

"Yeah," I told him. "For as much or as little as she wants to put up with me, and I got it—" I motioned to all of them. "I have to ask her to dance."

None of this was how it was supposed to have been. None of it. But Jake was right. This was my fault. So tonight, tonight I started making it up to her.

What did Coach used to say? Being involved with the team didn't come with an engraved invitation. You involved yourself.

I almost had myself psyched up for it by the time Frankie walked in. Thankfully, we'd gotten the mums done and hidden—even mine. I'd done mine a little less elaborate, but very much with her in mind, right down to the pen trinket I slid on it.

'Course, once I got a good look at her, I damn near swallowed my tongue because even in a tank top and shorts, she looked stunning. Her hair was smoothed out and hung beautifully, and her eyes were bright.

"Holy crap," Coop exhaled.

"Wow." Archie said a beat before he wolf-whistled. "You could start a whole new Homecoming trend in that outfit."

Jake just grinned. "I think I hate Coop right now."

"Yep, too bad, so sad." Coop laughed.

But when Frankie glanced at me, the hesitation in her eyes? That flash of worry? It hit me right in the nuts.

That was what I'd done.

"You look amazing," I told her, meaning every word. "How do you feel?"

The tremulous smile on her lips inched upward. "A lot fussier than I ever imagined. It was kind of fun and…wow, people do that all the time to get ready for stuff?"

There she was with a teasing roll of her eyes and shake of her head.

"It's a memory," I reminded her and held up my phone. "You want a picture?"

She laughed, then spread her arms. I got one snap of her, then Coop slid in miming hugging her, and she mugged for the camera. I snapped the shots as they all got in there for ones with just her and Jake, or her and Archie.

When she curled her fingers and told me I needed to be in the group selfie too, I didn't argue.

It was a step.

I had to involve myself.

Chapter Twenty-Two
ALL OF YESTERDAY'S PARTIES

Thankfully, some of the awkwardness of Ian's presence diminished as I devoured pizza. We still had another hour before we had to get ready, and all I had left was to put on a dress. When the guys teased me like they were gonna give me a kiss, I fended them off.

There was no way I wanted to mess up all the work Carol had done with my hair and my face. Sitting on the floor, legs crossed though, I kept studying them one at a time. Between what Maria had told me about someone roofying her and the other girls, and the fact that she'd mentioned Cheryl in the same breath as one of the girls who'd…

Yeah, I couldn't do this. I couldn't spend the whole night wondering which of them Cheryl had slept with. I *liked* Cheryl. Arguably, I had liked a lot of them, but Cheryl had been going out of her way to be my friend, and the idea she had sex with one of the guys and they'd never mentioned it just turned my stomach inside out.

Fuck, did I want a list?

As nauseating a concept as that might be, I kind of did.

"Guys…" Yeah, there was no way I wanted to spend my night turning myself inside out. I was already biting my tongue about Maria. She'd confided in me something that was really personal and horrible, but the other…

One by one, they focused on me, and some of the humor fled Coop's expression. "What's wrong?"

"Just want to ask something straight up." I glanced down at my drink and then set the can on the coffee table. There was a bit of glitter on the carpet, but I didn't want to focus on that. "Um… I'd prefer a straight answer, too. No sugarcoating."

Scratching his jaw, Archie eyed me. "You're going to ask us about a girl."

"Pretty much."

Exhaling, Jake set his own can on the table. "Shoot."

Ian frowned, but he didn't say anything to dissuade me. Which was good, he'd been all about telling me uncomfortable stuff, including the points thing.

"Was Cheryl one of your points girls?"

The immediate distaste on Archie's face sent relief through me. Coop opened his mouth, then shut it with a grimace.

"No," Jake answered swiftly. "Hell no."

Dropping his shoulders, Ian ran a hand over his face and then shook his head with a short, but firm, "No." I couldn't tell if the answer relieved him or not.

"Babe," Archie said, blinking as though he couldn't quite wrap his mind around the question. "One, she talks *way* too much."

"Two, she has no filter," Coop added. "And she's…"

"Sweet," Jake intoned that word like it was a bad thing. "The kind of too sweet that rots your teeth. Three, she doesn't have a mean bone in her body and…she and Mitch were already hooking up." Though he glanced at Ian for confirmation. "Right?"

"Far as I know, I wasn't really paying attention to what they were doing—they were *at* a lot of the parties. But she was there with the other girls first, he started showing up later."

Had they been at Ian's birthday? A lot of that night had been laser-imprinted on my brain, but it was more in sharp relief as to where the guys had been and who they'd been with. Everything else was kind of a background blur.

"Frankie," Coop captured my attention. "I'd have told you before the dress shopping. I swear."

"I didn't know about the points before the dress shopping," I reminded him. Ian winced, and Jake shot him a dirty look before focusing on me again. "I didn't want to think about it, I've spent the last few hours telling myself it didn't matter…"

"…but it does," Jake finished for me, and I nodded. "Baby girl, we're assholes, but we're actively trying to not be dicks. I wish I could tell you we hadn't screwed around as much."

"But we did," Archie said, owning it. "Cheryl, however, was never on that list. And at the risk of painting myself as a bigger asshole, I'll say it was because we wanted a challenge and she would have been too easy."

That was a horrible thing to say, yet, I had to be a horrible person, too, because I was grateful to hear it. "You swear?"

"Yes." Four, solid, unflinching answers. Even Ian. Looking at him, I tilted my head. Of the four of them, he'd probably show every ounce of that guilt on his face.

"No lie," he said, spreading his hands. "Why are you asking?"

"It came up today."

Aggravation flashed across Jake's face. "Who the fuck brought it up?"

"It doesn't matter," I told him. "It really doesn't. Just—someone who knew about it, and they mentioned her along with a few others."

Ian dropped his head, and his shoulders slumped. "Frankie…I don't want to give you some kind of list."

"Why not?" Archie asked. "You're the one who told her in the first damn place."

"Stop," Coop said before I could. "We're not turning this into a fight. She asked a question, we answered it. She needed to know…for what it's worth," Coop continued, focusing on me. "If…if I think you need to know because you're getting close to someone and they were on the list, I'll tell you. Otherwise, I don't really want to give you that list either."

The idea that there *was* a list was nauseating enough. "I don't want a list."

"I want to know who told you," Jake gritted out. "No one gets to try and hurt you like that."

"They weren't trying to hurt me." Of that much, I was pretty certain.

"Who tells you something like that if they aren't trying to get a dig in?" Archie's challenge was fair, but…

"Because it wasn't what they were trying to tell me. It came up in passing and without going into details…" While I wanted to ask them because what happened to Maria shouldn't have happened to anyone, I couldn't without betraying her. "I promise," I said before Archie could press the point on it. "So, in a weird way, maybe it's better that Ian told me when he did."

Even if I'd never wanted to know.

Doubt echoed on three faces, but Ian actually gaped. "What?"

"I'm glad I heard it from one of you and not from someone else." Blowing out a breath, I reached for another slice of pizza. "I'm sorry if I killed the mood. Like I said earlier, I kept trying to tell myself it didn't matter, but it did. I like Cheryl. She's…been really great the last few weeks, and as much as last summer seems to be hanging over all of us, I'm doing my best to not make it a thing."

"It's the past," Jake promised. "It's never going to happen again."

Hard to ask that really, especially when I was still dating three of them. No, I wasn't going to press my luck at the moment. How much of a hypocrite was I?

"I believe you," I told him, and guilt assailed me at his harsh exhale. "I'm really sorry if I…"

"No, babe," Archie said. "You don't have to be sorry. Our fuck-up. We deserve the bite in the ass. And you haven't ruined anything, especially if you feel better."

"You do, right?" Coop caught my hand and studied me.

I nodded. I did. "Yeah. I do. Weird, right?"

"Nope," Ian said, surprising me. "Can't really say it's weird when you have to ask us in the first place, you know?"

"True." Head tilted back, I exhaled. "Okay, for the future…no more crazy sex parties."

"Only crazy sex party I plan to have is with you," Jake stated, and when he dropped a kiss on my lips, I laughed.

"Am I invited?" Coop teased.

"Depends," Jake retaliated.

"On?" Archie leaned forward.

"Yeah, on what?" Not that the idea wasn't crazy, because it really, really was—and at the same time, I had to admit, Jake's possible responses intrigued me.

He grinned. "The venue. The hostess. The rules."

"Venue can be arranged," Archie said with just enough seriousness that the curl of lust in my gut immediately went taut.

"Rules can be coordinated," Coop added, linking his fingers with mine.

"So that just leaves the most important part," Jake finished with a wink, then gave me another kiss. The heat flash firing through me probably boiled my face like a cherry tomato. I might even have been charmed by the teasing between the three if I hadn't been so damn turned on by the idea. The glint in Jake's eyes suggested he had a pretty damn good idea of what he was doing, too.

And on that note…

I gave him a shove. "No touchy boys, I cannot reapply the magic here."

"Ha!" Coop snorted. "You don't need anything to look fantastic. But…" He held up his hands. "This is me backing off. You'll notice I wasn't the one to smudge the lipstick."

"Hey." Jake popped him in the arm lightly, but both were laughing.

Beyond their antics, Ian stared at all of us with a kind of hungry intensity that made me blink. When his gaze snagged on mine, he looked away, and I sighed.

With a shrill whistle, Archie cut through all of the antics. "Car is here in forty minutes. Who wants to get ready first?"

Everyone looked at me, and I motioned to myself. "All I have to do is put on my dress. Why don't you boys get ready and I'll clean this up and feed the cats."

"I'm going to borrow your shower," Archie said as he stood. "I hope you have a lint roller ready after I'm in my suit." His words and wink reignited the fire they'd lit earlier with their sex party comments.

Laughter burst out of me. "I'll see what I can do."

"Yay."

"Do I want to know?" Coop asked, playful suspicion in every syllable.

"You do," Archie called as he walked away. "But you're not going to."

I laughed again and reached for the pizza box on the table. Ian closed his hand on mine as we both grabbed for the same one. Frozen, I met his gaze, and he yanked his hand back. "Sorry."

"It's fine." Not like I was trying to take his hand. That little tendril of disappointment needed to just die. We were friends. "I'm just gonna get rid of the empties."

"I can do that." He was gathering the others and grabbed the one from my hand. "Want me to just consolidate all the leftovers into one box?"

"Um, sure, it's not like anyone here cares if their food touches the others."

"This is painful," Jake commented. "I'm gonna change, baby girl." He rose and pressed a hand to my lower back. "You good?"

"I'm fine."

Coop just shook his head. "I'll take care of the cats." Then both left me in the living room with Ian, who took care with setting the pizza together and carefully not looking at me.

Folding my arms, I shifted my weight from one foot to the other. Then I snagged the last box with pizza and added it into the one he'd been compiling. He glanced at me.

"You really okay with me going tonight?"

"Why wouldn't I be?" Eyebrows raised, I dared him to challenge me. "We just hung out for the last hour, and we were fine."

"Yeah but…"

"Friends, Ian."

"Angel…"

I shook my head. "No. Frankie. Angel was sweet when we were dating, but we're not."

"And if I want to again?"

Was he serious right now? I stared at him.

"If I screwed this up, then you'd have every right to tell me to…"

"Stop."

He grimaced.

"We're not doing this." Breaking up with him had been hella hard. Having him here right now and trying to be friends was hard. "You said you couldn't do it, and that you just wanted to be friends. Well, that's what I'm doing. Don't… don't make this a thing."

Tears burned in the back of my eyes, and I grabbed the empty boxes from his hands.

"Frankie…"

"Ian, please don't." Pivoting on my heel, I headed for the kitchen. Coop stood there, his expression tight and worried. He eased aside as I brushed past him and didn't try to stop me as I carried the pizza boxes out. The ground was hot against my bare feet, and I probably screwed up all the softening they did at the nail place, but I didn't care.

All the way to the dumpster, I fought off the tears. Where the hell did he get off just launching that at me tonight? Was that why he wanted to go? Because he changed his mind?

Well, la-de-fucking-dah.

I threw the boxes in the dumpster. The cardboard didn't have enough weight to actually land with any kind of a bang, and that robbed it of any kind of satisfaction. The stink of the trash didn't help either.

Turning around, I locked gazes with Coop, who stood waiting on the sidewalk. "He means well," he said as I approached. "He's an idiot, but he means well."

"I don't want to talk about it." Arms spread, I tilted my head back toward the sky. It was still this absolutely perfect day. The sun was warm, the air was cool, and away from the dumpster, it didn't smell like garbage. "I just want to go and dance and have fun and pretend…"

Did I really want to pretend? Or did I just…

"Hey," Coop murmured, catching my hands. "Tell me. What do you want to pretend?"

"I don't want to pretend," I told him, finally meeting his gaze. "I have three amazing boyfriends." Three. "I want to go and have a great time tonight. I want to dance with you guys. I want to laugh. I want to enjoy that dress I got after the fashion show at the store."

He grinned.

"I just want to be us."

"Then that's what we'll do."

"I don't want to pretend." The second time was as much for Coop as it was for me. I didn't want to play this game with Ian. "He said he couldn't do this…"

"I know."

"And now he's asking what if he wanted to try again? What the hell kind of question is that?"

"A dumb one," Coop murmured.

"It's not even saying he does want to, it's just—what if he did. I'm supposed to try and unsettle everything for a hypothetical?" Irritation scraped through me. "And he's asking me this *right now*?"

"Want me to have Jake kick his ass?"

The question stopped me in my tracks, and I glared at Coop. "Don't make fun of me."

"I'm not," he promised. "But you really are cute when you get pissed."

"Ass."

"Sometimes," he agreed, then grinned. "Tonight is about exactly what you want it to be about. This boyfriend, for one, can't wait to dance with you."

"We really haven't danced like that. Have we?"

"Nope. It's always been as buds, even when the other boys still thought girls were icky and gave us cooties." He looped his arms around me and pulled me close. "I already had your cooties, what were they going to do to me?"

I laughed, and just like that, all the anger leached away. "You're such an idiot sometimes."

"Ah, but for you, I can be an idiot all the time."

Now I rolled my eyes.

"Feel better?"

"Yeah."

Coop did that, he could take the sting out of the rage.

"I do."

"So, do I get a verdict on whether Jake should kick his ass?"

"They're already bruised up enough, don't you think?"

With a shrug, Coop said, "It's Jake, what do you think?"

I thought if Jake heard me be this upset, he'd have already gone to kick Ian's ass. "He didn't hear, did he?"

"Bubba was still breathing, so I'm going to take that as a firm no, he didn't hear."

"Then let's keep it that way."

"You got it." Tapping the tip of my nose gently, he said, "Can I make you smile, beautiful?"

The corners of my lips curved. "You already did."

"Then hold onto that and to me. Okay?"

"I think I can do that."

"Now, I'm going to smudge the lipstick." He dipped his head.

"It's okay," I breathed as his lips were a centimeter from mine. "She promised it was smudge-proof."

The kiss sent tingles cascading through the unsettled chaos of emotions rioting through me. Gripping his shoulders, I dug my fingers in and held. The lick of his tongue against mine grounded me, even as it lit me up again. We were both panting when he finally lifted his head.

"Well," he murmured, tilting his head. "Definitely smudge-proof. Good to know."

The wry remark punctured the tension, and I chuckled as he looped an arm around me and we headed back to the apartment. Ian stood by the back door, hands in his pockets staring at us.

His pained expression cut at me, but I lifted my chin.

"Go on inside," Coop murmured against my ear. "I'll take care of this." Did it make me a chicken that I would rather Coop dealt with it? I didn't want to fight, but I also didn't want Ian yanking my heartstrings around.

"Thanks."

Ian stood aside for me and as I closed the door, Coop said, "Dude, rule number two, let's back it up, okay?"

"We aren't there yet, and it just kind of…popped out."

Great, he really hadn't even meant it. I shut the door firmly and headed for my room. Jake stood in the living room, dress pants, dark shirt, dark vest and a red tie that would match my dress. No jacket.

Holy hell.

He looked…

"Wow."

He grinned as he glanced at me. Some of his hair tumbled over his forehead. It wasn't quite combed, more rakish than normal. The faint bruises added to the effect. At the same time, he was gorgeous.

"You look amazing."

"Baby girl, all for you."

That just pumped my heart right up.

"Unfortunately for him," Archie said as he sauntered out, his shirt was white, with a deep red vest and no tie over a crisp pair of dark slacks. "I look so much better."

Jake's snort just made me laugh.

They were adorable.

And sexy has hell.

Did we really have to get dressed up and go out?

"See?" Archie said, his grin smug. "She's speechless."

"Ha. That's because I'd already taken her breath away." Jake grinned, absolutely unabashed. They both looked amazing. "Yo, Coop," he bellowed. "Get the lead out, I wanna see Frankie in her dress."

When Coop and Ian came in, there was no evidence of the earlier issues. They headed back to my room to change, leaving me to drool over Jake and Archie. It also gave me time to get pictures to add to my phone.

Coop's suit was lighter than the others, but he'd gone with a jacket instead of a vest and he a dark red shirt without a tie that would go with my dress, too. They had really color coordinated.

Like Coop, Ian had gone with a deep red shirt, but he had dark navy almost black slacks and a dark tie to match.

They all looked…different, and yet awesome. "Wow," I said when it was my turn to head back and change. "No one is going to be looking at me tonight."

I didn't turn to see their faces, but the fact that four snorts followed me told me enough. Still, my nerves were rioting, even as I reminded myself—these guys liked me in ripped jeans, tank tops, shorts, and sweats. Dressing up was fun, but what I liked about them wasn't their clothes, either.

The pep talk only lasted so long as I slipped into the under things I'd bought for this outfit. I had to go with a thong—which I hated—but it would leave no lines on the dress. The strapless bra fit like a second skin, but at least I didn't have so much I was gonna pop a boob.

That would be horrifying, and I'd actually jumped around in the thing to make sure.

The dress slid on like floating silk—another reason I liked it, and my hair held up as I slid into and out of clothes.

I wore the bracelet Archie had given me with all its new charms, then looped the charm like layers of necklace on. Three strands that dipped in varying lengths. Finally, I tucked the earrings in and stared at myself in the mirror.

I'd never looked less like me and at the same time…

I didn't even know I could look like this.

It might all be way too much work for everyday, but it was kind of fun.

Huh…Coop was right. The lipstick was smudge proof. I had an extra tube of it that Carol had given me, since she used a brand new one. The small wristlet would let me carry my keys, phone, and ID, so I slid the lipstick in there and then glanced at myself once more before I put on the shoes.

They were the strappiest things I'd ever owned, but I hadn't gone for high heels. They were gold, so they'd match the jewelry and they showed off my feet.

Prissy, right?

Heart racing, I headed for the door. Every step had the skirt swishing against my legs, and the air seemed cooler everywhere. Technically, I had more covering me than I had in the shorts and tank, but the barely there feel of the material left me more exposed.

"Ready or not," I called out with a hell of a lot more bravery than I really possessed. "Here I come."

The low hum of conversation cut off abruptly a full two seconds before I cleared the end of the hall into the living room. Standing, all four faced me and it took a moment for their stunned expressions to register. Coop held a giant mum in his hands, and they each had a garter on their sleeves that matched it.

Even Ian.

I forgot how to breathe.

I'd forgotten all about the mum. Cheryl mentioned the thing about her mom making hers, and that moms did that, and my mom…

"You guys made me a mum?"

Archie grinned slowly, and Coop's eyes brightened. Jake slid his hands into his pockets and let out a low whistle.

"It's beautiful."

"No where near as beautiful as you are," Coop said. "That dress looks every bit as good on you as I remember…but you're…"

"Stunning." Archie nodded. "Frankie, you look like a million bucks."

Face hot, I flapped my hands at my cheeks. "Stop it, I'm going to cry, and then the mascara will run and I'll get snotty."

That pulled a laugh from them, even Ian, who stared at me with something like wonder and maybe a touch of sadness. Yeah. I couldn't focus on that. I just—I couldn't. Instead, I closed the distance to look at the mum.

"We wanted you to have the full experience, baby girl," Jake said. "Coop organized it, and Archie over there fried his fingertips off."

It was beautiful, the purple ribbons created a sunrise effect around the fat white mum and the ribbons had our school colors and red to go with my dress. There were even trinkets hanging on it. Like my charms.

Fuck, I really was going to cry.

"No tears," Coop said. "Don't do it. Laughter, not tears."

My cheeks ached from my smile as they worked to safety pin the thing to the strap of my dress. It weighed a ton and stretched almost to my knees with the ribbons.

"Perfect," Ian murmured. "You look perfect."

Dipping my chin, I glanced down at it and then at all of them. "This… thank you."

"My pleasure," Archie said, then gave me a kiss before Coop winked and gave me another, but it was Jake who cupped my face gently and very carefully wiped his thumb against my lower lashes stealing away the tear that defied me.

"You ready to party?"

Was I ever!

"I can't wait," I whispered.

"Pictures," Archie said abruptly, and phones came out.

"You better send me copies." But we took turns standing together. This mum would not make the whole night. In fact, I kind of wanted to keep it here so it wouldn't get damaged. At the same time, my ping-ponging emotions carried me skyward again.

They'd made me a mum. Dressed up. And we were all going to Homecoming.

Hair, nails and makeup? A couple of hundred dollars.

Fancy dress? Way too much.

A night with my guys? Even Ian?

Priceless.

Chapter Twenty-Three
EVERYTHING I WANTED

The limo arrived exactly on time, and we locked up and headed out together. It was fun to take more pictures on the way, the mum stayed, and even though I loved it, I did not want it ruined. So the guys hung it up in my bedroom for me.

I sat between Coop and Jake with Archie and Ian opposite us as the limo carried us over to the Garden Hotel and Convention Center one town over where the Homecoming dance was being held. As we pulled up, I got my first good look at the Hollywood theme work the committee had done, including the red carpet leading up to the doors, the velvet-rope lining the walkway, and the silhouettes of paparazzi—it was both ridiculous and adorable.

When the driver opened the back door, Jake slid out first and then held a hand out to me. The perfect weather of the day was turning into the perfect evening. The breeze tugged at my hair, but it wasn't hot at all. The sun was dipping on the horizon, but it would be another hour before it went down.

We waited until everyone was out before following the red carpet inside. We weren't the first to arrive, but we were definitely not the last. Cars were pulling in to the parking lot, and other kids were walking up. Other cars were lining up behind the limo to deposit their passengers too.

Jake threaded his fingers with mine as we headed inside. There was a star wall set up with the school name and in our colors along with a photographer to take our picture.

"We're gonna take a little time here," Archie informed the photographer. And we did—we got individual shots of me with each of them, then one of all of us together. The only couple shot we didn't take was me and Ian.

Whatever Coop said to him seemed to have worked. Holding onto that, we were still laughing from the last picture when we headed inside.

"Woah," Jake said as we made it into the lobby area. The music pulsed from beyond the doors, but someone had taken the time to create "sets" all over and there were a couple more photographers.

"Classic car pic!" Coop said, catching my hand and tugging me over to the replica of James Dean's Porche 550 Spyder. They even had a fan to create wind.

I slid into the driver's seat and Coop made a face before he hopped over into the passenger side.

Snap.

The King Kong set was next, and Jake and I played like we were hanging off the Empire State Building.

Like I said, ridiculous.

Snap.

Archie wanted the shot with the faux casino and James Bond. I hung off his arm like some Bond girl. But I was pretty sure the fact I couldn't stop laughing as we cut up didn't help.

Snap.

The last set we got to was a horror movie set up, right down to the "bloodied knives" and faux bodies. At my grimace, Ian said, "Hard pass."

I almost said "sorry" because he hadn't gotten to do the movie one, but I didn't do horror movies, and thankfully, none of them questioned that.

We followed the hall toward the double doors.

"You ready?" Coop asked, the thrumming beat vibrated the air around us. It had to be loud in there, and I grinned. It was weird, how many dances had I gone to with all of them? Usually, they'd had dates of their own, but more than once, I'd been the defacto date, if for no other reason than one of the guys went stag.

Still, tonight, it was just us.

"You know what?" I said with a grin. "I really am."

Jake and Ian grabbed the doors, and there was a wall of gold glitter streamers we had to pass through to get inside. The music rolled out on a wave. Inside, it was all glittering lights and moving strobes. A DJ occupied the corner and rocked out to the music filtering through the oversized speakers.

There were already people out dancing, tables were set up scattered around the dance floor, and there was a station to get drinks—water and soda. No punch bowls. It was kind of funny, you always saw punch bowls in the movies, but I'd never seen a single one at a dance in real life.

"You're here!" came the squeal of a voice warning me of Cheryl's approach before she launched at me. Coop steadied me with a hand on my back as I hugged her back.

Laughing, I pulled away to see Cheryl in all her finery. She'd pinned her hair up save for two tendrils falling on either side of her face. It made her look like a real doll.

"You look gorgeous," Cheryl continued catching my hands. "Doesn't she, Mitch?"

Mitch grunted a response, or maybe he said something else, but I barely got a glance at him before Cheryl did a twirl.

"What do you think?"

"I think you look perfect." I had to pitch my voice higher to carry, and she grinned.

"Oh…" She thrust her phone at Mitch. "Take our picture." Then she hooked arms with me as Coop and Jake dropped back a couple of steps, both guys were shaking their heads, and it gave me my first good look at Mitch. Despite the dressier clothes and neat hair, he wore a faintly sour expression. Kind of like he'd smelled a fart in church.

Then again, maybe Cheryl had just had him snapping a lot of pictures this evening. It was a Cheryl thing to do. Wrapping an arm around my waist, she tilted her head in, and I laughed as we leaned toward each other.

Two flashes from the camera on her phone and she let me go with an excited titter to grab the phone and look. "Oh we look awesome, see?" She showed me the picture and, you know, it wasn't half bad.

"Hey," Coop said as he caught my hand. "I'm stealing Frankie for a dance. We'll see you later."

"Okay," Cheryl said. "We'll join you!" She grabbed for Mitch's hand, and he actually rolled his eyes with what I hoped was exasperated affection or I might have to nut punch him.

The guys were right, Cheryl was sweet. Mitch had better be nice to her.

"We'll catch up," Coop said to the guys as he tugged me toward the dance floor. There were shoes under a lot of the tables. Half the girls had already ditched their heels.

Not that I blamed them, it was why I hadn't worn them. The music shifted as Coop weaved his way through the room for the dance floor. Beyond Cheryl, I recognized a few other seniors. Most of those already here were likely juniors or sophomores. Seniors tended to arrive later...

Or so it seemed.

The song changed as we got to the floor, and I laughed. I loved this song. I think I bounced the last couple of steps to the dance floor itself. It was crowded, and for once, I didn't care. Turning to Coop, I grinned at him. He'd ditched his jacket already, and we moved together to the music. Laughing, we mouthed the words at each other as we moved. When he spun around and danced back at me, shaking his ass, I laughed and lifted my arms as we rocked.

When "Shut Up and Dance" segued to "Moves Like Jagger," I shifted to dance backward and ended up bumping into Jake. While Coop didn't sit it out, I was dancing between them. As the music cycled through and Archie hit the dance floor with us, I rotated between them until it was just all four of us dancing.

I lost track of the songs they were playing and just moved with the beats. Sweat, cologne, and fragrances perfumed the air around us. When they finally gave us a slow song, it was Jake I ended up dancing with.

"I'm glad you guys kept track," I told him a little breathlessly.

We were both a little sweaty, but Jake didn't pull away, just kept his arm around my lower back as he dipped his head to talk against my ear. "Always. Besides…I'm faster."

Head back, I laughed because he sounded so damn smug about it.

"Having fun?"

"I really am," I promised. Somehow, while we'd all been dancing, more people had filtered in. Though the crowd had thinned a little with the slower songs. The Homecoming court had also arrived. I didn't know half the kids who got elected to it, and I didn't care.

"What?" Jake asked, and gave me a squeeze.

"Hmm?"

"You have the tiny little Frankie-frown. What are you worried about?"

I had a *Frankie-frown*? I opened my mouth to ask, then snapped it shut again. "Did you vote for the Homecoming court?"

He shot me a bemused look. "Of course you were thinking of something utterly random."

Well…duh.

Chuckling, he navigated us slowly toward the edge, and I was okay with that because I really was getting hot now that we'd slowed down. Even my hair was sticking to the back of my neck. So not sexy. "Probably," he said with a shrug. "I wasn't paying that much attention. Didn't they have ballots out at lunch the second week?"

Had they?

"No clue," I admitted, and then laughed when Jake hugged me a little closer. We were supposed to moderate the PDAs, but it was nice to just dance with him. "So much for my *normal* high school stuff, huh?"

"Pfft," he scoffed. "Do you care that you didn't vote or don't remember it if you did?"

"No." Not at all. Not really.

"Then, I say again…pfft." The song was winding down. "C'mon, water break."

He tugged me off the dance floor, and I was fanning my face as I followed his weave through the crowd.

"Frankie!" Rachel's voice had me twisting, and Jake stopped as I pulled back. Wearing a dark green dress that hugged her like it had been painted on, Rachel leaned in and gave me almost an air hug before she motioned her hand up and down. "Damn. You look good enough to eat."

"Too bad. She's not on the menu," Jake interrupted, and I rolled my eyes. When I gave him a light nudge with my elbow, he slung an arm over my shoulders. God, we were both so sweaty.

"Yeah, dickhead. You clean up nice, too. Definitely not edible though." Rachel flicked her fingers at him as if dismissing him before she focused on me again. "Can I steal you for a minute?"

When she cut her eyes to the right, I saw the slender Asian girl hovering a few feet back.

Oh.

"Jake, I'll meet you guys…" Where were they?

He frowned then pointed toward the tables nearer to the door where we'd come in. "Bubba grabbed us a spot over there. You want a drink?"

"Anything cold," I told him.

"You got it." Then he glanced at Rachel. "I've got my eye on you, Manning."

"Oh, I'm feeling all warm inside. It's probably bile."

Laughing, I gave Jake's hand a squeeze before I bumped Rachel. "Behave, or I'll give your girlfriend the same kind of stink eye."

"You would never," Rachel teased. "You're way too nice."

"Ha," I countered as we made our way over. "Just you wait, I have it on good authority that I'm adorably the worst."

Her snort just made me grin wider. "Skylar, this is Frankie," Rachel said when we reached her. We all kind of had to huddle to be heard over the music. "Frankie, this is Skylar."

"Hi." I debated offering her my hand 'cause that might be weird, but then just stuck it out anyway. "It's really great to meet you."

Shy smile growing a little brighter, Skylar clasped my hand. "It's really nice to meet you, too. You really are every bit as nice as Rachel said you were."

"Oh, I was going to say don't believe a word she says, but if I'm supposed to be nice, I can totally live with that."

Skylar laughed, and Rachel grinned.

"You having fun?" I glanced between them. Like me, they were a bit sweaty.

"Actually," Skylar said, as she took Rachel's hand. "More than I expected. I go to private school. We do not have dances like this. It's kind of like in the movies, but not."

Spreading my hands, I paused my response when a body collided with my back, and then Cheryl leaned over me. "Rachel," she scolded. "Why didn't you introduce me to her?" Then without waiting, she stretched out a hand to Skylar. "I'm Cheryl, I'm a little obnoxious, but I'm sure we're going to be amazing friends. Rachel only likes amazing people."

Cheryl still had an arm around me, a bottle of water fisted in that hand. Her perfume tickled my nose, but her light-hearted spirit proved infectious.

"It's good to meet you, too," Skylar said, some of the shyness in her expression eased. "Rachel has told me about both of you. But what she didn't tell me was how pretty you are.”

“Eh,” I said with a half-shrug. “This…” I made a motion toward myself, “does *not* happen everyday, but thank you. Besides, I’m betting she’s too tongue-tied by how pretty you are.”

“Nice,” Cheryl complimented me and offered a playful fistbump. “I was just gonna say because Rachel’s not an idiot.”

Amusingly enough, Rachel seemed a little flushed and her eyes overbright as she gave us both a look. “And now we’re going away before you two get any more ridiculous.”

“Awww,” Skylar teased with a grin. “Maybe I want to hang out with them and get all the dirt on you.”

“Sorry, no can do,” I told her. “Dirt is definitely a third meeting aperitif.”

Cheryl giggled, and Rachel rolled her eyes. When she mouthed *I hate you*, it was like my life was just a little fuller. I blew her a kiss as they wandered away and then eased Cheryl from leaning on me quite so heavily.

“You okay?” I checked with her.

“I’m good. Tell you a secret, my shoes were killing me. You were so much smarter to come in flats.”

I shrugged. “More like a safety concern. I teeter in heels, and dancing in them sucks hard.”

“I get that—well, I don’t, but I can appreciate it.” She grinned. “You know, I’m going to go grab a soda. You want this? I only had one drink.” She passed me the water bottle. I did actually.

“Thanks.”

“You having fun?” With a nod behind me, she added, “You’ve been dancing since I got here.”

“I am. You?”

“Not too bad. Mitch is being kind of a buzzkill. He doesn’t want to dance as much, so don’t mind me if I join you the next time you’re out there.”

“Deal.” Waving at her, I unscrewed the top and drank a good third of it before pivoting to head to the table. My mouth was a little too dry. The water tasted more like tap than bottle, but whatever. Probably too warm. The guys weren't alone, but I recognized a couple of the football players who had dropped in and dragged Jake and Ian into a conversation.

Archie and Coop looked more amused than anything as I circled the table and downed another couple of gulps of the water. It was great on my throat and at least I'd managed to cool off some while talking to Cheryl, Skylar, and Rachel.

"That's Rachel's date?" Archie asked as I sat.

"Yep, she was nice."

He slid another bottle of water in front of me and a soda.

"Thank you." The fresh water bottle had condensation on it, and I screwed on the cap of the first one and popped open the second. Oh. Colder. So much better.

"You've been working it out there," Coop said. "I forgot how much you like to dance."

"Me, too," I admitted. "And it's good music tonight."

"I don't disagree." Archie said, bumping my shoulder. "Next slow song, it's my turn."

Coop snickered, and the brush of his pinky against mine sent a little thrill through me. I tapped my foot in time to the music; I liked the new song the DJ put on. Seriously—he had great taste.

"Where did they find this guy?"

Archie shrugged. "Bubba might know, but…" He motioned to where he and Jake were talking. Jake caught my glance and winked once. I grinned. Gaze snagged on Ian's, I swore I could feel his sigh.

"You want to get back out there?" Coop asked. I took another couple of gulps from the cold water, then stole a drink from the soda.

The sugar and caffeine were almost as welcome as the cold.

"Yes," I said, grinning. "Do you mind?"

"Nah," Coop said as he shoved his chair back and stood. "C'mon."

"I'll be there in a minute," Archie told us as he drained the last swallow in the first water bottle, then grimaced and washed it down with the soda. My thoughts exactly, however, I didn't say anything.

"Hey," Jake called as Coop and I circled the table. "Where you going?"

"To dance," I said with a finger wave, then motioned to the table and all of us. "We can talk anytime. This DJ is awesome!"

The corners of his eyes crinkled as he grinned. "I'll catch up in a sec."

Giving him a thumbs up, I caught Coop's hand and we slid out onto the dance floor just as "Happy" started to play and I laughed. That was perfect. Arms up in the air, I twisted and danced to the beat. It didn't take long for others to pour onto the dance floor, all of us clapping our hands. Well, I was.

Rachel and Skylar appeared in my periphery, and I bumped hips with Rachel once. Cheryl hopped toward me, and Coop rolled his eyes as I made room for her in the little circle we were making.

Archie slid up behind me, and we swayed together, hips rocking from side to side in tandem. Jake weaved through the girls, and they expanded a little and then he chuckled as he caught my hands and spun me into him and then out. I stumbled a half-step, but Ian was right there, and he steadied me. I slowed for a beat, then shook it off. We were all dancing, and it was the first time he'd gotten out here all night that I'd noticed.

Flushed and overheating, I didn't care as "Happy" segued right into "Last Friday Night." Cheryl leaned in, lip-syncing, and then Rachel and I were singing it, too. Coop was laughing and clapping. Jake wrapped his arms around me from behind, and we swayed together as the crush on the dance floor increased.

But it was the dance version and the techno beat and chanting had us all screaming. Best. Night. Ever.

I lost track of the songs and who was really dancing with who. It didn't matter, we were all out there. When the song switched again, I tapped Jake to wave him closer. "I'll be right back. I gotta pee," I told him in his ear, and he chuckled.

"Okay," he answered, and it was more a matter of reading his lips than actually hearing him.

The flashing lights were so bright and the music loud. It was like actually being in a movie a little. Fanciful thoughts or not, they made me giggle. The tension of the last few weeks had been bled away while we danced.

Swaying, I fanned myself as I strode across the room for the doors. The bathrooms were outside, and it was much brighter with the overheads on outside and so much cooler. I was burning up. Head back, I paused for a moment, free of the pounding beat.

It was like stepping into another world. Glancing around, I searched for the restroom signs and had to pass the faux sets area toward another hall that twisted around to find the girls.

The music faded even more to a distant hum as I slid into the bathroom. The colder air felt so good against my overheated skin. It was like someone had me sucking on a jalapeño. There were a couple of girls checking their makeup in the mirror when I came in.

One was a junior—Brittany? Bella? B-something or other, and Maddy. I only remembered Maddy's name because of Mom. They cast me grins, and I gave them a little finger wave as I did the happy pee pee dance into a stall.

If I'd had to pee when I was on the dance floor, I was about to burst by the time I got in here. The dress stuck to me in places, and my hair was damp, but I just shifted things so I could empty my bladder.

Seriously, peeing should never feel that good, but it did. The girls' voices faded as they left the bathroom. After I finished, I stumbled a little getting the dress straightened back out.

Damn, it wasn't this hard when I put it on earlier. It was a dress, not a body suit. Out of the stall, I braced a hand against the door. The overheated feeling wasn't fading, despite the cooler air, and dizziness assailed me for a minute. Ugh.

Food. All that dancing. I needed to eat.

With care, I walked over to the sink and washed my hands. A glance at myself in the mirror made me feel a bit better. The cosmetics Carol used had held up well, even if I had been sweating. Sliding a wet hand against the back of my neck, I sighed at the coolness.

Hair down might look pretty, but it was too warm. I leaned against the counter and blinked slowly. Tired swamped me all at once. Maybe the dancing and the lack of stress were just what I needed. Another couple of dances, and I bet I could talk the boys into heading out. Though…

Disappointment crept in. I kind of didn't want it to end. Tonight was like the first really right thing in a while. It was perfect.

Soda. Maybe a snack. Then more dancing. Decided, I rinsed my hands again before blotting them dry with a paper towel. I wandered back out and the dizziness hit. Pausing, I leaned against the wall outside the bathroom.

"Hey, you okay?" A warm arm slid around my waist, and I blinked slowly.

"Yeah, I'm just…" The flush of heat hit again. The last time I felt like this, I'd had way too much of the whiskey at one of Archie's parties. I'd puked that night, too.

Not pretty.

But all I'd had was some water. We hadn't had any drinks.

"Here, why don't you sit down?" He guided me farther down the hall. Maybe there were benches or something. "You want me to get anyone?"

"I can text the guys," I said. "Really, I'll be okay." But he didn't slow, and it was like stumbling through molasses. "Just pause for a sec…"

"You don't look so good, hot stuff, we need to cool you off."

I blinked, and my vision wouldn't unblur. The music had all but faded. I tried to dig my heels in, but he kept moving.

"Hey," I said twisting against his arm. Not that my body cooperated.

"Just cooperate," he said. "Really, you don't look so good. I'm going to take care of you. I promise."

What the hell?

He pushed me through a door, and I gripped the wristlet. I still had my phone. This wasn't right. Panic scrabbled through me.

"Really," he said pulling me right up against him. "It's going to be fine." I pushed my hands against his chest.

"Let go."

It was too hot. And I didn't know him…

Then he kissed me.

Where the Hell...

Coop

She's not with Rachel or her girl.

Archie

Not outside.

Jake

Not in the girl's bathroom. Bubba said there was another around the corner. He went to look.

Archie

WTF

Coop

We'll find her. Check lobby?

Archie

OMW

Chapter Twenty-Four
EVERY BREATH IS A BOMB

He shoved his tongue in my mouth, and my arms were like lead. Pushing against him was like pushing a wall. But I had teeth. Even dizzy, I could still bite down.

The taste of copper flooded my mouth, and he let out a shout. The grip on my arms turned even more painful a split second before he jerked his head up.

"Bitch." Spit hit my cheek, and I squinted up at the guy who'd just been kissing me. I knew that voice. My eyes wouldn't focus, and every limb seemed weighed down by heavy bricks.

Fumbling, I pushed again, and this time, he shook me. My head snapped forward and back. Crab walking my hands up his chest, it was so much effort. Then I hooked my right hand and my pretty new red nails against his face and dragged the hand down.

He swore again.

Pain exploded through my cheek, and I toppled sideways. It was like I was stuck, I couldn't move, I couldn't do more than blink. I couldn't even make a sound 'cause it hurt.

"You little… You're a fighter, huh?"

The hands grabbed me and slammed me onto my back. Why the hell weren't my eyes working? This was worse than being drunk. I managed to get another hand up and tried to yell. It was getting harder though.

Hot breath in my face, and I couldn't turn away from him trying to kiss me again, but I got my fingers on his ear. Metal. There was metal on his ear.

I yanked on the earring for all I was worth, because I was falling down in a hole. He let out another shout and wrenched my wrist. It kind of hurt, but I didn't care.

"What the fuck…" The weight on me and the looming presence suddenly vanished. A harsh grunt of sound followed by the meaty thunk of fists impacting against flesh. "You *son of a bitch*. What the hell did you think you were doing?"

Ian? Fury lived in that voice. I'd never heard that much rage in him before. He almost sounded like Jake.

But not Jake.

"Hey…" Oh. Jake was there.

Something crashed to the floor. Shouting.

"Woah, woah…babe…" Someone picking me up.

Why couldn't I focus?

Blink.

I tried to open my eyes.

Blink.

They wouldn't stay open.

"Easy, beautiful, I got you." Coop.

Blink.

Cold air.

Blink.

"What the hell is going on?" Archie.

Blink.

Flashing lights.

Blink.

"Only one of you can ride with her." Who?

Blink.

"I'm going," Coop said.

"We're following."

Blink.

"Can you tell me what happened?"

"This asshole was all over her." Ian.

Ian was there, too…what happened to his voice?

Blink.

"We really need to get in touch with her mother."

"I'm eighteen, and I'm not going. I have no idea where her mother is, and she hasn't answered the calls we've made."

Turning my head, I focused on Coop. He had his arms folded and looked pissed. Where…

"Hey," the nurse said, pushing past Coop. Why was there a nurse here? My face hurt. "Take it easy, you're at East Mercy. Can you tell me your name?"

"Frankie," I said, and oh my voice sounded like I'd swallowed glass, and my throat hurt like hell. "Frankie Curtis. Was there an accident?"

We'd been at the dance. Had something happened on the way home?

"I'll answer your questions in just minute, okay, hon?" The nurse gave me a really kind smile. Just past her shoulder, Coop stared at me with a tense expression. He didn't look hurt. That was good. Where were the other guys?

"Is everyone okay?"

"One more sec, can you tell me how you're feeling right now? Any pain? Any discomfort?"

"Face hurts." I lifted my hand, and then paused at the I.V. in the back of it. Oh that was why it hurt. I tried for the other one and winced more. Oh that really hurt. "What happened to my wrist?" It was wrapped in some kind of splint and ace bandage.

"Any other pain?"

"Coop," I focused on him. "What's going on? Where's Jake and Archie? Where's Ian?"

"Right here, baby girl," Jake said from the doorway.

"I told you it can only be one at a time right now," the nurse scolded.

"She's also upset, so bite me," he retorted.

"Please," Archie tacked on to the end of it. Oh, he looked like he'd been ill. "We're all worried about her. It's been hours."

Hours?

What the hell…?

"Fine, but please wait." Finally, the nurse looked at me again. "What's the last thing you remember?"

"I was at Homecoming." My bracelet was gone. And I was in a hospital bed. The guys didn't look too bad. Jake still had some bruises from before, but they looked yellow under the lighting. Archie looked a little sick and pale. Coop's expression seemed inflexibly angry, except when he looked at me. They were all still in their nice clothes, though Coop's looked like he'd spilled something on his shirt.

Images flashed as I tried to think.

"I went to the bathroom. I didn't feel good."

Coop came around to the other side of the bed and put a hand on mine carefully because of the I.V.

Everything after that was just…fuzzy. "Did I fall?" I'd fallen. But I didn't remember how.

"Okay, that's good, Frankie," the nurse said. I looked for a nametag, but she didn't seem to have one on. "Really good. The doctor will need to see you, and there are police here who want to talk to you, too, but before we do any of that, your friends are all going to have to wait in the hall for a minute."

There was some disagreement with the guys, but Coop pressed a kiss to my forehead. "We'll be right back," he promised. "We're literally going to be right out there.”

I nodded. Not that I really seemed to have a say in anything. Once the door closed behind them, I focused on the nurse again.

“First, my name is Denitra Hunley, you can just call me Denitra.”

She seemed to be waiting for me to respond, so I nodded. Her close cropped dark hair curled against her scalp, but she had a really kind smile.

“I’m a nurse here at Mercy General, but I’m also a SAFE advocate. So I’ve been with you since they brought you in.”

Safe?

“Stop Abuse for Everyone,” she continued. “Have you heard of that before?”

I shook my head slowly. “I’m not going to like where this is going, am I?” Between my wrist, my face, and this whole situation, my head had started to pound.

“Probably not. You were admitted from emergency room unconscious and for treatment in a suspected sexual assault.”

I definitely didn’t like where this was going.

“Someone roofied me.” That was why I couldn’t remember.

Ice slithered through my veins. The vague flashes seemed to come and vanish before I could grasp them. My eyes burned. “Can we turn the lights down?”

“Of course.” She rose and turned off the main overhead, leaving only one on across the room, and it was much dimmer. That helped. “And yes, it was suggested you had been drugged by the young men who found you. You have very good friends.”

Maria had told me that someone had been doing that. But… Guilt stabbed at me. “Did…did someone…?”

“As far as we can tell with a cursory exam, no. Because you were unconscious, another nurse and I, only, removed your clothes and jewelry and bagged it for evidence. I also cleaned out under your nails…” She continued talking in that very easy tone, explaining everything, and as unsettling as the information was, it also helped to have it laid out for me.

A shiver went up my spine, and I wanted to fold my arms, but the IV pulled and my wrist protested, so I put them back down.

"You said I wasn't…"

"Without a full exam, I can't guarantee it," she said gently. "However, your underwear did not appear to have been disturbed."

Fuck. Humiliation crawled through me. I'd been in a thong.

"Also, the boys indicated that the assailant was still dressed, those are both positive signs."

"I don't remember." Nebulous flashes. That was it. "I don't…" I shook my head.

"That's pretty standard in a case like this. One of your friends consented to a urine test because he was feeling off and said he'd drunk the same water as you. We found a very small amount of flunitrazepam in his system."

"Archie finished my wa—" That hadn't been my water. "Is Cheryl all right?" I shook my head to try and clear it. Bad idea. "I'm sorry. The water I drank…Cheryl gave it to me. She said she wanted a soda instead, she'd had a drink from it, and it was warm and tasted off. I was hot and sweaty and really thirsty."

"I don't know about your friend, but what I want to do now is perform an exam so we can confirm whether you were assaulted, and I'd also like to collect a urine sample. We're pretty lucky to be right in the window for this, because a lot of people wait and the sooner we test, the better it will be."

Did I want to know?

My stomach seesawed. Chest tight, I tried to suck in a deep breath. Sweat dotted my brow, and my mouth went dry—or dryer. "Can I have…" Did I even want water?

"How about some ice chips?" Denitra offered, and she held out a small paper cup already boasting the melting ice. Every action she took was utterly patient.

"So I have to have the test?"

"You don't have to do anything," she told me. "But every piece of evidence we gather can help with the prosecution of your assailant."

My assailant.

I had an assailant.

"What exactly do you do?"

Her explanation didn't make me feel better. It was invasive, but she promised me complete privacy, and they would take care of everything. "You can say no to the exam, no one is going to compel or force you. I'm here to help. I can discuss the options and recommend therapy and what we can do after, but you have to make the decisions. The urine test though, I think you can handle that, yeah?"

Sure. Pee in a cup. How hard could it be?

"I know this is difficult."

"It's hard to be difficult if I can't remember it." The guys had found me?

"Not remembering doesn't make it less traumatic," she assured me. "It doesn't make it less invasive. Even if nothing happened, someone still hurt you. That feeling right now—the confusion and the distance—some of that can be after effects of the drug. It's also shock. This is going to take time to process. It won't go away over night."

"You're saying I'm going to need therapy." Curtises didn't do therapy. No, they got involved with inappropriate men real or intentioned, and flaked out on their kids.

My mom wasn't here. That was what they'd been talking about.

"Therapy wouldn't hurt, but everything is one step at a time. That's how we get through this. I'm going to be right here for you…"

"Are you just going to tell the cops and the doctors what I said?"

"No," she told me so firmly, I didn't question it. "Unless you specifically ask me to, I won't be speaking to them at all. I'm *your* advocate. I'm protected by confidentiality. What you tell me goes nowhere else unless you give me permission. I'm SAFE."

"That's kind of cool." I blinked hard and looked down at my hand. "I don't—hurt like he did anything. But I feel kind of funny all over."

"That's normal, but I'm glad you aren't experiencing that kind of discomfort. So would you like to start with the urine test? Or would you like some time to just sit here and think? We're not in a hurry. This happens on your schedule."

"How long… how long have we been here?"

"It's Sunday morning."

Sunday morning.

God.

The cats.

"Your friends have been here all night. They've been taking turns sitting with you, policy is only one at a time."

"The police?"

"When you're up for it, I'll call the detective, and he'll come take your statement."

"Do you know…you said they stopped it? They caught him?"

She nodded. "That's what your friends told me. I haven't spoken to the police other than to inform them they would have to wait until you were ready to talk."

I licked my lips. "Did they tell you who?"

"I'm sorry, no. We can ask them, when you're ready. I can stay with you while you talk to them, too. If it will make you feel better."

"They won't hurt me." They knew already. If they found me, they knew already.

"I believe you," she said with a smile. "But like I said, it's what makes you comfortable."

When she offered me the ice chips again, I took them and sucked on a couple. My mouth really was so dry, and I felt—off. "I'll do the urine test."

"We can wait for your mom if you want," Denitra offered, and I shook my head.

"It's fine. I'm old enough to make that decision for myself, right?"

"You are," she said carefully. "But it might be easier for you to wait for your mother."

"No," I said firmly. "Do you know where my phone is?"

"Your friends have it. We had to take the little clutch purse though."

That meant they had my keys and my ID and stuff. "That's fine." I tried to sit up more and winced. Oh. Wow. It felt like someone had piled me on the football field.

"Careful," she said. "You want some help?"

Everything about Denitra was warm and caring. She didn't just reach over and help me up, she asked.

"I think I got it."

"Okay. I'm right here."

With her monitoring me, I made it to my feet. She disconnected the tube from the IV and hung it up.

"We're just hydrating you at the moment, but we'll put that back in when we are done, all right?"

I nodded.

Every step seemed a little rocky, especially since the hospital gown seemed to gap. She didn't try to help me, just followed me to the bathroom and then she put on a pair of gloves and got out a little plastic cup.

With a marker, she wrote something on the side of it.

"Do you have to watch me?" I'd really rather just pee on my own.

"You good to do this?" She nodded to my wrist, and I looked at it all wrapped up. It was my right, and it would make it a little tricky, but I could do it one-handed. I really wasn't going to have her hold a cup for me to pee into.

Not. Happening.

"I'll be fine."

She didn't argue with me or try to persuade me otherwise. Instead, she moved to the door and pulled it mostly closed. "I'll be right here. Just call me if you need help."

Yeah.

No.

My left hand trembled as I sat down and pulled the gown out of my way. It was an uncomfortable prospect, but I managed without sloshing it anywhere. I set it on the little tray where she'd left it and then finished. Glancing down at my thighs, I bit my lip. There was a bruise, but it was nearer to my knee. There were more bruises on my arm. After I finished and used the rail to help myself stand, I moved to the sink.

My left cheek had a fat, puffy bruise and a cut. That looked—wonderful. My eyes seemed huge. The non-smeared makeup was definitely looking worse for wear, and my eyes had black smudges under them.

The trembling in my hand seemed to move all over me, and I tried to remember. But the flashes didn't seem to gel into anything more than a shadow. I didn't remember being hit. Or hurting my wrist.

Or if anything actually happened.

"Frankie?" Denitra called.

"I'm all right," I said, not meaning a word of it. I wanted to be all right.

I was not all right.

Even breathing seemed to hurt at the moment. Rinsing my hand carefully, I wiped it off with a towel from the wall dispenser, then dropped it in the trash before I moved to the door.

"I'm done." She opened it gently and the look on her face was so damn understanding, I just wanted to cry. "If you do the exam, can you tell if…if he did anything?"

"Yes," she said. "We can. It will be uncomfortable for you, but I'll be here every step of the way."

I nodded.

"I don't want the guys to know."

"No one has to tell them."

I swallowed.

"But I would recommend one more time that we try to call your mom, hon. You're going to need support."

Yeah. My mom would be the last person to give that. "Call her. But she won't be coming. She'd have to care to show up and right now…I'm not the priority." I don't think I ever had been. "But I don't want to wait for when she decides to answer."

"Let's get you back in the bed, then I need to get a couple of things."

"Is it going to be anyone else?"

"No," she said. "I can do the kit collection if you want. I'm a registered nurse, too."

"Thank you."

It didn't take her long. It was humiliating. She explained everything, and not once did it feel like she was judging me. Not even when I answered if I was sexually active, what kind of prophylaxis I used, and a dozen other uncomfortable questions.

At the end of it, I had a definitive answer. As definitive as she could be.

The assault had never made it as far as penetration. So while he had bruised me, he hadn't penetrated.

That was something.

It was also when the dam broke and the tears started sliding down my face.

I don't know when she got the gloves off or moved her stuff aside, but she sat down and hugged me while I cried against her shoulder. The sobs hurt almost as much to let out as they had to hold in. But she didn't rush me or try to tell me it would all be all right, she just let me cry. When I finally slowed to just sniffles, she eased back and then got a cool cloth to help wipe my face.

After she got me tucked back into the bed and the IV reattached, she promised to get me some water and asked if I wanted anything to eat. I really didn't want anything.

I'd have to see a doctor, but she would be with me for that. When she brought up the police again, I just wanted to pull the blankets over my head, but I nodded. I'd talk to them.

"When can I go home? I have to look after my cats."

"You might need to stay here overnight. I want to get the urine test done, and we want to monitor you for any adverse reactions to the drugs and medications. Plus…you really shouldn't be alone yet."

I didn't want to stay in the hospital. I'd ask the doctor. "Thank you."

"Frankie." The firm note pulled my gaze up to her. "This isn't your fault. Nothing that happened was your fault. You are going to be all right. You will have support. I'm going to be here for you, and I'm going to help you find someone you can talk to."

That sounded great, but… "Thanks," I said again. "I'm just tired. Sorry."

"Do you want to see your friends? Or should I send them home?"

They weren't going to leave just because she told them. They'd been here all night. All night.

I still couldn't wrap my head around that.

"In my stuff there was a bracelet…"

"After we process everything, I'll make sure you get it back."

At the moment, I didn't care about the rest of it, but the bracelet was important.

"Frankie, what can I get you?"

"The guys…can they all come in?"

She nodded. "As long as they keep it calm in here, yes. They'll have to go out again when the doctor comes. Okay?"

"Okay."

I hoped I didn't look as bad as I felt, but the looks on their faces when Denitra let them back into the room dashed my chances of covering up my tears.

"I'm going to take this down, I'll be back in a few. You three will behave while I'm gone." Denitra gave each of them a stern look. "She needs calm and rest."

"We got this," Coop told her, but he was already across the room and carefully taking my left hand. When the door closed behind her leaving the four of us alone, I leaned my head against the pillows and stared at them.

"Who?"

"Baby girl, you don't need to worry about…"

"Who?" I asked again. "Someone from school? A stranger? Who?"

Archie raked a hand through his hair, and the three of them looked at each other. Finally, Coop said, "It was Mitch."

I closed my eyes. I barely knew Mitch. "Is Cheryl all right?"

"She's fine," Archie said. "Nothing happened to her." The harshness in his tone worried me. He still looked rough.

"They were dating," I told him. "That water…"

"It was hers," Jake said, almost like he had to ground it out between his teeth. "We know."

I glanced at each of them. "Cheryl didn't do this."

"No one is saying she did," Coop said gently. "Pretty sure Mitch gave her the water, and then she ended up giving it to you."

"Ass probably waited until you wandered out to follow you." Jake's knuckles were white where he gripped the edge of the bed. "If Bubba hadn't heard something…"

"Where is he?"

"Getting questioned," Archie said, and then he eased down on the side of the bed. "Is this okay?" He was careful not to touch me, but he looked like hell.

"Are you okay? You drank some…"

"I know, babe. Started feeling a little woozy about ten minutes after you went to the bathroom. When you didn't come back, we got worried. I mostly have a headache, I didn't pass out…" He sucked in a breath and blew it out. "One of us should have gone with you."

"That's on me," Jake snarled. "She told me—you told me—and I just let you go."

"It was the bathroom guys…you can't exactly go in with me."

Coop stroked his thumb against my palm. "It's no one sitting here's fault," he said steadily. "It was Mitch. Let's put the blame where it belongs. Right now, we're going to keep this nice and calm. What do you need?"

"I want to go home," I admitted. "The cats…"

"I fed them," Jake said. "I left for a little while earlier, drove back, made sure they were all right, and then came back here."

Relieved, I closed my eyes.

"I'm sorry, babe," Archie said quietly. "You really shouldn't have had to go through that."

"For what it's worth, I don't remember it." My eyes still stung, and it was almost easier to talk with them closed. The concern on their faces choked me. "But I'm really glad you're here now."

"Not going anywhere," Coop said. "I called my mom—after we couldn't get ahold of yours." Reluctance crept into his voice. "Just in case, you know she used to be able to sign for you at school so maybe…"

"Did you tell her?"

"Just that you got hurt," he said gently. "No other details."

"Everyone knows though...don't they?" Before they could answer, I said, "Never mind. I don't care. I just…Denitra, she did an exam. He didn't…he didn't do much more than…" I didn't even want to say the words, so I held up my wounded wrist and motioned to my face carefully.

"I still want to break his legs," Jake said almost conversationally. "To start."

Making myself open my eyes, I looked at them and blinked rapidly at the sheen of tears in their eyes. Like me, they seemed to be blinking them back. "I'm really tired."

"Then get some sleep." Coop let go of my hand long enough to drag a chair over. "We're right here."

"Not going anywhere," Archie said. "Unless you're hungry. I can go get you something."

I really didn't want food. "Not yet." I licked my lips. "I just want to sleep." And then to wake up and have this all be a bad dream.

"Then sleep," Jake said softly, and he touched my foot through the blanket. "No one is going to bother you."

I believed him.

Chapter Twenty-Five
ALMOST EVERYTHING I WISH I'D SAID

ARCHIE

The doctor was in with her, and the cops wanted to talk to Jake. They'd already interviewed Bubba. He sat in a chair across from me in the waiting room. Coop wouldn't move from her door. Even if he couldn't be inside it, he planted like a damn oak. Where I would have argued or Jake would have bellowed, Coop just stood his ground.

As much as I envied his calm, I couldn't embrace it. Every time I looked at Frankie's bruised and pale face, rage flooded me. Not even the fact Bubba had broken Mitch's jaw satisfied my need for violence.

That son of a bitch was on another floor in this hospital with his jaw wired shut and a handcuff on his wrist. Coop and I already had to keep Jake from going down there once. Personally, I'd been fine with letting Jake take another pound of flesh, but Coop held his head and reminded us that Frankie needed us *here* and not in jail.

Someone had cleaned up Bubba's hands. The knuckles on both had been split open and bloody when we'd gotten in the car. The ride back to Frankie's place where we got our own vehicles had been dead silent. Coop texted us the whole way. Not that any of the updates made us feel better.

Frankie was unconscious.

Frankie had suffered abrasions and contusions.

They were pretty sure she'd been drugged.

No. Shit.

The wooziness had hit then. The sick feeling. It had been coming in waves since just before we realized Frankie hadn't come back from the bathroom.

At the hospital, getting answers was like pulling teeth. No one would talk to us. It was why Coop wouldn't leave.

The cops showed up.

The nurse advocate.

Tough lady. I liked her.

She didn't take crap from anyone, the cops, the doctors, us…and then Frankie finally woke up.

Even after I'd given them a urine sample and confirmed there'd been drugs in the water, the answer hadn't helped. It just made me angrier.

Angry some fucker had done it.

Angry some fucker turned out to be Mitch.

Angry the fucker did it to Frankie.

Maybe he hadn't *meant* for her to have the water, but that didn't matter. He'd taken advantage of it.

He'd hurt her.

I was so fucking over people hurting her.

"Hey…" Bubba's voice pulled me out of those dark thoughts. Not far really, they were right there. The violence in his eyes promised me he wasn't pulling me out. Not really. He followed me right in. "Did we ever find her mother?"

"Yes," I said spitting out the word. "Jeremy confirmed it for me. She and

Eddie are in Prague."

Bubba closed his eyes. "Bitch."

"Pretty much."

Not only had the bitch moved out, she'd left the country. No word. Not even a fuck off. Fine. Screw her.

I'd called Wittaker. He promised to file an emergency brief to get her emancipation rolling. It was a sticky process. I didn't care what it cost. Frankie deserved so much better than this crap.

If Wittaker couldn't get it done, I'd call Grandfather.

I owed the old man a call anyway.

He could do anything.

"Do you need a lawyer?" I should have asked earlier.

"No," Bubba said with a shrug. "Not yet. They aren't charging me with anything as far as I know. I don't care if they do. Asshole had it coming."

Yes. Yes he did.

"If they want to talk to you again. We get you a lawyer."

"I don't care about me…" Bubba said, and looked up the hallway. "How is she?"

"She's Frankie," I told him. "She endures." That was the worst part of all of it. The pain in her eyes and the fact that she put on a brave face for us. But I'd heard her crying. We all had. Jake looked like he wanted to take the door down, but Coop kept a hand on his shoulder.

How the fuck did he stay so calm?

I hated him.

I envied him.

Nauseated, I leaned forward and dropped my head. Elbows on my knees, I tried to suck in a deep breath. I was not going to puke. They'd offered me something for this earlier.

I refused.

If Frankie had to endure this, then I could. I didn't want to forget one miserable second.

A hand settled against my back. "Easy, man, what can I get you?"

"Can you get me that twenty minutes back for her? So one of us is at the bathroom when she comes out?" So that asshole never put a finger on her.

"I wish."

Yeah. Me too.

We sat there for a while, and when Jake came back, he looked like hell. The rage in him seemed to shimmer in the air around him like heat rising off the pavement. "They want to talk to you, Arch."

"I don't fucking care."

I didn't.

"Be faster if you talk to them. Sooner we get this done, maybe the sooner we get out of here."

Take Frankie home. Try to make this better somehow.

"Fine."

Bubba gave me a pat on the shoulder as I stood.

"You need to eat," Jake told me, and I just stared at him.

"Can you eat?"

He shook his head.

"Me neither."

The next hour blurred, but I answered the cops' questions. They were pretty basic. Who was I? What had I noticed? When had I drunk the water? Did I see how Frankie got it? When did we notice she was missing? Were we aware of some long-standing problem with Mitch?

On and on.

After, it was Coop's turn, and I took his place outside her hospital room. It seemed like the doctors and cops had been in there forever. But she wasn't alone, the advocate was with her.

Still, by the time they cleared out, it was mid-afternoon and someone had to think about getting back to feeding her cats. Bubba volunteered. He hadn't gone anywhere near her room. Instead, he'd been the one running to get drinks, talking to the cops, or just sitting down the hall. Waiting.

He wanted to be there, but he wouldn't go.

Coop gave him the keys. Bubba said he'd bring food back, then he left.

"He blames himself," Coop said.

"What?" Jake looked at us. We'd be in with Frankie, but the advocate was helping her shower now that they'd done everything.

"He blames himself," Coop said with a sigh. "He pulled back, she broke up with him, and last night when he was supposed to be her date, she got hurt by someone on the team. He blames himself."

"Well, he can get in line," Jake snapped. "I'm the one who let her go to the bathroom, and I let her get water from Cheryl. I was supposed to be getting her a drink, I should have just taken it over to her while she was talking to them."

We all blamed ourselves. As much as I wanted to tell Jake none of this was his fault, I didn't disagree with him.

We could have done things differently.

On all fronts.

Things I should have said to her, to them. We should have made it clear from the beginning. We shouldn't have been competing at all. Jake was right, there was room for all of us.

"He saved her," Coop said with a certainty I wanted to share.

"Not soon enough."

There was no response to that.

What could they say?

We'd all fucked it up.

JAKE

One day later…

"I can do it," she told me as she climbed the stairs. We'd all blown off school.

Fuck 'em. They'd kept Frankie overnight, and none of us left except to come back here and feed the cats. Bubba brought back a change of clothes for her the night before.

It was smart. She didn't want to be in that hospital gown, and they'd taken her dress and her jewelry. Coop had her phone and keys and stuff. But…she didn't want us hovering. Frankie had never been frail or fragile, even if I treated her like spun glass. I wasn't an idiot—she was tough as they came. She put up with all of us, didn't she?

Still, she looked somehow far more delicate, especially with her wrist all bound up and her face bruised. Every single time I saw that bruise, I wanted to kill something.

Bless Coop's mom, she'd come to the hospital that morning and helped us wrangle with the staff to discharge her. Archie had been ready to call the lawyers in. Hell, even Jeremy showed up and, though a little more worrisome, so had Joe, Bubba's dad.

Between them, they managed to work it out.

I'd called Mom the night of the incident at the dance and again yesterday. She and the girls were making food, I had to go over and pick it up. Ready-to-heat meals, stuff that would be easy for Frankie to fix.

Bubba's mom had sent stuff already, and Coop's mom said something about doing the same.

Frankie would have food. She loved to eat, even if she'd barely said a word as she picked at the breakfast sandwiches we'd picked up. The fact that she didn't touch the hash brown worried me more than anything.

Ahead of us, Archie unlocked the door and Coop followed. Bubba hadn't come with us to bring her home. I didn't think his reticence had anything to do with not seeing Frankie hurt. The guy didn't think she wanted to see him, and he didn't want to bother her.

It was stupid as fuck, she needed all of us, but I'd kick his ass later.

Frankie moved slowly through the apartment. The cats rushed out to greet her, the volume of their meows climbing as she made her way to the sofa.

I half-thought she'd go to her room, but she settled on the sofa, and the cats jumped up. The fact that there were fingermarks on her arms just fueled the fury that seemed right at the edge of boiling. Every single mark on her, I wanted to erase and then pound into Mitch three-fold.

Walking around that corner to see Bubba tearing into Mitch had been like a slow-motion horror movie. Because right behind them, I caught a glimpse of Frankie's red dress, sprawled on the floor like blood.

I'd also never seen Bubba like that before. Even seeing red and ready to tear into Mitch—which trust me, the kidney shots I gave him probably had him pissing blood—the fact Bubba kept hitting him after he was down gave me a small sense of satisfaction.

Until the moment Coop stood, cradling Frankie, and the world just stopped. It sucked all the oxygen out. There were voices in the hall. Staff from the center were there. Someone called the cops and an ambulance.

They called two really, one for Frankie and the other for Mitch. Not that I cared. They could have left him.

They should have left him.

I snagged a blanket from the back of the sofa and draped it over her. A flicker of a smile faded almost as soon as it pulled on her cheek. "I'm all right," she told me, and I eased onto the sofa next to her. I wanted to pull her in my lap and just hold her, but I also didn't want to hurt her again. There was a bruise on her shoulder and another on her back. I'd seen that one this morning when I helped her change.

She must have landed on something on the floor in that room. It was another conference room from the looks of it, filled with chairs and tables. Just an innocuous place, and he had been going to…

When her hand touched mine, I turned my hand over so I could cradle her fingers. Why couldn't time turners or shit like that be real?

"You want coffee, babe?" Arch asked. At least he didn't look quite like hammered shit today.

"You guys have already done a lot…"

"Uh huh. You want coffee?" Archie even managed a real smile.

"I'd kill for some coffee."

"Done." Keys in hand, he glanced at me, and I nodded as did Coop. "Awesome. I'm grabbing some pizza, too while I'm out."

"Archie…"

We all focused on her.

"Thank you."

"Always."

After he left, Coop said, "I'm going to take a shower. You need anything?"

"I'm okay," she told him. "Really. Jake is staying with me, right?"

"Like I'm attached," I told her, and that almost got a real smile.

Coop lifted his chin toward me, and I nodded. Of all of us, Coop had kept his cool. Sooner or later, he was going to burst, and we'd have to watch for it. But I had this. I'd stay calm.

Frankie needed calm. That was what the advocate said. The doctor said. Hell, even the lady cop who'd interviewed me pulled me aside after and said that.

I wasn't planning on throwing a rave, but I got the damn message.

I'd be calm.

Alone, I focused on her. "Movie? YouTube? Book? Stand up comedy?"

She laughed at the last, it was a real if faint, and she grimaced as she put a hand to her chest. "Don't make me laugh."

"Okay," I said, hanging my head. "So horror movie right?"

When she swatted me, the first real sense of relief hit me. There she was. There was my girl. "How about a tearjerker?"

"Fuck. No."

Her sigh tugged at me, and I was ready to capitulate before the corners of her mouth turned up again. "Blowing shit up and shooting people?"

"Now you're talking my language."

I grabbed the remote and turned on the TV, flicking it over to Netflix, we hunted for something. I had an idea…

"Jake?"

"Hmm?" I cut a look at her.

"Could…could I have a hug?"

The remote fell out of my fingers, and I twisted to ease an arm around her immediately. She shouldn't have had to ask. "Tell me if I hurt you." With care, I tugged her over. The cats scrambled away as she leaned into me.

"You're not," she whispered, and rubbed her undamaged cheek against my shirt. Cradling the back of her head, I rested my cheek against her hair.

"I'm sorry, baby girl," I whispered. "I should have done more."

"You're here," she told me. "You guys came."

Eyes closed, I held her. "Always," I promised. "We're always going to be there."

Nothing like this was going to happen to her again.

Ever.

"Now, we can watch something blow up."

"You got it."

COOP

Coffee and pizza helped. The shower helped. Frankie smiling, maybe not huge smiles, but little ones, those helped, too. Everyone was on edge. Archie, Jake, even Bubba, though Bubba kept tabs via text message. Rachel and Cheryl had both called. We'd intercepted those and kept them at a distance for now. I didn't doubt Frankie could use a visit from her friends, Rachel especially. But she'd want to look after a devastated Cheryl. When I mentioned that to Rachel, she told me she was already on it without even an ounce of bitchiness.

What do you know, miracles did happen.

"No," I told him on the phone. I'd walked over to my apartment to grab the things my mom had made and to check on Sis. It felt like an eternity since I'd been home. "Get off your ass, and come and see her."

"Coop…she doesn't want to see me."

"You don't know that," I told him. Swallowing back the urge to yell, I headed in to our kitchen. There were two trays of lasagna. Mom had cooked them that morning and left them out to cool. "Seriously, you don't. You were there, you actually got that ass off of her, and you put him on the ground. You say you care, I *know* you care. She needs to see it."

His sigh echoed over the phone.

"Bubba…you want to be here, don't you?"

"Yes." Fervent. No hesitation. "I love her."

Yeah. I knew that.

"Then I'm not the person you need to be telling. She needs to see you. She needs to see all of us. That's our job right now. We're the rocks. She's always been there for us, now we're there for her."

The sigh he let out resonated with me. "I wanted to kill him. I still want to kill him."

That, I understood perfectly. "Then channel that into being there for her. Jake's managed to make her laugh once. Archie's doing a great job of distraction. Come be her teddy bear."

His snort made me smile. "That sounds sexy."

"It's not, but we're all in boyfriend territory. You may not like it, but being her friend right now might be the best thing for her. She needs to know we don't see her any differently, and that starts with you."

Quiet. Then. "How do you know all this?"

"Turns out studying psych is useful," I told him. I'd also been doing a lot of reading on my phone, and I had a long conversation with Denitra. She'd given me her number and some other resources. "Frankie's gonna need to talk to people, right now it's us, eventually, she's going to need others. Real help. Real therapy."

"You sound like my dad."

"Well, your dad wasn't all wrong." I stared at the ceiling. "And while I want to sound like I know what I'm doing…I really don't. I just don't want to screw this up. We can't afford to—she really can't afford it. Her mother's a no show useless bitch. That means it's us. We're the family. So get in or get out. But choose, Bubba."

Then I hung up.

Harsh? Maybe. The guy wanted to do the right thing, but he wasn't sure what the right thing was. When push came to shove, he'd absolutely been there, and he was fighting to be her friend.

Now he just needed to fight for her.

"Coop?"

I cut a look to the doorway where Sis stood. She looked painfully young to me. Younger than the last time I saw her. Or maybe it was me, maybe I'd gotten older. My eighteenth birthday already felt far in the past.

"Hey, Sis," I gave her a smile as I straightened. "Just came to grab the lasagnas. Mom said your asthma was acting up and you didn't want to go to school today."

She folded her arms. "Is Frankie going to be okay?"

"Yep," I told her, not missing a beat. "She's going to be fine. Give her a couple of days, and I bet she'll even want to hang out."

They hadn't in a while. Something that Sis noticed over the summer. Not that Frankie had ever been mean to her. Far from it. While she'd distanced herself from us, she'd made time for Sis when Sis needed her.

"Come here," I said, and she hurried over to me for a hug.

"I was really worried. One of my friends texted me that her older sister said Frankie got hurt at the dance."

Yeah. I'd seen the rumors flying around. At least the one thing they'd gotten right—*Frankie* had been hurt. The assholes kept their mouths shut.

Probably good, 'cause Jake just needed one person to say the wrong thing and he'd probably explode.

Fuck. Maybe we all needed therapy.

"She's gonna be fine," I told Sis again, and rubbed her back. She'd always been an affectionate pain in the ass. Always wanting hugs or to snuggle. I put up with it, even grumbled about it, but I didn't mind. The last year or so, she'd been more reticent about it. Growing up, Mom had called it. Teenagers suck, she used to tease me. But they're worth it.

"Cool. You staying over there tonight?"

"Probably, as long as she needs me."

"Is Frankie really your girlfriend now?"

I kissed the top of Sis's head and eased back to look at her. "What do you think?"

A sly grin crossed her face. "That you finally got the balls up to ask her 'cause you've had a crush on her forever."

"Wow, don't let Mom hear you say that."

Sis laughed. "Mom's the one who said it."

I chuckled. Fair enough. "Yeah," I said, then tapped her nose. "She's my girlfriend. That does not mean you get to tease her."

"I won't. I like Frankie." Then she gave me another impish look. "More than I like you, and leave one of the lasagnas!" She backed off. "Mom made one for us, too."

"Cool. How's the asthma, for real?"

"It's fine," she said, waving her hand. "It bugged me yesterday. Probably allergies. I just…I wanted to be here when you got home."

I got that. "I'll be down at her place. Text if you need me."

"I will…you know, unless you ignore me cause you're kissing her."

I snorted, but she'd already escaped back to her room and seemed in a much better mood.

Yeah, kissing might be a while.

Shoving my phone in my pocket, I grabbed one of the lasagnas and headed for the door. "I'm going."

"K-I-S-S..."

"Ignoring you," I added, and her laughter followed me out the door.

Brat.

The sunshine and breeze were almost as nice as it had been on Saturday. It seemed weird to be such great weather. At the same time, we needed the sunshine. Maybe I could take her for a walk later. Even if it was just down to the park...or a drive.

The lake would be nice, especially if she didn't want to see people.

One step at a time.

Back at her apartment, she was curled up with Jake, her feet in Archie's lap, and they'd switched to superhero movies. When she looked up at me and smiled, relief worked through me. "We were just gonna start an X-Men marathon."

I made a face. "All of them?"

"Yep," Archie said. "All of them."

"Hey," Frankie said, nudging Archie with a toe. "Some of them are so bad, they're good." Then she smiled.

Yeah, we were definitely watching all of them.

"Popcorn?" I offered, and a little light flickered in her eyes.

"Candy?" she and Jake said in unison, and I chuckled.

"On it. I'll see what you have."

That worked, too.

IAN

I wanted to see her. Badly. I wanted to take back every stupid damn word I said to her. Every dumbass mistake. I wanted to go back to when I was taking her to Homecoming and before Mitch got within a mile of her. I wanted to make it all better.

While I couldn't do that. I could be there, just like I said I would. Jake's text gave me something to do, so I swung by the store and stocked up on all her favorites.

When I got there, Coop let me in, and he nodded. The guys and Frankie were in the living room. Surprise flickered across her face when I came in, and the bruises she had rekindled my rage. Jake paused whatever they were watching.

I wanted to break that asshole's jaw all over again.

Holding up the candy, I said, "I come bearing gifts."

Then she gave me a real, if tentative, smile. "My favorites."

"I thought you might need them." Need me. But it wasn't about me.

"Are you staying?" The question hung there, and the guys were all quiet.

I met her gaze evenly and said what I should have said all along. "Nowhere else I want to be. No one else I want to be with."

No matter what it took, I wasn't going anywhere. I didn't know how long it would take or what I would have to do, but I would to fix this.

I wanted her back.

I just had to earn it.

Frankie and the boys return in *Whispers and Wishes*.

To keep up with Heather and all her series join her reader's group:

https://www.facebook.com/groups/HeathersPack/

Afterword

What happened to Frankie, to Maria, and the other girls mentioned but not named should never happen to anyone. It happens more often than people like to address. I struggled with that chapter, even knowing what was coming and I struggled, again, when I wrote the aftermath.

I struggled with whether to put a warning on the story, though I fought to address it with as much sensitivity as possible. As a rape survivor, I understand that it's a topic that makes even people who have never experienced it uncomfortable and for those who have, I hear you.

Thank you for trusting me. Frankie and the boys will be back in *Whispers and Wishes*.

About Heather Long

USA Today bestselling author, Heather Long, likes long walks in the park, science fiction, superheroes, Marines, and men who aren't douche bags. Her books are filled with heroes and heroines tangled in romance as hot as Texas summertime. From paranormal historical westerns to contemporary military romance, Heather might switch genres, but one thing is true in all of her stories—her characters drive the books. When she's not wrangling her menagerie of animals, she devotes her time to family and friends she considers family. She believes if you like your heroes so real you could lick the grit off their chest, and your heroines so likable, you're sure you've been friends with women just like them, you'll enjoy her worlds as much as she does.

Follow Heather & Sign up for her newsletter:

www.heatherlong.net

Also by Heather Long

UNTOUCHABLE

Rules and Roses

Changes and Chocolates

Keys and Kisses

Whispers and Wishes

Hangovers and Holidays

Brazen and Breathless

Trials and Tiaras

Graduation and Gifts

Defiance and Dedication

82ND STREET VANDALS

Savage Vandal

Vicious Rebel

Ruthless Traitor

Dirty Devil

ALWAYS A MARINE SERIES
Once Her Man, Always Her Man
Retreat Hell! She Just Got Here
Tell It to the Marine
Proud to Serve Her
Her Marine
No Regrets, No Surrender
The Marine Cowboy
The Two and the Proud
A Marine and a Gentleman
Combat Barbie
Whiskey Tango Foxtrot
What Part of Marine Don't You Understand?
A Marine Affair
Marine Ever After
Marine in the Wind
Marine with Benefits
A Marine of Plenty
A Candle for a Marine
Marine under the Mistletoe
Have Yourself a Marine Christmas
Lest Old Marines Be Forgot
Her Marine Bodyguard
Smoke & Marines

BRAVO TEAM WOLF
When Danger Bites
Bitten Under Fire

BOOMERS

The Judas Contact

Deadly Genesis

Unstoppable

Chance Monroe

Earth Witches Aren't Easy

Plan Witch from Out of Town

Bad Witch Rising

Her Elite Assets

Featuring:

Pure Copper

Target: Tungsten

Asset: Arsenic

Fevered Hearts

Marshal of Hel Dorado

Brave are the Lonely

Micah & Mrs. Miller

A Fistful of Dreams

Raising Kane

Wanted: Fevered or Alive

Wild and Fevered

The Quick & The Fevered

A Man Called Wyatt

Going Royal

Some Like It Royal

Some Like It Scandalous

Some Like It Deadly

Some Like it Secret

Some Like it Easy

Her Marine Prince

Blocked

HEART OF THE NEBULA
Queenmaker

Deal Breaker

Throne Taker

LONE STAR LEATHERNECKS
Semper Fi Cowboy

As You Were, Cowboy

MADISON, THE WITCH HUNTER
Every Witch Way But Floosey's

MAGIC & MAYHEM
The Witch Singer

Bridget's Witch's Diary

The Witched Away Bride

Mongrels

Mongrels, Mischief & Mayhem

SHACKLED SOULS
Succubus Chained

Succubus Unchained

Succubus Blessed

SPACE COWBOY
Space Cowboy Survival Guide

WOLVES OF WILLOW BEND
Wolf at Law
Wolf Bite
Caged Wolf
Wolf Claim
Wolf Next Door
Rogue Wolf
Bayou Wolf
Untamed Wolf
Wolf with Benefits
River Wolf
Single Wicked Wolf
Desert Wolf
Snow Wolf
Wolf on Board
Holly Jolly Wolf
Shadow Wolf
His Moonstruck Wolf
Thunder Wolf
Ghost Wolf
Outlaw Wolves
Wolf Unleashed

www.ingramcontent.com/pod-product-compliance
Lightning Source LLC
Chambersburg PA
CBHW060633310726
48982CB00003B/755